SUSAN MALLERY

meant to be yours

HQN™

Recycling programs for this product may not exist in your area.

ISBN-13: 978-1-335-04149-4
ISBN-13: 978-1-335-65100-6 (Walmart Exclusive edition)

Meant to Be Yours

Copyright © 2019 by Susan Mallery, Inc.

A Very Merry Princess
First published in 2017. This edition published in 2019.
Copyright © 2017 by Susan Mallery, Inc.

www.HQNBooks.com

Printed in U.S.A.

CONTENTS

MEANT TO BE YOURS

CHAPTER ONE

JASPER DEMBENSKI COULD accept an idiosyncratic GPS, the blown tire and the five hailstorms he'd driven through yesterday. It was the lack of coffee that was going to do him in.

He shook the empty coffee can, as if the action would magically produce results. Not shockingly, no coffee appeared. He was going to have to head to the grocery store, which was easier said than done, given that he was driving a thirty-six-foot RV. Or maybe there was coffee up at the main office. If he could grab some there, he could put off having to shop until later in the day.

Jasper was on the last leg of a three-month book tour for his latest suspense novel. Rather than trying to convince him to deal with dozens of flights, rental cars and hotels on the multicity tour, his publisher had enticed him with the idea of traveling via RV. Jasper didn't mind driving long distances, he enjoyed the solitude and time to think, and the RV parks were actually pretty decent.

He was about eleven hundred miles from home. Once he joined up with Interstate 10, it was a straight shot back to Happily Inc. All he needed was a large cup of coffee. He would find a Walmart or Target close to the interstate and get enough food to see him through the next two days.

He walked out into the warm September morning

and started for the main office. Along the way, he nodded at people who waved or called out greetings. RV parks were friendly places. As he wasn't one for unnecessary chats, he'd learned to keep moving while offering a brief wave. Otherwise, he might get trapped in a lengthy and tedious conversation about the viability of a certain back road or a discussion about the best kind of bait for catfish.

"You git, you hear me? Go on out of here or I'll get my shotgun."

The angry words came from his left. Jasper instinctively went on alert, his body tensing as he spun in that direction. Using the RV he'd just passed for cover, he backtracked so he could come around from behind and see what was happening.

"You heard me," the man yelled. "Get out of here."

Jasper stayed close to the RV as he circled around and then stepped into view, prepared to get between some jerk and whoever he was threatening. Only the short, round, old man wasn't taking on his kid or his woman, instead he was raising his hand to a dog. An old dog with ribs showing through dirty fur. A dog who flinched and backed away.

"Problem?" Jasper asked, using his *tell me your story before I kick your ass* voice, the one he'd perfected during his time with the military police.

The old man glared at him, as if wanting to take him on, then seemed to think better of it. "It's nothing. Just that dog who's been hanging out here for a few weeks. Somebody dumped him. If you don't want a dog, just shoot him. That's what I say."

The kindness of strangers, Jasper thought grimly. Or lack thereof. He knew there were more good people than bad, but every now and then he was forced to question his faith in humanity.

The dog—some kind of Lab-shepherd mix—looked at him with sad, knowing eyes, as if he didn't really expect better of life. He stayed out of reach and, despite the heat, shivered a little. He was obviously starving and might be sick. Who would just dump a dog at an RV park?

"He begs for food," the old man added, his tone defensive. "I don't have time to deal with him."

Jasper thought about the coffee he hadn't had yet and the eleven hundred miles between him and home. He thought about the book he was trying to write and how slowly it was going. He thought about the nightmares he often had and that there were still enough bad days to keep him humble. The absolute last thing he needed in his life was some old dog.

"If you were him, you'd beg for food, too," Jasper said. "Don't shoot him."

"You don't get to tell me what to do."

Jasper sighed before squaring his shoulders and staring down at the old man who was maybe five-five to Jasper's six foot three.

"Seriously?" he asked. "You're going to go there with me?"

The old man shook his head. "I'm just saying…"

"I know what you're saying. Don't shoot the dog."

Jasper walked to the office. Sure enough, they had a huge carafe of coffee that he used to fill his travel mug. While he drank down the dark, hot liquid, he asked about the dog and confirmed it was indeed a stray. A few attempts had been made to catch it, but no one had been successful.

Jasper headed to his RV. He would spend no more than fifteen minutes looking for the dog. If he found it, he would lure it back to his RV with food. Once it was inside, he would take it to a local vet and have it checked for a chip. If there wasn't one, he would drop it off at a shelter and be on his way. It would take him two hours, tops.

Or less, he thought as he approached his RV and saw the dog sitting outside the side door.

"Good morning," Jasper said, opening the door.

The dog jumped inside and made his way to the small refrigerator, where he sat again.

"Somebody's messing with me," Jasper grumbled.

He pulled out lunch meat he was going to use for a sandwich and gave that to the dog, who gulped it down. Jasper quickly scrambled a couple of eggs. Less than ten minutes later, the dog was stretched out on the sofa, completely relaxed and nearly asleep.

Jasper looked up the closest vet's office and called to explain the situation. The perky receptionist told him they'd just had a cancellation and could see him right away.

"Of course you can," he muttered.

The drive was easy, there was parking for his RV and damn if the dog didn't follow him inside the vet's office with no problem.

Jasper explained the situation to the smiling older woman with a name tag that read Sally. When he got to the part about him giving the dog to a shelter, her smile faded.

"You don't want to keep him yourself?" she asked.

"Ah, no. I'm not really a pet person."

Both she and the dog stared at him. Jasper shifted uncomfortably. He wanted to explain that he wasn't being cruel—rather his reluctance was realistic. He'd been in a really bad place when he'd gotten out of the army. After tons of therapy, medication and stumbling onto the one thing that could get him halfway back to being able to exist in polite society, he was healed enough to pass for normal. But he knew the truth—he would never fully get there. More than one therapist had warned him he was broken beyond repair.

They hadn't used those exact words—they were too professional for that. But the truth had been clear enough all the same.

But the woman in front of him wouldn't want to hear that and he certainly didn't want to tell her.

"I'd like him checked for a chip and maybe given an exam to see if he's all right," Jasper said.

"Sure. Let me take you to one of the rooms."

He and the dog followed her. She paused by a floor scale and motioned for the dog to step on it.

"Come on, boy. Right here."

The dog obliged. He was forty-eight pounds. Sally winced.

"He should be closer to seventy-five pounds," she said. "He's really skinny. Poor guy."

Jasper and the dog went into an exam room.

"I'll get one of the techs to come in and scan him. If there's a chip, we'll take it from there. If there isn't, we can talk about whether you want to pay for an exam when you're just going to take him to the shelter."

Her tone was pleasant enough but Jasper heard the judgment, all the same. Instead of speaking, he nodded. The woman left and he was alone with the dog.

They both sat and stared at each other. Jasper looked away first.

"You can't stay on your own," he said, shifting uneasily in his chair. "Look at you. You need someone to take care of you. A shelter would mean three squares and a bunk, right? And you'd find a family of your own."

Without wanting to, he recalled reading somewhere that older dogs had trouble getting adopted. Which wasn't his problem.

"I've never had a pet," he added, glancing at the dog, who still regarded him steadily. "I don't know how to take care of you."

He supposed there were books on the subject. Plus, the old guy wasn't a puppy. He would know how to deal with humans. Between the two of them, they might be able to get it right.

"I'm not a good bet," he added in a low voice. "I was in the army for eight years and I saw things. Sometimes I have flashbacks and I just… I'm better off alone."

The dog's head dropped as if he realized what Jasper was trying to say. As if he'd given up hoping and had accepted he was going to be abandoned—again.

Jasper stood up and glared at the dog, who still didn't look at him.

"I didn't want any of this. It's not my fault. I'm not the bad guy."

The dog didn't move—he sat there all hunched, as if the weight of the world was just too much for him.

Jasper thought longingly of his quiet house, the sameness of his life when he was home. He had friends, but on his terms. He had relationships with women. Sort of. He just wasn't like everyone else and wanting to be different didn't change the truth.

The dog raised his head and looked at him. In that moment when their eyes met, Jasper would swear he saw down-to-the-bone sadness and despair. It was so real, so visceral, that he felt the anguish as actual pain.

The door to the exam room opened and a petite, pretty, gray-haired woman in a white coat entered.

"I'm Dr. Anthony," she said with a smile. "For once all my techs are busy and I'm free." She crouched down and gently patted the dog's back. "Hey, old guy. How are you? Where'd you find him?"

"At an RV park a few miles from here. They told me he was abandoned a few weeks ago. Apparently he's been avoiding people, except to beg for food, but he came right into my vehicle."

Dr. Anthony petted him a little more, before running her hands up and down his legs and along his back as if gently checking for wounds or injuries.

"People can be cruel," she said as she stood. She pulled a handheld device out of her coat pocket and turned it on. "All right, let's see if you have a chip."

Jasper found himself tensing, not sure if he wanted the dog to have one or not. Dr. Anthony ran the reader back and forth a couple of times, checking him closely, then straightening and shaking her head.

"No dice," she said. "I didn't think so. Someone who cares enough to get a microchip doesn't walk away from their pet. Sally said you were going to take him to a shelter?"

Jasper hesitated.

Dr. Anthony gave him a sympathetic glance. "Look, it's better for him to be there than on the streets. We have a good one nearby. They'll take care of him. He's not your responsibility. You did the decent thing, bringing him in. That can be enough."

Which sounded like permission to do what he knew

made sense. Great. He would take the dog there and be on his way.

He opened his mouth to ask for the address, but what he said instead was, "What if I wanted to keep him?"

"You sure?"

Jasper looked at the dog, who stared back at him. He thought about his house up in the mountains and how every now and then, the quiet got to him. He thought about the loneliness he'd seen in the dog's eyes.

"No, but I think giving him a good home is the least I should do."

Dr. Anthony smiled. "Okay, then. Are you from around here?"

"California. I'm heading home today."

"Then I would suggest a brief exam to make sure he's relatively healthy. I can give you a collar and leash and food that will be easy for him to digest. When you get to your place, find a vet and get him a more thorough exam. You and your vet can discuss what to do as far as vaccinations. He'll need a few chew toys, maybe a ball and a bed of some kind. He's an old guy, so he's going to want to take things easy. Still interested?"

"I am."

"Good. Now why don't you put him on the exam table there and we'll get started."

"It might just be okay," wedding coordinator Renee Grothen murmured softly to herself as she surveyed the wedding reception. She wouldn't risk admitting everything had turned out as planned until the last guest had left, but four and a half hours in, things were going really well.

Jim and Monica Martinez were a sweet couple with

a fun firefighter theme for their big day. There was a long tradition of firefighters on both sides of the family and plenty of cute touches in the wedding and reception.

Monica's dress laced up the back and instead of white ribbon to cinch her gown, she'd used bright red. The centerpieces were ceramic boot vases painted to look like firefighter boots, filled with red, orange and yellow flowers. There was even a walk-through fountain at one end of the reception area, created with fire hoses, a pump and a lot of engineering.

Renee walked around the perimeter of the indoor reception space, looking for problems. So far, so good, she thought with cautious optimism. The cake had been cut, the bar service was about to end and the tone of the party had faded from raucous to comfortably tired— exactly as it should. With a little luck, things would wrap up on time and without a crisis. This was Monica and Jim's day—Renee wanted it to be as perfect as possible. While she always took care of her clients, she tended to unleash her mother bear instincts for her special couples and Monica and Jim certainly qualified.

She spotted Pallas Mitchell, her boss, walking toward her. It was nearly ten on a Saturday night and Pallas, a pretty brunette only recently returned from maternity leave, yawned widely. When she spotted Renee she held up her hands, palms up.

"What can I say? I've been home with an infant. These wild late-night hours are going to take some getting used to."

"No one's judging," Renee told her. "As I said at seven, at eight and again at nine, *go home*. I can handle this. You're barely back and you need to give yourself time to adjust to the schedule."

"You've been running things for nearly six months. You need a break."

In truth, Renee *was* a little ragged around the edges, but she'd loved handling Weddings Out of the Box while Pallas had been gone. She'd enjoyed the challenges each unique wedding presented and watching all the details fall into place on the big day.

"I had lots of help," Renee pointed out. "Hiring college students on summer break was a good idea." And what they'd lacked in experience, they'd made up for in energy and enthusiasm.

"Now that I'm back, things can return to normal," Pallas said, covering another yawn.

"Go home," Renee urged. "Please. I can handle things here. I promise."

"Okay. I will. Thanks. Don't you dare come in tomorrow." Pallas's voice was firm. "For once, we don't have a Sunday wedding. Enjoy the break."

"I will." Renee would probably pop in to do a little paperwork, but she wouldn't stay long. "Are you coming to The Boardroom on Monday night?"

In a wedding destination town, the rhythms of the residents were determined by weekend weddings. Happily Inc's workweek started on Wednesdays as the businesses geared up for the dozens of nuptials that occurred in multiple venues. Which meant the town's Friday night was actually on Monday.

The Boardroom, a local bar, hosted game nights on Mondays. Board games ruled and tournaments were heated and fun as friends crushed each other at everything from Candy Land to Risk.

Pallas shook her head. "I'll admit to being a bit of a worrier. When we went a couple of weeks ago, I couldn't stop thinking about Ryan. He's only five months old. It's too soon to leave him at night."

Renee held in a smile. "Sure. I get that."

"I know you don't, but thank you for pretending. Have fun for me, too. Oh, Jasper's back, so tell him hi, if you think of it."

Jasper was back? Renee hadn't heard. She liked knowing he'd returned from his big book tour. Not for any reason in particular, she amended hastily. Sure, he was nice, but there were a lot of nice guys in the world. There was just something about Jasper. Maybe it was because in addition to being good-looking and just a little dangerous, he wasn't a forever kind of guy.

"I saw that!" Pallas grinned. "I totally saw that. You did the predatory smile thing I was never good at. You want to use him for sex! Did I know this?" She stomped her foot. "Did this happen while I was on maternity leave? What else went on while I was off having a baby?"

Renee laughed. "You're reading way too much into my smile. I'm happy he's home from his book tour. That's all."

"I don't believe you."

"Jasper and I are not involved. I doubt we've had more than a three-sentence conversation."

Not that it took many sentences to ask *Your place or mine?* And while the description of predatory was nice, it gave her too much credit. Would she stalk him and pounce? Not even on her best day. Would she say yes if the man asked? She smiled again. Oh, yeah, she would. Definitely. Okay, probably. *If* she was feeling brave. Because while she worked her butt off to give her couples their perfect happily-ever-after day, she knew it was never going to happen for her. Those who could—did. Those who couldn't became wedding planners.

Avoiding relationships might be the smart choice, but it was also a lonely one. She knew Jasper was into the long-term, monogamous, not-serious kind of thing and she was pretty sure she could handle that. Assuming she was his type and he was interested. They could have some laughs, lots of sex and walk away completely unscathed in the heart department. Where was the bad?

"There's something going on and you can't convince me otherwise," Pallas said. "You have depths. I'm very impressed. Okay, use Jasper and then tell me the details because hey, he's got to be great." She yawned again. "I'm such a lightweight. I'm leaving now."

"Good night. Hug Ryan for me."

"You know I will."

Pallas walked out of the reception hall. Renee continued to circle the space, looking for any forgotten handbags or phones, and noting how long it would take the cleaning service to return the huge room to order. Doing her job and not thinking about the fact that Jasper was back—that was her.

A loud whoop got her attention. She turned and saw three teenaged guys running through the fountain at the far end of the big, open room. Each of them jumped, trying to touch the arc of water dancing overhead.

The younger brother, she thought as she made her way toward them. And his friends. No doubt they were bored after so many hours with not very much to do. Regardless, she was not going to have them disrupt the reception when it was so close to being over.

As she approached the running, jumping teens, she saw both sets of parents, along with the bride and groom, still dancing. They swayed in time with the music, oblivious to the fountain and the idiots messing with it. Then several things happened at once.

The younger brother started an extra long run toward the fountain. Jim let go of Monica and spun her out the length of their arms. Monica bumped her mom, who stumbled a little. Dad grabbed Mom, moving all of them closer to the fountain and the younger brother running, who had to swerve suddenly to avoid them. As he swerved, he lost his balance and slipped, tumbling into the fountain mechanism. One of the hoses broke free, wiggling and spraying water everywhere.

Renee saw it all happening and knew there was no way she was going to allow her beautiful bride to get soaked. She lunged for the hose, caught it and held it tightly against her chest as the bride's father rushed to turn off the water to the hose. It took only seconds, but by then the entire fountain had spilled over and Renee was drenched, shivering and had water up her nose even as she wondered if she looked half as ridiculous as she felt.

The new Mrs. Martinez hurried over. "Renee, are you all right?" She turned on her brother. "How could you? This is a wedding, not a water park."

Aware that end-of-wedding exhaustion could easily lead to emotions spiraling out of control, Renee quickly faked a smile.

"Monica, it's fine. Don't worry. Keeping you and the rest of the wedding party dry was my only concern." She glanced at the water draining onto the floor and realized part of the fountain was still pumping out water. That couldn't be good. If she couldn't get everything turned off, she was going to have to call in one of those companies that took care of disasters like flooding. "Really. It's no problem."

"You're dripping and the water's rising. My dad went to find the main shutoff."

Renee wrung out her hair and hoped her makeup wasn't too badly smudged. Then she realized the water level in the reception hall was indeed climbing and hoped Monica's father found the shutoff soon.

She was just about to go help him when he returned.

"All turned off." He glanced at the mini flood. "Sorry about this."

"It's fine," Renee lied, her tone soothing, because that was part of her job. To pretend all was well even when they needed to be figuring out how to build an ark.

The rest of the guests were heading out. Nothing like the threat of an unexpected flood to get people moving, she thought, trying to find the humor in the situation.

"I'm so sorry," Monica told her as she held her dress out of the water and slipped out of her shoes.

"Don't be. You had a wonderful wedding and reception. Why don't you and Jim start gathering your things? I have a spare set of clothes in my office. I'll get changed, then help you make sure you have everything."

As she spoke, she noticed the water seemed to have settled at about the six- or seven-inch level. Yup, she was going to have to call someone. No doubt she would be here all night. Oh, joy.

"I'm really sorry," Jim said. "We thought we'd planned for every contingency." He glared at his new brother-in-law. "Except for stupid." He turned back to her. "Let us know the cost of cleanup. We'll pay for it."

"Thank you. I think the deposit should take care

of it but I'll let you know if there's a problem. Now if you'll let me go get changed, I'll be back with you in ten minutes."

Monica nodded.

Renee slipped out of her shoes and walked through the ankle-deep water. When she reached her office upstairs, she carefully closed the door behind her before undressing, then slipped on jeans and a T-shirt. No exactly professional, but she wasn't going to worry about that right now. Before she returned to her bride and groom, she looked up the local disaster cleaning service. The number was in her files, but wasn't one she had had to use before.

They picked up on the first ring.

"Happily Inc CleanUp. This is Hilde. How can I help you?"

"Hi. I'm Renee Grothen at Weddings Out of the Box. We had a firefighter wedding tonight with a big fountain. There was an accident with one of the hoses and now our main reception hall is flooded."

There was a pause. "Um, did you say firefighter wedding? Never mind. How much water?"

"About six inches."

"That's a lot."

"It was a big fountain."

"Give us thirty minutes and we'll be there."

"Thank you."

Renee hung up, gave herself a second to catch her breath, then headed back to deal with the bride, the groom, the flood and anything else that might happen tonight. Because with a wedding, it was always something.

CHAPTER TWO

SIX DAYS INTO pet ownership, Jasper had no idea how he was doing. He and Koda—a name that had just kind of shown up in his brain and seemed to suit the dog—appeared to be getting along okay. Koda had slept most of the drive back, waking up for meals and for easy walks while they both stretched their legs. Along the way, Jasper had bought dog beds, some toys and more food. Koda's appetite was good and he looked better every day.

Once they'd reached Jasper's mountain home just outside of Happily Inc, Koda had explored the house before quickly settling into a routine. When let out to do his business, Koda didn't stray far from the house and he seemed to prefer to be inside rather than out. They took a couple of walks a day, going slowly, Koda sniffing and Jasper thinking. Koda slept quietly while Jasper worked. When they left the office together, Koda brought his favorite toy—a stuffed rabbit—with him.

From Jasper's point of view, Koda was pretty easy company. He slept on his dog bed in Jasper's bedroom at night. Once, Jasper had awakened from a familiar nightmare, to find the dog on the bed, pressed hard against him, as if offering comfort. As Jasper got his bearings and was able to slow his breathing, Koda hopped down and returned to his own bed where he quickly went to sleep.

Jasper had installed an electronic doggie door so Koda could come and go as he wanted without Jasper having to worry that local wildlife could also wander into the house. Koda had figured out how to work the doggie door in about ten minutes. They had a vet appointment later in the week and Jasper had downloaded a book on having a dog as a pet to make sure he had it all covered.

He still didn't know why he'd brought the old guy home—nor did it matter. Koda was here now and Jasper would take care of him. He had to admit, the quiet company was nice.

"I'm going into town," he told Koda as he set out the bowl of kibble mixed with canned food. "It's Monday night and I like to hang out at The Boardroom. It's a bar that caters to locals. On Mondays they have board game tournaments. Most of my friends go."

He had no idea why he was explaining any of this to the dog—it wasn't as if Koda could understand him. Still, he couldn't help going on.

"I won't be that late," he continued. "You have water and your bed. I'll leave the radio on that classical station you like. There's the doggie door if you need to go out." He paused, not sure what else to say.

Koda finished his dinner, then looked at Jasper, as if processing the information. After a couple of seconds, the dog retreated to his bed in the family room and lay down.

"All right." Jasper put his food bowl in the sink. "I'll see you when I get back."

He got in his truck and started down the mountain.

The road was familiar and when compared with the RV he'd been driving, the 4X4 truck was practically sporty.

The thought made him smile. The long book tour had been good for him. The RV had given him a home base. Although his publisher had offered to rent a fancy bus with pop-outs and an onboard washer and dryer, Jasper had decided to buy an old, used RV instead. He'd thought he might want to use it again, for a tour and maybe a trip of his own. He'd liked being on the road.

As he headed into town he wondered if Koda would enjoy another trip or if he'd been too traumatized by what had happened to him in San Antonio. He supposed he could take an overnight trip and see how it went. Although any time away would have to wait. He was getting back into his book and had a deadline looming. For the next few months, his primary focus would be getting the story right, then getting it down on paper. Well, not paper, exactly. He used a computer, but the concept was the same.

He reached the main part of town and turned into The Boardroom's parking lot. He saw plenty of familiar cars and smiled. His friends would be there, as would other local residents. He would kick a little ass on the board game front, have a beer and a burger, talk to his buddies, then head home. A perfect evening.

Four years ago, if someone had told him he would settle in this quirky wedding-based town, he would have said that person was crazier than him, but here he was— doing better than anyone could have expected. Forward progress, he thought as he made his way inside. It beat getting left behind.

"Jasper! You're back."

"Hey, stranger. How was the book tour?"

"When'd you get home?"

The calls came from every corner of the bar. Jasper nodded at his buddies, waved at a few people he knew by sight and scanned the room, looking for an open spot at the tables set up for four.

Mathias Mitchell, an artist who worked with glass, walked past him, a beer in one hand and a glass of wine in the other.

"Hey, man, you made it. Good to see you." Mathias nodded toward a table. "Come sit with us. Carol's friend, Renee, is hanging out with us, so you'd make a fourth."

"Will do."

Jasper walked around for a few minutes, greeting his friends and giving a brief account of his three-month book tour. When a gong sounded, giving the ten-minute warning before the game started, he walked to the bar and ordered himself a beer. He figured he would get the burger later.

As he took his drink, he glanced around the room and caught sight of a petite redhead talking to Carol, Mathias's wife. Renee Something, he thought. The woman Mathias had mentioned. She was maybe five-one. Despite her slight stature, there was something powerful about her. As if she would do whatever was necessary to get what she wanted.

He held in a grin. Right. Because he was just that good at assessing women. The truth was he knew nothing about her, which was fine. Even though it had been nearly a year since he and Wynn had ended their not-quite relationship, he wasn't looking for anything else right now. Still, there was something about a woman with long hair. Especially long, *red* hair.

As if aware of his scrutiny, Renee turned toward him. For a brief second, their eyes met. Jasper was about to offer a wave when Renee surprised him by flushing slightly and looking away. As if she'd been caught doing something she shouldn't.

He glanced around, trying to figure out what could have caused her discomfort. When nothing obvious showed itself, he figured he'd simply misinterpreted the situation. Hardly a surprise—he wasn't just a guy, he was a guy who knew diddly about women. A fact proven by his inability to create a love interest for the hero of his latest novel. He knew the guy needed a woman in his life—it was a great way to wrap up the series—but he had yet to figure out who she was and how she fit into the story. Or how to write her. So far the only sentence he'd managed to write and then not delete was: She was tall, with short, blond hair. Oh, yeah, the royalty checks were going to roll in on that one.

He was still chuckling when he approached the table. Carol rose and hugged him.

"You made it back! Welcome home. Did you miss us?"

"I did."

Mathias held out his hand. "Good to see you. How was the tour?"

"Good. Long. Plenty of stops."

"And adoring fans?" Carol asked, her voice teasing.

"There were some." Jasper turned to Renee. "Mind if I join you?"

She smiled and waved to the empty chair. "Please. Your reputation precedes you, so I'm happy to be on the same team."

Whatever weirdness had existed before—or hadn't existed—was obviously gone.

He raised a shoulder. "I haven't played board games in a few months. I'm probably rusty."

"I doubt that," Carol said as she sat down. "Speaking of rusty, I want to warn everyone that this is my first night away from Devon. I've been away during the day, but never at night."

Jasper wanted to ask how one was different from the other, but knew there was no point. Her reasoning might be based on the fact that her baby was maybe five months old, or it might be a female thing, or it could be something everyone else understood intuitively.

Mathias reached across the table and squeezed her hand. "You know she's fine, right? And it's not like she's with someone we don't know."

Renee smiled and leaned toward Jasper. "Pallas and Carol share a nanny. With their kids only ten days apart in age, it makes sense. The woman is terrific and does a great job, but they're both uncomfortable being away from their babies." Her tone softened. "You know what new moms are like."

He nodded rather than say something along the lines of "not really." He knew even less about young mothers than women in general. His stint in the army had given him a range of skills that could be useful in a wartime situation but they hadn't been much on training him for life with regular people. As for that small town where he'd grown up…well, that was eight lifetimes ago.

He studied Renee, taking in her freckles and the cute way her nose turned up a little at the end. She had green eyes—although hers were more gray than his. There was something about her smile he liked. If he were to describe her in a book he would probably mention her long bangs and…

And what? Her height? Her eyes? The shape of her mouth? Did anyone care about that kind of crap? Dammit—he was a number one *New York Times* best-selling author and he couldn't describe a woman? His career was obviously over.

He pushed that thought away. He would dwell on his inability to write later. Tonight was about having a good time.

"What's the game?" he asked as several of the servers started passing out board games. "Ah, Monopoly. Excellent."

Carol picked up the piece of paper that had been left on the table. "Traditional rules," she read. "Whoever has the most money at the end of an hour goes on to the next round. After that, rounds are thirty minutes." She glanced at her teammates. "That sounds easy enough."

Renee nodded and turned to Jasper. "While you were gone, we had a Monopoly Junior tournament and odd number rolls didn't count. Things got quite heated."

"I'll bet."

Her conversation was completely normal. He must have imagined whatever had happened before. Only was she leaning toward him or was he imagining it?

They unpacked the game and chose tokens. Mathias counted the money and passed the right amount to everyone, then they rolled to see who would go first. As usual, Jasper rolled the highest number and got to start. He rolled double sixes, followed by a five. He bought the Electric Company property, then collected two hundred dollars from the Community Chest card he drew from the top of the stack. Carol was on his left, so he handed the dice to her.

She stared at him. "I'd forgotten what it was like to play against you. I don't think I like it."

He flashed her a smile. "What can I say? I'm a lucky guy."

She made a huffing sound and rolled a seven. "How did the cleanup go yesterday?" she asked Renee.

"We are back to normal. The water is gone, everything is dried out and there's not really any serious damage." She glanced at Jasper. "We had a little accident at the firefighter wedding on Saturday night. Someone bumped the hose fountain and nearly flooded the place."

"What's a firefighter wedding?"

She took the dice from Mathias and rolled. "Weddings Out of the Box does theme weddings. In this case, the theme was firefighters. The wedding colors were red, yellow and orange. The flower girl carried flowers in a fireman's helmet. That sort of thing."

"People do that?"

Renee grinned. "Jasper, you've driven by Weddings Out of the Box. One side of the building looks like a Tuscan villa and another looks like a castle. What did you think was happening there?"

"I thought Pallas was quirky."

"Theme weddings are big business," she told him. "There are the usual ones. Princess, pirate, weddings based on books or movies. This fall we're having a Halloween wedding, a football wedding and an apple wedding."

"What's an apple wedding?" he asked.

"They're apple lovers." She laughed. "It's kind of hard to explain."

An apple wedding? Was that really a thing? He felt as if there was a whole world out there, about which he knew nothing. First women and now weddings. He needed to work on his life skills education.

Mathias rolled the dice and then moved his token. "I'm going to make a quick call to our nanny," he said, then shrugged sheepishly. "Like we said before, it's the first time we've left Devon at night, so…"

"You should absolutely check in," Renee told him. "You'll feel better."

Carol watched him go. "It's funny. All the things I worried about before we had Devon haven't been a problem. Instead there are so many *other* things to worry about. Like leaving her alone."

Renee patted her arm. "It will get better. You're a terrific mom. She's lucky to have you."

"Thanks."

Jasper looked at Renee. "Do you have kids?"

"Me? No. I'm not married." She flushed slightly. "Not that you need to be married to have children. I wasn't saying that. Or judging. I just mean…" She cleared her throat, lowered her gaze, then looked at him. "Um, no. You?"

He shook his head.

Okay, there was *something* going on with her. He was sure of it. Fairly sure. Reasonably sure, at least. He really had to get out more. He hadn't felt the need before, but being around people again made him aware of his solitary state. Not to mention the lack of sex in his life.

He looked at Renee. She was small, but everything was in the right place. She had a sense of humor and he liked her smile. What were the odds she was looking for a brief but satisfying fling that would go absolutely nowhere?

Mathias returned and took his seat. "Everything is fine," he told Carol. "Devon's asleep and nothing is wrong."

Their eyes locked. "I want to go home," Carol said softly.

"Thank God. Me, too." Mathias sprang to his feet. "Sorry about this, but it's a baby thing."

Renee waved her hand toward the door. "Go be with your beautiful baby. Great progress was made tonight. Next time you'll stay the whole first hour."

Carol laughed. "Thanks for understanding. See you at lunch tomorrow."

"You will," Renee told her.

Seconds later, they were gone. Jasper looked at Renee. "I guess the odds of one of us heading to the finals just went up."

"They did."

She held his gaze a second past what he would consider normal, friendly interaction, shifting them into the *maybe I'm interested* category. Or was that just wishful thinking on his part? He really had to get this whole man/woman thing figured out. At sixteen, being socially awkward could be considered a little charming. At his age, it was pathetic.

"Monopoly is less fun with just two players," he said. "Could I buy you a drink instead?"

RENEE TOLD HERSELF there was absolutely no pressure. Jasper had invited her for a drink and she had said yes. Big whoop. Men and women met for drinks hundreds of times a day and it was all completely normal. Boring even. Only sitting across from Jasper wasn't anything she would describe as normal, and it could never be boring.

For one thing, the guy was hot. He was tall, with broad shoulders, but more than that, there was an air of casual strength about him. As if he could handle himself in any situation. Should scary-looking bad guys burst into the place, Renee knew Jasper would handle the situation. She, on the other hand, would run screaming into the night. Or hide. Or faint.

He also had that hint of slightly wounded male about him. He'd been damaged in his past and it showed. It took a stronger woman than her to resist that kind of yumminess. Although this was just a drink, she reminded herself as Jasper walked over to small corner table they'd moved to. He set a cosmo in front of her and before taking a seat across from her and picking up his gin and tonic.

He took a sip, studying her over the glass. She had no idea what he was thinking, nor did she know what to say. Nerves gripped her tightly, making her feel awkward. She hadn't been on a date since moving to Happily Inc, and before that she'd been getting over a shattered heart, and before that she'd been in a nearly three-year relationship, and before that...

"So, how was your book tour?" she asked brightly, hoping the question and his answer would distract her brain. "You were gone a long time."

"I was. My publisher tried something new, sending me out in an RV."

"I'd heard something about that but I thought maybe people were kidding. You really traveled the country in an RV for a month?"

"Three," he said with another one of his sexy smiles. "Before that I spent a few weeks in Europe. Traveling more conventionally."

"You must have a lot of fans. I knew you were a successful author, but you're internationally famous."

She meant the words to be teasing, but didn't think they came out that way. Probably because she hadn't actually put together who Jasper was. In her mind, he was the slightly mysterious, former military guy who kept to himself and provided plenty of *take me now, big guy* fantasies. Apparently he was a little too close to, say, Chris Pine territory for her purposes.

Not that she was going to smile brightly and offer a night of hot sex. Because while everything went fine in her head, in real life, there were serious pitfalls. Hysterical laughter followed by a look of extreme pity. Not that Jasper seemed like the hysterical laughter type. But the pity was a real possibility. Or revulsion. That would be depressing and she wasn't looking for another boy-girl setback.

The smart decision would be to enjoy the drink, pretend she'd never once undressed him with her eyes and retreat to her charming apartment where she would tell herself she didn't care that she was never going to have sex with a man again.

"I've been lucky," he said easily. "The books have to work for people, of course, but there are a lot of authors who struggle in obscurity. I had breaks early on."

"Like I said—internationally famous. What's touring like? Is the Europe part different from the US part?"

"Very, especially with the RV. Here I was able to drive from place to place. I'd park near a big city, then head in for the events. Sometimes I'd do a morning show, or drive-time radio. I might have media interviews during the day or drop in to a few bookstores and sign stock. In the evenings I would have organized book signings where I'd talk for a few minutes, take questions, then sign books. Then back to the hotel or RV and start it over in the morning."

"That's less glamorous than I thought. What about in Europe?"

"That's a different schedule. I would arrive in a city, usually in the morning, have lunch with whomever the publisher wanted me to meet, do media, then have a signing, followed by a late dinner. Get up in the morning and drive, fly or take the train to the next city and do it all again." He flashed her another smile. "All while not speaking the language. It's an endurance sport."

"It sounds like it. What's the best part?"

"Meeting the readers. It's hard not to like people willing to line up to tell you how much they love what you do."

"I hadn't thought of that. I get the occasional thank-you note, but there's never been a line." She picked up her drink. "Anyone creepy? Didn't Stephen King write a book about a crazed fan?"

"Yes, and we're not going to talk about that." He chuckled. "There are fans who know way more about my books than I do and want to talk themes and what I could do instead. Sometimes readers want to give me story lines, which I have to sidestep because of potential legal problems."

"Your life is really interesting."

"No, it's not. Ninety percent of the time I'm sitting at a computer, trying to figure out what to say next. It's a lot of hours by myself, sometimes with swearing."

She liked him, she thought with some surprise. She hadn't really spent time with him before, so had filled in the blanks with her own fantasies, which were more about his body than his personality. It was nice to know there was an actual person behind the gorgeous eyes.

Funny how she'd been thinking about him on and off for the past couple of days and tonight he'd walked into The Boardroom and sat down at her table, as if fate were stepping in.

"Tell me about the apple wedding," he said, leaning toward her. "No one dresses up in an apple costume, do they?"

She laughed. "No. I promise, nothing like that. An apple wedding is more like a Christmas wedding. The theme inspires the decorations and the colors, not the clothing. Let's see. The bridesmaid dresses are apple green, there are crab apples in the bouquet and the floral arrangements on the tables. The signature drink is an apple martini. That sort of thing."

He stared at her, his expression blank. "I have no idea what you're talking about."

"What's confusing?"

"All of it. I get the bridesmaid dresses. I've seen women in those before. But the rest of it? You're speaking a foreign language."

"What about all the weddings you've been to?"

He took another sip of his drink. "I haven't. I joined the army when I was eighteen. None of my friends were even thinking about getting married then. I got back for a few visits, but no weddings. After my dad died—it was always just the two of us—I never went back. My military friends went home to get married and I usually couldn't get leave."

Now he was the one speaking a foreign language. "You've never been to a wedding?"

"Nope."

"That's not possible."

"It's no big deal."

"It's a rite of passage. It's how this town supports itself. Happily Inc is a wedding destination town and you have actually never been to a wedding?"

"Pallas and Nick got married in Italy and I was gone when Carol and Mathias got married."

She stared at him. "Come by Weddings Out of the Box sometime and I'll show you a video," she told him. "They're all variations on a theme, so once you've seen one, you'll be wedding literate."

"But not fluent?"

His voice was low and teasing. It sent ripples down her spine and made her wish she was the kind of woman who could look a man in the eye while inviting him back to her place. But she wasn't and she couldn't. She might want a *let's get naked* night with Jasper, but the truth was she'd never once had sex with a man she wasn't half in love with and it seemed unlikely she could find the skill set to change that now.

"I think fluency is a ways off," she said lightly, hoping he couldn't hear the disappointment in her voice. As he had no idea what she was thinking, the emotion would only be confusing and misleading. Man, even without a relationship, the whole boy-girl thing was really hard to navigate.

"You help brides plan their weddings, right?" he asked.

"Yes, although it's better when the groom is involved, too. Weddings Out of the Box is a wedding venue. We specialize in theme weddings. We've done princess weddings and cowboy weddings and apparently the world's greatest alien wedding based on a computer game, but that was before my time."

"Interesting."

She wasn't sure it was, but it was nice of him to say it.

They looked at each other, then away. Silence stretched between them, grew awkward, got bigger and started making Renee uncomfortable. Crap, crap, crap, this wasn't going to work. Who was she kidding? She was only confident in limited situations—like work. She was never going to be the kind of woman who could tell a guy she thought he was attractive and ask if he would like to have his way with her. Which left her sad and depressingly aware of the fact that she might never do the deed again, which made her want to stomp her foot. Or cry.

Neither response would go over well in public, so it was definitely time to go home. She looked at Jasper.

"It's getting late. Thanks for the drink. I had a nice time."

He studied her for a second before nodding. "I did, too. Let me walk you to your car."

They went out into the night. It was mid-September, so still warm, but they'd passed through the burning heat of summer. In a few more weeks, there would be an actual nip in the air. At least in those hours close to midnight. It rarely got cold-cold in Happily Inc.

They walked to her black Mini with the white racing stripes on the hood. A silly car, to be sure, but one she loved as much as she could love a car. It was cute, it was zippy and with the back seats down, it held as much as she needed.

"This is me," she said lightly.

Jasper glanced from the car to her and back. "It suits you."

She smiled. "Thank you. I try to be worthy of its sassiness, but I don't always succeed. I suppose that's a metaphor for my life. I want to be wild, but I'm not quite sure how."

"You mean that?"

She looked up at him. Literally. With them both standing, she was aware of how tall he was, how strong. He exuded power and confidence. He was all things male and maybe that should have scared her, but it didn't.

"Renee?"

"What?"

"You didn't answer the question."

"There was a question?"

One corner of his mouth turned up. "I may be reading this all wrong, but just in case I'm not..."

He put his hands on her waist and pulled her toward him. The move was unexpected and she would have instinctively resisted, only there was something about the feel of his hands and her growing sense of anticipation. Because he was holding her exactly like a man holds a woman he means to kiss and kiss well.

She looked up to confirm her theory, which gave her exactly half a second to prepare herself for the impact of his lips on hers.

Her first impression was of heat. His mouth was warm, as was his body, but she was on fire. Need erupted long before he deepened the kiss. Just pressing against him, having him hold her and holding him back was unbearably arousing. When he actually got busy with the kissing part, she wasn't sure if she was going to melt, scream or fall apart right there in the parking lot.

His tongue stroked her bottom lip. She parted, then groaned when he slipped inside. They circled and danced and explored. She raised herself on her tiptoes to get a better angle. He nipped her lower lip, then ran his hands up and down her back.

Everywhere he touched blazed with hunger. She was nearly shaking with need. He might not know much about weddings, but he sure could kiss and right now that was the superior skill.

But just when she was really getting into it, Jasper pulled back. He was breathing heavily and looked slightly dazed.

"That was unexpected," he murmured.

"Good unexpected?"

He cleared his throat. "You have to ask?"

"Just checking."

They stared at each other. Here it was, she thought. The moment of reckoning. She could wimp out and walk away or she could be strong and self-actualized by asking for what she wanted.

"Come home with me."

The words came out more question than statement, but she'd said them, so good for her. Unless he said no. Then she would die—right there in the parking lot. They would find her stiff body in the morning and no one would know what had happened.

Jasper raised an eyebrow. "You sure?"

She hunched her shoulders. "I've used up all my courage, so I can't ask again."

He chuckled. "I'm not looking for you to repeat the question. I'm confirming this is what you want."

She looked at him, starting at his very large feet and working her way up. It was too dark in the parking lot for her to be sure, but she was fairly confident he had an erection. She took in his broad shoulders, his handsome face and then thought about how sad and lonely her girl bits had been.

"This is what I want," she told him.

That corner of his mouth turned up again. "How far is your place?"

"About six minutes from here."

"Then we'd best get going."

CHAPTER THREE

SEVEN MINUTES AND maybe twenty seconds later, they were in her small apartment. Renee managed to turn on the lamp by the door and kick off her shoes before Jasper reached for her. Their lips clung even as he tugged at the hem of her T-shirt. It was impossible to pull off her shirt while kissing, but they tried before finally breaking apart.

"Bedroom," she said, thinking of the box of condoms she had in her dresser. A box she'd bought when she'd moved to town and never had the opportunity to open until now.

Movement out of the corner of her eye caught her attention. She turned and saw Jasper had pulled off his shirt, leaving his broad chest bare. He was muscled and male and she couldn't help moving closer and pressing her mouth to his warm skin.

She'd barely had a chance to do more than register the slightly salty taste of him when he was unfastening her bra and reaching around to cup her breasts. The feel of his fingers against her hungry flesh was perfection. He caressed her curves before brushing against her tight, sensitive nipples. At the first stroke, her breath caught. At the second, she cried out as pleasure burned through to her center. She was already wet and swollen. In seconds she shifted to downright desperate.

"Bedroom," she said weakly, still thinking of that condom and him inside of her and oh, please could they get on with it.

"You *are* focused on getting up there," he said, his voice teasing.

She managed to open her eyes and look up at him—a challenging task considering how he was playing with her nipples, rubbing them between his thumb and fingers and then squeezing just tightly enough to make her groan.

"Unless you walk around with protection in your pocket which, I confess, will make me think less of you, we should head to the bedroom."

"Well, damn. You're right."

Before she could say anything, he shifted, bending over and then scooping her up in his arms. She shrieked at the sudden loss of control and grabbed on to him.

Renee couldn't remember the last time she'd been carried. She assumed she'd been maybe eight or nine. Yes, she was small, but she was mighty and she didn't take kindly to being—

He lowered her onto her bed. Before she could complain that she did not enjoy being picked up like a sack of potatoes, he lowered his head and drew her left nipple deeply into his mouth. He flicked his tongue against the taut skin before sucking hard enough to make her writhe with need and delight. Heat poured through her. Wanting grew until she couldn't think about anything else. Even as he shifted to her other breast, she was unfastening her jeans and pushing them off.

He drew back and watched her. "That much of a hurry?"

"It's been decades."

"You're not old enough for it to have been decades."

"It feels like decades." She pointed to his jeans. "Take your clothes off."

He grinned. "Yes, ma'am."

He stood and quickly did as she requested. Renee gave herself a moment to study his naked body. The man looked good and was, ah, well proportioned.

"Condoms?" he asked.

She rolled over to get them out of the far nightstand drawer. When she shifted back, Jasper returned to the bed.

"How would you like this to go?" he asked.

"Fast."

He chuckled. "What I meant was you're kind of small and I'm a big guy. Until we figure out what works best, do you want to be on top?"

She had a brief image of impaling herself on his erection, sliding down until he filled her all the way.

"Done," she said, tossing him the box. "Hurry."

"You're bossy."

"Yes, I know. It's part of my charm."

He put on the condom, then motioned to his covered dick. "Whenever you're ready."

She supposed she should spend a minute thinking about the fact that she barely knew the man, yet here she was, naked and prepared to do the deed. While she'd never been particularly prudish during sex, she wasn't exactly wild, either. Maybe it was because there was no emotional risk, or maybe she was simply that horny, or maybe it was Jasper himself. At this point, she genuinely didn't care.

She straddled him and positioned herself over him, then closed her eyes as she slowly lowered herself. He was long and thick and filled every inch of her in the most delicious way possible. She shifted that last bit all the way in, then let her body remember what all this was about.

Jasper swore. She looked at him.

"What?"

"You." He swore again. "You're naked, sexy as hell, all-in with how it feels and I'm just supposed to lie here without losing it like some kid? I'm not sure I have that much willpower."

Really? *Really?* She smiled. "So this is arousing?" She wiggled a little, then contracted her muscles.

He inhaled sharply. "That is not a game you're going to win. Not if you want what I think you want."

He had a point, but she couldn't help teasing him with another squeeze. He groaned.

She laughed. "Okay, I'll stop, for now. What if I do this?"

Without thinking, she slipped her fingers between her parted thighs and found her swollen clit. She'd only meant to tease him with a quick show of her touching herself, but the second she rubbed herself, her need climbed from desperate to unbearable. The combination of her touch and the fullness of him inside of her was too much to resist. She told herself she had to stop, that she couldn't do that kind of thing in front of him, but the sensations building inside of her were powerful and amazing and…

"Don't stop," he said quickly. "Renee, don't stop. Please."

She looked at him and saw him intently studying her. His pupils were dilated, his body stiff. He moved his hands to her hips, guiding her up and down in the rhythm designed to take them both over the edge.

Still watching him watch her, she rubbed harder, faster, with each circle, she brushed against the base of his erection, she felt how hard he was, how ready.

"Tell me it's not going to take long," he breathed.

"It's not."

She was so close already. Her orgasm was just there, on the fringes. Still holding his gaze, she moved up and down faster and faster. She could feel her breasts bouncing, her face flushing, her release getting closer. Need built and built until she was overwhelmed and had no choice but to give in to her orgasm. She cried out, her body contracting around him, forcing him over the edge. His hands tightened on her hips, holding her still as he pushed in even farther, pressing against the very heart of her and groaning as he came.

Renee stayed where she was for a few seconds. Reality returned and she had to face the fact that she was naked, straddling a man she barely knew and his penis was still inside of her.

Just as her afterglow was about to crash and burn in a sea of humiliation, Jasper smiled at her. It was a very self-satisfied male smile that spoke of his own pleasure at everything that had happened.

"You're not all that," she said, shifting off him and standing. Her legs were a little shaky and she'd been stretched every which way, but she had to admit, she felt good. Better than good.

"I'm all that and so are you."

He got up, as well. They cleaned up and went looking for their clothes. Once they were dressed, Renee braced herself for the speedy departure. It was what guys did, or so she'd been told. This was her first one-night stand. No regrets, she told herself. She wasn't looking for anything but easy sex. She was a disaster at romantic relationships and knew the smartest decision was to avoid them completely. Jasper had given her everything she'd wanted.

"Got any beer?" he asked when he'd tugged on his T-shirt.

"I do."

She moved toward the kitchen. As she passed him, he reached out and lightly stroked her arm. They paused to stare at each other. One corner of his mouth turned up in a boyish half smile that left her feeling oddly…floaty.

She grabbed a bottle for each of them and they went into the living room. So he was going to stay for a bit. That was unexpected, but nice. Really nice.

He settled on the sofa. She hesitated a second before sitting in the chair opposite. While snuggling next to him sounded appealing and something she could get into, she didn't actually know him that well. The truth of the statement nearly made her laugh.

Sex?

Why, yes, thank you. Now what was your name again?

"Something funny?" he asked.

"Um, no. Just thinking about stuff."

He studied her for a second. "You know I'm not the marrying kind, right?"

She'd nearly taken a sip of her beer. Grateful she hadn't, so she wouldn't choke to death, she set the bottle on the coffee table between them and stared at him. So much for feeling floaty.

"What are you talking about? The marrying kind? Why would you say that? Why would you think it?

Who do you think I am? I don't want to marry you. It was just sex. It was good sex but it wasn't in the—" she held up both hands and made air quotes "'now we have to get married' category."

She didn't know if she should stand up for emphasis or just glare convincingly.

Jasper grimaced. "Sorry. I didn't mean to upset you. It's just, you plan weddings for a living."

"That is my job, not who I am. You write about people getting murdered. I don't assume you're planning to murder me. Not the marrying kind. No wondering you're not in a relationship."

"Hey, don't judge."

"That line deserves judgment."

"Can I have a do-over?"

"Sexually or conversationally?"

An eyebrow rose, as his expression shifted to slightly predatory. "Give me a few minutes and you can have both."

"You wish." Although in truth, she thought it was a good idea, too.

"I kind of do."

They smiled at each other. There was a moment of silence, but this time it was comfortable.

"How'd you end up here?" she asked. "You don't strike me as a Happily Inc kind of guy."

"My car broke down. I was living in LA and I had just driven to New York to visit my publisher and agent."

"You drove from LA to New York and back? Why didn't you fly?"

"I didn't fly well back then. I still don't like it, but I can do it."

Why wouldn't he fly well? Oh, right, she thought.

While she didn't know the details, she'd heard rumors about his time in the military and how he'd escaped without physical injury but still had suffered from significant PTSD.

"So you were stuck in town while they fixed your car?" she asked.

"I was. It was an old clunker and it took a while to get the parts shipped in. I stayed at one of the hotels."

She picked up her beer and grinned. "Oh, please, please tell me you stayed at the Sweet Dreams Inn."

"Why would you care about that?"

"I want to picture you hanging out in one of the themed rooms. The princess room or the Heidi room or the woodland creature room."

"There's a woodland creature room? Why?"

"It's fun. I'd love it."

He shuddered. "That must be a girl thing. For what it's worth, I was in the pirate room."

"I know that one. It's nice."

When she'd first taken the job in Happily Inc, she'd made it a point to visit all the local businesses that supported the wedding industry. She wanted to be able to offer recommendations because she knew what she was talking about. To that end, she'd toured all the rooms at the Sweet Dreams Inn, so she knew the pirate room was actually fairly masculine, with a huge sailing ship doubling as a bed.

"But still—no little woodland creatures to keep you company?" she asked, her tone wistful.

"I'm afraid not. Argh."

She laughed. "Okay, I'll accept the pirate room. So you were stuck in town and decided to stay?"

"I didn't have a plan. I drove around to kill time. The

people were friendly enough. I was here over a Monday night, so the clerk at the front desk suggested I head to The Boardroom for game night."

"And you were hooked?"

"I was intrigued." He shifted so he rested his bare feet on the coffee table. "I contacted a local real estate agent about places on the market. I knew I wouldn't want to live in town, so I wasn't expecting much. My house is the first place we saw. I looked at a half dozen more, realized I'd already found what I wanted and made an offer."

"And here you are."

His gaze locked with hers. "Here we both are."

She felt the tension rising between them. It was nice. Sexy and insistent. Inside, heat began to build.

"So I'm not looking for a relationship," she said. "I haven't ever had good luck in the romance department." Which was putting it mildly, she thought. Her love life had been a disaster, and while she wanted to say it was her mother's fault, in truth there were other reasons.

"Giving up on your own happily-ever-after?" he asked.

"Pretty much."

He lowered his legs and rested his feet on the floor, then put his beer on the table. "But a woman has needs."

His tone was low, sexy and intriguing. Renee felt herself flushing. Stupid red hair, she thought with a sigh. "A woman does. As does a man."

"Yes, that's true."

She kept her gaze on his, even though she desperately wanted to look away. "But, ah, I've never really done anything like this before."

"Had a sex-only relationship?"

She winced. "Could we not call it that?"

His voice turned teasing. "But you *do* want me to be your booty call."

In for a penny and all that. "Yes."

He nodded slowly. "So you'd be using me for sex?"

"I could say the same thing about you."

"I didn't ask you to be *my* booty call. I don't know." He raised and lowered his shoulders. "I've never been anyone's sex toy before."

"You didn't really just say that."

He dropped his gaze to the floor. "I feel used."

"Just stop it. No one believes that for a second."

He looked at her again and grinned. "Sex without the promise of anything more," he said. "I'm in." His smile faded. "Having said that, I'd like to keep things exclusive. Otherwise it gets confusing. Unless you want to invite one of your friends to join us."

"What?" she shrieked.

He stood and pulled her to her feet. "I'm kidding. I know them too well. Worse, I know the men in their lives. It would be weird. So just you and me, for as long as it's good for us, then when it's over, we walk away. No regrets, no bad breakup."

It sounded so mature and modern, she thought. And was exactly what she wanted. And while she was fully aware that it could all end horribly, because her boy-girl things always did, at least she was starting from a position of clarity and honesty.

"Agreed," she said firmly, raising herself on tiptoe so she could kiss him. "Now, if it's been long enough, I think I should let you use me for sex. To keep things fair."

"I like how you think."

He pulled a condom out of his jeans pocket and

tossed it onto the coffee table. "I grabbed that from your bedroom. I say that so you don't think less of me." He grinned. "Your sofa is very comfortable. Why don't we start here and see where things go."

RENEE HAD BEEN HEALED. Despite her lack of sleep and the generally achiness from unused muscles getting a workout, she felt happy and energized and just a little bit weightless. It was amazing what a night of great sex could do for a woman. And with a little luck and some schedule planning, it was exactly what she intended to experience again and again. Yup, she would be enjoying her booty call bonanza for as long as it lasted.

Jasper had left around two in the morning. Even though she technically could have slept in, she'd been awake by six, happy and practically humming with the glory of the day. After clearing up her work emails, she'd gone to the grocery store for ingredients for one of her favorite pasta salads. She'd fixed that, showered, done a little more paperwork, then just before noon she headed for Willow Gallery, where she would meet her girlfriends for lunch.

She had a large group of friends in town. Their schedules were complicated and everyone was busy, so the weekly lunch was a priority. They rotated locations and whoever hosted provided an entrée. Everyone else brought whatever they were in the mood for. Mostly the menu worked out but every now and then they ended up with three veggie plates. Still, Renee was far more interested in the conversation than the food. She enjoyed the chance to hang with other women. In the past, she'd worked hard to keep herself a safe distance from the people around her. But since moving to

Happily Inc, she'd realized it was safe to connect and fit in. She could relax here and that felt good.

Willow Gallery, a beautiful venue close to the river, housed amazing art pieces. Happily Inc was home to several successful artists. Renee had moved to town in time to see her friend Natalie grow from struggling unknown to rising star. Natalie had been able to quit her office manager job to concentrate on her art full-time.

Renee pulled in next to two familiar cars. Pallas and Carol were both already inside, and if previous lunches were anything to go by, they would have brought their babies with them.

Just as difficult as accepting she would never have love in her life, was the realization that she would never have a traditional family. While children weren't an impossible dream, if she wanted kids, she was going to have to go it alone, and being a single mom wasn't an easy road. Renee had watched her own mother deal with being both parents while raising a child and it had been hard for her. On the flip side, Renee also knew what it was like to be left by a father and that was a pain that didn't go away. So while she could have a child on her own, she didn't want to go that route, and what with her finally accepting she was never going to trust her heart to a man again, she was stuck.

"I'm not going to think about that," she said aloud as she got out of her car. She'd had great sex the night before, she was going to enjoy hanging with her friends and she would hold Devon and Ryan as much as she could until the other women wrestled the sweet infants from her arms.

She was still smiling as she walked into the gallery. Natalie already had Ryan, so Renee dropped her tote on the buffet table set up by a display of a massive blown glass garden filled with exquisite glass flowers.

"How's my best girl?" she asked, gently taking the sleeping baby from Carol.

"I'm fine," her friend said drily. "Thanks for asking."

Renee grinned. "Good to know." She gently rocked Devon, enjoying the weight of her and admiring her rosebud mouth and velvety soft skin.

"We need more babies around here," Pallas said as she unpacked Renee's insulated tote. "Pasta salad. At some point I need to get off carbs, but I'm not quite ready. What's in this?"

"Cheese tortellini, bacon, tomatoes, diced cucumber, broccoli all tossed with an avocado ranch dressing and sprinkled with cheese."

Pallas raised her eyebrows. "That's a lot of work, young lady."

Renee thought about her early start and good mood. "I was inspired. It's a recipe my mom used to make, only she used regular ranch dressing."

"Sounds delish. I brought brownies," Pallas said with a sigh. "It's the carb thing. I can't help it."

Silver and Bethany walked in together. Silver dumped her container on the table and headed for Natalie.

"Hi, everyone. Pass him over."

Natalie reluctantly passed Ryan to Silver.

"I guess we really do need more babies," Natalie admitted, pushing up her glasses.

"You first," Silver, a pretty platinum blonde and the owner of a mobile bar called AlcoHaul, told her with a grin.

"Not me." Natalie shook her head. "I want another year at least before I get pregnant. I'm working on my art and enjoying being married to Ronan. I'm more interested in aunt status right now."

Renee looked at Bethany, expecting her friend to hurry over and claim Devon, but Bethany stayed by the buffet.

"Hi, everyone," Bethany said with a wave. "The lunch looks great. I brought a veggie plate."

Pallas made a face, then forced a smile. "It's always good to have something healthy on the table."

Renee lowered her voice and whispered, "Liar."

Pallas took Devon from her. "I meant it. Sort of."

Wynn arrived, a plate of brownies in her hand. "Sorry. I got on a call with a client and he was a talker. How is everyone?"

As she spoke, she set down the brownies and reached for Devon.

"Go hug your own baby," Wynn said with a smile as she cooed at Devon. "Mine is way too old to rock."

Renee felt an unexpected stab of guilt and worry rip through her. Jasper and Wynn had once been a couple. Sure, things had ended nearly a year ago, but still, they'd been involved. Wynn was her friend and did that make things awkward?

Renee told herself she would talk to Wynn after the lunch—there was no way she was going to discuss it in front of everyone. Not when it was new and she had no idea what having a man available for a booty call actually meant.

The still-sleeping babies were placed in their car seats and the friends filled their plates before sitting at the table that had been set up in the center of the gallery.

"How's everyone?" Silver asked. "Bethany, weren't you and Cade planning a trip to El Bahar next month?"

Bethany, the adopted daughter of the king of El Bahar, looked startled by the question. "Nothing is finalized. We're still figuring it all out. Leaving the horses for that long is always difficult."

"Don't you have a manager and several people helping out in the stables?" Renee asked.

"We do, but it's still complicated."

Not exactly an answer that made sense, Renee thought. She looked at her friend and wondered if something was going on. Bethany didn't seem like herself.

"I can't find anything better than an appletini for the apple wedding," Silver said. "I've tried a bunch of different cocktails and I'm not sure our bride is going to love any of them."

Pallas looked around the table. "We have an upcoming apple wedding. The bride wants appletinis but the groom's mother wants a different apple-based drink. So far they've been unable to agree on anything. We have one final tasting this week."

"This whole thing is putting me off apples," Silver grumbled. "And I like apples."

"Give yourself an apple-free month and your love will be restored," Carol told her.

Everyone laughed.

Conversation flowed easily. Renee remembered the first time Pallas had invited her to the girlfriends' lunch. She'd been nervous and not sure she would get along with the women, but they'd welcomed her and now were an important part of her life. She knew that her friends would be there for her. She liked being a part of something—belonging. She hadn't had that in a while. Certainly not in high school where the other girls had mostly avoided her. College had been a little better, until someone had figured out the truth about her mother.

Nothing she had to worry about now, she reminded herself. She was keeping Verity far, far away from Happily Inc.

"Great salad," Wynn said, waving her fork at Renee. "There are just enough vegetables to make me feel righteous."

Renee smiled and ignored the guilt. She would talk to Wynn later and get any issues resolved. It was the right thing to do.

But ninety minutes later, all Renee wanted to do was bolt. Instead, she forced herself to walk out with Wynn and ask if they could talk for a moment. Wynn looked surprised, but immediately agreed.

"Want to go grab coffee or can this be talked about in the parking lot?"

Renee glanced around. Everyone else had already left and the gallery was closed on Tuesdays, so customers would not be arriving.

"I just need a second," she said, not sure how to begin. Or what to say. Or... "I had sex with Jasper."

Wynn, a gorgeous woman with curly, dark hair, raised her eyebrows. "Interesting."

"Sorry. I didn't mean to blurt it out like that. It's just you two used to, you know, be friends, and now you're not and I wasn't sure if you were still, um, thinking about him and if it was all right that I..."

"Had sex with him?" The corners of Wynn's mouth twitched. "Aren't you asking a little late? The deed is done."

"I know, but it was unexpected, so I didn't really have time to text you."

Wynn grinned. "That would have been a really note-worthy text for sure." Her expression turned serious. "Our relationship ended last year. We're completely done and what he does with you is great with me." The smile returned. "I mean that in a not awkward way."

Relief erased the guilt. "You're sure?"

"Very. Jasper and I weren't right for each other. He's a great guy, but not *my* great guy."

"Oh, this isn't serious," Renee said quickly. "Neither of us is looking for that. This is very much a no-strings kind of thing." No way she was going to mention the booty call aspect of things.

"That's how it always starts." Wynn tilted her head. "Just as an FYI, Jasper isn't as broken as he thinks. You might want to be careful about that."

Renee had no idea what she was talking about. "Meaning?"

"Most normal guys eventually reach a place where they want more. If you're sure that's not in the cards for you, great. But Jasper just might want to change the rules."

"I can't see that happening."

"Maybe I'm wrong." She smiled. "I'm glad you two found each other. It's nice to be a part of something."

"What about you?"

Wynn shook her head. "Yeah, I'm not really that girl. I try to be, but I'm not."

CHAPTER FOUR

JASPER THOUGHT ABOUT throwing his laptop out the window, but as always, talked himself down. The urge occurred fairly regularly and so far he'd resisted destroying his computer. No good would come of it, he reminded himself. It wasn't as if getting rid of the piece of equipment would solve the problem. It wasn't the keyboard's fault that he couldn't write for shit.

"Dammit," he growled, pounding on the table.

Koda raised his head, as if asking what was wrong.

"Sorry," he told the dog. "Go back to sleep. I'll be more quiet." Jasper saved the pitiful three sentences it had taken him the entire morning to write and leaned back in his chair.

"I can't write women," he told the dog. "Never knew it was a problem. After six years of being published, you wouldn't think that would be news, but it turns out I've never tried to write a woman before. Not one who isn't a victim or a one-night stand."

He rested his head in his hand. "Please don't repeat that to anyone. It makes me sound like a misogynistic asshole and I'm not. It's just my detective had been single through the entire series and now that I'm wrapping things up with him and moving on to another character, everyone thinks I need to leave Vidar in a better place, and that means involved with a woman."

His editor had suggested the idea more than once, and Jasper knew she was right. But who was the woman and how did they meet and when they met, what did they talk about? So far all his dialogue had been stilted and unrealistic. Book dialogue was not like normal human-to-human conversation. It was high points and information and moving the plot forward. In real life…

He smiled, thinking about the conversations he'd had the other night with Renee. Now those had been fun. Especially the parts where she'd gasped "More" or "Harder." Neither of which was going to make it into his book. Writing a woman was difficult enough—no way he could write sex. He wrote about serial killers, and unless sex was part of the ritual murder, he absolutely was not going there in his novel.

Jasper looked at Koda. "I am one sick guy," he admitted. "I need help."

Koda got up and stretched, then picked up his stuffed rabbit and carried it over to Jasper.

"Thanks," Jasper told the dog, before tossing it across his office. Koda trotted over and picked up the rabbit, carrying it back to Jasper, who threw it again.

They played the game for a few minutes before Jasper gave up pretending to work. He stood and headed for the door, Koda at his heels. They both went outside. Koda headed off into the woods to take care of business while Jasper looked around, wondering if there was any inspiration to be had or if he should simply accept his limitations and hope his career continued despite them.

He was deep in self-flagellation when he heard a familiar voice calling his name. Hunter Beauchene walked around the side of the house.

Wynn's son was thirteen now, and getting taller by

the day. He was at that awkward stage where his arms and legs didn't fit with his torso. His voice was in the process of changing and every now and then, Jasper caught glimpses of the man he would eventually grow to be.

"Hey, you," he said, holding out his hand. Hunter did the same as they greeted each other with their elaborate handshake, a ritual that had been established nearly two summers ago. Back when he'd first started seeing Wynn.

Not that she'd introduced him to Hunter. Instead she'd insisted their sex-only relationship be kept secret—especially from her son. If Hunter found out, it was over. Well, Hunter had figured it out almost immediately and had wanted to be friends with Jasper. The kid knew the rules and wanted to keep their hanging out time off his mom's radar. Jasper had resisted at first but eventually Hunter had won him over and they'd started hanging out. He supposed his willingness to break her only rule had been a sign they weren't going to make it as a couple. Ironically, as soon as they'd broken up, she'd stopped minding if he hung out with her son. Yup, women were confusing as hell.

"Is it afternoon already?" Jasper asked, glancing up at the sun. It felt earlier.

Hunter looked at him. "It's barely eleven. I have the day off. The teachers are doing some training or something. You really don't know what time it is?"

"I've been working."

Hunter nodded, getting the explanation. He was used to Jasper's odd ways.

Koda broke through the trees and raced toward Hunter. The teen dropped to his knees to greet the dog. In a matter of seconds, they were on the ground, tumbling over each other. The combination of happy yips and human laughter comforted Jasper. At least this part of his world was as it should be.

"You hungry?" Jasper asked, when the two broke apart.

"Got any cookies?"

Jasper and Hunter shared a weakness for Cheryl's Cookies, and Jasper ordered them frequently. They agreed that the sugar cookies with buttercream frosting were the best.

They went into the kitchen and Jasper pulled four cookies out of the freezer. Hunter poured himself a glass of milk while Jasper refilled his coffee mug. Koda settled in his bed in the kitchen where he could watch everything going on.

The dog was doing well, Jasper thought. Putting on weight, sleeping and settling in to his new life. He was good company.

"How's school?" Jasper asked as he opened the plastic wrap around the first cookie. "Classes going okay?"

"Jasper, you always ask that."

"I'm interested. So answer the question."

Hunter rolled his eyes. "I'm doing fine. I get good grades."

"You better."

"Or what?"

Jasper grinned. "You want to go there with me, kid?"

Hunter laughed. "No, I don't. But in a couple of years I'll be able to take you."

"In your dreams."

"Mom says this year if you hire some guy to teach you a new fighting style I can come to the lessons. As long as they're after school." Hunter's expression was hopeful. "So maybe you could think of something really cool for the book you're writing."

Jasper found it easier to write about something if he could actually do it himself. He'd learned to throw knives and use fighting sticks for previous books. And shoot a crossbow. Hunter had begged to be a part of the lessons, but while Jasper was willing to cross some lines, there were others that needed to stay in place.

"I will think of something cool," he said, "but I will also run whatever it is past your mom."

"She really did say that."

"I believe you." He flashed a grin. "Sort of."

Hunter laughed and tossed Koda a piece of cookie.

"So what's going on for the rest of your day off?"

Hunter finished his second cookie and picked up his milk. "I'm going to go over to a friend's house."

"You ride all the way up here?"

"I got a ride partway from a park ranger."

Jasper thought about the pages he hadn't written. He was behind on his book and if this morning was any indication—and so far, it was—without doing something drastic, he was never going to make forward progress on his story. Maybe he needed a change of scene and a chance to observe women in their natural habitat.

"I'm heading to town," he said. "We can throw your bike in the back of the truck and I'll drive you to your friend's house."

"Thanks."

Thirty minutes later Jasper stood in the center of town and tried to figure out what he was supposed to do now. Walk around and watch women going about their lives? That wasn't going to be good for anyone. He wasn't some crazed stalker guy and would watching a random female do grocery shopping or walking her baby get him any closer to solving his problem? He honestly didn't know where to start. Or how to start. Or what he wanted to do.

He walked over to a bench by the river and sat down. Detective Vidar needed a love interest. He didn't want the woman to be a cop, so not anyone he worked with. Which was limiting because Vidar, like Jasper himself, didn't have much of a social life. Dating a victim seemed tacky. Plus, most of Jasper's killer's victims ended up dead. So someone involved on the fringes of the crime? Or what? A neighbor? A...

He stood up. This was ridiculous. He knew women. Lots of women. All he had to do was talk to one of them. He looked around and saw the large wall that defined the boundaries of Weddings Out of the Box. Renee. He would go see Renee. Not only could they talk about his book, he would get to see her smile and that alone was worth a trip down the mountain.

"WE CAN DO an assortment of different kinds of apples to hold the place cards," Renee said, scrolling through photos of apples on her computer. "That adds variety. However if you want consistency and to be in line with your color palette, then I would say stick with the Granny Smith apples."

She paused and glanced at the speakerphone. There was a moment of silence, followed by the sound of breathless female laughter.

"I've hit a wall," Stacey Treadway said. "I can't make one more decision. I just can't."

"Someone has to," Renee said gently. "And it's not going to be me."

"And I thought apples would be easy. Let's do the Granny Smith apples for the place cards. They'll go with the glass towers we'll have around the space and it will look nice."

"Done and done," Renee said, studying her list. "Stacey, I don't want to scare you, but I think we're finished."

"Really? So no more decisions?"

"Not today."

Stacey laughed. "Let me guess. You're not making any promises."

"Nope. But we're really close and your wedding is going to be beautiful. I'm very excited to see everything turn out."

"Thanks, Renee. You've been so wonderful to work with."

"You've been great, too. Just remember, I'm here for you. Call me if you need anything and I'll do the same. Otherwise, we are good to go."

"Wow. It's getting close. I guess I'll see you soon."

"You will."

They hung up. Renee wrote up the notes from their phone call, entering the information on her computer where it would automatically feed to her tablet. A happy wedding day was all about keeping track of the details.

She'd barely hit the save key when Jasper walked into her office.

He looked good, she thought as she felt a bit of tingling low in her belly. Tall and a little rugged. She hadn't seen him since their night together and wasn't sure what to say now. Or think. Or how to act. Unexpected nerves tightened her throat and chest and she had the strangest urge to both bolt and throw herself at him. She settled on doing neither.

"Hey," he said as he paused by the door. "Is this an okay time?"

"It is. What's up?"

"I was in town and I wondered if we could talk for a second."

"About?"

He motioned to a chair in front of her desk. She nodded and he sank down, then looked at her.

"I have no idea," he said.

"You have no idea why you're in town or you have no idea what you want to talk about?"

"Both."

"Okay. Do you want to take a minute and collect your thoughts?"

Instead of answering, he glanced around at her office. "You plan weddings, right?"

"I do."

"What does that entail?"

Not the question she was expecting. She smiled. "Are you asking for yourself?"

"You know I'm not."

"Just checking. You might have met your one true love in the last few days."

His gaze turned knowing. "I had someone on my mind, so no. Tell me what you do?"

"When a couple decides to hold their wedding here, I help them with as much of the wedding as they want. We provide a full service venue. We can arrange catering, bar service, flowers, an officiant and anything else they might want. In addition we have the unique ability to create nearly any kind of theme wedding the happy couple is looking for."

He nodded. "Say I want a movie wedding. *American Graffiti*. Do you know it?"

"I've seen it before. It's what, the 1960s? I'm kind of picturing the movie *Grease*, so I'd have to watch *American Graffiti* again to get the details right. We'd take liberties with the clothing. Some kind of poodle skirt bridesmaid dresses could be cute. We could do food from a diner for sure. Maybe a play on burgers and fries. Silver could come up with some fun cocktails—all variations on classics. You'd want a cutout of that white Thunderbird for guests to take pictures in. 1960s music, for sure. Oh, we could get a bunch of 45 records and use them in lots of different decorations. Maybe around the base of the centerpieces, or hanging from the ceiling. I think themed custom cookies would be terrific, too. If the groom was willing, we could really play on the poodle skirt idea and have poodles made out of flowers. And a soda fountain would be fantastic. Oh, we could do ice cream–based adult beverages. That would be unique and the guests would love it."

He stared at her. "You came up with all that in a minute."

"Probably more like five, but yes. Jasper, that's what I do. I might know what a bride wants before she comes in but often I don't. I need to be able to think on my feet." She leaned toward him. "Once we picked a direction, we would discuss who's providing the vendors and where she is in her process. Oh, we also need to know how long we have. Less time makes things frantic, but more time means decisions get changed again and again and that can be stressful for all of us."

She paused. "I can keep talking, but I'm not sure what you want to know."

"Me, either. You've given me a lot to think about. Thanks."

"You're welcome. This is for your book, isn't it?"

"Yes. Maybe. I don't know. I'm having some problems with one of the characters." He frowned. "Why aren't you married?"

She hadn't seen that question coming. "Excuse me?"

"Why aren't you married? You're smart, you're sexy and—" He glanced over his shoulder and lowered his voice. "I happen to know you're dynamite in bed."

She felt herself flush. "Thank you and that is off-topic."

"Too personal?"

"A little, but also confusing."

"I don't get women," he admitted. "I have this character and I can't figure her out. I can't even make her close to real. Why do women do what they do? What are they thinking?"

He got up and closed her office door, then returned to his seat. "That night at The Boardroom. Why me? Why then? I served for eight years and when I got out of the army I was so screwed up in the head. I've made my way back a fair amount but we both know I'll never be normal. I'm okay with that. But you're not damaged. So why aren't you with some great guy, popping out babies and living the American Dream?"

She could see he was genuinely confused, which was kind of appealing. Later she would think about how casually he talked about being damaged. According to Wynn, he wasn't as broken as he thought, but that was for another day.

As for his question about her single status, she wasn't sure what to say. There were a lot of reasons and many of them had to do with her mother. No way she was going to talk about that. So maybe something safer. And lucky for her, it was the truth.

"I've had two serious relationships," she began. "In college and then a few years later. My last one lasted almost three years. He was a little older, established. Nice. That's what I liked most about him. He was just plain nice. A thoughtful man who paid attention to the little things."

"I hate him already."

She smiled. "Don't bother. He's not worth the energy. Things were going great until they weren't. We were seeing each other regularly, when we could. He traveled. I thought we were in love and mentioned marriage. He said he needed time. He loved me but didn't see himself committing to one woman for the rest of his life." Her mouth twisted as she remembered the long talks. "He said if he was ever going to marry someone, it would be me."

Jasper looked concerned. "Did he cheat?"

"Not in the way you're thinking." She sucked in a breath and looked at him. "It turns out he was already married. With three kids. When I found out and confronted him, he admitted he totally adored his wife and his family and had no plans to leave them, but he loved me, too, and hoped we could just go on the way we had been."

Jasper swore under his breath. "You kicked his ass to the curb."

"I did. I felt stupid. Did he play me or did I allow myself to be played? And did it really matter?"

She still couldn't answer that question. She'd taken over a year to come to terms with his deception and her own foolishness. Falling for someone married after the disaster with Turner and their broken engagement, she'd realized love simply wasn't going to happen for her. Whether it was because she chose the wrong guy or because there was something fundamentally wrong with her, the end result was the same. Relationships ended. Men left—like her dad, Turner. Or they were total losers. Regardless of the how and why, she always found herself alone and shattered. She wasn't going to do that ever again.

"You weren't wrong to give your heart," Jasper told her. "You didn't know what he was doing. It's not your fault."

"I still feel stupid and ashamed. At least I did. Now I've moved on. Anyway, that goes in the column of reasons why I'm not married. I take issue with your assuming that a woman has to—" she made air quotes "—be married and pop out babies to be living the American Dream."

He nodded. "Yeah, I kind of figured that one out on my own. The woman thing is hard. Any suggestions on how to do better?"

She thought for a second. "Movies. Watch movies." She started writing on a piece of paper. *"Two Weeks Notice, Brooklyn, Juno, Steel Magnolias."* She wrote down several others. "These are all strong women in great stories. Watch them, then we'll talk."

He took the list and stood. "Thanks, Renee. I appreciate it. I'll start watching them today."

Before she could answer, he was gone. Just like that. No offer for a lunchtime quickie or even some idle chitchat.

"You are such a guy," she murmured, before turning back to her computer. Which, she had to admit to herself, wasn't really a bad thing at all.

JASPER WATCHED THE movies Renee suggested and a few more. He made sure he fed Koda on time and took the old guy for a walk every day. Otherwise, he was pretty much glued to his TV or tablet. He watched movies while jogging on his treadmill, while preparing and eating his meals. He fell asleep watching movies, then started fresh in the morning.

Several days later, he surfaced, realizing he'd watched all the ones Renee had suggested, and several more, and he still had questions. After checking the time on his phone and realizing it was barely seven in the evening, he texted Renee.

You around?

A bit later, she responded. Are you asking what I think you're asking?

He picked up his phone and called her.

"I was asking if we could talk," he said when she answered. "I watched all those movies you suggested and I have a lot of questions." And an interest in seeing her because it had been a few days and even while watching the movies, she'd been on his mind.

"Oh. Okay. I wasn't sure."

"What else would I be asking?"

"I thought maybe a polite version of 'u up.' You know—the texting question about a booty call."

"I didn't know that." He paused. "Maybe I knew that, but I wasn't thinking about that."

She chuckled. "Apparently we need a code word.

And to be honest, some foreplay, because I would need more than 'u up' to get me in the mood."

"I can be all about foreplay. What would you like?" Because while he had wanted to ask her some questions, they could wait until after. "Or I could come over and figure it out."

"I can't. I have my period and I feel awful. And while that probably falls under the category of TMI, it's true."

"I'm sorry. Can I do anything?"

"I wish, but this is my problem. However, I am available to school you on the mysterious ways of women. Did you really watch all those movies?"

"Yes, and a lot more. You sure you're up for company?"

"I would appreciate the distraction. Just ignore the soft whimpers."

"Would ice cream help?"

She sighed. "Actually, it would help a lot."

"I'm on my way."

CHAPTER FIVE

RENEE SPENT THE time between the phone call and Jasper's arrival alternating between wanting to see him and wishing she'd told him tonight wasn't going to work for her. She just plain didn't feel good and she wasn't sure trying to make polite conversation was going to go well. Only the second she opened her front door and saw him standing outside her apartment, she had the strongest urge to throw herself into his arms and be held in a strong, powerful, *I'm here for you* hug.

What was up with that? she wondered as she stepped back to let him in. Her hormones must be more out of whack than she'd realized.

"Hi," Jasper said, holding up a small white bag. "I didn't know what you liked, so I brought three different flavors."

"That's very thoughtful. Thank you."

He stepped inside and shut the door. She peeked in the bag and saw there where three containers of different flavors of Ben & Jerry's ice cream.

"Cherry Garcia is my favorite," she said, pulling out the pint. "What would you like?"

"The cookie dough one."

She got out bowls and served them each a generous portion, then led the way to the sofa. She curled up in the corner by where she'd plugged in her heating pad.

It wasn't glamorous, but when the cramps got bad, the heat helped. Right now she was only dealing with a low ache, but that could change at any moment.

He sat at the opposite end and angled toward her. "You really up to this?" he asked. "I could just eat my ice cream and leave."

She grinned. "I notice you're not willing to abandon your ice cream."

"I can if that would make you feel better."

"Sweet, but not necessary. So you watched the movies. What did you think?"

He took his time answering, as if considering his words. He was so large, so masculine, that he seemed out of place. She'd never thought of her apartment as girly, but with him sitting on her gray sofa, with all the throw pillows, and the pale mauve walls, she had to admit, the space had a decidedly feminine air.

Funny how last time she'd been so intent on getting him into her bed, and into her, that she hadn't noticed the absence of maleness.

"I liked nearly all the movies I watched," he said. "*Juno* was great. I never thought about what it must be like for a girl in high school to have to deal with a pregnancy. It's not easy."

He put down his ice cream and gazed at her intently. "*Steel Magnolias* was unexpected. Not what happened with Shelby but how the characters impacted the story. The guys were in the background while the women carried the plot."

She smiled. "Now you know how we feel a lot of the time."

"I can see that. I watched *Gilmore Girls*."

"The series?"

"I started with the one that covers a year in their life and then went back and watched a couple of seasons."

He was determined to figure out his female character, she thought, impressed by the time he was willing to put into his project.

"What did you think?"

He picked up his ice cream again. "I was confused. What happened to Rory? In the original series, she was strong and driven. In the later one, she had no direction. She was a character who always overprepared so to show up at that interview with nothing didn't make sense. That's not who her character was. And the ending." He shook his head. "If I did something like that, my readers would hunt me down. Actually they wouldn't have to. My editor would have already killed me."

He sounded passionate and engaged in the characters. "Did you like it or not?" she asked.

"I don't know. I was unsatisfied but I can't stop thinking about it. So there's a lesson in that. Plus, I liked how strong the women were in the movies. It's like in my books. The stronger the villain, the stronger the hero has to be to defeat him."

"Or her."

He sighed. "Yes, or her. Although statistically, there are very few serial killers who are women."

"That's because they don't get caught."

He flashed her a grin. "Touché."

"Thank you. So you're thinking a strong woman for Vidar?"

"I think that would work best with him. Not a cop. If she was on the force, he would have met her already. And a transfer seems too convenient. Not that it matters—I don't like the idea of a work relationship. He wouldn't do that."

"What about someone he meets locally? He goes to that coffee shop by his apartment," she said, trying to think of who else Vidar ran into regularly in the books. "She could work there, or have just moved to the neighborhood. They could accidentally grab each other's to-go cups."

Jasper looked surprised. "You've read my books?"

She laughed. "Of course I've read your books. You're a local author and the only writer I've ever met. Why wouldn't I read your books?"

"I didn't know."

He sounded both sheepish and pleased, which oddly enough made her feel a little teary, which was craziness on a stick. Hormones, she thought again. They were powerful little creatures.

He cleared his throat. "I like the idea of someone local. She works in an office, she's a dog walker."

"I don't see Vidar as a real dog kind of guy. He's too focused on what he does. I'm not sure he'd be a good pet parent."

"He could do it. He just hasn't had a chance."

Her lips twitched. "You're defending someone who doesn't exist?"

"Yes. He's my guy."

"Fine. He could love dogs." She held in a smile. "Or cats. What if he meets a crazy cat lady?"

"No. Definitely no."

"What about just one cat? I've always wanted a cat. They're so beautiful."

"No on the cat."

She smiled. "Okay, she owns a restaurant, she's a

plumber, she works in a bar, she's a teacher, she's a..."
She tried to think about what kind of career would make
sense for Vidar's lady friend.

"What if she's a wedding planner?" Jasper asked.

Renee finished her ice cream and licked the spoon.
"Really? That's both flattering and creepy at the same
time."

"It makes sense. You're creative and resourceful.
She could be, too."

"How would they meet? Vidar goes to a wedding?"

"He could. Someone from the force. Or a friend."

"Not family," she said. "He doesn't have any. I don't
know—a wedding planner is nothing like what he does.
Would they even get along? And while we're not on the
subject, where did you come up with his name? Vidar.
It's unusual."

"I found it in a baby name book. It's based on Norse
mythology. Vidar is the son of Odin and a giantess
named Grid. He's silent and known to be strong. I
thought it suited him."

"I can't get past his mother's name. Grid? Really?"

"It was different back then."

"Still. 'This is my mother, Grid'?"

"You're not helping."

Renee laughed. "Okay. Vidar, son of Grid. Oh, wow,
I just realized that Pallas's name comes from Greek mythology." She paused. "Or Roman. I think Greek. We
have two mythologically based names in town. What are
the odds? And back to your girl. She could be a florist,
an artist. Oh, make her a glass artist. You could totally
hang out with Mathias and Ronan and learn the trade.
It would be very method acting. Or writing, I guess."

"You're feeling better."

She smiled. "I am. The ice cream cured me, at least for the moment. Thank you for bringing it."

"Thanks for helping me with my book."

"We didn't accomplish anything."

"I have a lot to think about. That's progress."

"If you say so." She thought about all they'd discussed and how he'd watched all the movies she'd suggested plus more she hadn't. He was good at his job, doing the work and then some. He was handsome, funny, godlike in bed and successful.

"So why aren't you married?" she asked. "Why the serial monogamy?"

"You proposing?"

"Not today."

He grinned. "Okay, you answered my question when I asked it, so fair is fair. You know I was in the army."

She nodded.

"Before that I was just some small-town guy. I grew up in Montana. I liked the usual outdoor stuff, had a girlfriend in high school. There weren't a lot of opportunities and I wasn't excited about college so I joined up right after I graduated."

His gaze shifted past her, as if he was seeing something she couldn't.

"I got into the military police and that was good for me. I liked my work and I was serving my country. Some days were more difficult than others." He shifted his attention back to her. "I had several tours in Afghanistan. They got harder and by the time I was ready to rejoin the civilian world, I found myself physically intact but mentally and emotionally messed up."

"PTSD?" she asked.

"Among other things. I had nightmares, anxiety,

sleeplessness. I couldn't focus. Some days I couldn't stop shaking. I went through all of it. Therapy, drugs, group counseling, halfway houses. Everything helped a little but nothing helped very much. After a while I figured out I was never going to be whole. Not the way I had been. The doctors I saw talked about managing my symptoms. One day we were given an assignment to write about how we were feeling. I started writing and couldn't stop. Two years later, I'd finished a book that had nothing to do with the war and everything to do with someone else's problems. That was the first Vidar novel."

She thought about what Wynn had said—that he wasn't as broken as he thought—and wondered if it was true.

"So you're too wounded to love anyone?" she asked lightly.

"Something like that. It's okay. I've got a pretty decent life." He grinned and got to his feet. "I never thought I'd be a writer, that's for sure."

He moved close, bent down and kissed the top of her head. "Thanks for talking to me tonight. I hope you feel better soon."

"I will. The first twenty-four hours are the worst for me. By the morning, I'll be fine."

"I'm glad." He touched her cheek. "I'll show myself out. See you soon."

She nodded and he left. When he was gone, she stretched on the sofa and thought about all they'd talked about. Jasper was an interesting guy. Under other circumstances, she just might want to test her friend's theory about his condition. But as things were, she would be foolish to even try. Love was not happening—

at least not for her. Given her past, she was going to have to go it alone. But for this moment in time, Jasper was exactly right.

RENEE HUNG UP the phone and did a little shimmy in her chair. Having the disparate elements of a wedding start to come together always made her happy. When a seemingly impossible item—like a request for half the chairs at the reception to be black and the other half to be white, while all of them had gold cushions—worked out, she felt as if she could achieve anything. At least when it came to weddings. Ride in on a hot air balloon? Done. A vegan cake so delicious no one would guess its lack of dairy and eggs? Easy-peasy. Talking dolphins? Renee winced. Best not to go there, she thought, entering the information about the chairs on her computer and saving it so it flowed through to her tablet.

She was about to call yet another vendor about yet another challenging request when Jasper walked into her office and smiled at her. Her body reacted immediately, reminding her that it had really liked this man and the things he'd done to her and hey, her period would be over soon so maybe they should set up a date or something.

Instead of going down that path, she settled on the more conventional and safe, "Hi."

"Morning. You have a minute?"

If he was willing to take off his clothes and have his way with her, she had several, she thought dreamily, only to remember they were in her office and she should probably play just a little harder to get.

"I do," she told him, motioning to one of the chairs in front of her desk. "What's going on?"

"I've been thinking about what we talked about last night. I want Vidar's love interest to be a wedding planner. It gives her access to a lot of people he wouldn't normally come in contact with and it gets him out of the station. He was in there a lot in the last book. We both need a break."

She was still processing his announcement so could only ask, "You and Vidar need a break?"

"Uh-huh. I thought I could follow you around for a few weeks, learn about the business and—"

"No," she said firmly, as all thoughts of them having another close encounter faded from her mind. "You're not getting your serial killer cooties on my weddings. I'm a big believer in keeping the energy positive and flowing forward. Do you know what a serial killer would do at a wedding?"

Jasper stared at her, his gaze intense. "That's what I was thinking. I want the serial killer to be a wedding crasher."

"No," she said firmly. "Just no."

"No what?" Pallas asked, walking into the office. "Oh, hi, Jasper. Did I know we had a meeting with you?" She frowned. "You're not getting married, are you? I mean of course you could if you wanted, I just didn't think you were seeing anyone right now. Are you?"

Renee tried to act normal. She had no idea what he would say to that question and was incredibly grateful when he simply smiled and said, "I'm doing research for a book. I want to give my hero a love interest in the last book of the series and I'm thinking she'll be a wedding planner."

"Oh, Vidar's going to fall in love?" Pallas sighed. "That's so great. I love that. He needs a woman for sure. He's way too alone all the time and with his dark thoughts and all. A wedding planner would be perfect. Weddings are positive and upbeat and happy." She smiled at Renee. "Are you going to help him? That's a terrific idea. Let him follow you around and stuff. Jasper's the kind of writer who gets the details right."

Renee held in a groan.

"If it's not too much trouble," he said, smiling winningly at Pallas. "I'd really like to follow her around and get to know the business."

"Sure. Whatever you need." Pallas turned to Renee. "I'm assuming you're fine with it. Being married to an artist, I know how important it is to go with the flow when they get an idea in their head. So we're good?"

Renee sighed. "We're good." She waited until her boss left before glaring at Jasper. "If I didn't know better, I would swear you'd planned that."

"You know I didn't." He leaned back in his chair and rested his ankle on his opposite knee. "Sometimes I get lucky."

"I'll say," she muttered, ignoring the potential double entendre.

"You could have told her no," he pointed out. "You could have said I would be in the way and you didn't want me around to taint everything with my serial killer cooties."

An excellent point. She could have and she hadn't so this was partially on her. While Pallas might not have understood Renee's reluctance, she would have respected it. So why had she just sat there like a lump? Did she want to spend the time with Jasper? Did she want to help with the book? Did she not want to have to think about that question right now?

"I'm not in a place to discuss that," she told him firmly. "So let's set some ground rules. Weddings are incredibly stressful for everyone involved. It is a special day for the bride and the groom and no matter what, they come first."

"Agreed."

"You will not offer suggestions or opinions, make faces or otherwise indicate you think what they're doing is anything but magical."

"I'd never offer an opinion."

"You say that now, but when Wendy and William want to get married while riding the prize pigs they both raised, you might find yourself with a thought or two."

"Prize pigs?"

"It's an example." She glared at him. "I'm serious, Jasper. For you this is work, for them, it's their lives. They will remember their wedding forever. You can't get in the middle of that."

"I know that, but why do you think I'd want to get in the middle of anything?"

"You get involved in your research. You learn by doing. I've heard about the fighting sticks and who knows whatever methods you use to figure out how to do stuff. I don't want you getting into that level of detail with my weddings."

"You're really protective of them."

"Of course I am."

He put both feet on the ground and leaned toward her. "Renee, I give you my word that I won't get personally involved in any of your weddings. All I want to do is observe you and learn about what you do."

"It all sounds fine," she grumbled.

"You don't believe me?"

"Oh, I believe you mean what you say now. But I don't trust you not to change the rules."

"That will never happen."

"Sure. You go to hell for lying, same as stealing."

He grinned. "I haven't heard that one in a long time."

"The point is still valid."

She knew she was going to regret allowing him into her world and at the same time she was oddly excited about the idea of Jasper learning about what she did. Later, she would have a serious talk with herself and figure out what exactly was going on with her brain. But until then…

She unlocked a drawer in her desk and pulled out a tablet and charger.

"You'll need the tablet to keep up with what's going on with the various weddings," she told him. "I have a firm 'you break it, you bought it' policy, so respect the property."

He studied her. "You're tough."

"Yes, I am. You need to respect that, too."

"Yes, ma'am." He picked up the tablet and turned it on, then waited while it booted. "How did you get to be a wedding planner? Is it something you study?"

"Not exactly. I was a marketing major in college." After her attempt to get into fashion had failed spectacularly, she thought sadly. "I liked marketing but I didn't love it. On a whim, I applied for a job as a wedding planning assistant in Bel Air."

"Fancy."

"It was. I discovered I had a flair and one thing led to another. After I learned the business, I started looking for a different location. That led me to here."

His gaze settled on hers. "I'm glad it did."

The quivers in her tummy were unexpected but very nice. "Me, too."

He glanced at his tablet. "It's ready." He looked again. "How many weddings are in this thing?"

Renee picked up her own tablet and glanced at the index. "We average one and a half weddings a week or about seventy-five a year. We can hold as many as three a week—Friday night, Saturday and Sunday—but we try not to. Everyone gets too tired and cranky."

He shook his head. "That's a lot of weddings."

"It is. Most of the weddings we're doing these days are multiday events. With the entire wedding party coming into town from somewhere else, it makes sense. We can host a rehearsal dinner on Friday night and a brunch on Sunday morning with the wedding as the main event on Saturday. As soon as bride and groom sign with us, they have their own file. You'll see their names listed in alphabetical order, bride first."

She looked at him. "We usually have the most contact with the bride. If we have two men getting married, or two women, we list under our point of contact. All right, click on Jackson/Kincaid."

Jasper did as she asked, then looked at the display. "I get it. There are tabs for every category. Guest list, flowers, catering, decorations. Huh." He touched the display. "So the calendar tells you what needs to be done when. Green means it's good, yellow is pending and red is trouble?"

"Exactly. I can easily print the calendar. I can also print out a to-do list for each wedding. Every week I print out a master list, so I know where we are on each wedding and what needs to be done and the status on pending orders. Because Happily Inc is a wedding destination town, our vendors work with us all the time. I don't have to worry that Silver won't show up with the bar, or Gary won't deliver the right number of chairs. In some ways, we're able to pass on some of the work directly to our vendors, which keeps costs down."

She showed him a basic contract and talked about the various weddings coming up in the next few weeks.

"I'd like to go to one," he said.

"You're not crashing a wedding. It wouldn't be right."

"Could I work at one?"

Renee pulled up her wedding calendar, then tabbed through the various menus. "The apple wedding is coming up. The drinks are all premixed, so you could talk to Silver about helping her. If you know how to be a waiter, then you could talk to the catering company."

"I'll go see Silver," he said. "I think I'd do better with drinks than food."

"There *is* less to go wrong."

He flashed her a smile. It was a good one that had her toes doing a little curl in her sensible pumps.

"What other themes do you have coming up?"

"Can't get excited about the apple wedding?" she asked, her voice teasing.

"I'm going to see it for myself, and that will be plenty."

She looked at the calendar. "It's fall so we have some that are just seasonally based. There's a Halloween wedding, which should be interesting, and a football wedding." She looked at him. "It's more Dallas Cowboys–based than generic football. I was a little nervous, but it's turning out beautifully. The wedding colors are the silver and blue. The bridesmaids are all in silver and the dresses are gorgeous. I'm getting excited about it. We're also doing a Scottish wedding. That couple lives in Sedona so we have most of our meetings in person. With the other couples, most of the meetings are teleconferences."

She paused, not sure what else he wanted to hear about. Before she could ask, he said, "What's wrong with the Halloween wedding?"

"Nothing. Why?"

"Your voice was different when you mentioned it. As if you didn't approve or something."

"What? No. It's fine. There are a lot of fun elements. The best man is the bride's dog."

His gaze didn't waver. "There's something, Renee. I can hear it."

How could he have guessed? Was it a writer thing or was she not hiding her feelings? She bit her lower lip.

"It's not anything," she said slowly. "At least it's not anything I can define. I just don't…" She glared at him. "This is just between us. You can't tell anyone or put it in your book."

He set down the tablet. "I won't betray you."

For a second she wondered if he meant something else by his words, or had a different meaning. She told herself not to be ridiculous.

"I don't have a good feeling about them," she admitted. "I can't explain it beyond that. Sometimes, when I'm working with a couple, I get a sense of whether or not they're going to make it. Maybe it's how they treat each other. I don't know."

"They're not going to make it?"

She hesitated before shaking her head. "I don't think so. I hope I'm wrong. I hope they live long, happy lives together."

"But you don't think so."

"No."

"It's okay. People have intuition about different things. This is your area of expertise. You've seen a lot of couples come and go. Of course you'd have a sense of them."

He rose. "Thanks for all the information. I'm going to head home and process it. I promise not to show up again without giving you a little notice."

"That would work."

He surprised her by closing the door, then circling around her desk and drawing her to her feet. When she was standing, he cupped her face in his large hands and kissed her.

"Thank you for your help," he murmured, his mouth moving against hers.

"You're, ah, welcome."

He chuckled, kissed her again, then walked to the door. "I'll be in touch," he promised.

"I look forward to it."

And then he was gone. Renee sank back in her seat and pressed a hand to her chest. The man had skills. With nothing more than a very fleeting kiss, he'd made her heart race.

Work, she reminded herself. She had to focus on work. She glanced at the tablet and saw she'd pulled up the Halloween wedding. Instantly her good mood vanished. She did not want to be right about Andrew and Asia, but she was afraid she was.

Intuition, he called it. She could accept that. At least she wasn't doing anything crazy like claiming she could see ghosts or talk to animals and wasn't that a good thing?

CHAPTER SIX

THE NIGHTMARE BEGAN as it always did—on the edge of a road, with the rocky, brown hills behind him. Everything was familiar, but even though he knew what was going to happen, he couldn't stop his heart from racing as he braced himself for the unfolding chain of events.

The open pickup rounded the corner. Jasper walked toward the driver to check his ID. Jasper's men were already inspecting the truck. The details were all there—the chill in the winter air, the scent of distant cooking fires, the crunch of his footsteps on the gravel.

Even as he went through the motions, he tried to stop himself, warn his dream-self that there was danger. That there was going to be an explosion and—

A soft whine broke through his dream. Unexpected weight shifted on the bed, drawing him back to the present. He opened his eyes and found himself in his darkened bedroom, Koda stretched out beside him. The dog watched him anxiously.

"Hey you," Jasper said, feeling his heart pounding and the sweat on his body. The physical manifestations of the nightmare weren't that bad this time. Koda had awakened him before the really bad stuff started. Before everyone died.

He reached out and rubbed the dog's head, then sat up so he could catch his breath. It was nearly dawn.

Getting up made more sense than trying to sleep again. Safer. He leaned his head against Koda's strong back and told himself it was just a nightmare. It wasn't real—not anymore.

"WHEN DO YOU close on the house?" Jasper asked several hours later.

Garrick McCabe stretched out his long legs, picked up his beer and shrugged. "In ten days. I've never bought a house before. My real estate agent tells me it's going really well, but I have to admit the amount of paperwork is staggering. Weren't we supposed to be a paperless society long before now?"

Jasper grinned. "Try being self-employed. When I bought this place, I thought the bank was going to ask for a blood sample or something. I was lucky—I'd just signed a great deal with my publisher, so I dumped my advance into the down payment and that helped."

"Makes sense. At least I have W-2s from the city to flash around. Plus, I think being a cop makes me a decent bet. The odds of me taking off and not making my monthly payments seem unlikely."

Garrick was with the Happily Inc police department. Jasper knew he'd been born in the area and had grown up here. He'd moved to Phoenix to go to ASU and had taken a job with the Phoenix Police Department before moving back two years ago.

He and Garrick had gotten to know each other over games at The Boardroom. Jasper had asked for his help with a couple of details for one of his books and since then Garrick had been a part of the cadre of people Jasper called on to get it right for his characters. Just before the book tour, he and Garrick had gone off to a weekend conference in rural Virginia where cops came from all over to learn about new kinds of weaponry and body armor.

The front door to Jasper's house opened and a familiar voice called, "Sorry I'm late."

Koda stood and watched, his hackles raised.

"It's just Cade," Jasper told the dog. "You remember him, don't you?"

Koda stayed on alert until Cade appeared. When he saw the tall man, his tail wagged and he walked over for a greeting.

"Hey, big guy," Cade said, dropping into a crouch and petting the dog. "You're looking good. You've put on more weight. Another month or so and you'll be where you should be."

He stood and nodded at his friends. "I see you started the party without me."

"Go grab a beer and join us," Jasper said, hoping he didn't sound as nervous as he felt. He'd invited his friends over to read pages from his new book. Normally he only needed help with new fighting skills or police procedures, but this time was different. This time he had to deal with *Mandy*.

Vidar's love interest, whom he'd named Mandy, was going to be the death of him. So far he'd written and rewritten their first scene eight times. In half, they already knew each other and in the rest, they didn't. None of them had gone well. He really hated to send his agent crap if he didn't have to so he was hoping his friends could give him some insights.

Cade returned from the kitchen, beer in hand. He sank into one of the oversize chairs and glanced at Garrick.

"Close on the house yet?"

"In ten days."

"Let me know if you need help moving."

"Me, too," Jasper added.

"I'm good. The place I've been staying is furnished, so I only have a few boxes of personal things. I'll live on a futon for a few weeks, then figure out what I need."

Cade grinned. "A futon? You're such a guy. Come on, man. Grow a pair and buy a big-boy bed."

"In time, in time."

Cade shook his head. "You losers. You both need a woman in your life."

"We're not going to share," Jasper said mildly.

"Fine. You *each* need a woman in your life." Cade sipped his beer. "Being friends with a writer is a pain in the ass."

"You love being on the fringes of my fame."

"Fame?" Garrick chuckled. "Is that what we're calling it now?"

Jasper wanted to continue the banter, but he was too concerned about his story. "So," he began, then cleared his throat. "I have some pages I'd like you to read. For the new book."

He told them about the plot—as far as he knew it—and explained that Vidar would be finding a love interest as Jasper wrapped up the series.

"That's new," Cade said, studying him. "You don't put women in your books."

"Not unless they're being killed," Garrick added. "Or they're a one-night stand for Vidar. Even in bars and stuff, the walk-ons are nearly always men."

"They're not," Jasper protested before wondering if it was true. Given the trouble he was having writing Mandy, it made sense that he'd avoid the whole "female" thing. Write what you know and all that. Which said what about him? That he was so uncomfortable with half the species that he avoided them, even in his books? Was that what he wanted with his life or who he was? He tried to tell himself he'd had a relationship with Wynn, only it hadn't been much more than someone to have sex with. And how well did he know Renee? So far he liked her a lot, but it had only been the one night.

"Jasper?" Cade's voice was soft. "You okay?"

"What? I'm fine."

Both his friends were watching him with studied concern.

"I'm fine," he repeated. "I'm not having a flashback or anything. I was just thinking." Damn—the problem was worse than he thought.

He pointed at the pages in the center of the coffee table. "That's them. Make notes if you want or just set them on fire. Either way, I'd like to know what you really think. No holding back. Being nice isn't going to be doing me any favors."

With that, he rose and called to Koda. "We'll be outside. Let me know when you're done."

With that, he walked out of the family room, through the kitchen and toward the back door. Koda followed, his nails clicking on the hardwood floors. Once they were clear of the house, Jasper found a good-sized stick and threw it as hard as he could. Koda raced after it, returning it a few seconds later. He politely dropped it at Jasper's feet for him to throw again.

While he didn't know exactly what his friends were going to say, he was pretty sure there wasn't going to be any praise for what he'd written. He simply didn't understand Mandy enough to write about her. He couldn't get in her head or imagine her dialogue. She was as much a mystery to him as the moon.

He liked that she was a wedding planner and, based on what he'd learned from Renee, he'd been able to figure out where Mandy worked, but he needed more details. What did a wedding planner talk about with her clients? What was the happy couple interested in and where did his serial killer make his appearance?

After throwing the stick a few more times, Jasper set off with Koda at his heels. They did a quick circuit in the forest. As always the combination of movement, nature and quiet did its thing and his mind calmed.

Obviously he was going to have to follow Renee through one of her weddings. Go to meetings, watch the decision-making process, meet with the bride and groom. That would clarify the work aspect of things. He would also have to observe women more closely. He needed to figure out how they talked. Maybe he could record some conversations to get the right word usage and cadence.

He and Koda headed back to the house. Cade and Garrick were sitting on the back porch, beers in hand. Both of them tensed when they saw him.

"That bad?" he asked, deliberately keeping his tone light.

His friends shared a glance before Garrick looked at him. "In my version, Mandy's part robot, part Soviet general during World War II. She's barking out orders and telling people to be calm."

"The bride was nervous," Jasper started, then told himself to shut up. He was here to learn, not justify.

"She wasn't sympathetic," Garrick told him. "And

the way you describe her walking was just plain weird. Do authors really talk about how a person walks? Don't we just picture what we want in our head?"

"Sometimes a walk shows character," Jasper muttered, hoping he didn't sound defensive. "Thanks for the info."

"I made some notes on the page." Garrick shrugged. "I was honest."

"I appreciate it." He looked at Cade. "You must have read the kiss scene then."

Cade shifted uncomfortably. "Yeah, well, that wasn't a kiss. Damn, Jasper, up against the wall and sucking out her lungs? Where did you come up with that?"

Jasper couldn't remember the last time he'd been this embarrassed. He wanted to remind them both he was a number one *New York Times* bestselling author. Several hundred people lined up at his book signings. He was successful and a hell of a writer. Or at least he had been.

He swore silently. "I was trying to show passion."

"It was either rape or porn. I couldn't decide which. Sorry, man."

"No, I need to hear the truth." He absently patted Koda. "It's just tougher than I thought it was going to be. Women are hard."

Cade sighed. "Actually women are soft and they smell good. Not knowing that might be your problem."

Jasper laughed along with his friends, but deep inside he felt a cold knot of worry. He was totally and completely screwed and he had no idea how to fix the problem.

RENEE DIDN'T KNOW how to tell Jasper that with her period finished, she was more than ready to have another night of whatever he wanted to do with her. A phone call was out of the question. How exactly was she supposed to start *that* conversation? The same with texting. It would just be too weird.

On the bright side, she had an appointment with him this morning, so maybe she could work it into the conversation somehow. She could mention she was feeling much better. *Much*, much better. Although she shouldn't be too enthused. She didn't want him to think they were going to do it in her office. But their meeting was at eleven, so maybe when they were done talking, they could head to her place for a noontime quickie.

She cleared her emails and confirmed everything she needed to get done for the week, all the while doing her best not to think yummy Jasper thoughts. He strolled into her office right on time, looking all tall and Jasper-sexy.

"Hi," she said, trying not to sound too excited. Interested was appealing. Desperate didn't look pretty on anyone.

"Hey."

She waited for the obligatory "How are you?" to which she was going to say something like "Much better," as per the plan, only instead of saying anything like that, he paused for a second, then blurted, "We need to talk."

Nooooooooooo! She mentally stomped her foot. She didn't want to talk. She wanted hot kisses, big man hands and him having with his way with her, none of which she was comfortable sharing so she wasn't sure what to say, which turned out to be fine because he spoke first.

"I can't figure out Mandy."

Mandy? There was a Mandy? Disappointment and a bit of hurt formed a powerful knot in her stomach. "Who's Mandy?"

"Vidar's love interest. I finally named her."

Okay—she was fine with women who weren't real. "You mean you don't understand her character?"

"I don't get anything about her." He walked to her desk and sat down. "I can't get a handle on any part of her. Not her background or how she talks or what she's thinking."

"Do you have to be in her point of view?"

"I don't know. I think so. At some point she's going to be alone with the killer, so we'll have to know what's happening. Unless I did it from his point of view, but that seems like cheating." He glanced up at the ceiling and then back at her.

"I think it would help if I could be more involved with a wedding."

Coldness settled on her. "What, exactly, does that mean?"

"I need more details about Mandy's work. Your work. I think if I followed a couple from concept to ceremony, it would make a difference. What are the decisions being made and why? What do they fight about? Where could the serial killer come in? Is he with catering? Is he the officiant? The groom's father? A guest? I've been considering—"

"No."

She spoke the word firmly, meeting his gaze with as determined a glare as she could muster.

"Just, no. You are not going to get involved in one of my weddings."

"Why not? I'm following you around anyway. How is this different?"

"You're following me around in general. Now you're asking for something specific. Sitting in the corner while I'm on a teleconference is very different from being involved. You're asking me to insert you into a wedding where you'll be in all the meetings and possibly influencing the bride and groom so you get what you want rather than them getting what they want."

"I wouldn't do that."

She stared at him without speaking.

"I wouldn't," he repeated. "I don't want to be in the wedding party. I just want to be on the fringes."

"And if you decide that changing the colors from yellow and green to gold and silver would help your plot, you wouldn't say anything? Oh, please. Of course you would—in a hot second."

All her soft, gooey, sexy feelings disappeared, leaving behind a protective anger she was going to put to good use. She didn't know Jasper very well, but she understood he was a man who was used to getting his way. Only not this time.

"We are talking about the most significant day in a couple's life together. Weddings often take a year of planning. I'm willing to show you what goes on behind the scenes and you're already going to help serve drinks at an upcoming wedding, but you will not get involved in the process. The wedding isn't about you or your book, it's about the bride and groom. You don't get to mess with that."

"I wouldn't be messing with anyone. I don't understand. I learn by doing. I need to do this."

She rose so she could better make her point. "Jasper,

let me be clear. I will not have you destroying a beautiful wedding with your serial killer research."

He looked completely baffled. "I wouldn't do that. I'm kind of famous. They might be honored."

"Or horrified."

He stood—all six-foot-whatever of him—and looked down at her. "You really willing to take me on?"

"Oh, please. I'd take on you and the devil himself to protect my clients. My job is to give them the wedding of their dreams and I will do everything in my power to make that happen. Standing up to you is nothing."

She spoke with conviction, aware that, with each word, she was most certainly putting an end to any afternoon delight on the Jasper front. On a purely *I enjoy a man-induced orgasm as much as the next girl* basis, everything about this pissed her off. But none of that really mattered—not when it came to her couples. She could always get a vibrator and a supply of batteries. Her brides and grooms had only one shot at their wedding day.

He started to respond, then simply shook his head and walked out. When he was gone, Renee sank back into her seat and drew in a breath. She'd done the right thing—she knew that down to her bone marrow. But doing the right thing often came with a price and this time that price was Jasper himself.

JASPER STARTED TOWARD his truck, then changed course and went looking for Pallas. He had a feeling she would be more reasonable than Renee.

He had to admit—he hadn't gotten the reaction he'd been expecting. Yet more proof that he knew less than nothing about women. Were all guys this clueless or was he more lame than most? A question he would have to answer another time, he thought grimly as he stepped into Pallas's office and looked around.

She wasn't there and, based on the fact that her computer was off and her desk was clear, he would guess she wasn't in the building either. Probably for the best, he told himself, as he headed back to his truck. Going over Renee's head was kind of weaselly on his part. She'd been very clear on her feelings and while he didn't understand them, he had to respect them. And her. She'd been fired up for sure.

Now, away from the situation, he had to admit she'd been kind of sexy when she'd been yelling at him. She hadn't been intimidated by him at all. She'd been willing to take him on, no matter what, to protect her clients.

He reached his truck and slid onto the seat, but instead of starting the engine, he pulled out a pad of paper he kept in the glove box, along with a pen and began scribbling notes. He described how Renee had looked as she'd taken him to task—the fire in her eyes and the determined set to her body. Small but mighty, he thought. She was a woman who wouldn't take crap from anyone—at least not when it came to one of her weddings. He wondered if she was that brave on her own behalf.

Mandy would be the same way, he thought absently. Strong and willing to take on the world. He wasn't sure a wedding disaster would resonate with his readers but there had to be something… Did she have a baby sister who needed… Did she have a kid?

He looked out the window but instead of the wall of Weddings Out of the Box, he saw Mandy walking a little boy to school. No, a little girl. Mandy would take on the world for her. She would be fearless and determined.

And if she was a single mom, getting involved with Vidar would mean higher stakes. She couldn't bring just anyone into her daughter's life. Plus, at the end of the book, when her life was in danger, the stakes would be even higher—she had to stay alive for her daughter.

Jasper scribbled notes as quickly as he could, all the while feeling that sense of rightness he got when he finally figured out a problem with his book. He was barely aware of a car pulling in next to his truck until the doors opened and the conversation drifted to him.

"We have to finalize the colors today," the young woman said with a laugh. "If we don't, Renee is going to fire us for making her crazy."

The man with her smiled at her across the roof of the car. "I don't think a wedding planner can fire the people who hired her."

"Did you read the entire contract, word for word? I'm guessing there's a 'they make me crazy' clause for situations just like this one."

Jasper set down his notepad. The man was maybe thirty, about five-ten and wearing a suit. The car was a late model BMW. His bride-to-be was only a couple of inches shorter, with blond hair and a curvy build. They looked successful, happy and in love.

Even as he told himself a smart man would respect what Renee had told him, he was getting out of the truck and closing the door behind him.

"Morning," he said. "You're here to meet with Renee, right?"

They looked at him. "We are."

"Great. I'm Jasper Dembenski."

The couple exchanged a glance. "I'm Hanna and this is my fiancée, Graham."

They both looked faintly puzzled and a little concerned as if they were wondering if he was going to try to steal away their business or tell them something bad about Weddings Out of the Box.

He offered them an easy smile. "You're going to love working with Renee. Her weddings are magnificent."

Hanna smiled. "That's what we've heard. We've only started and we're on a tight schedule, but so far, so good." She tilted her head. "Wait, you wouldn't be *the* Jasper Dembenski would you?"

"You mean the author?" He raised a shoulder. "I am."

"Really?" Hanna turned to Graham. "I love his books. They're the ones you read, too. What are you doing here? Are you getting married? You should so have your wedding here. You'll love working with Renee."

"No wedding, at least not the way you mean." He glanced at the building and knew there would be hell to pay, and yet he was going to do it anyway. "But I am writing a book."

Hanna's eyes widened. "A new one? A new book?" She clutched her hands together. "Are you doing research? Is that why you're here? Say yes! Please say yes."

Jasper chuckled. "You guessed it. My serial killer will be involved with a wedding. I don't have all the details yet."

She waved Graham closer and grabbed his hand. "Do you need to research a specific wedding?" She looked at Graham. "Is it okay if he uses ours?"

"Sure. Can one of us be the serial killer?"

Hanna jumped up and down. "Yes! Pick me. Or Graham. Or my dad! He loves your books, too. We're doing a Scottish-themed wedding. Does that work for you? Do you want us to change something?"

Because they would, he realized. They would do pretty much anything he asked, which was exactly what Renee had been worried about. That he would turn their wedding into his.

"What I'd like is to observe," he said. "Just stay in the background and take notes. Maybe ask questions."

"Anything," Hanna said. "This is so exciting. I can't wait to tell my dad. Come on. You have to meet Renee. She's the best. She's going to be so thrilled."

Reality landed like a sucker punch to his gut as Jasper realized Renee was going to be many things, but thrilled wasn't one of them. Less than twenty minutes after she'd shut him down, he'd managed to get exactly what he wanted. He was still trying to figure out how he was going to explain himself when they walked into her office.

"Hi," she said, coming to her feet. Then her smile collapsed when she saw him. "What are you doing—"

"You'll never guess," Hanna said happily. "This is Jasper Dembenski. He's an author."

"Oh, I know exactly who he is," Renee said, staring at him. "You three know each other?"

"We just met in the parking lot," Graham said. "Jasper's writing a book about a serial killer at a wedding and he needs to do some research."

"He's going to use our wedding as the backdrop." Hanna clapped her hands together. "I really hope one of us can be the serial killer."

Renee's gaze sharpened as she stared into his eyes. He saw anger and frustration but what hit him the hardest was the disappointment. Then she blinked and the calm, organized wedding planner Hanna and Graham knew was back.

"A serial killer bride would be interesting," she said pleasantly. "Now about your wedding—let's go into the conference room and review where we are. As I recall, we were going to have our color choices made by today. How are we coming on that?"

Jasper stepped back so Renee could lead the way. He followed Hanna and Graham down the hall. He knew she was mad now, but it would be worth it. At least that was what he told himself. Whether or not he believed it was another story.

CHAPTER SEVEN

RENEE GOT THROUGH the meeting with Hanna and Graham by focusing on them and pretending Jasper wasn't in the room. A reality made difficult by Hanna deferring to him on every decision. On the bright side, they'd chosen medium blue and mauve as their colors and they'd set up meetings to discuss food, drinks and decorations.

With all that decided, Renee printed out the details and handed a copy to Hanna and Graham before reluctantly passing one to Jasper.

"I'll be in touch next week with the information we're waiting for," she said as they prepared to leave. "We're on a tight time frame, so we need to get going on everything."

"This is so wonderful," Hanna told her. "I can't thank you enough." She turned to Jasper. "You have our email addresses, right? So if you need anything you'll be in touch?"

He looked faintly uncomfortable as he shook hands with them. "You know I will be."

Renee was hoping his uneasiness came from the fact that he had to now face her. She hoped he was feeling like the worm he was, but she had her doubts. If he cared about anyone but himself, he wouldn't have done what he did. It wasn't a lesson she wanted to learn, but better early in their nonrelationship.

Hanna and Graham left. Renee half expected Jasper to duck out with them to avoid her, but he stayed where he was. She waited until she was sure the other couple was out of earshot before turning her attention on him.

"That was lucky timing," she said, careful to keep her voice calm when she really wanted to throw a chair at his head. "It took you what, fifteen minutes, to go behind my back?"

"Renee, it's not what you think."

"It's exactly what I think and you know it. You understood everything I was saying and when you didn't agree, you did what you wanted. You never gave a thought as to why I felt as strongly as I did. You didn't care that I would be upset or feel betrayed. You wanted what you wanted and that's all that matters to you."

She closed her tablet. "Your book is nowhere near as important as their wedding. It's their day, not yours. You were thoughtless and selfish and you have proven that I was a fool to think we could be friends or that I could trust you. Neither is true. Now I would like you to leave."

"I don't get to say anything? What about my thoughts on what just happened?"

"Your opinion doesn't matter at all to me, Jasper. Not anymore."

When he made no move to stand, she got up and walked out of the conference room. She went to her office, where she closed and locked the door. While it was unlikely he would follow her there, she wanted to make it clear she was done talking to him.

She leaned against her door and closed her eyes for a second. Disappointment didn't begin to describe what she was feeling. While their relationship was never going to be about more than sex, she had thought he was a decent guy and now that was ruined forever. He was just some thoughtless jackass who had wormed his way into one of her weddings and there wasn't a damn thing she could do about it.

"I'LL BE THERE at the end of next month, Mom," Renee said as she turned on the road that would take her to the animal preserve. Her friend Carol had asked her to stop by, without saying why. A reason to be concerned, Renee thought, hoping everything was all right.

"I'm glad we'll get a few days together," Verity Grothen, Renee's mother, said, her voice perfectly clear over the car's speakers. "I've found a lovely little spa in the neighborhood. Let's have a girls' day out."

"I'd like that, Mom."

"Then it's a date. You take care, sweetie."

"I will. You, too."

They hung up. Renee breathed a sigh of relief that her mother hadn't mentioned visiting Happily Inc. There had been a few murmurings when Renee had first moved here, but she'd claimed she was too busy to have anyone visit and had instead promised a trip to her mother's place in San Diego.

Not that she didn't love her mother—she did. Verity was the only family she had. It was just having her mother around was complicated. Especially here, she thought as she parked at the animal preserve.

The Happily Inc Animal Preserve was on the outskirts of town—by the dump and recycling center. Carol's father and her uncles, Ed and Ted, had bought the dump and all the surrounding land years ago. After establishing a healthy savanna, they'd brought in nonpredatory animals such as zebras, gazelles, giraffes and a water buffalo.

The nonprofit was supported by donations and a trust that had been established the previous year when artist Ronan Mitchell had donated several glass pieces that were sold at auction.

Whenever Carol hosted a girlfriend lunch, she had it at the preserve, weather permitting. While everyone else enjoyed being outside and catching sight of the animals roaming free, those lunches always made Renee nervous. She preferred to live her life wild animal–free. Not that she didn't love nature—she did. Just from a safe distance that was definitely out of earshot.

A cat would be different, she thought wistfully. She liked cats. At least she thought she could, if she was ever brave enough to get one. But whenever she considered it, her mind reminded her of all the potential disasters that could follow.

Renee pushed those thoughts away and instead wondered why Carol had asked her to stop by. As Carol was happily married and the mother to an adorable baby, Renee didn't anticipate them having to discuss a problem.

At least not a problem of Carol's, Renee mentally amended as she walked toward the main offices. She, on the other hand, was still fuming from her encounter with Jasper two days ago. His complete disregard for her job, her clients and her specific request that he not get involved in a wedding had made it clear he was a definite candidate for jerk of the year. Her only regret was that she'd ever thought he was a decent guy. Obviously her ability to find the worst guy in the room was still alive and well. Note to self—avoid men forever.

Easy enough, she told herself firmly. She wouldn't

look, wouldn't date and certainly wouldn't touch. Any attempt to get along with a man on a romantic or sexual level would only lead to disaster. It was just…she'd really liked him. And now she couldn't and that made her both pissy and sad.

Pushing all thoughts of Jasper and his dickishness from her mind, she walked into the main building and was surprised to find both Carol and Bethany waiting for her.

"Hi," Renee said, smiling at her friends.

Carol and Bethany both rose and hugged her. Carol was a pretty, down-to-earth redhead who favored cargo pants and T-shirts. Bethany, a gorgeous blonde, was equally casual in her dress code. While Carol worked with the grazing animals that roamed the Happily Inc savanna, Bethany and her husband, Cade, were co-owners of a horse ranch outside of town. Bethany's claim to fame was that she was the adopted daughter of the king of El Bahar and therefore an honest to goodness princess complete with tiaras and bodyguards. While she was in Happily Inc, she lived pretty much like everyone else, but when she returned to El Bahar, she was living the princess life.

"So what's up?" Renee asked, then paused as the two women exchanged a glance. Her first thought had been maybe some kind of group party they needed help planning, but now she was thinking it wasn't anything like that at all.

Her stomach clenched as she braced herself for bad news. Was someone sick? Was it worse than that?

"Let's go back to my office," Carol said, leading the way down a short hall.

They went into her small, messy office and she shut the door behind them.

After clearing files off chairs, they all found a seat. Renee looked at each of them.

"Just say it," she told them. "I can handle it."

"It's nothing bad," Carol said quickly. "I'm sorry. We didn't mean to scare you."

"It's actually good news." Bethany offered a fake smile. "Really."

"Uh-huh. Why don't I believe that?"

"I have no idea." Bethany sucked in a breath. "I can't do this."

"You have to," Carol said gently. "The news is going to come out eventually and the more people you tell, the better you'll feel."

"I'm not sure about your logic," Bethany muttered before looking at Renee. "I'm pregnant."

Renee blinked. She hadn't seen that coming. "You are? That's wonderful. But you're not happy. Is there something…?"

Bethany quickly shook her head. "The baby is fine. It's not that. I'm thrilled, Cade is over the moon. We're both so excited. It's just…"

Renee had no idea what she was talking about. If they were happy and the baby was healthy, then what could possibly be wrong? They were going to be parents. There would be a new generation and—

"Your parents," she said flatly. "You have to tell your parents."

Bethany dropped her head. "I'm having the first grandchild of the king and queen of El Bahar. My brothers are still kids, so it's going to be years before any of them gets married, let alone has a kid. My mom will be excited, but my father is going to ruin everything."

She looked at Renee. "He'll fly over and wrap me in bubble wrap himself. He'll want me monitored and protected and life as I know it will never be the same." Tears filled her eyes. "What if he orders me back to El Bahar?"

"Can he do that?"

"He's the king. He can do anything he wants when it comes to his family. I wasn't born in the country, so I'm not in succession to the throne and neither is my child, but that won't matter to him. He's going to want to make sure his first grandchild is taken care of from conception, or from the second he knows I'm pregnant."

Renee grinned. "He's going to be a grandfather. Of course he'll be excited."

"He's a grandfather with superpowers. There's a difference."

Renee glanced at Carol. "Am I here to offer advice?"

Carol nodded. "You're the most honest, sensible, pragmatic person we know." Her mouth curved up. "I mean that in a good way."

"Then I'll take it that way." Renee touched Bethany's hand. "Tell your parents. This is their first grandchild and they deserve to know. Plus, you're making yourself miserable keeping it from them and that's not fun."

Bethany scowled. "That's it? That's your advice?"

"Not quite. Before you call, take some time to come up with a phrase that defines how you feel and how you want to be treated. For example, something like, 'Dad, I appreciate that you're worried about me, but right now I need to focus on taking care of myself and our baby. I need to stay calm and centered and the best way for me to do that is to be with Cade in Happily Inc.'"

Renee shrugged. "Or whatever your version of that is. Then you write it down and keep repeating it until he gets the message. Oh, and have a point of compromise ready. Let him fly over a doctor or invite him to listen to the baby's heartbeat or something. Ask for what you want, then offer him something he wants that you can live with."

Bethany stared at her. "That could work. I like what you said." She turned to Carol. "Can I have a piece of paper and a pen? I want to write that down. It was perfect. And you're right about offering him something. I'll say no to everything first, then compromise later. That way he feels as if he's winning."

"I told you she'd be good," Carol said as she handed over a pad and pen.

"It comes from years of working with feuding wedding parties," Renee said, her voice teasing. "Sometimes what Mom wants and what her daughter wants are not the same thing." She smiled at Bethany. "I think I forgot to say congratulations. I'm so happy for you."

"Thanks. We're both thrilled. There's just the big royal thing to get over and then we'll be fine. Now tell me again what you said."

Renee worked with Bethany to get the statement how she wanted it. They talked for another thirty minutes or so, then Renee drove back to her office. On the way, she thought about how lucky Carol and Pallas were to have their babies. Now Bethany was pregnant. She would guess it was just a matter of time until Natalie and Silver were pregnant, too. She and Wynn were the only ones not married and Wynn had her son, Hunter, so she wasn't totally alone.

It was hard to be left behind, Renee thought sadly as she waited at a light. She wanted it all—husband, kids, a normal life—and she couldn't have it. She'd thought just sex might be enough but even that had gone spectacularly wrong. The universe was trying to tell her something and she should probably listen. When it came to a happily-ever-after, she was doomed to nothing but disappointment.

JASPER WAS WILLING to admit that he'd reached the virtual bottom of guydom. He wasn't sorry about what he'd done, but he was sorry Renee was upset with him. The moral equivalent of not regretting the crime while disliking the consequences.

In the three days since it had all gone to hell with Renee, he'd emailed with Hanna three times, getting more details about their wedding, along with several stories about how they met and two pictures of their cat. They were a cute couple and he knew they would be a great resource and he should have been happy only he wasn't. He felt guilty and possibly ashamed, although he wasn't ready to admit the latter. Not yet. And if all the emotional angst wasn't punishment enough, he couldn't write.

This wasn't the *I don't understand women so Mandy is a one-dimensional cliché*. Nope, he actually couldn't put words to paper.

He'd been trying. He had lots of ideas. He'd worked on the plot, had developed Mandy's character a little more, all of which went fine, but when it came to writing the story, he sat in front of his computer and thought about how he'd screwed up with Renee.

Not that he was going to take it back. He wasn't. He needed Hanna and Graham to help him. Plus, he wasn't going to mess with their wedding. Not in a serious way. They were excited to be a part of his book, so it was possible he'd added to the wedding. They were special and didn't everyone want to be special?

None of which helped with the lack of writing, so he finally gave up and drove to town. He went up and down the main streets, circling closer to Weddings Out of the Box but never actually getting there. At the last minute, he made a left turn and found his way to Wynn's print shop. He parked and went inside.

He had no idea what he was going to say to her or why he was even here, which turned out not to be a problem. She took one look at him and called for one of her workers to man the front desk, then motioned for him to follow her into her office.

"What?" she demanded when she'd closed the door behind him. "What did you do?"

"Maybe I didn't do anything."

She put her hands on her hips and glared at him. "Really? Then why are you here?"

She had the whole mom-stare down cold—no doubt due to years of practice. She looked good in black pants and a multicolored short-sleeved sweater. Her hair was long and curly, her eyes were dark and thickly fringed with lashes.

Funny how he'd never noticed her lashes before. Should he talk about Mandy's lashes in the book? Did guys notice lashes? He hadn't until just now, so probably not, although—

"Jasper!"

He returned to the present moment. "What?"

"Tell me what's going on." Her gaze narrowed. "It's Renee, isn't it? Do not tell me you've messed that up already."

"What? No. How did you know about Renee?"

"She told me you two had gotten together and wanted to make sure I was fine with it."

Damn—women really did talk about everything. Renee had told Wynn about their night together? He hadn't said a word to anyone. Not that he was keeping a secret—it simply hadn't occurred to him to say anything.

Wynn's sharp expression softened. "I told her it was okay. You and I were over months ago."

There was something in her tone. At least he thought there was. "What aren't you telling me?"

She smiled. "Nothing."

He didn't believe her but wasn't sure he really wanted to know. The whole woman thing was so much more complicated than he'd ever realized.

"I'm sorry about before," she told him. "When we were going out. I was wrong to be so arbitrary about Hunter."

"You mean telling me he and I couldn't be friends? You *were* wrong."

She laughed. "Yes, I was. I was scared of you becoming too important to him and then us breaking up. I should have seen that you would stay friends with him no matter what."

He didn't know what to do with that. While the apology was nice, he had a feeling it wasn't free. There was something else coming—he was sure of it.

"So you don't mind Hunter and I hang out now?"

"It's good for him. You were right. He needs a man in his life. As much as I want to be everything to him, that's not realistic."

"Maybe you'll meet someone and get married."

She rolled her eyes. "No, thank you. I'm not interested in anything permanent."

They'd had that in common, he thought. He knew his reasons—he'd been damaged in the war and would never be healed enough to fall in love—but what about Wynn? What were her demons?

Before he could ask, she said, "This conversation is not about me. You're the one who showed up on my doorstep."

"I didn't know where else to go. Do you really think you're going to be alone for the rest of your life?" Did Mandy? Did she want more? And if she didn't, why not?

"Sometimes love isn't practical," she told him. "It's not about wanting or not wanting, it's about what can be. You assume you can't fall in love because you're too broken from what happened in Afghanistan."

"I was warned it was a likely outcome."

"Maybe then, but you've changed a lot. When you first moved to town, you kept to yourself. We barely saw you. Then you started making friends. We got together. It was nearly a year, Jasper. That's a big deal."

"It didn't work out."

"It was the best we could do at the time. My point is you've come a long way. Hunter said you even have a dog."

"I didn't plan on getting a dog."

"You still have one, even without a plan. You're getting better by the week. I think you're a lot closer to normal than you want to believe. Now tell me what happened with Renee."

He wanted to say that she was wrong, that he hadn't healed as much as she claimed, that he would never be right and he was okay with that. Only he didn't want to fight with her and suddenly the need to know what to do about Renee seemed more important than anything else.

"I told her I wanted to be involved with one of her weddings. Sit in on the meetings, understand why the bride and groom were making the decisions they were, listen to them pick out stuff."

Wynn frowned. "Why on earth would you want to do that?"

"In the book I'm writing Vidar's love interest is a wedding planner and the serial killer is somehow involved with the weddings."

"Oh dear God, you're not subtle, are you?" She rubbed her temple. "Let me guess. Renee said no way, no how because she would never agree to that." She looked up at him, her eyes wide. "Tell me you didn't go behind her back and charm some couple into letting you get involved."

He shifted his weight, then shoved his hands in jeans pockets. "Maybe."

"You are the dumbest of the dumb. She must be furious with you. Personally I'd hire someone to beat you up and then set you on fire. How could you? And don't tell me you needed it for the book. Yes, it's how you make your living, blah, blah, blah. We're talking about the woman you were sleeping with. We're talking about a friend. You dismissed her feelings and violated everything she cared about. She let you into her world, she trusted you, and you betrayed that trust and her."

He opened his mouth to say it wasn't like that at all, only before he could speak, he realized it was exactly that. He'd done those things and more. He'd acted as if what she thought didn't matter. He'd treated her badly, then he'd rubbed her nose in it.

"I see the light bulb," Wynn said.

"I was terrible," he breathed. "I messed up everything."

"Yes, you did."

She opened the door and pushed him into the hallway.

"What are you doing?" he demanded. "We have to talk. You need to tell me what to do to fix this."

"Sorry. That's not my problem. I suggest you go home and think about everything you did wrong. Revel in your wrongness and when you feel you understand it fully, wallow just a little more. Only then can you go and apologize to Renee."

Before he knew what was happening, she'd pushed him out onto the sidewalk and turned and walked away. Jasper stood there, the self-loathing growing by the second. He felt awful and he had no idea what he was supposed to do now.

CHAPTER EIGHT

RENEE HADN'T SEEN Jasper in nearly a week. She'd passed through the stages of grief at least three times and then kept circling back to anger. Probably because it was such an energizing emotion. She was dealing with all her weddings, enjoying her work with only occasional flashes of how much she really disliked him when he surprised her by walking into her office at two in the afternoon.

She glared at him, ignoring the huge bouquet of flowers he placed on her desk. Flowers didn't come close to making up for what he'd done.

They stared at each other. Renee was determined not to speak first. She might have to deal with him on the Scottish wedding, but she wasn't going to make it easy. She wondered if it was still possible to have someone tarred and feathered and if so, what that entailed. Could you buy feathers in bulk and did they have to be a certain kind?

"I'm sorry."

Renee allowed her face to shift from unreadable to disbelieving.

Jasper sat across from her. "Renee, I mean it. I apologize for what I did. I was wrong. You told me you didn't want me involved in a specific wedding and instead of listening, I went behind your back. I betrayed your trust. I get that."

"Do you? Or is this where you tell me it was worth it because you have a book to write?"

He drew in a breath. "You told me these are people's lives. That they'll remember their weddings forever and I have no right to get involved in that. You were right and I was wrong and I'm sorry."

"But?"

His gaze locked with hers. "I was wrong."

She felt the first crack in the emotional wall she'd erected, followed by a second crack and a few bricks tumbling down.

"I'm going to contact Hanna and Graham and tell them I won't be bothering them anymore."

"It's too late to do that. They're both excited. If you back out now, you'll disappoint them so I'm stuck and you get what you want."

He looked a lot more miserable than triumphant, which almost made her feel better. Almost.

"I didn't want to hurt you," he said.

"You didn't care about hurting me."

"I didn't, but I do now." He put his hands on her desk. "For me, writing is capturing the movie I see in my head. It has to be clear to me before I can get it on to the page. When it's not going well, I'm constantly scrambling to solve the problem and when I get into problem-solving mode—"

"You don't give up."

"I don't."

"We need a safe word."

His eyebrows shot up. "We do?"

She did her best to keep from smiling. "Not for that.

For when you get too involved in your story. I need a word or a phrase that will remind you to stop being a crazy writer and start being a human being again. I can't work with you if I can't get through to you."

"I know. I'm sorry."

There were more cracks and more tumbling bricks until the wall was pretty much gone and she was left with wanting to tell him everything would be fine. Only she didn't because while she believed him, she wasn't totally sure she could trust him.

As if reading her mind, he asked, "Am I forgiven?"

She wanted to say he was, only she wasn't all the way there yet. "That's going to take some time and work on your part."

"Fair enough. Are you sure about keeping me on the Scottish wedding?"

"Yes. Just don't try to influence them. Let them do what they want to do." Her voice was sharper than she meant it to be and she sighed. "Let them have their wedding."

"I will. You have my word."

"Are you sure you want to offer that?" she asked. "If you break your word, you're leaving me with nothing."

She tried to keep her tone light so he wouldn't guess how close her statement was to the very heart of the problem. She liked Jasper, she wanted to keep liking him, but if he broke his word again, she couldn't. And there wouldn't be a third chance. She just didn't have that in her.

"I give you my word I will not knowingly influence Hanna and Graham. What I ask in return is if I accidentally start down that path that you kick me in the shins to help me remember."

One corner of her mouth turned up. "You've seen my shoes. You sure you want to risk that?"

"Yes."

"Okay. Kicking it is." She pulled a file out of a stack on her desk. "The apple wedding is this weekend. By now I assume Silver's been in touch about that."

He frowned. "You're going to let me help at the apple wedding?".

"I was always going to do that, Jasper. I was pissed but I'd said you could."

He grimaced. "You're saying you don't go back on your word."

"Something like that." She opened the folder. "You know what to wear. You'll be walking around with a tray of premade drinks and that's all. Respect the wedding and the participants. Don't initiate conversation with anyone. You've been to fancy parties and events before. The servers are invisible. Observe all you want but don't engage. Agreed?"

"I'll be a ghost," he told her. "I really am sorry."

"I believe you."

She did believe him. But trusting him—that was something else entirely.

JASPER ARRIVED AT the apple wedding a full two hours before the ceremony started. He was still feeling guilty about his behavior, which he didn't like, and figured the only way to make things better was to let his actions show Renee he wasn't a total loser.

He parked at the far end of the parking lot, as instructed, and made his way toward the Airstream trailer set up by the gate on the property.

He could see into the open, outdoor area of Weddings

Out of the Box. Dozens of round tables had been set up on the grass. The chairs were a stained light brown, the linens a bright apple green and white. Flowers and some kind of small apple made up low centerpieces at some tables while others had tall clear vases filled with Granny Smith apples. Place cards were attached to apples, continuing the theme.

He'd been reading up on weddings and receptions and had even bought a few bride magazines. He'd ordered those online so he wouldn't have to explain himself to a grocery clerk he would have to face again when he bought groceries.

He knew about place settings and charger plates and the issues with votives (they burn out quickly) versus tapers (tall candles were an inherent danger, what with people brushing up against them). Stacey Treadway and her fiancé, Felix, had chosen votives but instead of using a traditional holder, they'd place them in hollowed-out apples.

He spotted the table where the cake would be set up and wondered what kind the bride and groom had chosen. Something apple-y, he would guess.

He still wasn't sure who his serial killer would be. Not the bride and groom—that he knew for sure. It seemed too complicated. From what he'd read, both would be extremely busy on their wedding day. Plus, they couldn't be a bride and groom over and over, which made being a serial killer more complicated. The same could be said for the family members, which left the catering staff, the officiant and anyone else who worked around weddings, such as the cake baker or florist. He was also still considering a random stranger who crashed the party.

But this was not the time for him to be thinking about that, he reminded himself. He was here to work. He made his way to the Airstream, where he would report for duty. Silver Lovato, a platinum blonde with great business skill and some serious attitude glanced at him before pointing to a stack of aprons on a small table by the rear wheels of the trailer.

"You're early. That's encouraging. Put on an apron and then wash your hands. You can help me set up. We'll start with martini glasses."

As instructed, he'd worn a white long-sleeved shirt and khakis. He rolled up his sleeves and washed his hands, then began pulling out trays of martini glasses from storage lockers in the trailer.

The Airstream had been converted into a traveling bar—in keeping with Silver's business name: AlcoHaul. The previous year she'd taken on her now-husband, Drew, as a business partner and they'd expanded from a single trailer to a total of three, allowing them to grow the business. From what his friend Drew had shared, these days Silver was more into overall management than handling specific events, but every now and then she worked a wedding.

Silver showed him where to stack the glasses.

"We have two hundred guests," she said. "The drink list is simple. Appletinis and beer. There will be champagne for the toast, but the catering staff is handling that, so not our problem. There is nonalcoholic apple cider for those who want it. Water, iced tea and soft drinks are also handled by the catering staff. If anyone asks for that, point them to the far side of the room. That table there will have pitchers of water and iced tea along with tubs filled with canned soda."

He nodded, wondering if he should be taking notes.

"There is a dishwasher in this trailer," she continued, her blue eyes staring intently into his. "You will load it the way I tell you. You will check with me before starting it. The wash cycle is fifteen minutes. We will need to run the dishwasher continuously for the second hour of the reception. I brought four hundred glasses. That will not be enough."

He stared at her. "We'll go through more than four hundred glasses?"

Her expression turned pitying. "You really don't know what you're doing, do you? According to Renee, there aren't children at this wedding. That means two hundred adults. I always assume two drinks in the first hour and one drink per hour after that. Assuming the usual five to six hours, that's at least eight hundred glasses, not taking into account people leaving their glasses somewhere, or changing their mind about what they want."

"Eight *hundred*?"

"Uh-huh. Back in the day, we washed them by hand." She flashed him a grin. "Be glad you're not going to have to do that."

She motioned to the large portable bar she'd set up in front of the trailer. "I'm cheating. I'll be premixing batches of the appletinis and storing them in pitchers in the refrigerator. When we get the high sign that the ceremony is nearly over, we'll pour them into shakers, add a little ice and start filling glasses. The first twenty minutes will be the worst. However many drinks we have ready, it's not enough."

She pointed to the kegs sitting in ice. "I have more helpers coming. They'll handle that. No guests touch the keg. If you see it happening, come get me." Her eyes narrowed. "Do not take on a drunk guest yourself. You don't know what you're doing and you'll only escalate the situation. Do I make myself clear?"

Jasper thought about pointing out not only didn't he work for Silver, he, in fact, wasn't getting paid. He was helping out to learn about weddings. But as her gaze held his, he thought maybe that was not the smartest thing in the world to be saying right now.

"Yes, ma'am."

"Good." She started toward the building. "Let's get our update."

He had no idea what she was talking about, but obediently followed her toward the main building. When they were in the paved courtyard, Renee stepped out, tablet in hand.

He'd seen her dressed for the office, but not working a wedding. He was used to tailored dresses and suits, but there was something about the short-sleeved dark green dress she had on. Maybe because he knew she had dressed to be invisible and had failed miserably.

The muted color of the dress made her eyes an even deeper green. She'd pulled her long red hair back into a sleek ponytail that he would guess was easy and wedding-appropriate yet gave her a sexy-librarian air. Even her low-heeled shoes were oddly appealing and he had no idea why.

But while he was having all kinds of inappropriate thoughts, she barely acknowledged him, instead focusing on Silver.

"Catering is good to go. The cake is delayed. They're claiming traffic, but I have my doubts. The baker is in Orange County. Once they clear Palm Desert, there's nothing between them and Happily Inc but a few jack-rabbits. I think they got a late start."

Silver winced. "How late?"

"We're hoping they arrive during the ceremony." Renee pointed to the waiting table with small plates, a large carving knife and no cake. "The design is supposed to be simple so they say setup will be less than thirty minutes, but that still means they're setting up during the reception."

Renee drew in a breath. "The alternative is to have them work in a private room, then carry the completed cake out during the reception."

"That could go very badly," Jasper said, picturing a towering wedding cake falling to the ground.

"Tell me about it," she said. "I explained to Stacey that a Friday delivery was preferable but she was afraid something would happen to it in the night. As if we haven't kept hundreds of wedding cakes safe before."

"If the cake people need help carrying anything, I'm available," he told her.

She flashed him a quick smile. "Thanks." She looked back at Silver. "Please tell me you're in good shape."

"I'm in great shape. I'm about to start mixing up the appletinis. The kegs are set up and ready to go. My staff will arrive in the next fifteen minutes and I have extra help from Jasper. Go back to your wedding."

"Thanks. I can always count on you." She looked at the empty cake table. "Stacey is going to have to decide what she wants to do about the tardy cake."

With that, she turned and went into the building. Jasper watched her go.

"Does that happen a lot?" he asked. "Things being late?"

"There is always a disaster somewhere," Silver said cheerfully. "The key is good planning so whatever it is, it's mitigated. A few years back we were all robbed at gunpoint." She chuckled. "Turned out it was only a flare gun, but still. Scary in the moment. Oh, and another time there were zebras that got loose."

They reached her trailer.

"Want to learn how to make great appletinis?" she asked.

"Sure."

"Good answer. Some people go straight for the apple-flavored vodka, but I think that's cheating. Mine use regular vodka, lemon juice, apple liqueur, apple juice and simple syrup. More work for me but a better product for the client. And as you know, it's all about the bride and groom."

NEARLY THREE HOURS later Jasper stood holding a surprisingly heavy tray, waiting for guests to walk out of the ceremony. Across the reception area, the cake people were frantically setting up a three-tiered cake frosted in pale green and decorated with flowers and small crab apples. He only knew they were crab apples because Silver had told him. Otherwise, he wouldn't have had a clue.

The doors to the main building opened and people flowed out—most of them heading for him. He held his tray steady and murmured, "Appletini?" as they grabbed glasses.

"Got anything else?" a tall older man asked, glaring at the green drink.

"Beer over by the bar."

"Thank God." The man looked at the woman next to him. "Can you believe it?"

"It was a little upsetting," she said, taking an appletini and finishing nearly half of it in a single swallow.

Seconds later, Jasper's tray was empty. He set it down but before he could pick up the second one he had ready, the guests swarmed around and emptied it, as well.

Sixty drinks in less than a minute, he thought, a little stunned by the realization that Silver hadn't been kidding about the post-ceremony rush.

Fortunately she and her team already had two more trays ready. Jasper stepped in to help at the second keg and quickly filled glasses, all the while listening to murmurs of outrage. Obviously something had happened, but he had no idea what.

When the initial drink rush was over, Silver set him to work mixing more drinks. Renee hurried over to check on them.

"We're good," Silver told her. "No problems here. What happened during the ceremony? Everyone's talking about something."

Renee winced. "The officiant was a friend of the family, from the groom's side. He called the bride by the ex-girlfriend's name twice during the vows. The best man forgot the rings back at his hotel and he's not staying in town, so there wasn't time for him to rush back and get them."

Jasper might not know anything about weddings, but even he could guess that using the wrong name was not a good sign. Before he could say anything, the bride and groom appeared and everyone applauded.

For the next hour, he circulated with appletinis while

the guests mingled and snacked on appetizers. The best man appeared with the rings and there was an impromptu second ceremony where the bride and groom slipped them on, then kissed.

He returned to the trailer only to have Silver whisper, "Are you listening to the music?"

"I haven't been." He'd been too busy trying to take in all the activity while still doing his job.

"The DJ is only playing breakup songs. Someone told me his girlfriend dumped him last night. This wedding is turning into a disaster. Poor Renee."

He searched the crowd and saw Renee heading purposefully toward the DJ. She looked plenty determined and if Jasper were a betting man he would put his money on the fiery redhead. As far as she was concerned, this was her couple's special day and no one, not even a heartbroken DJ, was going to get in the way of that.

RENEE DIDN'T BOTHER drying her hair after her shower. She combed it out and then quickly braided it to get it out of the way. She pulled on yoga pants and a T-shirt before walking barefoot to the kitchen. After getting out plates and napkins, she poured herself a big glass of water and then slumped into a chair.

Her feet hurt, her back hurt, her head hurt, but the apple wedding and reception were behind her. She didn't have to think about anything for the next forty-eight hours and she planned to take full advantage of that. And lucky for her, after the wedding, Jasper had offered to stop by with dinner—which made him fifteen kinds of hero in her book.

She heard a knock on the door.

"It's open," she called, then watched Jasper walk

in with a big pizza box and a six-pack of beer. Whatever misgivings she might have still harbored disappeared when she saw him. Right now, she would forgive nearly anything if someone fed her and got her a little liquored up.

He opened a beer and passed it to her, then slid a slice of pizza onto her plate.

"Eat," he told her. "You've got to be starving."

"I am. This is great. Usually I have to forage around for leftovers. I keep telling myself to plan ahead and have a simple meal waiting, but so far that hasn't happened."

She took a bite of the hot pizza and tried not to moan at the deliciousness of it. They ate in silence for the first slice, then took a second to catch their breath before diving in again.

"What did you think?" she asked.

"It was overwhelming. There are so many moving parts. I know you have that program and all, but I still don't know how you do this every single weekend. The cake disaster, the DJ, the guy who choked on a piece of apple. There was something happening all the time."

"We don't usually have guests choking," she said, reaching for more pizza. "Thank goodness we had people there who knew what to do. I can perform the Heimlich maneuver, but that guy was huge. I wasn't sure I could get enough leverage. But he was fine and the party went on."

"What about the parents fighting? They got loud."

"Parents fight all the time. It's a way to release tension after months of dealing with their baby getting married. At least the DJ's song selections got more upbeat." She grinned as she spoke.

He studied her. "What did you do to make that happen?"

She raised a shoulder. "I might have mentioned his predicament to one of the bridesmaids who thought he was really cute. They started talking and I'm pretty sure they stole away for a quickie."

Jasper's mouth dropped open. "You're kidding."

"I'm guessing, but I'd put money on it. They were both holding hands and smiling a lot after his break."

"I had no idea."

"Now you do." She reached for her beer. "No more wedding mysteries for you. Now you've seen one up close and personal. Well, not the ceremony, but the rest of it."

As she spoke she realized she probably should have told him he could watch the ceremony from the back. The next one, she told herself.

"It was a learning experience for sure," he said. "Silver hustles with the drinks. She said there would be a rush, but I had no idea what she meant until it happened. I enjoyed being thrown in the deep end. I really do learn by doing." His gaze locked with hers. "I want to apologize again, for going behind your back. I am sorry."

"Stop apologizing. I believe you. Of course if it happens again, I'm going to hire someone to beat you up."

"I'm sure you have the name of someone in your contact list."

She smiled. "I just might."

"I wouldn't be surprised. So was this a typical wedding?"

"There is no such thing. They're all different. Not just the themes but the people involved. The families generally set the emotional tone and that makes a difference. I've had bitchy brides like you wouldn't believe but if everyone else is normal, then it's not so bad. Weddings are highly stressful so we often see the best and worst of people. Every now and then either the bride or groom surprises me on their wedding day, but usually not. I generally know who's going to be easy to work with and who is going to make me earn my paycheck."

They'd finished the pizza and beers. Jasper opened a second bottle, then stood and pulled her to her feet.

"I learned a lot today," he said, drawing her close.

Renee slipped into his embrace and let a sense of anticipation wash over her. Yes, she was tired, but Jasper was exactly what she needed to end her night.

The thought of him touching her, arousing her, bringing her to climax had her on her toes and pressing her mouth against his. He kissed her slowly, deeply, as if they had all the time in the world. His hands moved up and down her back even as his tongue claimed her. She was just about to suggest they take this party into the bedroom when he stepped back.

He handed her the open beer and pointed to the sofa. "You need to relax and then get some sleep. I'll talk to you tomorrow."

He was leaving? He was *leaving*?

"What are you doing?"

He gave her a slow, sexy smile. "You said you wanted foreplay. That was foreplay."

Before she could say anything, he kissed her again, then left. Renee stared at the closed door, then shook her head. And people said women were complicated.

CHAPTER NINE

MONDAY NIGHT RENEE sat across from Jasper at The Boardroom. While they'd texted a few times yesterday and this morning, she hadn't seen him since the "foreplay" kiss at her place, Saturday night.

She still wasn't sure what she made of what had happened. While she respected his willingness to go along with her requests, she had kind of been interested in a little more. Maybe later tonight, she thought happily as Nick and Pallas joined them.

"Does anyone know what the game is tonight?" Pallas asked, concealing a yawn behind her hand.

"Rough night with Ryan?" Renee asked sympathetically. "Is he teething?"

"He was pretty good, but that wedding on Sunday about did me in."

Renee tried not to react as a jab of guilt pierced her. "I should have been there, Pallas. I'm sorry."

"No, you shouldn't have. You've been working six days a week for months now. It was a small wedding party of thirty people and it was a brunch. Everyone was gone by three in the afternoon. I'm not complaining, I'm just saying I'm out of practice."

"Weddings are a lot of work," Jasper said. "It's no wonder you're tired."

Pallas smiled at him. "That's right. You went to the

apple wedding. I heard there was some excitement. So what did you think? Did you find out who your serial killer is?"

"He's going to crash the weddings he goes to. That allows me to set them up however I want. I think he's righting wrongs—killing a cheater, or a child abuser. Doing the wrong thing for the right reason."

"I'm not sure there is a crime that deserves someone being killed by a serial killer," Renee said.

"That's because you're a good person," Jasper told her. "I look forward to being around more weddings to get a real feel for them. The level of drama means everyone is on emotional high alert. That's good for me."

He glanced at Renee as if expecting her to say something. She supposed she should mention his serial killer cooties messing up her couples' happy day, but she really didn't have it in her. He'd been great at the apple wedding. Stacey and Felix hadn't known he wasn't one of Silver's regular servers. He'd done his job and had observed in such a way that no one had guessed. Given that, she supposed there wasn't really a reason to object.

Pallas yawned again. "Sorry. I'll rally."

Nick looked at her. "You're being ridiculous."

"You don't think I'll rally? I really will."

He squeezed her hand. "Not that. You're working too hard. Ryan is still a baby and while I understand you want to be back at work, you also want to be with him. You're running yourself ragged doing both."

"But I need to be in the office. Renee has been doing both our jobs for too long already."

"Agreed." Nick smiled at her. "There's an easy solution. Make Renee a partner so she can manage things, then hire staff to take care of the day-to-day wedding business. You two can't keep doing it all yourself. The business is getting too big. You need help."

Pallas nodded slowly. "You have a point. I need to think about it."

She smiled at Renee, who was doing her best to sit there calmly, as if they weren't discussing her future. She had no idea what to say or do other than look normal and wait for the game of the night to be announced.

Take her on as a partner? Would Pallas want to do that? Would she want it for herself?

She knew the answer even as she mentally asked the question. Of course she did. She wanted to be a part of something. She wanted to have a place in Weddings Out of the Box and the town. Not just an "I work here" place but one that said she totally and completely belonged.

Hope blossomed. She told herself it was early days yet and a lot of things could change, but still, a partner!

The Boardroom servers began passing out the game of the night. Renee glanced at the familiar cover of Risk and tried to remember how to play. She was too excited to think.

She felt Jasper reach under the table and lightly squeeze her hand. She looked at him and he winked, as if he got what she was thinking and he was there for her. Which was a lot to read into a hand squeeze/wink, but she was going to go with it, regardless.

JASPER SAT IN the Weddings Out of the Box conference room and had no idea what to expect. Renee had texted him that she had a meeting with Hanna and Graham and that he was welcome to attend. But when he arrived, she'd told him it was a video conference meeting, which was how a lot of her prep meetings were handled.

"Not everyone can get to Happily Inc a dozen or so times before the wedding," she said, setting up her computer and tablet. "Hanna and Graham live relatively close, so we'll see them more than we see most of our clients, but even they don't want to drive in every time."

She had him sit across from her at the large table, then passed him an agenda. "We're hoping to cover all this today. Not every decision will be made, but we'll make a run at them. I have a few samples to show them but the most important issue is the timetable. They've booked the venue for an entire weekend. I want to work out the hours to make sure the contract doesn't need to be amended and that we're charging them the right amount."

She smiled. "Too much information?"

"Not yet but I'm sure we'll get there."

He'd never helped plan a wedding so he had no idea what to expect beyond what he'd read in the bridal magazines. He'd ripped out to-do lists to bring with him. Hanna and Graham's wedding had been fast-tracked so they wouldn't have the usual year or so to plan.

Renee set file folders on the table, then typed on her computer. The large screen on the wall lit up. He saw that Hanna and Graham would be on the left, while whatever material they were sharing with each other would appear on the right. Exactly at 10:00 a.m. Renee initiated the phone call that would conference them together.

Hanna appeared first, waving at them. Graham followed.

"Hi, everyone," Hanna called, waving. "Hi, sweetie. How's New York?"

"Busy," Graham said. "I miss you."

"I miss you, too." Hanna laughed. "We'll be done now with the lovey-dovey stuff and we can start the meeting."

"The lovey-dovey stuff is my favorite," Renee assured her. "You know Jasper's here for the meeting, as well, right?"

"Hi, Jasper," Hanna said. "We're so excited about the book. Thanks for the notes you sent. I love being involved in the process."

"Thanks for letting me sit in on this," he said. "Pretend I'm not here."

Renee picked up the first folder. "Let's confirm the events," she said. "Friday night is the rehearsal dinner. We'll have the actual rehearsal at five and the dinner will follow at six. Things will wrap up by nine."

She paused, as if waiting for them to respond.

"I want to go later," Graham said with a shrug, "but you and Hanna are right. The big event is the next night and we don't want to be tired or hungover."

"Exactly." Renee flipped to another page. "The ceremony will start Saturday at five, with the reception at five thirty and running until eleven. Then you're back here at ten the next morning for a goodbye brunch."

Hanna glanced down at several pieces of paper. "That's what I have, too. Jasper, does that work for you?"

Jasper thought of how Renee had warned him just being around the couple would change things. "I'm good with whatever you decide."

Hanna nodded. "Okay, then the times work. What's next?"

Graham sighed. "My mom really wants the bagpipes

to play 'Amazing Grace.' I know it's usually played at funerals, but this is important to her."

Jasper was more caught up in the fact that they were going to have bagpipes at the wedding. He wasn't sure he'd ever heard live bagpipes before.

Hanna smiled. "Honey, it's fine. I already told you it was."

"But you really didn't want that song at the wedding."

"It's not what I would have picked but she's your mom and you're her only son and it's important to you. I want you to be happy and I want her to feel good about the day, too. It's one song. I can live with it, I swear." She looked at Renee. "'Amazing Grace' at the wedding."

"Why don't we have him play one or two songs while everyone is being seated," Renee said, making notes. "That way it's not just a single song that everyone focuses on. We can have 'Amazing Grace' be the last song performed on bagpipes, right before you walk down the aisle. You'll still be in the bride's room, so you can hear it, but it's less, um, in your face."

Hanna laughed. "An excellent compromise."

"Perfect." Renee pulled several lengths of fabric out of a bag. "I have the table runner samples to show you. We have a simple blue that matches the color in the tartan we're using or we can just go for it and use the tartan itself. Keep in mind the fabric is the same weight regardless. We'd use a computer generated design to print the tartan on the runners so while there's a cost difference, we're not talking about a heavy wool fabric."

She held each sample up in front of the camera at the head of the table.

"What do you think?" Hanna asked.

"Tartan," Graham said.

"Oh, good. That's the one I like, too."

The meeting went on for nearly two hours. After a while, Jasper stopped taking notes and instead just listened. Renee kept things moving along, but also gave the couple as much time as they needed to make decisions.

They all agreed they would have the caterer at the next meeting, along with Silver, so they could nail down the food and bar menus. Hanna had already picked a local florist who would work directly with Renee as the decoration decisions were made. By the time everyone logged off, they were further along than they had been but there was still work to be done.

When the screen went blank and Renee closed her computer, Jasper handed her back the agenda.

"I don't know how you do this, week after week."

"It's a lot of work but then a wedding is often the biggest party a couple will ever throw together. Details matter, so does making sure it all comes together."

"Which is where you come in." He thought about what they'd discussed and what he'd observed at the apple wedding. "I see the similarities."

"Some elements remain the same. The dress, the flowers, walking down the aisle, the food." She smiled. "Some kind of drama. But every wedding has its own personality. This is going to be a fun one."

"I'm looking forward to it."

"Me, too." She glanced at him. "There are people who say getting married doesn't change anything for a committed couple. That a piece of paper doesn't matter. But I don't believe that. It's a rite of passage in our society and the choice to participate in that, or not, makes a statement."

He wouldn't have thought of a wedding that way, but knew that she was right. So what did it say that his serial killer wanted to destroy that moment in someone's life? Did he care he was ruining the memories forever? Did he not think of it that way? Was the killing for the greater good?

"And I've lost you."

He looked at Renee. "Sorry. I was—"

"Working on the book. Yes, I'm starting to recognize the glazed look. Go home and be brilliant."

"No. You let me be a part of this. I should at least…" What? Buy her lunch? Take her to bed? The latter was the most appealing, he admitted. But would it be tacky to ask?

She laughed as she stood. "Go," she repeated. "I will see you later. You're in the zone. Take advantage of it."

He grabbed his notes, circled the table, kissed her briefly, then headed for his truck.

Maybe the serial killer wasn't thinking about the damage he was doing. Maybe that was something he figured out along the way and it bothered him. That would give him some interesting angst as he plotted his next murder.

So many possibilities, Jasper thought happily as he drove home. Inspiration was everywhere.

"I'VE BEEN THINKING about what Nick mentioned the other night," Pallas said at their weekly update meeting.

Renee kept her expression neutral, waiting for Pallas to come down on one side of the issue or the other. She didn't want to assume good news.

"I don't know why I didn't think of it myself." Pallas smiled at her. "I'd love to have you as a partner, if you're interested."

"I am. I have a lot of ideas about how we could divide the labor—especially with you having Ryan. And I've been thinking about hiring people. Would we want one or two full-time employees who can do everything or more part-time employees who are specialized?"

"Oh, you mean like wedding specialists to help on the day? I think that would be great. Another pair of eyes and hands to help with whatever happens."

"Exactly." Renee leaned toward her. "I think you should stop handling wedding days completely. At least for the next few months. Why not manage more of the meetings and let me deal with the weddings?"

"Until we hire some people," Pallas said.

"Until then."

"You are exactly who this business needed. You're so reliable and creative and easy to get along with. I'd be lost without you." Pallas paused. "I really want to move forward with this. Let me think about the best way to bring you on board. In the meantime, I'd like you to be thinking about what you would like the partnership to be. We'll discuss it all in a couple of weeks. Does that work?"

"Absolutely."

Renee floated back to her office. On her next day off, she would take the morning to put together her thoughts. She'd been given an exciting opportunity and she really wanted to make it happen.

When she slipped into her chair, she had the brief thought that if Pallas knew *everything* about her, she might not be so willing to take her on as a partner. Not that she ever needed to find out. Renee was getting good at keeping that part of her life separate.

She finished up her paperwork and was about to head home when she got a call from Jasper.

"How's it going?" he asked when she picked up the phone.

"Good. Today was actually light and I was just about to go home." She hoped she sounded more casual than she felt. To be honest, she was hoping he was asking for a booty call because she was so over the whole foreplay thing. What had she been thinking when she even suggested that?

"I was wondering if I could get your help with something," he said. "Want to come by? I'll provide dinner."

"Sure. What do you need help with?"

He hesitated a second before admitting, "Kissing."

Renee started to laugh. "I can say from personal experience, that's not really true."

"Thanks for the endorsement, but I'm talking about in the book rather than in life. I don't know what to write or how to describe it. Writing 'he kissed her' seems like cheating, but if I go much further than that, it's too much detail."

"Porn?" she asked helpfully.

"So I've been told." His tone was a little defensive. "How do other writers do it? I could never write romance. Give me an action scene anytime. Shooting is fun or I can always do a nice scene where someone's throat gets slit. I'm good at that."

"Poor Jasper. Brought to his knees by touchy-feely emotions and a few kisses."

"I wouldn't say brought to my knees," he grumbled.

"I know and that's what makes it so fun. I'll wrap things up here and drive to your place."

Before she hung up, she got his address, then quickly finished her work for the day. She thought about stopping by her place to change clothes, but didn't want to take the time. She felt all fluttery with anticipation. She and Jasper hadn't really had much of a chance to hang out for a while now. Okay, they'd recently had dinner and before that they'd been working on wedding stuff, but it wasn't the same as just spending an evening together. Plus, there was the promise of kissing, at the very least. He was always saying he learned by doing and she was up for a fair amount of doing, wherever that might lead.

She put his address into her car nav system, then followed the directions out of town and up the mountain. She knew that Ronan and Natalie also lived well above the town, but thought their place was in a different direction. Despite having lived in Happily Inc well over a year, she hadn't done much exploring. Work kept her busy and it wasn't that fun on her own.

She went up the side of the mountain, occasionally glancing at her outside temperature gauge. In Happily Inc, the sunny afternoon had been ninety-seven degrees. Up in the mountains, the temperature had dropped to seventy-eight, which was a big difference. She would bet at night it got even cooler. Jasper could sleep with his windows open, if he wanted.

She was still fantasizing about cool breezes on bare skin when she spotted his house number on a mailbox and pulled onto the long, paved driveway. There were trees on either side and a sense of being a long way from Happily Inc.

She saw the house up ahead. It was plenty big, but in a hodgepodge kind of way, as if it had been added on to every generation or so, with no thought of symmetry or style. There was a big porch and what looked like the original cabin, then additions jutting out in all directions.

She parked and got out of her car. Jasper walked out to greet her, looking all tall and manly and sexy enough to make her whimper. Kissing was not going to cut it, she told herself. She was going to have to insist they go all the way or she was going to be really cranky.

He smiled and drew her into his arms, then pressed his mouth to hers. He tasted of mint and promise and just hanging on to his lean, strong body was enough to get her ready.

"Hi," he said when he drew back. "Thanks for coming over."

"Thanks for inviting me," she said, staring into his eyes. "Is this really about research or did you lure me up here?"

One corner of his mouth turned up. "A little of both."

"I like the honesty." She briefly rested her head on his chest, then turned to the house. "So this is great."

"It's a mess but it works for me. Come on inside and I'll give you the tour."

They walked up the front steps and moved into the house. It took a second for her eyes to adjust to the less bright interior. She had a brief impression of hardwood floors and big windows and really ugly furniture. She was about to tease him about it when something moved. Something large and dark and alive.

She jumped back and pressed a hand to her chest. "You have a dog!"

She knew she sounded horrified, which was pretty okay because that was how she felt. She swung to face him, hoping he would say she was wrong and it was just a big, hairy rocking chair or something.

Jasper looked surprised. "That's Koda. You knew I had a dog."

"No, I didn't. When did this happen? You never said you had a dog. You can't. You really can't. I don't do well with pets." Dogs especially, because they seemed so knowing and aware and what had he been thinking?

She risked a quick glance at the massive creature stalking her. "Okay, I have to go."

"Renee, what's going on? Are you afraid of dogs? He's just an old guy who's very gentle. You don't have to be scared."

Scared of a dog? If only it were that simple, she thought, all thoughts of kissing and sex and good times vanishing as she stared at the creature who would be her undoing.

It wasn't fair—not in the least—yet here she was, facing her worst fear and knowing the second she admitted the truth, nothing was ever going to be the same.

CHAPTER TEN

JASPER HAD NO idea what was going on. If he were to line up ten people he knew, he would assume Renee would be the last one to have an irrational fear of dogs. And while he still thought of Koda as *the dog* rather than *my dog*, he found himself feeling protective of his new family member.

He dropped to a crouch and called Koda to his side. When the dog sat next to him, Jasper looked at Renee.

"See, it's fine."

Her expression had faded from panicked to wary—an improvement, he supposed.

"He's a good guy," Jasper said, careful to keep his voice low and gentle. "I got him when I was on my book tour. Someone dumped him at an RV park and he was starving to death, so I took him in. He's very gentle. He likes it when I throw the ball or sticks and he has a stuffed toy rabbit he carries around in his mouth. He likes apples and cookies and sleeping by the fire. There's nothing to be frightened of."

Renee didn't look quite as worried, but she also wasn't getting any closer to Koda.

"I'm sure he's the perfect animal, I'm just not a dog person."

"But you're so softhearted."

"It's not anything I can explain. When I was little…"

She pressed her lips together. "I always thought maybe one day I could get a cat, but so far I haven't been able to. It's more about my mother."

"Was she attacked by a dog?"

"No. It's— You wouldn't understand." She kept her gaze on Koda as she backed toward the kitchen. "If you can accept my fear isn't rational, then you should stop trying to explain it away."

She had a point, he thought, giving Koda another pat before rising to his feet. "Do you want to go home?"

She shook her head. "I'll still help. Why don't you leave him here and we can work in your office? You do have an office where you write, don't you?"

"Out the back of the kitchen."

She glanced over her shoulder, as if judging the distance, then began inching in that direction. Jasper told Koda to stay until she'd escaped to the hallway leading to his office, then released him.

"I'm sorry about this," he told the dog.

Koda seemed more resigned than upset. Jasper gave the dog a doggie cookie, then left him in the house and made his way to his office. He wasn't sure what to make of what had just happened. Renee being scared of dogs bothered him. No—not her being scared. It was how she'd reacted. He was disappointed that she hadn't made more of an effort. He didn't want to think she was the kind of person who didn't even try.

He pushed his questions and concerns aside and joined her in his office. She stood in the center of the room, looking at his desk and the pictures and plotting cards he'd pinned to the giant corkboard against the far wall.

"I didn't read anything," she said when she spotted him. "I don't want to intrude."

"You're not and I invited you. You can look at anything you like."

She stayed where she was and gave him a tight smile. "So do you have pages you want me to look at or are we going to talk about where you are in the book or what?"

What he'd wanted was for her to help him figure out how to describe a kiss only right now that didn't seem likely. Neither of them appeared to be in the mood. Pages might be safer.

He'd already printed out the scene he'd been working on. He grabbed the sheets from the printer.

"There have been three murders at different weddings around town," he said, handing over the sheets. "Vidar can't figure out the connection. In the first wedding, the victim is the bride's mother. At the second, it's a guest and with the third, it's one of the musicians. He's worried about Mandy's safety because with nothing tying the victims together, he can't find the pattern. They've been arguing about it and then he kisses her."

Renee listened, then glanced at the pages. "You want me to tell you what I think?"

He nodded even as he realized he didn't want to know she thought they were crap. Not that he wanted her to lie about them. Honest to God, when this was over, he was never writing a woman again. It was just too difficult.

Renee set down her small handbag and took the pages, then quickly scanned the four pages before starting over and reading them more slowly. When she was done, she said, "Mandy isn't mad."

"Why would she be mad?"

"Maybe *mad* isn't the right word. I'm not a writer, so I don't know how to describe it, but there should be something more going on. Vidar's really worried. He's telling Mandy the problem and that he wants her to be careful. She listens to him, smiles and says 'Yes, I will.'" Renee walked to the window, then looked back at him. "I can't explain what I'm feeling, I'm sorry."

"You're saying there's no energy between them. He's trying to save her life and she's buying apple juice."

"I'm not sure I would have put it that way, but sure."

She was right, he thought grimly. Vidar was upset and Mandy didn't share his feelings.

"She's not in danger," he said more to himself than to her. "She could be but we don't know if the serial killer is going to be at one of her weddings and regardless, she wouldn't be a victim. She's not a bad person. She'll never be in danger."

He swore under his breath. "This book is a disaster. I need Mandy in danger and I'm keeping her as far away from the bad stuff as possible, which is what Vidar wants but if she's not involved then there's no tension and what happened to my talent?"

"What if the bad person is someone she cares about?" Renee asked. "Like her sister or her boss? So the killer will be close and she's in danger but without being icky?" She shrugged. "Unless that's dumb, in which case forget I said it."

Jasper stared at her. "That would do it. Her business partner. Not her kid but someone else. Having it be her sister would work. What if her sister *is* her business partner?" He stalked toward her and grabbed her by her upper arms. "What if they're twins?"

"Twins is good."

"Twins is perfect. And just now—" He jogged back to where he'd been and retraced his steps, trying to maintain the right amount of energy as he looked at her.

"Vidar is trying to get her to understand she could be at risk and she's not buying it. He's frustrated. He cares about her as a potential victim, of course, but it's more than that. He cares about her and she won't listen."

He looked at Renee, trying to feel what his character would feel. He grabbed her and held on, letting the emotions flow through him. He was focused on where his hands gripped her and how hard he held her and, when he kissed her, what her mouth felt like against his.

"That," he said eagerly, racing around to his laptop. "Just let me make a few notes. The kiss, the twin thing, all of it. Fifteen minutes tops."

He struggled to type fast enough to get it all down. His mind was flying as he made notes on various possibilities. He wrote until it was too dark to see his keyboard and suddenly realized that it had been a whole lot more than fifteen minutes and it was very unlikely that Renee had waited for him.

He got up and hurried to the house. After letting Koda out, he checked for her car, but it was gone. She'd left a note on the counter saying she was going to let him work and that she hoped it went well.

"Way to screw up," he muttered as he texted her an apology. Some days it seemed as if he couldn't get anything right. Worse, he'd really wanted to spend the evening with her. He'd missed them hanging out.

Koda walked back into the house and looked at him as if asking the state of meal service that evening. Jasper petted his dog as he headed to the pantry.

"I'll get right on that."

As for Renee and her reticence about animals, there was something there. Something she didn't want to tell him. He was going to have figure out a way to get her to trust him enough tell him the truth.

RENEE BERATED HERSELF the entire drive home. She shouldn't have reacted the way she did. She should have been more accepting of Jasper's dog. It was just…did it have to be a dog? Couldn't he have gotten a fish? She was pretty sure she could survive a fish. After all, what could it possibly have to say?

She got back to her apartment in time to realize not only wasn't she getting that booty call she'd been hoping for, she also didn't have anything for dinner. She debated the sensible decision of the grocery store where she could get a nice lean protein and some salad, but decided today was not the day to be sensible. Instead she ordered takeout Chinese, getting enough for three so she would have plenty left over for lunches for the rest of the week.

After loading her plate with a scoop from each of the containers, she went into the alcove/study where she had a small desk. She opened her personal laptop and checked to see if she had email (she did not) then went on Facebook to check out the happenings.

She smiled at the requisite postings of toddlers discovering something they hadn't encountered before, be it grass, a puddle or snow, then read up on her friends' lives. Her friend Nell had posted a link to a video of a party. Renee clicked on it, then found herself watching yet another video and another until she unexpectedly came across a gender reveal party.

A pretty brunette with an obvious baby bump motioned for two sets of parents to pull a cord. When they did, pink balloons floated down from the ceiling. There was lots of hugging and happy crying and plenty of laughter. The proud parents-to-be stood arm in arm, obviously thrilled with the news. The camera panned across the excited guests to a sign someone was putting up on the wall. *It's a Girl!*

Renee set down her plate and told herself it didn't matter. So Turner and his wife were having a baby. It was bound to happen. Turner had always wanted kids. He loved children and couldn't wait to be a dad. He'd always said he wanted a girl first because he'd read a study in one of his psych classes that fathers bonded easily with the firstborn, regardless of gender, but if a daughter was born second, he might not make as much effort to connect with her.

Renee remembered how she'd pointed out that wasn't going to be a problem for him. He loved kids, wanted kids and he was going to bond regardless. Besides, unless he was going to have to stern talk with his sperm and get them to cooperate, there was no way to determine the outcome of any particular pregnancy until after the fact.

He'd called her Miss Smarty-Pants, as he had whenever he'd been teasing, then he'd pulled her into his arms and had kissed her.

"I want us to get married now," he'd whispered intently, as he'd undressed her. "I want us to get started on our lives."

His intensity had thrilled her and she'd nearly agreed. Only they both still had a year of college left and he hadn't yet met her mother. Renee knew however much she wanted to keep the two of them apart, she couldn't.

Before she and Turner made things permanent, he was going to have to know the truth.

Now, in her small apartment, she brushed away tears. Not that she still loved Turner—she didn't. The pain was more about what could have been than anything specific, but that didn't make it any easier to deal with.

RENEE HAD A difficult night of tossing and turning. The next morning she was exhausted and wished, just once, she could call in sick. But she had two weddings this coming weekend and a thousand details to deal with. She would suck it up and get through the day. And in a very few minutes, there would be coffee.

One shower and some leftover Chinese food for breakfast later, she was feeling a little more perky. The sadness had slipped below the surface where, she hoped, it would fade in time. If it didn't, she was going to have to get a few of her friends together to go out drinking one night. And wasn't it nice she had friends she could call to go out for an emotional emergency?

She hung on to that happy thought all the way to her office. After booting her computer, she threw herself into her work. Staying busy was the best distraction and it had the added benefit of getting things done.

By eleven, she'd made a serious dent in her weekly list and was feeling much better about everything. She was just arranging doggie day care when Jasper walked in.

He winked when he saw she was on the phone and quietly took a seat while she made arrangements for Buster to be kept company for six hours, including a long walk and dinner.

"Interesting," Jasper said when she hung up. "Given

your reaction to Koda, I wouldn't have thought you'd have a dog care service on the side."

She briefly thought about trying to explain about Koda, then told herself she simply wasn't up to it today. She was feeling too emotionally frail. Later, she would come clean and deal with the consequences, but not just yet.

"The Halloween-themed wedding has the bride's dog as the best man. It was the groom's idea, so Buster wouldn't feel like he was being replaced. It's all charming and wonderful, but then there's a huge golden retriever to deal with. I was arranging for him to be picked up here after the ceremony. He'll have company for the evening. Once the reception is over, the bride's parents are taking him through the honeymoon."

"You are a full service wedding planner."

"I try to be."

He studied her for a second before saying, "Thanks again for your help yesterday. I'm sorry I got caught up in my work."

"It's your process. I'm kind of getting used to it. And it's fun to be the source of inspiration."

"You were that and I appreciate it." He set several pages on her desk. "At the risk of being needy, would you mind letting me know what you think about those? No rush. Whenever you get a chance."

He looked hopeful, desperate and worried. Renee hid a smile. It was good to know someone as successful and impressive as Jasper had his own insecurities. It kept them on a semi-level playing field.

"I have a few minutes right now," she said.

He stood up. "That would be great. I'll just step outside so you don't feel pressure. It's okay if you hate them. It's been tough getting Mandy right. I'm not sure I have her all the way, but I think it's closer."

He ducked out before she could say anything, leaving her alone with the pages. She picked them up and saw he'd added a few notes, setting up the scene.

Vidar wanted Mandy to be careful. He had a gut feeling one of her weddings would be targeted. She didn't believe him.

> *"You're not going to come in here and mess with one of my weddings," Mandy said, glaring at him. "This is their special day. They'll remember it for the rest of their lives and I want those to be happy memories—not tainted by some detective lurking in the background."*
>
> *"They wouldn't know I was here."*
>
> *"You say that now, but what happens if you see someone suspicious in the crowd? Are you going to attack Grandmother Patricia because you have a nervous stomach?"*
>
> *Vidar told himself yelling at Mandy would accomplish nothing and it wouldn't help his case. He had to win her with logic, not bully her with brute force. But damn, she was bugging him.*
>
> *"I need you to see that my concern is for the wedding party and the bride and groom. I don't want to ruin anything, I want to protect them."*
>
> *"I'd be more likely to believe you if your teeth weren't clenched."*
>
> *"You are the most frustrating woman in the world."*
>
> *She surprised him by smiling. "You can't actually know that, can you? At most you've met one*

or two thousand women, so how can I possibly
take you seriously?"

Without thinking, he grabbed her by her upper
arms, drew her close and pressed his mouth to
hers. He didn't know how she felt about the kiss,
but it shocked the shit out of him. Then it made
him want to push her onto her desk and—

Renee flipped the pages, looking for more, but that
was where the scene ended.

"What?" she shrieked. "You're kidding."

Jasper appeared in the doorway. "What? You hate
it?" His mouth turned down. "It's okay. I can fix it.
What didn't you like?"

"Where you cut me off." She flung the pages at him.
"You are such a guy, leaving a woman hanging right as
things get good."

"What are you talking about?"

He grabbed the pages and flipped through them, then
started laughing. "Sorry. I didn't mean to end things
there. I wanted you to read through the scene. I must
have entered the wrong page numbers when I printed
everything out."

"I'm not sure if I believe you," she fake grumbled,
then grinned at him. "They were great. I like him and
I like her. Probably because she sounds a lot like me."

"She's based on you. Sort of. Parts of you. How you
protect your clients. I like that part, how you're always
there for them. So it reads okay?"

"It's way better than okay. You've always known
Vidar but now it feels like you know her, too."

"Thanks. That's a relief." He sank back into the chair.

"You've been great, Renee. I couldn't have gotten this far without you."

"I'm happy to help. It's interesting watching your process. I have learned that there is no way I could write a book. It's too intense. When you get into a scene, that's all that exists for you. I like my life a little more balanced."

"I do what I have to do. Which you said last night. Again, I'm sorry I got lost in what I was doing."

"It wasn't a problem. I had a quiet evening at home."

Which was absolutely the wrong thing to say, she thought, as she remembered the shock of finding out about Turner becoming a father.

Maybe it was exhaustion or hormones or just bad luck, but whatever the reason, Renee was horrified to realize her eyes were filling with tears. One second she was fine and the next she was sniffing and blinking and reaching for a tissue.

"Hey," Jasper said, coming to his feet. "What's wrong? If you're mad about yesterday, you have every right to be."

"It's not that," she said, struggling for control. But the more she tried not to cry, the more she actually did cry, which was embarrassing and so not her.

She half expected Jasper to bolt, but instead he circled around her desk, drew her to her feet and held her.

"Whatever it is, we can fix it together."

A wonderful sentiment, but not at all true. In fact the thought of her explaining and him *helping* had her laughing through her tears.

"What?" he asked, stepping back enough to stare into her eyes. "I'm lost here."

"Yes, you are." She sniffed. "It's okay. You didn't do anything wrong. In fact, no one did."

He took the tissue from her and gently dried her cheeks. "Then tell me what has you so sad."

"I'm not sad—not really." She drew in a breath. "I used to go out with this guy. Turner. Back in college."

"So not the married guy?"

"No. Turner and I were engaged. We were happy and planning our lives together and—" She hesitated, not sure what to say about how things had ended. No, not ended. How Turner had dumped her, breaking her heart into a thousand pieces.

"He ended things and it was hard. I'm not still in love with him or anything, but it took me a while to get over him and last night I accidentally stumbled on a video." She squared her shoulders because she was strong and capable and she would be fine. "He and his wife had a gender reveal party. They're having a girl." The tears returned. "Turner wanted a girl first. He talked about it a lot. I'm glad he's getting that now. I really don't care. It's not like I want him back or anything, it was just unexpected."

"Sure it was." Jasper pulled her close again, then kissed her before brushing away her tears with his thumbs. "Turner was always a jerk, but you're the kind of woman who overlooks that."

She managed a slight laugh. "Thank you."

"He's got to be sorry he let you go."

"I doubt that."

"You're wrong. I'm a guy and I know about these things. He wonders about you."

She knew he was mistaken, but the words were nice to hear. "Thank you."

"You're welcome." He kissed her again, lingering this time. "So, I was thinking, we need a do-over. Why don't you come up to the house after work? Koda will be on his best behavior and I'll cook and maybe you could spend the night."

She had no idea if he'd had those plans in mind when he'd first arrived or if they were in reaction to her story. She told herself it really didn't matter—either way, Jasper was a good guy and she wanted to be with him.

"Is there going to be sex?" she asked teasingly. "Because I'm really only in it for the sex."

He laughed, then leaned close to whisper in her ear. "You get more amazing by the day. There will be dinner and wine and sex."

"Then I'll be there."

"And you'll spend the night?"

She thought about the large dog who would be lurking and how much she wished Jasper had taken him somewhere safe that wasn't his house. But she knew she couldn't say that—there was no way he would understand and she really didn't want him thinking less of her. Koda seemed like a very nice dog—seriously, what was the worst that could happen? A question she knew she shouldn't tempt fate by asking.

"I'll spend the night," she said. "Oh, I went shopping a few days ago. I probably should have asked first, but where do you stand on the issue of sexy lingerie?"

His eyes immediately dilated and his eyebrows rose. "I'm in favor of it."

"Oh, good. Then I'll bring what I bought."

He kissed her again, the pressure a little more intense. "You are an amazing woman. I'll see you after work."

"Yes, you will."

CHAPTER ELEVEN

RENEE ARRIVED AT Jasper's place a little before five. Her morning productivity had meant she could leave early. She'd gone home, showered, packed a bag and had driven up the mountain. Whenever her thoughts had threatened to slide in the direction of Turner or Koda, she'd reminded herself that she was about to have hot sex with a guy who knew where all her buttons were and exactly how to push them. Thinking about that was just the distraction she needed.

She parked and got out her overnight tote. She'd left her work dress on a hanger. Before she could even close her car door, Jasper was heading toward her.

"You're here," he said, sounding happy. "I'm glad." He took the tote from her. "I'm going to barbecue ribs."

"You know how to do that?"

"As a matter of fact, I do. I marinate them in big batches and freeze them, then pull out what I want for the evening and cook them on the barbecue."

"Impressive."

"Tell me about it. Now a lot of people would consider ribs man food, so I made a pasta salad in deference to your fair gender."

"Because women like pasta?"

"Yes. I say that with great authority."

She laughed as they walked into the house. "I'm not

going to argue. Sounds delicious. I brought a bottle of merlot, which should complement the menu very nicely."

He closed the door behind them and motioned for her to lead the way down the hall.

As she walked, she was aware of a clicking sound following them. Koda, she thought grimly, telling herself she would simply ignore the dog. It wasn't as if she were afraid he was going to attack her. Nothing that simple. She would just pretend he wasn't there. Hopefully, with time, he would sort of blend into the background of the house.

She'd been so busy with her dog thoughts, she hadn't paid attention to the house and unexpectedly found herself in a huge master bedroom. The space was one of the new additions, she thought, taking in the large windows and big fireplace on the far wall. There was a king-size bed, several rugs scattered on the hardwood floors and a massive dog bed in the far corner.

"You can put your stuff in here," Jasper said, motioning to an open door that led to an apartment-sized master bath with his and hers closets. There were double sinks, a steam shower, jetted tub and one of those fancy toilets with lights and a remote control.

In the "hers" closet, Renee found built-in drawers, glass doors protecting shelves and a floor-to-ceiling shoe rack, along with what seemed to be miles of hanging space.

"I'm in love," she breathed, turning in a slow circle. "Who knew I could be bought for the price of an amazing closet, but apparently I can be and I don't even have that many clothes."

"Really? It's just a few shelves and hanging space."

"Silly man. It's so much more. It's the stuff of dreams."

She sighed happily, then quickly unpacked. Jasper only used one side of the long vanity, so she set her makeup case on the other and glanced longingly at the tub. For a second she allowed herself to wonder what it would be like to live here permanently—not just to enjoy the magical closet, but to be a part of all of it.

That wasn't happening, she reminded herself. She wasn't willing to go there ever again. She was going to be smart and sensible and that was going to be more than enough for her.

While he made them cocktails, she peeked in the refrigerator and saw that yes, indeed, there were ribs and pasta salad and some kind of chocolate cake thing that looked delicious.

"You know how to show a girl a good time," she said, closing the refrigerator door. "I'm going to have to up my exercise program to make up for tonight's dinner."

He pushed a button on a wall panel and soft music immediately filled the space. "Or we can work it off another way," he said, pulling her into his arms and moving to the beat of the slow song.

She relaxed in his embrace. "You know how to dance."

"A little. My dad made me take lessons one summer. I was maybe fourteen and at that gangly stage guys go through. I kept tripping over my own feet or stepping on my partner or giggling uncontrollably or getting an erection. It was horrible."

She smiled. "You were charming."

"I was a teenager, so no. Not charming."

She wondered what he'd been like before he'd gone into the army and served so many tours in a war zone.

How had he been different? What traits did young Jasper share with the man in front of her?

She relaxed against him, resting her head on his chest. "This is nice."

"I'm glad. I might not be able to give you babies, but I can seduce you."

Renee knew exactly what he meant and appreciated the sentiment behind the words, but had a feeling he would immediately freak out. Or the manly-Jasper version of freaking out.

She didn't have to wait long. There were maybe two beats of silence, then he slowly, carefully, drew back. His eyes were wide and filled what she would guess was panic. His mouth twitched, no doubt from him trying to figure out which words would get him out of the trouble he found himself in.

He cleared his throat. "What I meant was…"

She watched him, thinking she would let him flounder for a couple of minutes before saving him. "Yes?"

"I'm not saying I can't have children."

"Good to know."

"Just that we're not going there and this is about…" He half turned away and muttered something she was fairly sure was at least R rated. "The thing is… It's not like we're looking to fall madly in love and I know—"

"Wow." She kept her voice soft. "You really are just using me for sex. I don't know what to say to that."

Jasper stayed upright on the outside, but she had a feeling he was crumbling on the inside. "Renee, no! What I meant was—"

"No babies for me." She sighed dramatically. "No love, no anything. Just whatever the night brings."

She'd been teasing him right up until she realized she

was telling herself the truth and it wasn't pretty. She knew love wasn't in the cards—she'd tried and failed too many times. She didn't have another heartbreak in her. But did being sensible have to hurt so much?

None of this was Jasper's fault. She'd wanted to keep things light between them. She'd chosen him because she knew that was what he wanted, too, and it avoided anything messy. So why, at this moment, did that feel like a bad idea?

She was sure the answer was all wrapped up in Turner and his on-the-way baby and the reason he'd broken things off and that sometimes she felt life really wasn't fair, but again, none of that was Jasper's fault. He was playing by the rules they'd mutually established. The rules she still totally supported. She was just having a bad day.

"Renee." Jasper sounded worried, probably because he thought he'd hurt her.

He hadn't, not really. In fact he was a really sweet guy who looked out for her. Her feelings were her responsibility and so was the remedy.

"You are the most ridiculous man," she said softly, then raised herself up on tiptoe and kissed him. "Take me to bed and have your way with me, then feed me ribs and chocolate cake."

"Done!"

He shocked her by sweeping her up in his arms and carrying her to the bedroom. She hung on to him, not liking the sense of being so out of control.

"We should have talked about this before," she gasped. "You need to put me down."

"Probably, but I won't."

He bypassed the bedroom and walked directly into

the bathroom. She had no idea what he was thinking. Steamy shower? Tub time? Either way, sign her up. But his final destination was the vanity, which she found confusing.

He slowly, carefully, lowered her to her feet, then patted the smooth countertop.

"I've been thinking," he began, his tone suggestive.

"Interesting." She glanced from the counter to him and saw the heights were perfect. "How much have you been thinking?"

"A lot."

She laughed and kicked off her shoes, then tugged her T-shirt over her head. She pushed her jeans to the floor and shimmied out of her panties. Seconds later, her bra went flying.

Jasper took care of his own clothes, all the while glancing at her, as if enjoying the show. When they were both naked, he opened a drawer and set a box of condoms next to the sink, then he pulled her close.

She went into his embrace, but instead of just feeling the heat and strength of his body, this time she got to enjoy the way his bare legs felt against hers and how her breasts flattened against his chest. Even as he claimed her mouth with his and slipped his tongue inside, she reached between them so she could take his erection in her hand and stroke him.

He was unbelievably hard—the silky skin of his penis contrasting with the tension just below the surface. She explored the length of him before sliding her hand between his thighs and gently stroking his testicles.

In retaliation, he drew back just enough to lightly nip on her lower lip before kissing his way along her jaw.

At the same time he cupped her breasts in his hands and rubbed her hard nipples.

As she had before with him, she found herself going from "this is nice" to "take me *now*" in about eight seconds. Wanting grew until it was unbearable. She was wet and swollen and hungry for him and there was absolutely no way to get friction. She was just too short to ride his erection and rubbing against his leg seemed sad.

"Condom," she said, thinking that should get the message across.

"Yeah, no."

Before she could fully absorb what he'd said, he grabbed her around the waist and set her on the counter. The cold surface shocked her into gasping. The second gasp happened when he placed an openmouthed kiss on her very center, then sucked her clit, all the while filling her with at least two fingers.

It was the most perfect combination of sensations. She couldn't think, could barely breathe as all her attention focused on the feel of his tongue and lips and fingers moving in tandem, teasing her, testing her, going slow then fast, then faster still until she lost control and screamed as she came.

The shock waves crashed into her, causing her to arch her back and push toward him. He continued to love her until the last shudder faded and she could breathe again.

He gave her clit one last flick of his tongue before he stood and reached for the condom. After putting it on, he pushed into her, filling her, stretching her and making her nerve endings sigh happily.

He grabbed her hips, locked eyes with her and began pumping.

"This is not going to be long," he said between gritted teeth. "Doing that was incredible."

She drew back her knees and braced herself as he pumped in and out. "Yes, it was."

She was just settling in for part two when he called out her name and stiffened. Caught off guard, she couldn't help laughing.

He groaned. "I know. Unimpressive."

She ran her hands up and down his arms. "I think I would have liked you at sixteen," she teased.

"Thanks. It's your fault."

"Then I'll take the compliment."

He touched her cheek. "Do-over after dinner?"

"Absolutely."

THE NEXT MORNING, Jasper paused at the entrance to the "hers" closet and studied the single black dress hanging there. On the hanger it was kind of shapeless—at least to him—but he recognized the simple style and could imagine it on Renee's petite frame. The sleeves would come to her elbows, the scoop neckline was modest and the skirt part would end at her knee.

It was just one dress, hanging in the large closet. There was a pair of plain pumps on a shoe shelf and her tote bag tucked in a corner. Whatever else she'd brought, she'd put away in one of the drawers. Still, he liked seeing her things there. Wynn was the only other woman he'd had over to the house and her visits had been about having sex and then getting back to their lives. Sometimes she'd stayed long enough to have a quick meal, but they'd never lingered over anything and she'd never spent the night.

He found he enjoyed having a relationship that demanded a little more from him. He liked rolling over in bed and finding Renee next to him. He liked her using the other sink and how they worked together to cook dinner and then clean up after. He appreciated that she understood how he worked and wasn't mad when he disappeared for a few hours to work on his book. If he had to explain the combination of attraction and familiarity, he would say they fit together.

Funny how when he'd first moved to Happily Inc he'd barely been able to nod at people when he went to town and now he was enjoying having a woman spend the night. The mind's ability to heal was an amazing thing.

He went into his closet and pulled on sweatpants and a T-shirt, then made his way to the kitchen. Renee was hovering over the coffee maker, as if willing it to brew more quickly.

"Rough night?" he asked, his voice teasing.

She glanced at him over her shoulder and smiled. "A good night, but not a lot of sleep."

She looked well-loved. Her hair was mussed, her skin glowing. She had on some short robe thing and a pair of slipper socks that looked like bright green mice.

When the coffee maker's steady stream of brew turned into a hissing, gurgling splutter, she gave a sigh of satisfaction, then turned to reach for a mug.

At that exact moment, Koda crossed her path. She spun, nearly ran into him and then jumped back as if any kind of contact with the gentle dog would be fatal. Jasper felt his happy mood evaporate.

What was up with her and the dog? She wasn't a mean person. She was caring and kind and thoughtful so why was she so apprehensive when it came to Koda?

He waited until they both had their coffee and were seated at the kitchen island.

"Tell me what happened with the dog."

He spoke softly and deliberately made his tone coaxing. He wanted information, not a fight. There was something she wasn't sharing with him and he wanted to know what it was.

Renee cradled her mug in both hands. "Nothing. I'm fine. He just, ah, startled me."

"Were you bitten as a kid? Did someone you know get attacked? There aren't any scars, so I don't think a dog came after you. What was it?"

"You don't want to know."

So there was something. "I do. Renee, please. You can trust me."

"Oh, I doubt that." She set down her coffee and shook her head, as if she were arguing with herself. "It's not that I don't like animals. It's all animals, by the way, not just your dog, and personally I've always wanted a cat. There's just something about their fur and the way they purr. But I can't and I really don't want to tell you the reason. It will change everything."

She looked at him as she spoke and he saw the truth in her eyes. At least the truth she believed. He touched her arm. "Nothing will change. You have my word."

Her mouth twisted. "You say that now." She drew in a breath. "Fine. You want to know what my problem is? It's my mother."

Jasper hadn't been expecting that and had no idea how to respond. "Okay," he said slowly. "What did she do?"

"It's not what she did, it's who she is. My mother is… She's kind of…" She squeezed her eyes shut, then opened them and groaned. "My mother has a psychic ability to communicate with animals. No, that's wrong. It's not a two-way communication. She looks at them and knows what they're thinking, which wouldn't be horrible. The part that makes everything complicated is once she gets whatever information they want to share, she's compelled to blurt it out."

Jasper stared at her and waited for the punch line. The "No, really, here's what it is," only Renee stopped talking and stared at him—as if that were it. She was done talking.

He wasn't sure how to react. Annoyance flared—he was trying to be serious, trying to help her or at least understand. Her response was dismissive and…

She looked at him. "I'm not kidding."

"Your mother talks to animals?"

"No. She can hear what they're thinking. It's a thing. It was cute when I was a kid but then it became a problem, as you can imagine. As I got older, I started to worry that I had it, too, and it's not anything I want in my life."

She glanced at Koda and then away. "So far there hasn't been an indication and my mom swears she had her talent or whatever you want to call it from the time she was born, so I should be safe, but I worry. I don't want to hear some squeaky voice in my head."

It was like being back in group therapy at the VA, he thought grimly, listening to the really bad ones try to explain what was happening to them. Or talk to someone who wasn't there. Only with those wounded in war, he'd been understanding and patient. With Renee he leaned a whole lot more toward pissed and disappointed.

"You are afraid you're going to start talking to animals, too?" He tried to sound like he was listening instead of fighting anger and he was pretty sure he failed miserably. "Dammit, Renee, I'm serious."

"So am I." She slid off the stool and glared at him. "I didn't want to tell you and you insisted it would be fine, yet here we are. You think I'm lying. Or if you do believe me, you're now worried that I'm taking a train to Crazytown." Frustration sharpened her tone. "I'm serious, too, Jasper. This is real."

She turned and ran for the bedroom. He wasn't sure what to do, so he gave her a few minutes to get herself together. By the time he followed her, she was already dressed and was throwing her things into her tote bag.

"We have to talk," he said, wondering when it had all gone wrong. He liked her. He liked being with her, and now this?

"What are we going to talk about?" she asked, her voice thick with emotion. "I shouldn't have said anything. I knew better and I did it anyway. Well, fine. Now you know. You can believe me or not." She faced him. "If you have any feelings for me at all, do me one favor. Don't say anything. I don't want my life here messed up like it's been messed up everywhere else, okay? Just keep your mouth shut and everything will be fine."

He wanted to point out it wasn't fine now and that they still had to talk and he honest to God had no idea what to say.

Part of him wanted to demand she take it back and explain why she would play such a stupid joke on him, but the rest of him knew it was worse than that. The rest of him knew she believed what she was saying. And if that was true, where did it leave them?

"I'm going to go," she said.

She grabbed her things and walked out. Jasper told himself to go after her, but he couldn't. Or he didn't want to, and in the end, weren't those the same?

As SHE DROVE down the mountain, Renee chastised herself. She'd been stupid. No, she'd been what was stupid times a zillion to the millionth squared. She'd made a fool of herself in front a man she really liked and now she had nothing. No guy, no sex and the very real possibility that her life was about to blow up in her face.

She let herself into her apartment and dumped her clothes, then got undressed and stepped into the shower. When the water was flowing over her, she gave in to tears as she worried that she'd screwed up everything.

What had she been thinking when she told him? That he would be fine with it? That he would laugh and say "Hey, that's cool. What do you want for breakfast?" It didn't work like that—it never had. What if Jasper told people? What if she lost her job? What if once again she had to pick up the pieces and start over? Because it had happened again and again and again.

At six, her friends had loved that her mom knew what their pets were thinking but in high school it had meant being a freak. Later… Well, she didn't want to think about that.

She washed her hair and rinsed the tears from her face, then stepped out to start her day. Her stomach was in knots and her heart was heavy to the point of weighing her down.

The potential for disaster was going to follow her for weeks. She would never know if or when Jasper was going to repeat what she'd told him and then what? She loved Happily Inc. Pallas was talking about making her a partner. Everything could be lost if word of the crazy got out.

She got ready for work then drove to Weddings Out of the Box. At least there she could distract herself with various tasks. The weddings this weekend were low-key affairs that wouldn't require much more than the usual attention, so she would get ahead on the upcoming weddings. There was always plenty to do.

She spent her morning doing her best to get lost in her job. It was impossible to do, but she made the effort and went entire minutes without worrying. She didn't hear from Jasper, but then why would she? No doubt the man was changing his cell number and considering getting a security system at his house.

A little before eleven, just when she was thinking she should stop drinking so much coffee and eat something, she heard footsteps in the hallway followed by a shockingly familiar voice calling, "Renee? Are you here? Do I have the right place?"

Her mouth went dry, her heart physically stopped beating and her life flashed before her eyes. No. No! But there was no denying the identity of the visitor when her door was pushed open and her mother stepped into her office.

"There you are," Verity Grothen said with a smile. "Hello, sweetie, and surprise!"

CHAPTER TWELVE

"Mom!" Renee came to her feet and circled the desk. "What are you doing here?"

They hugged. Verity was exactly Renee's height with slightly darker red hair and blue eyes. She'd always been an attractive woman but after Renee's father had left, she'd never allowed another man in her life.

"I thought I was coming to San Diego in a few weeks."

"You were, but I needed to talk to you so I thought I'd pop by and surprise you."

Renee did her best not to panic. Her mother was in town. *Her mother was in town!* No and no! This was bad and it was going to get worse and there was literally nothing she could do to make things better. Even more upsetting, mentally screaming about it wouldn't accomplish anything because now she had to deal with the reality of it.

For months, there had been nothing, but in the space of a few hours, she'd told Jasper about her mother and now Verity was here—as if conjured.

"Is this your office?" her mother asked, looking around. "It's very nice."

The space was maybe ten by ten, with a desk, a file cabinet and two chairs. Hardly anything luxurious, but then Renee always had her client meetings in one of the two conference rooms and she and Pallas spoke wherever they happened to be and this was a mess!

"Thanks," she said, trying to focus. "Sorry, Mom. You threw me with your unexpected arrival. Let's go to the break room. It's more comfortable. On the way, I'll give you a tour."

"That would be so nice." Verity linked arms with her. "I want to see everything."

Renee let go of the fear and worry and told herself to simply enjoy being with her mom. Whatever else had happened, she knew her mother loved her and would always be there for her. The other stuff wasn't anyone's fault.

"As I've told you, we have theme weddings here. This weekend is a *Star Trek* wedding, complete with costumes." They walked downstairs.

Renee took her by the bride's room and then down the hallway into where the ceremony would take place. Instead of an arch, or an altar or anything signifying a church of some kind, there was a replica of the bridge of the Starship Enterprise.

"Oh, my. Is that where they're getting married?"

"It is. Both families worked on it, then had it delivered here. It's mobile so when the ceremony is over, we'll wheel it out to the reception area. We bring in another captain's chair and a small table and that will be where the bride and groom eat. They have some really fun things planned."

"It's quite elaborate."

"It is. Not every wedding is this complicated. Some are easier. We'll be having a Halloween wedding soon. That requires more props but less custom furniture."

Verity smiled. "It's lovely and you're doing such good work here."

"You can't know that."

"Of course I can. I know you."

Renee showed her how they could hang different panels to simulate different places. "We have gorgeous wood panels, but we don't use them much. They're too valuable. Plus printed paper is easier to deal with and a whole lot cheaper to customize."

They walked through the open courtyard where most of the receptions took place, then went back inside and headed for the break room. Renee poured her mother a cup of coffee and got herself some water. There had already been too much caffeine in her morning. After sitting at one of the small tables, Renee braced herself for whatever her mother had to tell her.

"So, you came a long way just to talk," she said brightly.

"I know." Verity worried her lower lip. "I needed to see you, and speaking over the phone just isn't the same. I thought I'd stay a few days, if that's all right."

So not a quick visit, Renee thought, hoping her disappointment didn't show. She wanted to suggest they both head back to San Diego, only there was no way she could simply take off, and making the suggestion would hurt her mother's feelings.

"That sounds great," she lied. "You'll love my apartment. It's small, but I can sleep on the sofa."

"Oh, no. I wouldn't want to get in the way. I've already booked a room at the Sweet Dreams Inn." She smiled. "I have the Harry Potter room. I think it's going to be very fun." Her smile faded. "A hotel is better, sweetie. I don't want to be a bother."

And there it was—the sense of being a terrible

daughter and horrible human being. "Mom, you're not a bother. I want to spend time with you. Stay with me."

"Thank you, but I'll be at the hotel." Verity looked at her and then away. She shifted in her seat.

Renee suddenly remembered there was a reason for the visit and from the looks of things, it wasn't happy. She went cold all over. What if her mother was sick? What if it was something bad?

"Mom, tell me."

Verity smiled. "It's actually good news. Very exciting. I've been in talks for a while now and I didn't want to say anything until I was sure…"

She picked up her coffee, then put it down. "It's not that I haven't loved being a hairdresser. You know my clients mean the world to me. But I'm not twenty-five anymore and the long days on my feet are getting to me so when I had this opportunity—"

"You're not sick?"

"What? Of course not. Oh, darling, is that what you thought?" Her mother grabbed her hand and squeezed. "I'm perfectly fine. And I'm getting a show on Animal Planet."

The world spun twice to the right, once to the left, then settled back in place. Renee told herself to keep breathing, that if she didn't she would pass out, possibly hit her head and then who knew what might happen.

"I'm sorry, what did you say?" she asked, her voice faint.

"I'm getting a show on Animal Planet."

What? "Talking to animals?"

"You know that's not what happens."

"Yes, I do, but you know what I mean. Is that what

you're going to be doing? Listening to animals then blurting out their every thought?"

She tried to sound curious rather than horrified. A show? Animal Planet was a big deal. If Verity had a show then her ability wouldn't be a secret anymore. It would be out there for all to see.

"It won't be like a talk show or anything," Verity told her. "I'll be visiting families to help them with their pets. I'm also going to do some shelter work. If I can let prospective pet parents know what they're dealing with, the adoptions will go more smoothly."

Which totally made sense, for those who believed in the whole I-can-talk-to-animals thing.

"I'm very excited," Verity continued. "This is a wonderful opportunity."

"It is. You're going to be a big success, Mom. I just know it."

Because why not?

On the one hand, she was thrilled for her mother. Verity had always worked hard to provide for her only child. She deserved something wonderful in her life. On the other hand, why?

"You can see why I wanted to tell you in person," her mother said. "Plus spend a little time with you. Once we start filming, I'm going to be so busy, we might not see each other for a while."

"You were right to come here," Renee told her, confident that at some point, she would even mean what she said.

Everyone was going to know. There was no hiding the truth now. It would come out and when it did, well, things would go badly because they always did. But Verity was her mother and she loved her and if only her stomach would stop writhing and she could have a moment to think…

"Renee? Who are you—" Pallas walked into the break room. "Oh, hi. Sorry. I heard voices, which was odd, but now I see you're visiting with someone." She paused, as if not sure what to do.

Renee smiled at her. "Pallas, this is my mom. Verity, Pallas is my boss."

"So nice to meet you," Verity said, shaking hands with her. "Renee has told me all about you. She does love working here."

"Good to know," Pallas said with a smile. "Because I want her to stay forever."

They both laughed. Renee wondered if she should try fainting. Maybe a head injury wouldn't be so bad.

"My mom's in town for bit," Renee said.

"That's so nice. Take the day off and get her settled. I can deal with whatever needs taking care of."

"Actually the weddings for this weekend are pretty much on track," Renee admitted. "Mom, why don't I help you get checked in to the hotel and show you around town?"

"Nonsense. I can handle that myself. You need to work and I need to make a few phone calls. But I would like to have dinner later, if that's all right."

Renee wasn't sure if her mother was really busy or if she was giving her kid an out. The former was acceptable and the latter made her feel crappy.

"Dinner is required," Renee said lightly. "Then I'll show you around. You'll love the town. It has a great history and the people are so friendly."

"We are," Pallas assured her.

"Then it's a date," Verity said.

They rose and Renee walked her out to her car. She hugged her mother, promised to call her later, then watched her drive away. As she retraced her steps, she told herself to be happy for her mother. The show was such a wonderful opportunity. Maybe no one she knew would watch it or put together the fact that Verity and she not only looked alike, they shared a last name. Uh-huh. That was likely.

Pallas was waiting just inside the main doors. "Your mom seems nice. I'm jealous."

Renee had met Pallas's mother. Libby was a stern, difficult woman who obviously preferred her son to her daughter. It was not an easy relationship.

"She's great," Renee said, thinking that except for the whole animal thing, Verity was fantastic. "After my dad took off, it was just the two of us. She's always been there for me."

"That's nice. I'm glad she's going to be around for a while. I look forward to getting to know her."

As Renee had no idea what to say to that, she simply nodded. "Uh-huh. So I'm going to get to work."

"Sure, but if you want to go hang with your mom, you should."

"And that makes you the best boss ever."

Pallas laughed.

Renee retreated to her office where she paced and mentally screamed and paced some more. The truth was her mother was in town and nothing was going to change that. Nor was the show going away, so Renee would simply have to deal.

Maybe it wouldn't be so bad, although if Jasper's reaction was anything to go by, she wasn't holding her breath on that one.

"Renee?"

She jumped and spun only to find Jasper standing in the doorway to her office. What was going on? Did she suddenly have the ability to make anything she thought of appear?

"I'm thinking of a million dollars," she murmured under her breath. "I'm thinking of a million dollars."

Jasper's look of concern deepened. "Are you okay?"

"No. I'm not. I'm really not." She glared at him. "Let me guess. You want to talk about it. You want me to admit I was lying about all of it, which you think is a really crappy thing to do. You don't believe me at all. Which is fine because you know what? She's here. My mother just showed up. Poof. One second she wasn't here and the next—"

"You're saying she transported in or something?"

"What? No! She drove, you idiot. I'm saying—" She shook her head. "Never mind. That's not the point. She's here because she wanted to tell me about getting a show on Animal Planet. That means everyone is going to know. Everyone. So telling you was just a practice session and we all know how that went, but who cares because you think I have a screw loose and…"

A thought formed. Of course. Why not?

She looked at him. "I will meet you at your place in an hour. I'll bring my mom and then we'll see who doesn't know what they're talking about."

He frowned. "Renee, I'm really worried about you."

"I'm sure you are. That's nice. An hour. Then if you're not convinced, we'll make an appointment with the doctor of your choice. Fair enough?"

"Sure."

She ignored his patronizing tone and the fact that he

still didn't believe her. It didn't matter now. She would convince him the only way she knew how. At the very least, she was about to have the satisfaction of watching Jasper eat his words. Metaphorically, of course.

RENEE KEPT HER attention on her driving as they headed up the mountain. Beside her, Verity looked out the window and admired the scenery.

"I can't believe how different the topography is up here," her mother said. "We're only a few miles from town, but it's totally different. How wonderful to live so close to the mountains."

"It is nice. I don't get up here often, but I really should make more of an effort."

She could start camping, she thought, holding in a laugh. Or hiking. Maybe she could commune with the wild animals. They could tell her about buried treasure or an abandoned gold mine. Only they didn't talk to her, they spoke with her mother and now everyone was going to know.

Renee had yet to find her zen center on the topic—obviously—but she was going to have to get there eventually. After years of ducking and weaving, of hiding, pretending and twisting the truth, the family secret was going to be exposed and then…well, she didn't know what was going to happen.

"So who is Jasper?" her mother asked. "Dare I hope you've met someone?"

Renee wanted to bang her head against the steering wheel. She'd been so intent on showing Jasper she wasn't a loon that she'd acted without thinking and now she had to tell her mother that she and Jasper were…were…

"We're friends," she said cautiously. "He has a dog, Koda."

"Friends? What kind of friends?"

"The kind who don't fall in love and get married. I'm sorry, Mom."

"Renee, you have to get yourself out there. You have to be willing to risk your heart again."

"No, I don't. You haven't. You haven't been with anybody since Dad left." She paused, realizing she actually didn't know all that much about her mother's love life. "Not anyone special enough to tell me about."

"That's different. I'm fine. You're the one I'm worried about."

"I'm fine, too."

Her mother looked at her. "Not everyone is going to be frightened of me," she said gently. "You need to give people a chance to surprise you."

Renee held in a sigh. "That's the problem, Mom. They rarely do."

JASPER HAD NO idea what was going on. He didn't want to believe Renee was unhinged, but she'd been acting strangely ever since telling him she believed her mother could talk to animals.

Nothing about the past few hours made sense. They'd had a great time together the previous night. The sex, the conversation, all of it. They'd laughed, they'd gotten to know each other better. Was she reacting to that? Was she so scared of getting involved that she was putting up barriers to keep them apart?

He didn't think that was possible or even likely and if she didn't want to see him anymore, why not just say so instead of inventing such a weird story? It wasn't like her at all and that was what troubled him the most.

He glanced at his watch. She should be here any minute, he thought, admitting he was unexpectedly nervous about seeing her. He didn't want there to be something wrong with her. He wanted them to go back to what they had been. He liked her and liked what they had—he didn't want to lose that. But in the end, it might not be up to him.

He heard a car pull up and hurried to the front door. Renee got out, along with an older woman who looked enough like her for Jasper to believe it was her mother. Verity Grothen was about her daughter's height, with a similar build. Her hair was darker, her eyes blue, but they definitely came from the same gene pool. While Verity was casually dressed in jeans and a flowy blouse thing, Renee still had on her work clothes.

"You made it," he said, moving toward them. He held out his hand to Renee's mother. "I'm Jasper."

"Verity." She smiled. "It's very nice to meet you."

They shook hands, then she glanced past him and raised her eyebrows. "Who is that handsome boy?"

"That's Koda," Renee said, leading the way inside. She hesitated just before reaching Koda, then seemed to steel herself before petting him.

So she wasn't afraid of dogs in the traditional sense, Jasper thought, not sure if the news was good or bad.

He and Verity went inside and followed Renee into the family room. Koda eased in behind Jasper, as if not sure what to expect.

"Renee tells me you're an author," Verity said easily. "While I'm sure I've heard of you, I have to admit,

I don't read suspense novels. I prefer a little less violence and death."

"Makes sense." He wasn't sure what to do. Stay standing? Sit down? Bolt?

He motioned to the sofa, then said, "Can I get you something?"

Renee ignored him. "Mom, could you talk to Koda, please?"

Her mother's looked sharpened, but she nodded and sank to the floor, then called Koda over. The dog crossed to her before sitting in front of her. Their eyes met.

Jasper didn't know what was about to happen. Renee wouldn't look at him and from the tension he saw in her body, he knew she was on the edge.

He returned his attention back to Verity and Koda. They just stared at each other for a few seconds, then Koda whined and lay down while Verity stroked him. She nodded, as if she were getting information and wanted the dog to know she understood. Which wasn't happening, he reminded himself. Whatever was going on, it wasn't—

"He's a sweet boy," Verity said, looking at Jasper. "He belonged to an older woman who got very sick. Koda says she went away. I don't know if that means they had to move her into a nursing home or if she died. She made her son promise to look after Koda, but instead he dumped him somewhere that frightened Koda. He was lonely and scared and starving when you found him."

"Everyone knows how I found Koda," Jasper said, trying not to sound disappointed in the badly done show. "The touch about the old lady is nice but—"

Renee glared at him. "Just listen," she snapped.

Verity looked between them before continuing. "He still misses her, but thinks she would approve of you, Jasper. He wasn't sure, at first. You almost didn't keep him, but he's glad you did. He likes living here. He likes the forest and the house and how you whistle for him when he's gone too long exploring. You have nightmares and at first they frightened him. He would get on the bed to calm you. Now he knows you're going to be okay. Sometimes he wakes you up so you stop screaming, but most of the time he only has to bump your arm to settle you. If he does wake you, he pretends he has to go out so you don't know it's really to help you."

She paused and looked at Koda. "He says you work too much and should take more breaks and you need more people in your life." She smiled at Renee. "He likes you and wishes you weren't so scared of him. He would never hurt you."

Jasper sank into a chair, unable to grasp what she'd told him. While she could make up a bunch of crap about Koda's former owner, there was no way she could know about the nightmares or the fact that Jasper had almost not taken Koda or how much he worked or any of the rest of it. No one knew. No one except Koda himself.

No, he thought, shaking his head. It was a trick. It had to be. Only it wasn't and with a certainty he couldn't explain and that sure as hell didn't make sense, he believed her. He *believed* her!

Holy crap—Verity could talk to animals.

He looked at Renee. "Why didn't you tell me?"

She rolled her eyes. "Really? Because I did tell you and you said I was lying. You thought I was insane."

She was right. He'd gotten angry because he'd been disappointed. He'd thought she was playing him. But she hadn't been. She'd been telling the truth and based on what he'd just heard, he had no choice but to believe her.

"I didn't get it," he admitted. "I mean I know you said the words, but this is incredible."

He glanced at his dog, not sure what to say to him. "Is he happy?"

"He seems to be."

All this time Koda'd been thinking those deep thoughts and Jasper hadn't known. He returned his attention to Verity. "How does it work? Do you hear words or get impressions or what?"

"There are some words. The ones the animal knows. Koda knows his name. It was Buddy before, by the way, but he likes Koda. The rest of it is feelings or images. I see what they see, feel what they feel. It's a one-way communication. I can't ask questions. They tell me what's most on their mind at the moment."

"Is it all animals or just some?"

"So far, it's been all animals. Domesticated animals are easiest. I've tried to communicate with wild animals, but everything is a jumble. We need a joint frame of reference." She rubbed Koda's ears. "He's a very good boy. You were lucky to find him."

"I was."

And now being a pet owner suddenly seemed like a much bigger responsibility.

Renee watched him cautiously. "So you believe me?"

"Sure. You heard what she said. How could I not believe you both?" He thought about how he'd acted before. "Man, I was a jerk. I'm sorry. It was just too incredible. But it's real." He grinned. "Damn."

She didn't seem convinced. "You seem okay with it. Are you sure?"

He thought about the question, wanting to let it all sink in. Was it unexpected? Of course. But the world was filled with things he had to take on faith—things that were real but that he couldn't see. Like gravity and quarks.

"Your mom can communicate with animals. That's fantastic."

She didn't look convinced. "I don't think it's sunk in yet."

"Renee, I'm not going to get upset. I think it's a great gift." He looked at Verity. "You're really lucky."

"That's what I think, too."

CHAPTER THIRTEEN

RENEE WASN'T SURE what to make of everything that was happening. Jasper had invited them to stay for dinner and Verity had agreed. Not that Renee minded—she enjoyed Jasper's company and was relieved he seemed to be accepting of what he referred to as "Verity's gift," but she wasn't quite ready to let go of her concerns. There had been too many consequences of the truth coming out for her to believe everything was going to work out so easily.

Jasper defrosted some hamburger patties. There were buns in the pantry and plenty of pasta salad left over from the night before. Verity helped with the prep work while Renee set the table.

Koda watched her and she had to fight the urge to ask her mom what he was thinking. If she had to guess, she would say he wanted to know if she finally accepted him. Not that she had a clue. So far she was blissfully unaware of animal thoughts, which should have allowed her to relax. Only she kept waiting for that to change and it wasn't a comfortable thought.

When they were seated at the table, Jasper continue to pepper Verity with questions about her "gift."

"Can you turn it off?"

"Not really. I still hear thoughts, as if someone is standing next to me, having a conversation." She smiled.

"It can get tiring after a while, which is why I've never had a pet at home. I need to be able to get away."

Renee added mustard to her bun. "Why are you so accepting? A lot of people have trouble believing in what my mom can do."

"Because of what she said. I was wrong before. I should have believed you, Renee. I'm sorry I didn't. What you said sounds far-fetched, but it's real."

He added pasta salad to his plate, then glanced at Verity. "I don't know how much Renee told you but after I got out of the army, I had pretty bad PTSD. I had different kinds of treatment. For some of it, I was in a hospital setting. Some of the guys there saw things. The doctors said they were hallucinations, but now I wonder if all of them were. Maybe they had a gift, too, because of their injuries or something."

"That's very open-minded of you," Verity said. "Not everyone can see it that way. There have been problems, especially for Renee."

"Mom, don't."

"It's all right, darling. Jasper should know."

"No, he shouldn't."

Verity ignored her. "Renee always wanted to study fashion. She was interested in the business end of things, working with the designers. While she was in college she got an internship with a famous fashion designer."

Renee sighed. "I was his assistant for the summer and I was perfectly happy to change directions. Marketing was a better fit for me."

"What happened?" Jasper asked, looking between them.

"I came to visit her," Verity said. "I was so excited.

I'd never been to New York before. She took me to her office and gave me a tour." She paused as tears filled her eyes.

"Mom, it's okay."

"It's not. I'm so sorry." She sighed. "I met her boss, who was a hideous little man with a Pekinese dog who was wonderful. She told me he was having an affair with three of the other interns and wanted me to warn Renee that she was next."

Renee turned to Jasper. "When my mom gets information, she can't help blurting it out. She not only told him she knew about the affairs, she told him off for taking advantage of college-age students and threatened to tell his wife."

"I couldn't help myself," Verity admitted. "I was so angry. Unfortunately, my temper cost Renee her internship."

"I wouldn't have stayed after learning that."

Verity picked up her wine. "It wasn't that she quit, it was that he ruined her reputation, telling lies about her so no one would hire her. And it's all my fault."

"You told the truth." Jasper looked furious. "He was the scumbag. I hope you told his wife."

Verity shook her head. "I didn't, but I heard later they split up so maybe she found out."

"It turned out for the best," Renee said lightly. "I'm where I belong. I love my job and my clients." And her new hometown, she thought, wondering how her mother's show was going to change things.

"But you would have loved working in fashion."

"Mom, let it go. I'm happy. That's what matters."

Jasper met her gaze. She wondered what he was thinking, but didn't feel this was the best time to ask.

"Tell Mom about the book you're writing," she said instead. "Jasper writes about a grumpy detective and now he has to write in a love interest. It's been a challenge."

Jasper chuckled. "He's not grumpy, but he does have an edge. I've learned that I don't write women well. It's very humbling."

"Men and women think different," Verity told him. "Men are very good at compartmentalizing. For women, it's everything at once. When a man has a bad day at work, he can decide to not think about it that night, but a woman has more trouble letting go."

Jasper stared at her. "You're right. I knew that but I never put it so concisely."

Renee smiled knowing that if her mother weren't having dinner with them, Jasper would have excused himself to go make some notes. He would promise to be back in five minutes and wouldn't resurface for hours.

"Renee mentioned you're getting a show on Animal Planet. What's that about?"

Verity waved her glass of wine. "I just had a wonderful conversation with my producer. They're very excited. They already have several families with pets lined up. I'll go into their home and observe the situation, then listen to what the pet has to say. After that, the whole family gets together and we try to work on whatever the problem is. We'll have animal behaviorists there, along with family psychologists. Our goal is to help the entire family unit, not just the pet."

She glanced at Renee. "I just hope it's not too difficult for you."

"It won't be," Renee assured her. "Mom, you deserve this. The show is going to be a big success and I want that for you."

"But everyone is going to know who I am. We have the same last name and you have a life here."

"I'll be fine."

"No one is going to mind," Jasper said. "If any of your friends figure out the connection, they'll be good with it."

Renee was less convinced, but she hoped he was right. Either way, they were here and there was no going back.

"WE'LL HAVE MILES of silver tulle," Renee promised from her seat at the conference table.

"And fourteen Christmas trees?" Katya asked anxiously.

"As requested." And life-size nutcrackers and centerpieces of wrapped presents and blown glass ornaments and all things seasonal, Renee thought. "Katya, your wedding is going to be a magical day. We're all excited to see it come together."

The slightly overweight blonde relaxed. "Thank you. It's just I want everything to be perfect."

"That's what I want, too," Renee told her. "So you'll get me your decisions by the middle of next week?"

Katya nodded. "I promise. Thanks, Renee. Bye."

Renee disconnected the call, then looked at Pallas. "That went better than I thought."

"Uh-huh. You handled her well but she is going to be trouble. I like how you didn't promise things would be perfect."

"Not a promise I can keep, but I can work in that direction."

Pallas gathered up her notes. "You don't like them."

"Who?"

"Katya and Jeremy. You think they're far more interested in the wedding than the marriage."

"There's no way you could know that without thinking it yourself."

Pallas laughed. "Fine. I feel it, too. It's the weirdest thing, how we get a sense about our couples. There must be subtle signals they're putting out. So far I've been right on every couple I thought wasn't going to make it."

"Me, too."

"So we're psychic. That makes us special. How's your mom?"

The change in subject, not to mention the recent mention of being psychic freaked out Renee just a little bit.

"She's fine."

"I saw her jogging through town on my way to work," Pallas admitted. "I so need to get back into exercising. What does she do?"

"My mom?"

Pallas tilted her head. "I asked the question casually, but now I'm really curious. Is everything okay?"

"It's fine. Completely. She's great. As for what she does…" Renee held in a groan. She wasn't handling the situation well at all. "She, ah, used to be hairdresser."

"She seems young to have retired. Did she hit the lotto? Because that would be so fun."

"No, not the lotto." Renee knew there was no point in not telling her boss the truth. "She's going to get her own show on Animal Planet."

"What? Really? Her own TV show? That is so cool! What's it about?"

"My mom knows what animals are thinking. So she can figure out if something's wrong."

She spoke as casually as she could, all the while bracing herself for derisive laughter or shrieking and pointing.

"She talks to animals?" Pallas asked.

"No, they talk. She just listens. It's not a two-way thing."

"I've never heard of that. It could be a really useful skill. Remember when we had the zebras at the black-and-white wedding? We could have used someone to intercede with them for sure."

"I wasn't here then," Renee murmured. "But I heard about it." The zebras had escaped and had to be rounded up.

"It would have been nice for someone to give them a stern talking-to." She rose. "A show on Animal Planet. Your mom's going to be a celebrity and I can say I knew her before it all happened. Cool."

With that she walked out, as if nothing had happened. They were just talking—sharing idle conversation. First Jasper and now Pallas. While the acceptance was nice, it was very unexpected. In the past, people finding out the truth had been a disaster. She'd lost so much, including her own father. But maybe things were different this time. Or maybe the disaster was lurking right around the corner.

As ALWAYS, WHEN the writing started to be a lot more work than usual, Jasper headed for town. Now that the summer heat had eased into slightly more reasonable fall temperatures, the tourists were back, so there was always something interesting going on. Maybe when it got closer to dinner, he would text Renee and see if she was available. With her mom in town, they might have plans. Still, she could invite him along.

He parked in one of the big public lots and headed for the river. Walkways lined both sides of Rio de los Suenos, as did stores and restaurants. The Boardroom was on the southeast side of the river, along with Chapel on the Green—competition for Renee's Weddings Out of the Box. On the northwest side were lots of shops, including the Willow Gallery.

He paused to watch a stretch limo cross the river, no doubt taking a wedding party to their hotel before the festivities began in a couple of days.

He paused outside Starbucks, not sure he wanted coffee this late, then headed down the block to get a slice of pie. He'd just taken a couple of steps when he heard someone calling his name. He turned and saw Verity walking toward him.

"I thought that was you," she said, waving at him. "You're in town."

"I am. Taking a break from the writing."

"I'm exploring. Happily Inc is a wonderful little town. So charming. Did you see that huge limo that just went by?"

"It's nearly the weekend. We're all about weddings here. It's big business."

"Renee has mentioned that but I had no idea it was so all encompassing."

He motioned to the 1950s-style soda shop up ahead. "I was going to get a piece of pie. Want to join me?"

Verity smiled at him. "I'm not much into pie but I would love a milkshake."

"You're on. Any flavor you want."

She laughed and let him guide her into the brightly lit café.

"Brace yourself," he said as they entered. "They take their time warp very seriously."

There was a long counter at one end and big, red vinyl booths in front of the window. A working jukebox sat against the far wall and "Rock Around the Clock" played on overhead speakers.

"I love it!" Verity told him.

A waitress waved toward the booths. "Take whatever's open," she said. "I'll be right with you."

They sat across from each other. Verity looked over the menu, her lips curving up as she read. "Now I'm sorry I already had lunch. I'll have to come back tomorrow for sure and have a burger. In the meantime I'll indulge myself with an Oreo cookie milkshake."

"Just avoid the place on the weekends," Jasper told her. "The wedding crowds pretty much take over. It's easier to hunker down and wait them out."

"Is it really that bad?"

"You'll see for yourself. My friend Garrick is a cop in town and he spends his weekends chasing down people who've had too much to drink and want to pick a fight because of something that happened at a wedding or one of fifty-seven other crimes that aren't much on their own but do tend to add up in volume. Come Monday, we return to our sleepy selves."

"How fascinating. Does everyone in town work in the wedding industry?"

"Most. There are all the service providers, that sort of thing. Three brothers I know are artists, and Cade and his wife have a horse ranch just outside of town."

Their server appeared. She wore a red apron over a

frilly white dress. "What looks good?" she asked cheer-fully.

"I'll have the Oreo cookie milkshake," Verity told her.

Jasper glanced at the specials written on a black-board. The pie selections were blueberry and apple.

"Blueberry pie with a scoop of vanilla."

"You got it. Want the pie warmed?"

"Sure. Thanks."

Their server left.

"Did you grow up here?" Verity asked.

"No. Montana. I got here via the army and my writing career. I was on a book tour, driving myself because I couldn't deal with flying." He paused. "Did Renee tell you about that?"

"No." Verity's expression turned sad. "She's learned to be very good at keeping secrets. She would never tell me yours."

"It's not a secret. I was in the army for about ten years. Military police. I saw a lot of crap you shouldn't have to see and when I got out, I was messed up in the head, big-time. I went through a lot of treatments. One day our assignment was to write. No subject, just try to get something on paper."

He smiled. "I started writing and writing. A few weeks later, someone gave me an old laptop. About a year in, I realized I might have something close to a story."

"The mind's ability to heal is a miraculous thing," Verity told him.

"I agree. I managed to sell my first book and they sent me on tour, but I was still too shaky to get on a plane." He shuddered at the memory. "Way too many people too close together, so I drove. My car broke down right here in Happily Inc."

He paused, wondering if Renee had told her Happily Inc's origin story. "You don't know how the town got its name, do you?"

Sadness flashed in Verity's eyes. It was quickly replaced by interest, but not fast enough. Jasper saw the emotion and wondered how much of her life Renee kept from her mother and why. Was it all about fear or was there something else going on?

The server returned with glasses of water and their orders. Verity unwrapped her straw.

"I don't know anything about the town. Not really. Tell me."

"Back in the 1950s, the town was going under. There was no industry, no tourists and no hope. Frank Dineen owned the local bank and he refused to lose everything, so he invented a history for the town. He talked about how a stagecoach taking brides to the gold fields back during the gold rush had a breakdown. Back then it took a long time to get parts and by the time the coach was ready to go again, all the brides had fallen in love and the stagecoach left empty."

"That's a nice story, but it's not true?"

"Not a word of it. Frank got the town to officially change its name to Happily Inc, then sold the whole thing in Hollywood. A few big stars came out here to get married and the wedding destination idea was born. The town's been growing ever since."

Verity smiled. "That's wonderful. Not the lie, of course, but the rest of it. So when your car broke down, you were experiencing your version of the origin story."

"I didn't know it at the time, but yes. I was stuck for a couple of days. The mechanic loaned me an old clunker car to get around. I went up the mountain and found a house for sale." He took a bite of pie. "I had my advance money burning a hole in my pocket. Between that and my savings, it was enough to buy the house. I bought the place, drove back to LA, packed up and returned here."

"You sound happy."

The statement surprised him. Jasper didn't think of himself as *happy*. He was broken or damaged goods or whatever variation of that made sense in the moment. But happy?

"I wouldn't say that."

"I would." Her tone was firm. "Have you been married before?"

"What?" He put down his fork. "No. I'm not the marrying kind."

"You don't like children?"

"What? No. Of course I like kids. Why would you ask that?"

"Just curious. It's a reason not to get married."

"You never remarried," he pointed out.

"That's different."

"How?"

Verity sipped her milkshake for a minute. "At first I didn't want to hurt Renee more than she had been already. You're very accepting of my…"

"Gift," he said firmly.

"Fine. My gift, but not everyone is. Renee's father left because of it. I'm not so sure he wouldn't have left anyway, but my abilities gave him something to blame." Verity looked away, as if trying to keep him from seeing what she was feeling. "It was hard on her. Renee loved her dad."

"They didn't keep in touch?"

Verity returned her attention to him. "No. He was simply gone. I suppose I could have forced him to visit her through the courts, but to what end? It wouldn't have been better for her. My point is, getting involved with a man seemed to invite more heartbreak into her life and I didn't want that. I suppose by the time she grew up, I was out of the habit of dating."

"You could start now."

Verity laughed. "I see. Because you're writing about a relationship, we all have to be in one?"

"Maybe."

"Do you expect us to be serial killers, too?" She shook her finger at him. "I've been reading up on you and I know what you write." Her humor faded. "There's darkness in those stories."

"There is, but to quote Shrek, 'Better out than in.'"

Verity laughed. "That's an excellent point. How do you know about Shrek?"

"I'm friends with a kid in town. His mother and I used to be involved. Hunter always claimed to be too old for animated movies but he would bring them up to the house for us to watch together." Jasper thought about Hunter's most recent visit and grimaced. "I miss the movies. He's growing up too fast. He's thirteen and the last time we hung out he mentioned a girl in his class. I'm not ready for him to be interested in girls."

"You can't stop time."

"I can try."

"Good luck with that."

He finished his pie. "Why didn't you ever go into animal consulting?" he asked. "You could have done well with something like horse racing. Or maybe helping with the big dog shows."

"I never thought about it," she admitted. "I suppose I could have…after Renee left for college, of course."

Because Renee didn't like that her mother was so different. No, he mentally amended. She didn't like the impact it had on her life. He wondered what other pain Renee had inadvertently suffered.

"I'm happy with the show," Verity said. "I want to help and I think it will be fun."

"You're going to be a big success."

She ducked her head. "I don't really care about that. I'm just ready for a change. I'm not getting any younger." She took another sip of her milkshake. "Are you in love with my daughter?"

Jasper nearly bolted. He felt his muscles tense as fight-or-flight kicked in. As there was no way he was going to fight Verity, and running was stupid and cowardly, he was left with an uncomfortable adrenaline rush and nowhere to put it.

Love? No and no. He didn't love Renee and they weren't going there. That was the point. Sex with a few laughs and nothing more. Not that he could say that to her mother.

"That's a pretty personal question."

"Is it?" She studied him. "You care about her a lot."

"She's, ah, great and we have fun together but I haven't known her very long. Besides, it's not like that for us. Renee doesn't want anything permanent and I can't."

"What do you mean you can't? You said you weren't married."

"I'm not. I'm single. It's what I told you before. About coming back broken. The therapists warned me I would get better, but I might never be normal."

"That's ridiculous. You might have had issues before, but there's nothing wrong with you now, Jasper. Anyone can see it." She sighed. "You young people today. Why are you so afraid of commitment? Loving someone is a wonderful thing. I would like to fall in love again at some point. Don't hide from one of our greatest blessings. The ability to love and be loved is what gives us our soul."

She sighed. "I'll stop lecturing you now, except for one thing. Please don't hurt my baby girl. I know she seems like nothing gets to her, but she has a heart and it can easily be shattered. Please don't do that to her."

He would rather she shot him than continue on the current topic. He didn't want to think about hurting Renee or who might have hurt her in the past or any of it.

"Yes, ma'am. I'll do my best."

"I suppose that's all any of us can ask."

She changed the topic, asking about Koda, and while Jasper answered her questions, he was still stuck on the love thing. Love? No way. Not him. He couldn't. But like Verity, he had to admit there was a part of him that wished it could be. Maybe just once.

CHAPTER FOURTEEN

BY SUNDAY AFTERNOON, Renee needed a break from her life. Having her mom around was much easier than it had been in the past and she was happy to spend time with her, but between the visit, her work and trying not to think about how her mother's new show would change everything, she was exhausted.

Both Friday's and Saturday's weddings had gone smoothly with only the slightest of hiccups. The Sunday morning "goodbye brunch" had ended when promised and the catering staff had cleaned up in record time, leaving Renee with a few extra hours she desperately needed.

Knowing Renee would be working pretty much 24/7, Verity had gone back to San Diego for the weekend with the promise to return on Monday, so Renee was off Mom duty until then. She had laundry to catch up on, bills to pay and an empty refrigerator, but she didn't want to complete any of her chores. She felt restless and uncomfortable and neither state had an explanation.

She went home and changed into crop pants and a T-shirt, then told herself she really had to tackle the growing pile of laundry. She'd nearly convinced herself to start sorting when she heard her phone chime, notifying her of a text.

How's it going? Want some company?

Hearing from Jasper immediately made her feel better. I'd love some. She looked at the mess that was her apartment then added, Why don't I come there?

Perfect. See you in a few.

She stepped over the laundry, grabbed her keys and was out the door in less than a minute.

When she arrived at Jasper's place, he was waiting for her out front. He walked over and pulled her into his arms. She sank into him, savoring the strength of him, the way he enveloped her entire body.

"You give good hugs," she said.

"Thank you. I've been practicing."

"On who?"

"I believe the correct question is 'on whom' and I meant that more as a feeling than a declaration."

She smiled. "Just checking."

They walked into the house. Koda was waiting. Renee glanced at the dog, told herself it was going to be fine, then reached out and petted him. He gave her a tail wag and a quick lick on the hand and that was it. There was no voice screaming in her head, no hint of his thoughts at all. She was pushing thirty—maybe she could let the whole "I can talk to animals" thing go. Maybe the gift skipped a generation, which meant she could never have children, but that was a different problem.

"You okay?" Jasper asked.

"Just tired. It was a busy weekend at work, plus my mom's visit. She's great and I'm happy to spend time with her, but I beg you, do not bring up her name while I'm here."

She expected Jasper to laugh and agree or nod or anything but shift his gaze and look guilty. Seriously? She couldn't even get past his foyer without there being something?

"What?" she demanded. "She said she was going home for the weekend. Is she secretly hanging out here?"

"What? No. That would be uncomfortable for all of us. I'm fine not talking about your mother." He pointed to the kitchen. "Why don't I make you a margarita?"

"You know how?"

"I can look it up. It needs limes, right? I have limes and tequila. We can fake the rest."

"What about my mother?"

He shifted his weight from foot to foot. "I hung out with her for a bit."

"What? When? What does—" she made air quotes "—'hung out with' mean?"

"I came into town because the writing wasn't going well and I ran into her. We walked around for a bit then got pie. Well, I got pie. She had a milkshake."

Which all sounded fine but there was only one thing they could have been doing the entire time. Talking.

"Yes to the margarita." She waved him toward the kitchen. "What did you talk about?"

"Lots of stuff. How the town got its name. How I ended up here. Whether or not I want kids."

She slid onto a stool at the island. "She asked you that?"

"It came up." He stood across from her, his hands on the counter. "She doesn't know much about your life."

Not exactly words designed to get her to like him more. "Don't judge me. You don't know anything about me."

"I know some. I know she loves you and misses you."

"You're taking her side?"

"There's no sides, Renee. I don't get it, is all. I never knew my mom. She died when I was a baby, so it was just me and my dad. He was a great guy. I know what that's like—being a team. I miss him every day. I guess I don't understand how you can cut her out of your life."

Annoyance flared. "Not that it's your business, but I don't cut her out. I stay in touch with her and I visit her."

"But you don't want her here."

"No, I don't. Or I didn't. It's not going to matter anymore. The secret's about to come out in a big way."

"Why does it matter so much? It's her thing, not yours."

Anger battled hurt. She shouldn't be surprised. It was always this way—at first everything was fine, but then it went to hell.

"It was her thing until all my friends found out. At first they were great. They would bring over their pets and ask her to tell them what they were thinking. So fun. But in high school, I was considered a freak. Even the weird kids avoided me. It was lonely. Eventually we moved so I could start over and that helped, but I was always afraid people would find out."

She could tell he didn't get it. Maybe he couldn't. Maybe it was something you had to live.

"My dad left because of her," she said.

"Maybe he would have left anyway. He didn't stay in touch with you, so he wasn't exactly a great guy."

Her eyes burned but she blinked back tears. "He was my father—you don't get to say that. You know what he told me the night he left? Do you know what he said? He told me it was just a matter of time until I was like her, too. That's why he couldn't stay and that's why he would never see me again. I never told her. I didn't want to hurt her more than she had been, but he told me that was the reason he didn't want to see me again."

"He was an asshole."

"Regardless, he left me because of what might happen." She sucked in a breath and tried to hang on to her control. "Turner, the guy whose wife is pregnant? We were engaged. We were in love. We had our lives planned. It was everything I'd ever wanted. Then he met my mother and it was never the same. Two weeks later, he ended things. He didn't want to risk whatever it was being passed on to our children, and then he walked out."

She slid off the stool and glared at him. "It's so easy for you to judge my life. It's easy to tell me what to think and how it should be, but you don't know. You can never know."

"I get that, Renee. I'm sorry for all you've been through and I'm not trying to hurt you, but I know you're seeing this all wrong. You don't have her gift. You can't know what Koda's thinking any more than I can. So let that go. Just deal with your mom. Worrying about whether or not you will suddenly get what she has is messing up your perspective." He softened his voice. "I wish I could know what you're afraid of. Is it being different? Being rejected? Being blamed?"

She knew in her head he was probably trying to help. He was doing a sucky job of it, but intellectually she was willing to give him the benefit of the doubt. But in her heart and her gut, she wanted to lash out. She wanted to verbally and emotionally slash him until he lay on the floor bleeding and in pain. She wanted to hit him in all his soft places so he was the one exposed and vulnerable and then she wanted to judge him.

"You first," she said sharply. "You get over your past, your pain, your nightmares. You heal yourself. You come to me and tell me you figured it all out and then we'll talk. Until then, stay the hell out of my life."

Jasper stood stoically, taking it all in and not saying a word. She grabbed her bag and headed for the door. The sound of nails clicking on the floor followed her. Just before she walked outside, she turned and saw Koda right behind her. He looked anxious, as if he sensed the tension.

She paused. "It's okay. You're a good boy. Only Jasper is the asshole," she told the dog before closing the door behind her and driving away.

TUESDAY MORNING RENEE had moved from fuming to hurt. She hadn't heard from Jasper since leaving his place Sunday afternoon and she really thought she would. For all his macho guyness, he was actually kind of self-aware and she had been sure he would figure out that he'd basically dismissed her feelings, told her she was wrong about everything and that she had to get over it.

But her phone had been silent on the Jasper front, making her think getting involved with him had been a huge mistake. Her mom's return to Happily Inc on Monday had been a distraction. They'd had a nice afternoon and evening. Renee had managed to sleep a little and now she was determined to have a good week with absolutely no Jasper thoughts getting in her way.

Her plans lasted until 9:01 a.m. when she arrived at Weddings Out of the Box only to find Jasper in the parking lot, leaning against his truck, obviously waiting for her.

She stayed in her car for a second, thought briefly about running him over, only she knew it was wrong and she would have regrets later. She'd never deliberately hurt anyone in her life. It wasn't smart to change that now, even if he did deserve it.

She got out and slung her bag over her shoulder. Maybe she could pretend he wasn't there and march to her office without acknowledging him. Not as satisfying as physical violence but certainly more morally correct. But still kind of cowardly. So in the end, she walked toward him, determined not to react to anything he said.

When she stopped in front of him, he surprised her by cupping her face in his hands and kissing her.

"I was wrong," he told her as he released her. "I meant well, but I was wrong. I jumped all over you when I should have listened. You're right. I can't know what it was like and after a couple of hours with your mom, it's easy to take her side, but how does that help? There shouldn't be sides. You went through things I can't begin to understand. You're a good person and you're doing the best you can, just like she is and I am. I messed up. I'm sorry."

It wasn't a *bad* apology, she thought grudgingly. "You mess up a lot."

"I do. Especially with you."

"Why is that?"

She expected him to smile or make a joke. Instead he looked away, as if he couldn't meet her gaze.

"I haven't been in a real relationship before," he said, glancing back at her. "I had a girlfriend in high school and a few flings in the army, but since then there was only Wynn and that was more about…" He shrugged. "We didn't talk much."

Relationship? They weren't in a relationship. They were sex friends. But even as the thought formed, she thought maybe it was wrong. After all, there'd been a lot more friendship and a lot less sex than she'd imagined. A relationship. Could she? Did she want to?

She told herself this was not the time to deal with anything like that. She already had plenty going on. But a relationship? Maybe…

"I liked your mom a lot," he said, surprising her with the shift in subject. "I feel bad for her." He held up a hand. "I'm not saying you're wrong. You're not. It's a difficult situation. I got carried away. I want to tell you it won't happen again, but it probably will. I'll learn from what happened and try to do better next time. I mean that."

She felt her tension easing. "I'm sorry, too. I shouldn't have gone on that 'you first' rant. I felt attacked so I hit back. I'm explaining, not justifying."

"Relationships are hard."

Why did he have to keep saying the *R* word? "We could go back to just sex."

"No, I like this better."

She thought maybe she did, too. "Thank you for coming to apologize."

"You're welcome." He kissed her again. "Now you have to get to work and I should be writing. Do-over on you coming by for margaritas?"

"Absolutely."

"Good."

He got in his truck and she walked into her office. Her mood had lightened considerably and the knot in her stomach was gone. She might not want a relationship but she had to admit if she was going to try again, Jasper almost made it worth taking the risk.

The morning sped by quickly. At eleven thirty, she went out in the lobby to greet Tara and Owen, who were finalizing their football-themed wedding.

They arrived right on time, Tara greeting Renee with a happy hug, while Owen shook her hand.

They were a handsome couple, tall, athletic and easy to be with. Tara was at least five-eight or -nine and Owen towered above her. Next to them, Renee felt like a miniature version of the species.

"It's nearly the happy day," Renee said, leading them to the conference room. "I think you're going to be very pleased to see how everything is coming together."

"I found this really great meditation app," Tara said, smiling at Owen. "To keep myself centered."

"Someone was getting a little snappy." His tone was more teasing than annoyed.

"I was, but I'm better now. It's a lot to think about."

Renee motioned for them to take seats. She settled behind the computer and activated the connection with the screen. "I'm hoping that today's wrap-up meeting will calm your nerves and allow you to simply enjoy the experience."

Owen grabbed Tara's hand and kissed her knuckles. "It's nearly here, baby. We're going to get married."

"We are."

Renee sighed happily. Her gut told her this couple was going to make it and that made her feel good about their wedding.

She pulled up the file and they went through the entire day from arrival to the final dance. The football theme—with a heavy emphasis on the Dallas Cowboys—had turned out perfectly. The silver-and-blue color scheme worked well for the reception. The food had been ordered, the drinks decided on.

Renee opened a box of jerseys that had been delivered for the wedding party and showed them to Tara and Owen.

Tara fingered the fabric. "It's really nice quality, just like you said. I like that they're not too thin."

"We'll have them all steamed and hanging by the time of the wedding," Renee assured her. "They'll be perfect. Do you want the steamer heated for your reception dress?"

Tara was wearing her great grandmother's wedding gown for the ceremony, then changing into a more contemporary party dress for the reception.

"I shouldn't need it."

Renee made a note on her tablet. "I'm going to make sure it's ready for you, just in case."

They went over the rest of the details. The groom's cake was in the shape of a jersey and instead of throwing the garter, Owen would be throwing a football signed by Dak Prescott. As he did every time the signed football was mentioned, he grumbled about giving something away that he would rather keep. Renee was careful not to look at Tara, afraid her amusement would give away the secret. What Owen didn't know was that Tara had two signed footballs and Owen would receive the other one after the reception.

The meeting took less than ninety minutes. Tara and Owen left reassured that their big day would go smoothly. Renee added a few things to her master calendar, then shut down the conference room and returned to her office. She'd barely started to think she should eat the lunch she'd brought from home when her friend Carol walked into her office.

Renee didn't bother hiding her surprise. "What's going on?" she asked. "You never just pop in. Is everything all right?"

Carol nodded even as she twisted her fingers together in obvious distress.

"What's wrong?" Renee asked. "Just blurt it out. We'll both feel better."

Carol hesitated a second before saying, "Pallas told me. I don't know if she was supposed to or not, but she did and now I can't stop thinking about it and is it really true? Can your mother talk to animals?"

Renee held in a groan. "She doesn't talk. She listens while they tell her what's on their mind." She braced herself for laughter and possibly derision, because really? Communicating with animals?

"Thank God." Carol moved closer to her desk. "I need her help. I'm desperate. There's something wrong with the giraffes. I don't know what, but they feel off to me and I'm responsible for them and I worry I'm not giving them enough attention with Devon and everything, and I could really use her help." She paused to breathe. "If that's not asking too much."

"You want my mother to communicate with your giraffes?"

Carol nodded vigorously. "Please. I know something's wrong, but I can't figure out what and I'm scared."

Renee had no idea what to say. It was not the reaction she'd been expecting, or had ever gotten before. "Um, sure. Let me call her right now." She pulled out her cell phone and dialed. When her mother answered, she explained the situation, listened for a second, then hung up.

"She says she will absolutely do her best. I'm going to get her right now and we'll meet you at the animal preserve."

"Thank you." Carol raced out, turned. "Really. Thank you so much. I can't wait to meet your mom."

"Give us twenty minutes."

Renee was still contemplating the unexpected turn of events as she parked in front of the Sweet Dreams Inn. Verity was waiting by the main doors and quickly hurried to the car.

"I hope I can help," her mother said as she fastened her seat belt. "I've never been able to understand wild animals because we don't share a language. Domestic animals are different, of course. I'm hoping your friend's giraffes have been around people enough that they can share their thoughts with me." She smiled at Renee. "This is very exciting."

"It's not how I spend my day—that's for sure."

Renee drove out past the dump and recycling center and entered the animal preserve. Carol was there, along with Ed, her father. Renee made the introductions.

"I put the female giraffes in their barn," Carol said, leading the way. "I've kept them separate so they won't distract each other."

"I have to warn you that while I'll do my best, I can't make any promises," Verity said before explaining how she couldn't communicate with wild animals. "We don't have a shared frame of reference."

"Makes sense," Ed told her. "What about birds and fish? Or is it just mammals?"

"I've never been able to tell what a fish is thinking.

I can get through to some birds. Doves are silent but swans don't shut up and they have opinions about everything. I've always wanted to try communicating with a dolphin, but I haven't had the chance."

"Fascinating," Ed murmured, holding open a large door. "Let's go see what the ladies think of you and vice versa."

Renee felt incredibly out of place in a dress and pumps. Her mother was in jeans and Carol and Ed wore what she would describe as safari gear—khakis and polo shirts. Given their work at the preserve, their wardrobe made sense.

The barn wasn't a barn at all, but a huge open building with big cages or stalls with wood and chain-link walls. The ceiling had to be at least twenty-five feet high, which made sense when one was housing giraffes.

There were tall windows, plenty of light and lots of ventilation. Renee inhaled the scent of hay and fresh air. Three beautiful giraffes watched them curiously. They were leggy and powerful with stunning faces and incredibly long lashes.

"The giraffes are usually kept outside during the day," Carol told them. "We bring them in at night to keep them safe. They're not exactly domesticated but they were all born in captivity and have a 'will work for food' mentality. I'm hoping you can tell me what they're thinking."

"Wonderful," Verity said. "They are simply wonderful. What a joy to work with them every day." She glanced at Ed. "You started the preserve?"

"My brother and I did. We'd had plans for a while and just needed the right location and an influx of cash." He shrugged. "We found this place right as a distant relative passed away, leaving us the heirs. It all worked out."

They smiled at each other. Renee couldn't help thinking this was the strangest afternoon she'd had in maybe forever.

Carol led them to the first giraffe. "This is Mrs. Santora. She's the one I'm worried about the most. She's just not herself lately."

Verity nodded and looked into Mrs. Santora's brown eyes. "You are a beauty, aren't you?"

The giraffe stared back, then took a step forward. The barn went silent. Anticipation crackled in the air. Renee desperately hoped her mother would be able to—

"Oh! That was very clear." Verity smiled at Carol. "Who is Dave?"

"Our male giraffe. I left him outside. He can be a little bit of an attention hog."

"Mrs. Santora doesn't like him at all. She wishes you'd stop putting them out together. She finds him annoying and just wants to be with her friends."

Carol's mouth dropped open. "No way! I was thinking of taking her off birth control so she and Dave could mate but first I wanted to see how they got along. That's why she's been acting so weird." She looked at Mrs. Santora. "Is that what it is? I'm sorry. I won't make you hang out with him if you don't want to."

"Well, I'll be," Ed muttered. "That's amazing."

"It is," Carol said, leading Verity to the second giraffe. "This is Ida. She and Mrs. Santora came together. They're Millie's girlfriends, her herd. I just want them to be happy."

Verity nodded, then stared at Ida. Once again the barn went silent. Renee watched her mother and saw her lips twitch, as if she were trying to hold in laughter. Verity listened for nearly a minute before looking at Carol.

"Ida doesn't have many concerns, except she would like you and the man I'm assuming is your husband to stop having sex in the savanna. She finds it upsetting and not anything she wants to see. You should stay in your own barn for that sort of thing."

Carol flushed. "Oh. I didn't know they could— Um, well, that's interesting. Let's go meet Millie. She was our original giraffe. We did some fund-raising to get her a herd so she could have friends."

As Carol approached Millie, the giraffe lowered her head over the gate. Carol rubbed her face while Millie nibbled her fingers.

"You're a beautiful girl, aren't you," Verity said, smiling at Millie. The giraffe looked at her.

This time there was no laughter. Verity's expression was intense and their conversation went on for a long time. Finally Verity looked at Carol.

"Millie is very worried that you're going to get distracted by your husband and baby and won't have time for her anymore."

"Oh, that would never happen." Carol looked at Millie. "You'll always be my girl. You have to know that."

"There's more," Verity told her. "Millie's pregnant."

Carol stared at the giraffe. Ed walked over and hugged his daughter.

"Did you hear that?" he asked. "Millie's pregnant." He looked at Verity. "We were hoping, but with a giraffe, it's difficult to tell. Plus the gestation is so long." He grinned. "We're going to have a baby."

"That's wonderful."

Renee felt as if she couldn't keep up. There was too much information coming at them too fast. Not liking Dave, Millie worrying about being abandoned, a new giraffe baby.

She squeezed her mother's hand. "You're doing great, Mom."

"Yes, it's fantastic." Carol hugged her. "Thank you so much. This means the world to me. I've been so worried and now I know what to do."

"You're welcome. I'm happy to help. Shall we go see what Dave has to say?"

"Let's."

Carol paused to give Millie one last pat before taking them outside where Dave stood in a large pen, dining on leaves. Several massive branches had been hoisted up and hooked onto a pole that was just the right height for him. As they approached his pen, he glanced at them before strolling over.

"He's quite the handsome man," Verity said.

Carol laughed. "Dave has some attitude, that's for sure. I'm curious as to what he's concerned about. He doesn't seem to have any problems in his life."

"Men are simple creatures," Ed said with a laugh. "I'll be the first to admit it."

Verity and Dave established eye contact. It was only for a couple of seconds, then Dave turned and walked away.

Carol glanced at Verity. "Anything?"

"He would like more of something called a leafeater treat. That was it. He was fairly insistent."

Carol laughed. "They're like giraffe cookies and Dave loves them. I'm not surprised he wants more."

She spun in a circle. "I'm so relieved. Thank you, thank you, thank you."

"You were incredible," Ed said. "This has been a big help. If I promise not to make you talk to any other residents, would you like to take a tour of the grounds?"

The question surprised Renee, as did her mother's response, "I'd like that a lot, but I'm afraid I came with my daughter and I would guess she has to get back to work."

"I can take you where you need to go when we're done," Ed said, as he smiled at Renee. "If that's all right with you."

"Of course." Renee hugged her mother. "Have fun on the tour. It's a wonderful place."

"I can see that."

"I'll walk you out," Carol said.

They returned along the same path they'd taken on the way in.

"Thank you for loaning me your mom. I'm relieved and happy and excited to know what my giraffes are thinking. I can't believe Millie's pregnant. I hate that she's been worried about me not being there for her. I'll take extra time with her. Maybe I should bring Devon out to meet her. Do you think that would comfort her or make her jealous?"

"I have no idea. Sorry."

Carol grinned. "That's okay. Giraffes aren't your thing the way they're mine. I wonder if there's any research on the topic. I'll have to go online and see."

Renee was more caught up in the total acceptance of her mom's ability and the fact that Carol believed everything she said. It hadn't ever been like this before. Not that she'd had many friends who'd needed help with their giraffes.

"I'm glad she could help," she murmured as they approached her car.

"More than helped. I can't wait to see her show. It's going to be amazing." Carol hugged her. "Thank you again. You're the best."

"I didn't do anything, but sure, thank me all you want."

They both laughed. Renee headed back to work, happy about what had happened and just a little confused about how easily her mother was fitting in. Maybe she'd been worried for nothing. Maybe it was all going to be just fine.

CHAPTER FIFTEEN

"ARE YOU SURE?" Verity asked for the third time as she set a stack of plates on the long table next to a cafeteria-size takeout container of enchiladas. "You're sweet to invite me, but this is your life. I don't want to interfere."

Not that long ago, Renee would rather have had root canal than invite her mother to hang out with her friends, but ever since the "giraffe incident" as she thought of it, Renee had found herself much more relaxed when it came to her mother. Maybe she'd just needed a few positive experiences to put things in perspective.

"You're only in town a few weeks," she said. "Once the show starts, you're going to be wildly busy and I'll never get to see you. The girlfriend lunches are a big part of my life. Of course I want you here."

"Thank you, sweetie. I appreciate that. So how often do you have these lunches?"

"Mostly every week. We rotate through the locations." Renee smiled. "When it's Carol's turn and the weather is nice, we eat out with the animals."

"Did that bother you?"

"At first. They got a little close but I never heard their thoughts." Something for which she would always be grateful. "When it's my turn or Pallas's turn, we eat here, at Weddings Out of the Box. Whoever is hosting provides an entrée. Everyone else brings what they want."

Renee and Pallas had already set up a long table with enough chairs in the shade. There were pitchers of iced tea, along with lemonade.

Pallas walked in a few minutes before noon. She set down a nine-by-thirteen casserole dish and waved a large bag of tortilla chips.

"To complement your enchiladas," she said. "Seven-layer bean dip. We are going to party today." Pallas smiled at Verity. "I'm so excited you're going to join us. This is fun."

"Thank you for letting me participate."

Wynn and Bethany walked in together. Renee made introductions all around, then poured drinks for everyone.

"I heard what happened with Carol," Bethany said. "It's so great how you were able to help her." She paused. "Cade and I have some horses we're concerned about. We have a horse ranch. Do you think you could come talk to them or am I asking too much?"

"I'd be happy to help if I can," Verity said easily. "I get along well with horses."

"Me, too, and I can usually guess what's going on, but a little direct communication would be helpful."

"You should open a satellite office here in Happily Inc," Pallas teased. "Verity's Animal Communication Network—East."

They were all laughing when the rest of the women arrived.

Everyone met Verity and got drinks, then they put food on their plates and settled at the big table. Renee quickly realized she didn't have to worry about her mother. Wynn sat on one side and Silver sat on the other and she had both of them laughing.

Carol was next to Renee. She leaned over and lowered her voice. "I hope you're okay with us stealing your mom like we did."

"Of course. She was thrilled to help."

"Are you upset—I guess you wouldn't be anymore—but when you were little, were you upset that you couldn't do what she does?"

"What?"

"Her gift or whatever you call it. You don't have it. That must have made you sad."

Something Renee had never considered. She hadn't wanted what her mother had, she hadn't wanted her mother to have it. But Carol's perspective was totally different. Not just because she hadn't lived through what Renee had, but because she had a practical application for the information.

"I wasn't sad," Renee told her, not sure what else to say.

"So Hunter's getting interested in girls," Wynn announced, drawing everyone's attention. "I can't believe it. He's only thirteen. I thought I had a couple of years left until I had to deal with that."

"Thirteen." Pallas looked shocked. "Don't tell me that. I don't want to have to deal with Ryan and girls for a while yet."

"He's barely six months old," Silver reminded her. "You have a ways to go."

"But still." Pallas sighed. "My baby."

"What did you do?" Renee asked. "Talk about it with him or lock him in his room?"

"I wish I could lock him in his room, but they frown on that now." Wynn grinned. "I told him to talk to Jasper."

Everyone burst out laughing. Renee chuckled as she thought of what she would guess was a serious case of panic on Jasper's part.

"I have an announcement," Bethany said. "I told my parents I'm pregnant."

"Good for you."

"Yikes, how did it go?"

"Oh, no. Poor you."

Verity glanced around the table. "I'm confused. Why wouldn't you tell your parents? Don't they want grandchildren?"

"Oh, they want them. There was shrieking and tears and a thousand questions about my health, and that's just from my dad."

"Bethany comes from an unusual family," Pallas told Verity. "How should I put this…"

"Oh, you're the royal one," Verity said. "Did I get that right?"

Bethany sighed. "You did. My dad is the king of El Bahar. Technically he's my stepfather, but he adopted me and I'm the only daughter and my brothers are much younger, so it's a lot of pressure. I wanted to tell them because they're my parents and I didn't want to tell them because he's going to be overprotective and make my life a nightmare."

"Ah, I see. He loves his little girl." Verity nodded. "That's lovely."

"You say that now, but you're not the one who's going to have fifteen bodyguards and a cadre of servants making sure I don't fall, trip or otherwise injure my delicate self and his very first grandchild."

"It's tough being royal," Silver said. "Bethany, be brave and endure the pain."

"Bite me."

They all laughed again. Conversation shifted to different topics. Renee enjoyed the time with her friends and appreciated how easily her mother fit in. She couldn't help wondering how everything would have been different if her mother wasn't…special. In some ways, a lot of ways, life would have been easier. But Verity's ability made her who she was and Renee knew that whatever happened, she wouldn't want her mother to change for anyone. Not even for Renee herself.

JASPER HAD NO idea what Verity wanted, but she'd sounded upset on the phone. He drove to town and met her in the lobby of the Sweet Dreams Inn.

She was pacing anxiously when he walked in and immediately hurried over to him.

"Thank you for coming. Something's happened and I just don't know what to do."

Jasper had just texted with Renee a couple of hours before so he knew she was fine. He led Verity to a quiet area of the lobby and pulled a chair close to hers.

"Tell me what's going on."

She bit her lower lip. "Odele, my producer, called. They've been brainstorming fun prelaunch ideas for my show. Something that would get the public's attention and get them interested. Odele wants it a little gimmicky, but not off-putting. I was fine with all that and said she could reach me here if she wanted to talk."

Jasper really wanted to hurry her along, but knew it was better to let Verity tell her story in her own way. Eventually she would get to the point.

"Odele called me this morning," Verity admitted. "They've come up with what they think is a wonderful idea."

He waited.

"A giant dog wedding."

Her voice was thick with emotion and he had the horrifying thought that she might cry. How many dogs would there be in a giant dog wedding? Twenty? Fifty? And why did it matter?

Her lower lip trembled. "Odele knows where I am and she must have done research on the town because she wants to have the ceremony or whatever it is at Weddings Out of the Box!"

Ah, so there was the problem.

"You're concerned Renee is going to be upset."

"Yes. I just got my baby girl back. We're getting along and she's letting me into her life and now this! She's going to hate the idea. What a nightmare. Dogs running everywhere, me talking to them, the TV cameras." Tears filled her eyes. "I tried to tell Odele we couldn't, but she was insistent and then she had to go. She's very determined and I don't want to jeopardize my show, but if I have to choose, of course I want Renee to be happy."

Jasper knew the situation was more complicated than that. He also knew Verity really wanted to make her show a success and that Renee wanted that for her mother.

"Has Odele booked the, ah, event?"

"Not yet. She's finalizing details before she calls. She said it would be a day to set up and a day to film. They're talking midweek."

"Then that's a good thing. Pallas gets more business

without a lot of work and none of the scheduled weddings get impacted."

"You're right. I hadn't thought of that. I'm sure the production company is paying very well." She brightened. "That will help. So all that's left is for you to tell Renee what's happening."

"Me?"

"Please, Jasper. She won't get mad at you."

He knew that Renee was more than capable of getting plenty angry at him, but that wasn't Verity's point. She didn't want to have to fight with her daughter now, when things were going well between them.

Damn, he thought grimly, seeing no way out of the situation. If he refused, he would upset Renee's mother. If he said yes, he would upset Renee. Either way, he was screwed, because Renee wouldn't like him upsetting her mother or herself so hey, no win for him.

"I'll do it."

"You will? Oh, thank you, Jasper."

"Uh-huh. In return, you're going to tell her how great I am until she's done wanting to back the car over me."

"I promise."

PALLAS AND RENEE met weekly to discuss the upcoming weddings and share leads they had about future clients. While Renee generally enjoyed the breakneck pace of their days, she found herself looking forward to the last three weeks of January, when Weddings Out of the Box would shut down for vacation. She didn't have any plans at the moment, but she was thinking somewhere quiet and peaceful with absolutely no brides or wedding parties or drama.

As Pallas reviewed the schedule, Renee took a second to wonder if Jasper would be interested in joining her for some of that time—just the two of them with no distractions except the ones they came up with together.

She had no idea if they were in a place where that was a question she could even ask. While he'd used the *R* word, she was less sure of their status. A relationship? But going away with him would be nice.

"You have it all under control," Pallas said, closing the calendar program. "We're also getting more and more busy. I used to have one wedding a weekend and I had the occasional weekend with nothing. Now we have at least two weddings or we have a wedding party booking us Friday through Sunday. I need to get serious about hiring help."

"The work is very steady," Renee said. "I would really like a couple of assistants on the days we have weddings. Someone to run and get things when we need extra thread or spot remover. I feel as if I'm forever racing back and forth across the property."

"Of course." Pallas nodded. "That would be easy enough. Most of our weddings are on Saturdays, so I could look at hiring high school kids who want a job on weekends. Of course they would have to be willing to give up their Saturday nights." She smiled. "Let me write up a job description. Once you agree I've captured what you're looking for, we'll post it and start interviews."

"That would be great." Renee knew she could always rely on her vendors to pitch in, but she needed more help than that.

"I think we need another wedding coordinator," Pallas said. "There are just too many weddings, and business doesn't seem to be slowing down seasonally anymore. I've been keeping track of your workdays and there are weeks you're here sixty and seventy hours. You should have said something."

"It's been a challenge, but you've been dealing with Ryan. I didn't want to get in the way of that."

"I'll admit taking on another full-time employee scares me, but it's necessary. If things keep going the way they have been, you're going to burn out. Worse, I could lose you."

Lose her? Renee wanted to blurt out that she had no plans to leave, but knew better than to say that. She loved working for Pallas, but she had to maintain a little bit of decorum. At least on the surface.

"I would like to work a bit less," she murmured. "But I know hiring someone is a big step."

"It is." Pallas's expression turned mischievous. "Which is why sharing the worry and pain is such a good idea. I've been thinking a lot about inviting you to be a partner in the business and I'd like to move ahead with that, if you're still interested."

Renee's heart thundered in her chest. "With everything happening, I'd completely forgotten about that possibility. But I'm interested. Very interested."

"Good. I've been talking with my lawyer." Pallas wrinkled her nose. "I can't believe I even have a business lawyer but I do. Anyway, she has come up with several ways to bring you into the business. First I'll have a professional business evaluation done so we both know what the business is worth. Then we'll discuss options. You can buy in outright or over time with a percentage of your salary going to the purchase. We'd detail the division of duties, so there are no misunderstandings."

She paused, drumming her fingers on the table. "What else? Oh, the profits. Right now they would be shared based on a percentage of ownership, but also a division of labor. That means if you buy in 50 percent, then obviously you'd get 50 percent of the profits. But if you have to buy in over time, then you'd get your percentage and an added amount because you're working more than me."

She frowned. "I hope that makes sense. The legal stuff and the accounting rules do not come easily to me. Oh, and if we move forward with this, I'm granting you 5 percent ownership as soon as we sign the paperwork, so you'd own that right away, regardless of how we move forward." She leaned toward Renee. "What do you think?"

Renee's head was spinning. Not only was there was lot of information to take in, she also couldn't believe this was really happening.

Pallas trusted her with her business. Pallas wanted them to be fifty-fifty partners! The concept was so impossibly wonderful that she couldn't take it in.

"I'm excited," she managed to say. "Yes, of course I'm interested. It's a wonderful opportunity."

"I'm glad you think so. You'll need to get a lawyer to look over everything. Nick says I can't recommend one because it would be a conflict of interest." She sighed. "He's such a guy. I'd say ask Wynn for a name. I'm sure she uses someone and I don't think she and I use the same person, so that would work."

"I'll text her today," Renee promised.

"And I'll get going on both job descriptions. For the part-time person and the full-time wedding coordinator. I really liked the hiring service I used when I found you, so I want to go with them again."

As they weren't yet partners, Renee was fairly sure Pallas was sharing rather than asking her opinion.

"What do you think about opening the place up to

midweek events?" Pallas asked unexpectedly. "Not more weddings. I'm not sure any of us could handle that, but other types of gatherings might be interesting."

"Like corporate events," Renee said eagerly. "That's what I've been thinking about. Meetings or seminars. We have the space. If all we had to do was set up tables and chairs, that would be easy. Almost no work for us but some income."

Pallas nodded. "That's what I was thinking, too. We'd only need a couple of caterers to work with. They provide their own servers, they do the cleanup afterward, so we're left with logistics and putting away whatever supplies we had to get out. I know our janitorial service would like more hours. We could find out if they would do the setup and takedown."

"We'd have to get a cut of the catering," Renee told her. "Because that's where all the money is. I suppose we could set up different menus so everything flows through us. Oh, what about themed events? We have the decorations from all the weddings. Depending on the type of business, we could offer different packages. It would add an interesting element to the event."

"A *Star Trek*–themed corporate getaway?" Pallas asked with a laugh. "I like it. You know, I was playing with this idea right around the time Nick and I got together. Then we fell in love and got married and I got pregnant and what is it they say? Life happens. I'm so glad you want to be a part of this."

"Me, too."

"Anybody home?"

Renee turned toward the open doorway. "That sounds like Jasper."

She got up and called his name. Seconds later, he came into view.

"You're not in your office," he said. "But your car is in the parking lot. I was starting to think you'd been abducted by aliens." He lightly kissed her, then waved at Pallas. "Am I interrupting?"

"We were just finishing up," Pallas told him. "Are you here to steal her away for a few hours?" Her voice was teasing.

Renee immediately thought that why yes, she could make the time, but before she could say that, Jasper looked at her. The second she saw the combination of regret and concern in his eyes, she knew he hadn't shown up to ask for a little naked time.

"What? I can see it's something, so just spit it out." She wanted to ask what her mother had done now, only she knew whatever it was Verity couldn't be involved. Since arriving in Happily Inc, her mother had been sweet and helpful and just plain—

"It's about your mom."

"Is she okay?"

"She's fine." Jasper looked past her to Pallas. "This is kind of about you, too. Her producer has come up with a really fun idea to promote the show."

Renee couldn't imagine what that had to do with her or Pallas. Unless...

"Did she find out about the giraffes?"

"What? No. It's a giant dog wedding."

Renee turned to Pallas who looked as confused as she felt.

"I don't know what that is," Pallas admitted. "How many dogs does it take to be a giant dog wedding?"

"That was my question," he admitted. "I guess we'll

find out when they get here. Odele, that's her producer, thinks it will be entertaining and visual and give them something to promote that will get attention on social media."

"Because 'we have a woman who talks to animals' isn't enough of a grabber?" Renee shook her head. "Sorry. I don't know the business and if my mom's excited then it's great that they're—" The pieces came together.

"Oh, no," she breathed. "They want to have the giant dog wedding here, don't they?"

"That's kind of the point of me stopping by. Your mom said things were good between the two of you and she didn't want to mess that up, so she sent me instead." He flashed her a smile. "This would be a good time to say don't kill the messenger."

Renee wanted to scream. This was so unfair. She and Pallas were in the middle of negotiating her joining the business. Talk about an off-putting twist in their relationship.

"It would be midweek," he added. "Odele said the show will cover all the expenses and make sure the property is back to normal by close of business on Thursday. Apparently they're willing to pay a premium for the use of the space."

Pallas looked at Renee. "Premiums are always nice."

"You're saying you can be bought?"

Pallas grinned. "When it comes to the business, money nearly always talks." She turned to Jasper. "I guess I need to speak with Verity's producer."

He pulled a business card out of his shirt pocket. "I happen to have her number right here."

CHAPTER SIXTEEN

RENEE AND JASPER left Pallas to call Odele and work out the details of the giant dog wedding.

When they reached her office, Jasper stepped in front of her to keep her from going inside.

"You need a break," he told her. "Let's go walk around for a half hour or so to clear your head."

She thought of all she had to do and all that had happened in the past hour. "I'd like that. I'm kind of reeling from too much input."

She collected her handbag, then led the way outside. She expected him to turn toward the Riverwalk but he went in the opposite direction. As she didn't have a particular destination in mind, she went along without saying anything.

"How are things with you?" she asked.

"Good. The book is progressing. Today was all about murder and gross bodies."

She laughed. "So an easy day."

"Yeah. None of that hard emotional stuff or dealing with Mandy's life. Give me a good dismemberment scene and I'm a happy guy."

"You're a weird guy."

"Maybe, but I'm okay with that."

He surprised her by taking her hand in his. She couldn't remember the last time she'd walked down a street, holding a guy's hand. Probably when she was with Turner, she thought wistfully. So many years ago. She didn't miss him at all, but sometimes the what-ifs of the situation were difficult to handle.

"Pallas wants to talk about me becoming a partner in the business," she said.

"That's great. Do you want to be a partner?"

"Very much. I like the business and I have some ideas about how we could grow things. It's a lot of responsibility and I'd have to buy in with a lump sum or over time. I have some savings, but I doubt it's close to enough, so I guess it will be over time."

"I have money."

She rolled her eyes. "I'm sure you have more than all of us, but that isn't relevant to the conversation."

"I could—"

"No."

"But I don't need it for—"

She glared at him. "No. Jasper, stop. There's no way you can just give me money to buy into Pallas's business without making things weird between us. Not only would it change things, it would completely freak me out. So just no."

He studied her for several seconds. "Fine. I will respect your wishes on this topic."

"Thank you."

"Even though you're wrong."

She made a low noise in her throat. "Boys are stupid."

"Liar. You can't get enough of me. Now no more talk of business." He pointed across the street. "See that building there? We're going inside. It's a magical place, so there will be no fighting."

Across the street was a very unassuming structure. It

was plain with big windows and large glass doors. The sign out front read Happily Inc Public Library.

"I don't understand. It's just the library."

"Not just the library," he told her. "When I was a kid, my dad worked a lot of hours. Our house got lonely so I would spend afternoons in the library, reading everything I could. The librarians watched out for me, made recommendations." He smiled. "Brought me cookies. Come on."

He tugged her along as he crossed the street. They went inside.

She looked around and saw thousands of books in rows of shelves. There were posters on the wall and signs pointing to various sections. It was, well, a library. But when she turned to Jasper, she realized he saw something completely different. His gaze was slightly unfocused as if instead of books, he saw journeys and possibilities.

He winked at her. "Let's go explore. I want to start in travel. It's over here."

He went directly to the travel section. This was not his first time here, she thought, wondering if the seeds of his writing career had been sown long before he'd realized.

He showed her an old book on Egypt, pointing out the sketched pictures and the original binding. There were coffee table-sized books of maps and books with shiny new photographs of different parts of the world.

At the end of the aisle, they went in different directions. She found herself in front of cookbooks from around the world. One published in the 1950s showed a sketch of a woman wearing high heels, pearls and an apron, as if that was the expectation.

"I would so fail at that," she murmured softly, flipping through the pages and finding an entire section of gelatin mold recipes.

Someone tapped her on the shoulder. She turned and saw Jasper standing very close. He leaned in and kissed her on the lips—a sweet kiss that unexpectedly made her eyes burn.

"Score!" he whispered. "I always wanted to kiss a girl in the library. It's been a fantasy of mine since I was fifteen and had a thing for a girl named Bambi."

"Seriously? Bambi?"

"I swear. She was so hot and she never noticed me."

"That's her loss."

"I like to think so."

Then he was gone, continuing his library exploration. Renee hugged the cookbook to her chest. Jasper was surprising in so many ways. She'd thought he would be brooding and quiet and a little scary, albeit good in bed. Except for that last one, he was nothing she'd imagined. Not that she was complaining. She really liked the funny, slightly quirky, affectionate man she'd come to know. He was a down-to-his-bones good guy and someone she was lucky to have in her life.

She'd been so frightened for so long, she thought as she shelved the cookbook. Afraid of getting hurt, afraid of being like her mother. She was nearly thirty and as Jasper had pointed out more than once, she had no hint of her mother's gift. There was no reason to think it would suddenly show up now. If she wanted to get on with things, she needed to let that fear go. Hanging on to it wasn't helping her at all.

As for not wanting to risk her heart, well, that was harder to deal with. She'd lost her father, friends, the career she'd wanted, Turner and maybe a piece of herself because of what had happened. The losses weren't her fault, but how she dealt with them was completely on her. She could be a victim and wallow in a lifetime of "poor me" or she could put on her big girl panties and figure out a way to move forward. The choice was hers. It always had been. It seemed like it was time to start acting like it.

She walked along the main aisle until she spotted Jasper poring over some car manual. She stopped in front of him.

"I would very much like us to go back to my place and make love for a couple of hours. What do you think?"

He shelved the book, grabbed her hand and practically ran out of the building.

"I knew the library would make you hot," he said as they headed back to where their cars were parked. "I love it when a plan comes together."

NINETY MINUTES AND two orgasms later, Renee felt a little melty and a whole lot more like herself. While she would have loved to spend the rest of the afternoon in bed with Jasper, he had to get home and do some writing and she needed to head back to the office. She still had some work to do before she could call it a day. But she would be smiling the whole time.

"Thank you," he said, kissing her as they picked up their items of clothing and put them back on. "Want to come over and spend the night?"

"Let me check with my mom. I don't know if she has plans or not. She's been pretty busy the last couple of days. If she's available, I really should spend time with her."

"If she's not, I'm happy to be your second choice."

She laughed and wrapped her arms around his neck. "You're not my second choice."

"I know."

He kissed her and she had a brief thought that being irresponsible had definite benefits. Then her better angels reminded her about her career goals and she reluctantly drew back.

When they were both dressed, they walked to his truck and he drove the short distance to Weddings Out of the Box, where she'd left her car. He'd just stopped at a light on the west side of the river when a helicopter flew overhead. A helicopter that was getting lower and lower, as if it were going to—

"The pilot is going to land in The Promenade," Jasper said over the noise, as he drove through the intersection and then pulled over.

They both got out of the truck and walked the few feet to The Promenade—an open area in front of stores by the Riverwalk.

Sure enough the helicopter was sitting on the concrete, its rotors slowing as the engine wound down. There were no markings indicating it was part of a law enforcement task force or even from a news station. Renee was fairly sure the Happily Inc police department didn't need or own a helicopter, so who could it be and why were they landing there?

More people spilled into the area. Renee saw several of her friends. Her mother came up, Ed, Carol's father, with her.

"Renee, this is so exciting. What do you think is going on?"

"I have no idea. We don't get things like this happening in town very much."

"Maybe it's a celebrity," Ed said.

Someone pushed through the crowd. "Oh my God!"

Renee saw Bethany running toward the helicopter.

"What are you doing?" Bethany shouted. "You can't act like this. You're disrupting people's lives!"

The engines were turned off. The sudden silence was nearly as shocking as the noise had been. Bethany stood with her hands on her hips as the doors to the helicopter opened.

"Oh, no," Renee breathed. "It's her parents."

"The king and queen of El Bahar?" Verity asked. "That's so thrilling. I've never seen anyone royal before. Well, I have, but only on television or in magazines. They look normal."

Renee recognized the older couple from the previous year's prewedding party for Bethany and Cade. The king was very handsome and just a little imposing. Liana, Bethany's mother, was a slightly older version of her daughter, with blond hair and blue eyes.

"Darling!" Her mother held out her arms. "There you are. We went to the ranch first, but they told us you'd come to town so we decided to surprise you."

"You couldn't drive?" Bethany asked.

"The helicopter was faster." Her father kissed both her cheeks.

"Where did you even get a helicopter?" Bethany asked.

"I bought it," her father told her. "It will be wherever you are, from now until you have your baby. There are pilots on call, 24/7. If you need to get to a hospital, they'll get you there in a few minutes."

Bethany looked horrified. "Please tell me you're kidding."

"Not at all. Now come. We'll fly back to the ranch together."

Bethany cast a helpless glance over her shoulder. "But my car is here."

The king waved and a man jumped out of the helicopter. "Give him the keys. He'll meet us there."

Bethany dug in her handbag and pulled out a set of keys, then sighed heavily and got in the helicopter. The engine started right up and then they all flew away.

Renee watched them go.

"That was quite the show," Verity said. "What an amazing town you have here."

"It's not usually like this, Mom." Renee said automatically, all the while thinking Bethany's worst fears about her parents were being realized. A helicopter standing by until she had the baby? What else was her father going to do to "help"?

The crowd began dispersing. Ed whispered something in Verity's ear. Verity nodded, then looked at Renee.

"Did you have plans for us this evening? Because I can keep myself busy."

"Not really. Did you want to have dinner?"

Verity hesitated. "Rain check."

"Sure. No problem."

They hugged, then Verity and Ed walked away. Renee was just thinking how nicely that worked out when she suddenly got what had happened. She came to a stop on The Promenade.

"No," she said, shaking her head. "No. It wasn't that."
She looked at Jasper. "My mother wasn't with Ed, was
she?"

"You mean like dating or something? I don't think
so. Didn't you tell me they met when she talked to the
giraffes? He would be interested in her gift. I'm sure
they're just friends."

He was right, she thought. That made sense.

Jasper put his arm around her. "So dinner and a
sleepover?"

"I'll be there."

HANNA REACHED UP and touched her hair. She'd had her
hair done at a local salon earlier that morning and the
complicated updo suited her face.

"It feels weird to have my hair up on my head like
this," she admitted with a laugh. "But I wanted to see
if I liked it."

Renee grinned. "You look great, but you have to be
comfortable with whatever style you decide on. Live
with it for the day, take some pictures, then decide."

"You're right. Okay, so champagne."

For once Hanna was the only one attending the planning meeting. Graham was out of town and Jasper had a
conference call with his publisher's marketing team. Not
that Jasper was an actual decision maker but he did want
to be as involved as possible. Or at least in the loop.

Thinking of Jasper made her happy inside. Things
were good between them—which, while interesting,
was not anything she wanted to have on her mind during an important meeting.

"Champagne," Renee echoed, then waited.

Hanna raised her shoulders up and down several times. "I can argue both sides."

"Then let me offer an opinion. No one is expecting a drink before the wedding. You have to pay for bar service along with the champagne and you're starting your guests on the road to getting drunk even earlier than usual. I'm not sure it's the best use of your money. Just as important, I don't think it adds to the experience of the ceremony."

"It seems so elegant," Hanna hedged. "Plus, not everyone likes bagpipe music so we thought it might help."

"Not everyone likes 'Ave Maria' yet you hear it all the time at weddings. This is *your* day, Hanna. My job is to help you and Graham have the most amazing wedding possible, so if you want champagne available to your guests ahead of time, then that is what you'll get. I'm just saying to think about it before you spend the money."

"You're right," Hanna told her. "What is it called? Gilding the lily? I just want everything to be perfect. I think I'm getting nervous because it's such a big deal." She wrinkled her nose. "Don't take this wrong, but I wish Graham and I hadn't started down this path. The whole big wedding, theme thing. I'm super excited about everything we have planned and we love that Jasper's using our wedding for his book, it's just we're kind of quiet, stay-at-home people, so this is a lot out of our comfort zone. We want our wedding to be significant to us and not just a big party."

"I totally get that. What you need to tell me is if you're just talking or if you really want to cut back on some of the things you have planned. We're about to reach the point of no return on a lot of things, so now is the time to decide."

Hanna briefly covered her face with her hands, then sighed. "I'm sorry. I'm being neurotic."

"You're not. You're spending a lot of money on a single day and while it's traditional, it's not exactly your style. Of course you're second-guessing yourself."

"Thank you for understanding. I don't mean to be difficult."

Renee smiled. "This is not the least bit difficult. Trust me. A three-hour conversation on the different shades of ecru and which one works the best for table linens is difficult."

"Thank you for saying that, even if it's not true."

"I wish it weren't, but I was there for every second of it."

"Okay. Then I'll accept my nerves as normal." She looked at the papers spread out on the table. They were printouts of the various elements that would be at the wedding. "I love it all. I don't want to get rid of anything."

Renee was used to brides having varying levels of freak-outs along the journey from proposal to ceremony. Hanna's was nowhere near noteworthy.

"Think about it. You still have a few days to change your mind on nearly everything."

"Thanks. I appreciate how calm you are." Hanna picked up her glass of water. "How did you and Jasper meet?"

The question was unexpected. Renee thought for a second. "We both live in town. Technically he lives on a mountain, but close enough. Happily Inc is small so eventually you run into everyone. We have mutual friends. It wasn't an actual meeting so much as at some point I knew who he was."

"How long have you been going out?"

Ack! Renee knew she couldn't say they weren't really going out in the conventional sense. They were, um, what? He would say they were in a relationship and she was still comfortable with not defining anything although she had to admit the man got to her in ways she wouldn't have anticipated.

"I didn't mean it to be a hard question," Hanna teased.

"It's been a couple of months now."

"The beginning is always fun. I remember when Graham and I were first together. We were crazy about each other from the start."

"How did you meet?"

Hanna laughed. "We were waiting in line for a movie. *Black Panther* actually. We each went with a group of friends who left us to hold their places in line while they got Starbucks. They were gone forever and we started talking." She sighed happily. "It was just one of those things. We sat together at the movie, we went out to dinner after and by the end of the weekend, we were in love."

She looked at Renee. "I'd never felt like that before. Not really. I was so sure he was the one and he felt the same about me. We really fit, if that makes sense. When my family makes me crazy, which is a lot of the time, he talks me down. When his twin sister expects too much from him, I'm a buffer. It works."

"That sounds lovely. You're going to have a wonderful wedding and a long, happy marriage."

Hanna's expression turned troubled. "I hope so. I

worry about that. Graham comes from a long line of people who stayed together forever, but not me. My parents have each been married and divorced four times. I can't tell you how many stepbrothers and sisters I have. My older sister has already been divorced once. She's engaged again and we can all see it's not going to last. I don't want to be like them."

Renee knew better than to offer a pat "you're not." That wouldn't help at all. "Do you know why any of the marriages failed?"

"Let's see. My sister married someone she barely knew, so they didn't have much of a chance. This guy is throwing up red flags, which she ignores. He's been unfaithful a bunch of times, he lies and he's kind of a jerk, but because he's really good-looking and has a great job, she's all about excuses. My mom keeps choosing the same type of guy over and over. It didn't work the first four times, but she can't seem to learn to avoid that type. My dad is more of a mixed bag. He married his second wife because she got pregnant. I'm not sure about the other two."

She paused. "Sorry. That was probably more information than you wanted."

"I can handle it," Renee said lightly. "But you've made my point. Hanna, you know exactly why nearly all those marriages didn't work out. You can see the flaws and you're not making the same mistakes. You know Graham and he knows you. You're clear on what each of you wants from your relationship. Isn't he a good guy?"

"He's the best."

"If you're just worried about repeating your family's pattern, that's one thing, but if you're genuinely concerned about your relationship with Graham, then you should see a therapist and get some counseling."

"That's good advice. Thank you. You're always so calming to be around." Hanna drew in a breath. "Okay, I'm ready to make some decisions. No champagne at the ceremony. Everyone can wait until we're married."

"Good choice."

"I'm pretty sure I like my hair up and I will work really hard to keep my family from making me doubt what a fantastic man I have in my life."

"Sounds like you have a plan."

"I do and it's wonderful."

CHAPTER SEVENTEEN

THE PLANNING MEETING for the "wedding of many dogs," as Jasper thought of it, took place in the same conference room as every other planning meeting he'd attended. What was different was the lack of bride and groom or any of their family members. Instead Renee was there, looking sexy and business-appropriate in a simple black dress, with Pallas, Wynn and Natalie also in attendance. Verity rushed in five minutes late, looking flushed and rattled.

"Sorry," she said, taking a seat across from her daughter. "I had a last-minute call from Odele, finalizing everything." She turned to Pallas. "Odele said she sent you the specs and a budget. Did you get them?"

"I have them right here." Pallas tapped a folder in front of her. "I have to say, for the record, I love TV weddings."

"Me, too." Renee grinned. "Their budget is very generous."

Which would mean lots of profits for the business, Jasper thought. Something Renee would appreciate now that she was going to be an owner.

"Good news for all of us," Wynn said. "Order lots of signage. I could use the business."

"We will." Pallas waved at Renee. "Take it away."

Renee flipped open a folder. "All right. First, the

giant wedding is turning into a medium-sized wedding. Instead of sixteen pairs of dogs, we're having eight pairs. A more manageable number. Odele's team has arranged for the care and feeding of the dogs. Each dog will have a handler, so we're only responsible for the ceremony and reception and the humans who will be there."

"Who are the humans attending?" he asked.

"The dog handlers, Odele and her team, the filming crew and I guess us." Renee flipped through her notes. "Oh, we have ten extras to be seated during the ceremony." She scribbled on a pad of paper. "I'm getting about fifty people. Does everyone agree?"

"That's my number, too, but let's plan on sixty to be safe," Pallas told her.

Renee entered the information on her tablet. "All right. So the dogs will come, have a little playtime to burn off energy, then get married. It's a group ceremony, so that should be quick. Again, assuming here, they'll need to do it a couple of times to get good footage. So say an hour?"

Pallas handed over a minute-by-minute accounting of the day. "That's what they say. An hour. Then a reception for another hour." She looked at Verity. "You're doing a one-on-one with each of the dogs. That's going to take a while."

Renee's mother shrugged. "It should be all right. They know there's no second take on that part of it. Odele's going to set up an area inside for me. A quiet room where the dogs can be comfortable."

"The groom's room," Renee and Pallas said at the same time.

"Not the bride's room?" Wynn asked. "It's so much bigger."

"We can't risk it," Renee told her. "We need it by midday on Friday and if there's any kind of accident, we can't be sure the smell will be gone or the carpet dry. The groom is just putting on a suit or a tux. The bride has the whole dress thing going on."

"I hadn't thought of that," Wynn admitted. "This is why you two are the professionals."

"You'll want to put down some kind of indoor-outdoor carpet to protect the floor," Natalie pointed out. "The filming situation could be stressful for the dogs, plus whatever food they're eating. Is there a cake or something?"

Renee typed on her tablet. "Floor protection. An excellent idea. Now, food." She read for a second. "Okay, they're providing doggie snacks. There will be a dog food cake and doggie cookies. We need to have catering for the humans. An easy lunch." She made more notes on her tablet. "I'll call the canine catering company and get information on what they're providing." She grinned. "We should either avoid cookies altogether or get sugar cookies with icing. That way we can have the bakery write 'human' on them."

Everyone laughed.

She looked back at her list. "I'm thinking we'll need to have the human catering inside. Otherwise it will be too tempting for the dogs. How about a salad and taco bar, two or three different kinds of sandwiches, water, soda and juices, plus dessert?"

Pallas nodded. "That sounds great. Odele told us we need vegetarian and vegan options."

"So no meat, no eggs, no dairy." Renee thought for a

second. "Sure. We can do corn tortillas and have beans and rice at the taco bar. I'll make sure the caterer provides a vegetarian sandwich and a vegan option. Maybe we'll do some kind of a soup."

She made more notes. Jasper reminded himself to avoid the vegan dessert.

"Decorations," Renee said and activated the screen on the wall. "Time is of the essence. Anything custom has to be easy to get. So I went on Etsy."

"I love that site," Wynn murmured.

Jasper had no idea what they were talking about. "What's Etsy?"

Pallas looked pitying. "It's a website with all kinds of crafts and different creations. We bought Ryan the cutest toy box. It's just gorgeous and really well made. You should check it out."

Renee's mouth twitched. "Yes, Jasper, check it out. It's very you."

"Uh-huh. You're just messing with me."

Renee was still smiling when she pressed a button on her laptop. A picture of a floral dog collar appeared on the screen.

"I spoke to the vendor. She's doing a rush job in eight colors. They'll be here by Monday."

Renee clicked the button again. A bow tie collar appeared. "These are for the boy dogs and will coordinate with the flower collars. We went with white, pink, blue, red, green, yellow, purple and orange."

"Not black?" he asked.

Verity glanced at him. "Black might not film well. There wouldn't be definition in the flowers."

All the other women were nodding. Were they just born knowing this kind of stuff?

"So no black," he muttered.

"I'd love to do cuffs for the paws," Renee said, "but we don't have enough time. So these will have to do."

"I could do paw cuffs out of paper," Natalie offered. "It wouldn't take any time at all. I'd use peel and stick dots to hold them in place, that way they can be adjustable, depending on the size of the dog. Read me the colors again. I'll have them match."

"Are you sure?" Renee asked.

"I think it would be fun."

Renee listed the colors. Natalie wrote them down, then the meeting moved on. Renee clicked the computer again. Rows of white chairs appeared.

"Odele wants flowers at the end of each row of chairs." Renee sighed. "I've already got a call in to the florist to make sure the flowers they send over aren't poisonous to dogs. We'll have ten tables that seat six." Another picture went up on the screen, this one showing a set table.

"I'm thinking white linens with black runners, seeing as we're not using black anywhere else." She glanced at Jasper. "Black will be a good contrasting color."

"Sure. But how do you use a runner? The tables are round."

Several more pitying looks were cast his way.

"We run them north-south and east-west, so they cross. It's pretty and simple. Flowers on every table. Black chargers instead of place mats."

She glanced at her notes. "Do we want a gift table? And if we do, should it be wrapped empty boxes or should we have actual gifts inside?"

"For the dogs?" Wynn asked. "Like toys and stuff?"

"I don't know," Renee admitted, then started typing. "I'll get a list together to ask Odele."

"Is there an officiant?" Pallas asked.

Renee scanned her notes. "I don't see one mentioned. I'll put that on the Ask Odele list, as well. It could really be anyone. The weddings aren't legal."

"It would be funny to have a cat marry them," Wynn said. "Although that is probably asking for trouble."

"I got the impression the wedding was supposed to be fun and charming rather than funny." Renee glanced at Verity. "Mom, what do you think?"

"I agree. Obviously it's not serious but it's not comedy, either."

"Oh, it might be," Pallas said. "Even with a medium-sized dog wedding, it's going to be hilarious. Or a complete disaster."

"Nick would point out that is you, being a ray of sunshine," Renee murmured as she typed. "It's on the list. Anything else?"

The meeting went on for a few more minutes. Jasper listened rather than said the wrong thing—again. So he wasn't Mr. Wedding Expert. At least he was participating.

Once they'd worked through all the items on the agenda, Renee reviewed their decisions and confirmed what she had to talk to Odele about. She excused herself and left for her office.

Verity disappeared just as quickly, leaving Jasper to walk out with Wynn.

"Do not even think about putting a dog wedding in your book," she told him.

"I wouldn't do that."

"You would, in a heartbeat. You enjoy putting real life into your stories, but the tone is wrong."

He knew she was correct, but really liked the idea of writing about dogs going crazy at a wedding.

"I couldn't have a dog wedding and a murder at the same time," he said. "That would be over-the-top. Still, it would be fun."

They reached the parking lot. He saw she'd parked next to him and they headed in that direction.

"Look how far you've come," she said, her voice teasing. "I remember when you would barely make eye contact when you showed up at The Boardroom. Now you're a social butterfly."

"That's extreme."

"Maybe but it's pretty close to the truth. You've changed."

They stopped by her SUV.

"Not that much," he said, hoping he didn't sound defensive, because he didn't feel it. Not really. Just a little apprehensive, because Wynn seemed to have something on her mind and he had a bad feeling it was more than helping Hunter with his fastball.

"Renee is really special," she said.

He held in a groan. "You and I shouldn't discuss that."

"Someone has to discuss it with you and no one else seems to be volunteering."

"We're doing just fine."

"I know and that's my point. Your relationship with her is a lot better than your relationship with me."

He had no clue what that meant, but figured the safest course was to keep his mouth shut.

"We were never going anywhere and we both knew it," she said.

"You set up the rules so we were bound to fail."

He hadn't meant to say that, but he wasn't taking it back. It was the truth.

"I did. Absolutely. I didn't want any more than we had and I was terrified you did."

"Why would you think that?" He'd been very clear on not getting involved. He couldn't.

"Because you were getting better every day. You were healing right before my eyes and I knew it wasn't going to be very long before you wanted something more." She offered him a sad smile. "I didn't realize that you would want it with someone else."

He'd gone from clueless to genuinely flummoxed. What was he supposed to say to that?

She held up a hand. "I'm not complaining. I get it. I was never going to be that important to you."

"That's not true."

"You never fought for me, Jasper." Her tone was soft, her gaze steady. "I'm not saying you should have, and I'm not complaining. I'm pointing out the fact that you never pushed back on my ridiculous rules and when I ended things, you let me go. I wasn't the one."

"I don't have a 'one.'"

"Of course you do. Don't be silly. Like I said, when you and I were together, I could see you getting better every day, but you're not anymore. You're healed. Whole. Whatever you want to call it." She touched his arm. "You're back among the normal, however you want to define that."

"I'm not," he managed through an uncomfortable combination of panic, fear and hope. "Things happened. I still have nightmares."

"You probably always will, but the band that defines

normal is pretty wide and you're well within it. What I mean by this is that while you'll always have crap from your past to deal with, you're still emotionally capable of being a functioning member of society. More important, you're more than ready and completely able to be in a real relationship. One with expectation and commitment and a future. That's my point here, Jasper. Don't assume what you have with Renee is like what you had with me. It's not. It's so much better and stronger. Don't blow it by thinking you'll be able to replace it. You and Renee have something really wonderful going on."

He wanted to ask how she knew any of this. About him, about him and Renee. He wanted to make her tell him why she would want him to think he was normal when he knew he wasn't. He couldn't be. Even his dog thought he had issues.

"You're wrong," he said, walking to his truck. "You're wrong."

Wynn didn't try to stop him. It was as if she knew he had to process what she'd said. As if she knew he was running away.

Well, so what? Bolting seemed the most logical next step, he thought as he drove out of the parking lot. Normal. No way. Not him. He was never going to be normal. He was always going to be reclusive and solitary and distant. He was broken—shattered—and he could never be right.

That settled, he made his way up the mountain, concentrating on the road and his breathing and doing his best to ignore the voice in his head that asked *What if Wynn was right?*

She wasn't. She couldn't be. Him healed? Because if he was, if he was at a place where he could be involved with someone in a meaningful way, didn't that change everything, including how he defined himself? And if she was right, where did that leave him? And assuming he could answer that question, then he had one more to wrestle with. What on earth came next?

RENEE WAS SURPRISED to find herself just as nervous the morning of the dog wedding as she was on any other day when she had a human wedding going on. Even though the brides and grooms wouldn't care about the decorations and if things flowed smoothly, she wanted to get it all exactly as it should be.

In deference to the fact that she might be called on to perform different duties at this event, she'd put on black slacks and a black blouse, rather than a dress. She had on flats and she'd pulled her hair back.

By eight forty-five, she'd confirmed the tables were set, the chairs were in place and the flowers had been delivered. By nine, the film crew had arrived to set up, as had the caterers.

Renee introduced herself to Odele, a tall, pretty African American woman with a take-charge attitude that Renee found comforting.

"This is exactly what I pictured," Odele told her, looking around. "I love it."

They walked the event, first going through the ceremony—to be performed by an Animal Planet celebrity dog trainer—then moving on to the reception.

"As you requested, we did only a couple of tables out here with the dogs," Renee said, pointing to the decorated tables. "The rest are inside, away from inquisitive canines."

"But there's a dog-friendly cake?"

"Yes, and cookies. There are a dozen or so water dishes around the perimeter of the reception area and I have someone who will be checking them regularly."

"Good." Odele scrolled through her tablet. "The pooper-scooper guy will arrive with the dogs."

"I'm glad you thought of that. I'm not sure I would have," Renee admitted.

Odele laughed. "I've done plenty of dog-based shows. You learn to expect that sort of thing."

They finalized all the details, then Odele went back to oversee her crew.

Close to ten, her friends started arriving. Not only would they be there to help with anything unexpected, they would also be extras at the wedding and ceremony.

Jasper had texted the previous day to say he couldn't make the wedding. Renee smiled as she thought of his excuse that he had to work on the book. She suspected he was thinking that a dog wedding could easily get out of hand and wasn't anything he wanted to be a part of. He was such a guy.

Carol, Silver and Verity all arrived at the same time. She showed them the layout and the incredible amount of food the caterers had already set up.

"I think it's called a craft table," Silver said, eyeing the Danishes. "Or maybe not."

"We're so Hollywood," Carol teased.

Verity looked around. "Renee, you've done a wonderful job."

"Thanks. Do you want to check out your room where you'll be doing the readings?"

Her mother smiled at her. "Has it changed from yesterday?"

"Odele was going to get the camera set up in it, so there's that."

"Then we should probably make sure it's as I remember."

"You think I'm overmonitoring the details."

"I think this is you doing your job, which you do very well."

"I appreciate that."

Renee told Pallas she and her mom would be right back, then they went inside to the groom's room. Sure enough, it was as it had been the day before, with all the furniture removed and cushions and a dog bed on the floor. A guy was setting up a camera. Two big lights had been placed at one end of the room and there was a chart on the wall, detailing the order in which the dogs would come in.

"You're going to be busy," Renee said. "That's a lot of dogs."

"I'll be fine. This will be good practice for me before the show starts."

They confirmed everything was in place before starting back to the main event area. Partway there, Verity came to a stop.

"I want to talk to you for a second."

Renee looked at her mother. "Is everything all right? You've been so busy working, I've hardly seen you for the past week."

Verity glanced away before returning her attention to her daughter. "Yes, well, there have been some things to deal with but it's all good. Very good, in fact. But that's not what I want to talk about. I've been thinking about what you told me about Pallas wanting you in the business."

"What? We didn't talk about that." Renee was nearly sure of it. She'd told Jasper, but that was it.

"Of course you did," her mother told her. "Anyway, I've been thinking that I would very much like to give you the money to buy in as a full partner."

"What? No. Mom, no. That's impossible."

"It's not. I have the money I made when I sold the salon, plus my payment for the show. I want to help." She smiled. "Renee, I've never been able to give you much financial support. You went to college on scholarships and before that we were always scrimping to get by. I want to do this. It would make me so happy."

Renee couldn't take it all in. "Mom, that is incredibly generous and I want to talk about it, but not right now, okay?"

"Of course. I just want you to know I love you and I'm so proud of you."

"Thank you. I love you, too."

They hugged before returning to the prewedding frenzy. Renee pushed thoughts of her mother's offer from her mind. She would deal with it later. No way would she take the full amount from her mother, but even the money for a quarter of her share would be fantastic.

They stepped outside in time to see Bethany arriving, with two tall men trailing her. She hurried over, her expression both apologetic and exasperated.

"These are my bodyguards," she explained. "They go with me everywhere and they make me insane."

"What about at the ranch?" Pallas asked. "They can't be there all the time. They'll spook the horses."

"They keep their distance, but there they are. Lurking. I hate lurkers."

"Poor you." Silver put an arm around her. "What are you going to do?"

"Endure. Be passive-aggressive with my parents. Plot my escape." She sighed. "If it's like this now, what is it going to be like when I have the baby? My parents are literally going to smother me with their concern."

"What does Cade say?" Renee asked.

"He says we should surrender to the inevitable and move to El Bahar when I'm about six months along. Then I can just be there for the birth before we come back here. But I don't know."

"Not a decision you have to make now," Pallas told her. "Although if you do go to El Bahar for three or four months, we are so going to visit."

That made Bethany smile. "Really? You'd do that for me? I'd have my dad send a plane."

Wynn put her hands on her hips. "Well, yeah. It's not as if we would go without your dad sending a plane!"

They all laughed. Renee excused herself to do one last check with Odele. They'd just finished when a couple of SUVs pulled up in the parking lot. Renee went out to meet the dogs and their handlers. As she waited, she realized she'd forgotten to ask Odele about the various breeds they were having. The collars were adjustable but if they had a pair of Yorkies, the collars might not be small enough.

The back door of the first SUV opened and two incredibly beautiful, incredibly large dogs jumped to the ground.

Odele came up next to her. "Oh, good. They're here."

"Wh-what are they?"

"Irish wolfhounds." She looked at Renee. "You know

all the dogs are large, right?" She checked her list. "We have the Irish wolfhounds, mastiffs, Great Danes—"

The second SUV opened and a Saint Bernard jumped heavily to the ground. A second one followed.

"Oh, no." Renee did her best to stay focused. If she started laughing, she might never stop. "A giant dog wedding. You really meant giant dogs."

"I thought it would be appealing to viewers. We debated tiny dogs, but that's a lot of close-up shots and we had the contacts for the big dogs, so here we are."

"A giant dog wedding."

The first giggle escaped. Then a second.

"Excuse me," she managed before running back inside the grounds. She found her friends all talking together. Pallas spotted her first.

"What is it? What's wrong?"

"Nothing," Renee said, trying not to give in to laughter. "It's just…" She pointed.

Two handlers led in the Irish wolfhounds, followed by the Saint Bernards. Apparently, the Great Danes had arrived because they were next.

"Oh, no," Pallas breathed.

"A giant dog wedding," Wynn said before starting to laugh. "I am so glad I brought my video camera. This is going to be fantastic!"

CHAPTER EIGHTEEN

BY MIDAFTERNOON THE film crew was packing up for the drive back to Los Angeles. The wedding and reception had gone reasonably well. The Saint Bernards had found a shady spot to nap and refused to be moved. The mastiffs had eaten all the flowers, then had promptly thrown them up, while the Great Danes had wanted to play and the wolfhounds looked bewildered.

Verity had done readings on all the dogs, including the Saint Bernards, both of whom had told her they just wanted to be left alone to sleep. The dogs had loved their cake, the pooper-scooper guy had kept up with, ah, production and the outdoor area seemed none too worse for wear.

Renee found herself just as tired as she was after an all-day wedding. Maybe it was because she hadn't known what to expect and maybe because she'd had so much to think about with her mother's generous offer.

"Patches. Patches! Here, boy."

Renee saw one of the handlers calling for the male Great Dane. He was close to Renee so she grabbed his leash.

He was beautiful—a black-and-white harlequin with long legs and an ever-wagging tail. Wearing flats, she was practically eye level with him, she thought humorously, leading him across the lawn.

"Did you have a good time?" she asked as he walked with her. "Did you have a good wedding?"

She reached out to pet him only to realize not only wasn't there an answer, she hadn't expected one. She'd simply reacted to being with a friendly dog. In fact, she hadn't once thought she had to worry during the entire day. She'd done her job, wrangled dogs when necessary, made kissing noises so they would look alert for pictures and that was it.

There was no gift—there never had been. Not for her. She had wasted so much time worrying about something that was never going to happen. How ridiculous.

"Thanks," the woman said, taking his leash. "He loves to explore. Okay, we're heading home. This was great. I can't wait to see the show."

Renee watched her go before returning to the reception area. She and Pallas did a quick walk-through to make sure there was no forgotten camera equipment, leashes or dog toys. Wynn had already headed back to work.

Mathias was with Carol, waiting to take her back to their place. He had Devon with him, the baby tucked in his arms.

They were a happy family, Renee thought wistfully. Like Pallas, Nick and Ryan. She doubted it would be very long before Natalie and Silver were pregnant.

Two by two, she thought. Then three by three, as they became families. She'd wanted that once, had hoped it could happen. She'd wanted to be like everyone else. Now, when she had finally realized she was totally gift-free and therefore normal, it was too late. She didn't have another heartbreak in her. She couldn't risk it.

Maybe if only Turner had hurt her. Or if she'd just fallen for the married guy. But those two combined were a massive hurdle to get over and when added to her father abandoning her...

Love meant stepping off an emotional cliff and waiting for someone to catch her so she wouldn't crash into the ground. What if no one was there? She couldn't take a chance. If her heart were shattered again, it would never be whole and she didn't want to be some sad, broken person for the rest of her life. Better to stay as she was. Lonely, yes, but functional.

Odele and her crew left, the catering staff packed up and by four, Renee was alone in the center of the courtyard knowing that the price of being safe was one she had to pay. She didn't have a choice—not when it came to her heart.

JASPER PUNCHED THE air twice, right, left, followed by a quick kick at knee-level. As he moved his foot, his chair slid back about a foot. He continued to work out the fight scene in his head, shifting in his seat as he punched again.

He repeated the sequence, pausing to reassure Koda, who stared at him from the safety of his dog bed. When he had the scene clear in his head, he rolled back to his desk and began typing.

In the book, Vidar had come into contact with the serial killer. They were in an empty warehouse and it was pitch-black, so Vidar wasn't sure of his identity, but he would injure him enough that there was a limp, which was what Jasper needed for later in the book.

Thud, punch, crack. He could see the scene in his head as if it were a movie, which meant he had it all the way it was supposed to be. It was only when he couldn't figure out what to say that he knew he was screwing up with the story.

He typed as fast as he could, mentioning the grit on the floor and the smell of something dead in the corner. He felt the impact of a blow on the side of his head. *Vidar's neck snapped to the left and he stumbled. The—*

"Hey, Jasper, you in here?"

The question, spoken just inside the office, jarred him from story world to real world. It took him a second to readjust his senses and remember where he was in space and time. He turned and saw Cade with two beers in his hand.

"You got a second or is this a bad time?"

Jasper knew if he said he had to work, Cade would understand and go away. He also knew his friend had something going on—otherwise he wouldn't have shown up with no warning in the middle of the afternoon.

"Sure. I'm at a good breaking point," he said, saving his work. He stood and called Koda, then walked toward Cade. "What's up?"

They went back into the house and sprawled on the big sofa in the family room. Koda jumped up next to Jasper and rested his head on his lap. Jasper rubbed his ears.

Cade set his beer on the coffee table, picked it up, set it back down, then stood.

"It's Bethany," he said, then shook his head. "Not her so much as her parents." He looked at Jasper. "What if I can't do it? What if can't deal with it?"

"What is *it*?"

"Royalty. Her father is the damn king of El Bahar. There are bodyguards at the ranch. They follow her everywhere she goes. If she's in the house, they stay outside, but otherwise, they're there. Her mother's called me three times already, begging me to let Bethany come home for the birth. As if I'm the one keeping her away. I'm not. I even told her we'd go back the last three months and she could have her baby there."

He paced the length of the family room, then faced Jasper. "I don't want to be gone that long but I could fly back every couple of weeks. We have a good manager and the business would be fine. It's just not how I saw my life."

Jasper had no idea what to say. He wasn't even sure of the problem. Was Cade simply chafing at the realities of being married to a princess or was he really concerned he couldn't make the marriage work?

"I know what you're thinking," Cade told him.

"I doubt that."

"You're thinking I should suck it up and deal. I knew who Bethany was when I proposed. I'd already been to El Bahar and I'd met her father and I knew he was going to be protective of her always. She's his only daughter. The man calls her the child of his heart. He's actually a really nice guy and I respect how much he loves her."

He returned to the sofa. "Being in El Bahar isn't that bad. I work in the horse stables. You should see their horses. They are incredible. They can trace the bloodlines back a thousand years. It's something. Her mom pointed out that Bethany's friends would be able to visit, so that would help. It's just tough, you know? It's not how I grew up thinking my kid would be born."

He picked up his beer. "It's mostly the bodyguards. They hover. Still, she's safe and I like that and if it makes her parents happy, that makes her happy." He shrugged. "I love her, Jasper. There's no denying that. I'd rather deal with this times a thousand than lose her."

Cade drank from the bottle. "I guess we're going to El Bahar in a few months."

"Sounds like it."

"Thanks. I feel better. How's the book going?"

"It's moving forward."

They talked for another hour, then Cade said he should get home.

"Thanks for helping me see the situation more clearly," his friend said. "I was really confused about what to do."

"You know I didn't say anything, right? You figured it out all on your own."

"Yeah, but you listened."

Cade left.

Jasper rinsed out the bottles and dropped them into the recycling bin, then looked at Koda. "Sometimes that's how friendship works. You're just there to listen."

He supposed he'd been used to that, back when he'd been younger, but in the military, he'd lost his friends in ways no one ever should. Dealing with that and everything else he'd seen, he hadn't been able to do much more than try to keep his head together. Being with other people had been impossible.

That had changed when he'd moved to Happily Inc, he thought, returning to his office. He'd changed. Grown. Healed.

Was Wynn right? Had he inadvertently started on the road to normal? He wasn't willing to accept her declaration that he wasn't broken, but he had a feeling she was more right than wrong on the subject. Five years ago, he couldn't have imagined having a place of his own, having friends, hanging out with them, having someone like Renee in his life. Five years ago, he couldn't have gotten on a plane or gone on book tour. Five years ago, he'd assumed he had one, maybe two books in him and that would be it. Now he couldn't imagine not writing books for a living.

His cell phone rang. He didn't recognize the number but picked it up anyway.

"This is Jasper."

"Hey, Jasper, it's Graham."

It took him a second to realize Graham was the groom in the Scottish wedding.

"How's it going?"

"Great. Look, I need some advice. I wasn't sure where to take Hanna for our honeymoon so I booked like three places. I need to make a decision about which one to go with and which ones to let go. Can I email you the links and then you tell me what you think?"

"Graham, why would you care about my opinion?"

"Because you're you, man. You know things about women."

"What I know about women wouldn't cover a postage stamp, but sure, if you want my opinion, you can have it. But I think you should go with your gut. You know Hanna better than anyone. Which place do you think would make her the most happy? Does she want a lot of activities or does she just want to hang out with you? Do you need to go exploring or would you rather be on a beach? You've spent time with her, you know what the two of you enjoy. I'm just some guy. You're the man she wants to spend the rest of her life with."

"Wow—that's really deep. You're right. I do know what makes her happy. Thanks. I know what to do."

"No problem."

Jasper hung up and shook his head. People were weird.

He looked at his computer and then back at Koda. "I'm not getting any writing done today. Want to take over?"

His dog looked at him as if to say, "You've completely slipped over the edge."

Jasper laughed, then turned to his phone and quickly texted Renee.

What's going on?

Her reply came in seconds.

I'm having a mini freak-out. I've decided you're right—I don't have my mom's gift and it's silly to spend the rest of my life waiting for something that is never going to happen. What a waste of time and energy.

He stared at the words. Good for you.

Thanks. So I'm going to the local animal shelter. I think I want a cat. A kitten, really, because it will be young and it won't judge me. Want to come along?

He looked at Koda. "If I say yes, it doesn't have to mean anything. It's not like I'll be bringing home a cat."

Koda didn't seem convinced.

"You like Renee. This is a big step for her. I'm going to tell her you're okay with it."

Koda sighed.

On my way now.

RENEE WONDERED HOW many people actually had a panic attack in the middle of an animal shelter. She was trying to control her breathing and ignore the adrenaline rush, but neither was working especially well.

"You don't have to do this," Jasper said quietly, standing close enough to offer support but not so close that she felt overwhelmed.

"I know."

"You can just look around and see what you think about the various pets they have here. Getting a cat is a big step."

She nodded, aware of her heart pounding in her chest. "But I think it would be good for me. I'm a responsible person. With us hiring someone to help at work, I'll be home more."

What she didn't say was that her getting a cat would make her a pet person. She liked pet people. She'd always wished she could have a cat. She liked the idea of being responsible for another life-form. She wanted to be able to say, "Hey, I have to get home to my cat." And at the end of the day, there would be someone waiting for her and she liked the sound of that, too.

An older woman in a shelter T-shirt hurried up, a clipboard in her hand. "Renee?" she asked.

"That's me."

"Thanks for coming in. We have a lot of kittens right now. I want to say it's the season, but these days, it's always the season. Spay and neuter! We're trying to get the message out but until everyone is a believer, we'll have more kittens than homes." She held out her hand. "By the way, I'm Brenda. Nice to meet you."

"You, too."

Brenda explained about the kittens they had that were ready for adoption. "Have you had a kitten before?"

"No, but I'm prepared to learn. I have a nice apartment that allows pets, a small den where I can keep the litter box. There's a window that gets plenty of sun and I won't be letting my cat go outside."

Brenda nodded as she spoke. "Sounds like you've thought this through. I'm not pushing, but if you're at work a lot, you might want to consider two kittens so they can keep each other company. Kittens need a lot of play and attention."

Two? Renee felt instantly nauseous. She couldn't possibly handle two little, living creatures. It was like asking for the moon.

Before she could run shrieking into the parking lot, Jasper reached for her hand. "You don't have to decide today. Let's go look at the kittens and see what we think."

Brenda led them toward the "cat" side of the shelter. The area was large and well lit, with several kittens to a kennel. Some were sleeping but a lot were awake and playing. Renee smiled at the big eyes and cute noses and little toes.

"Do you see one you like?" Brenda asked. "We have rooms where you can spend some time getting to know the kitten before picking the one you like."

Renee had no idea how she was supposed to decide which kitten was the one for her. Based on the color? The way it blinked at her? Weren't there personality characteristics that should be more important?

"Can you give me a minute?" she asked, hoping she didn't sound as rattled as she felt.

"Sure. Ah, I'll go help someone else and check back with you."

Jasper waited until Brenda had left to ask, "You

okay? We can leave and come back another time if this is too much pressure."

"They're kittens. They aren't supposed to be pressure. They're supposed to be cute." She looked at him. "What if all my years of worry and fear mean I can never have a pet? I want to have a pet. I want to be a normal person who has a cat."

"You will be. It's going to be fine. Let's go look at the adult cats."

They walked down the hall. There were cats on either side, a glass wall between them and visitors. Larger viewing rooms had three or four adult cats, while some were in small, individual kennels. Some of the cats watched her, but a lot were sleeping. She saw an orange cat alone in a kennel, glaring at her.

He was a big guy, with dark green eyes and serious attitude. There was something about him, Renee thought. Something she couldn't explain.

A volunteer walked past.

"Excuse me," Renee said. "Who is that cat?"

The volunteer—a teenager, with her hair pulled back in a ponytail—glanced at the kennel in question. "Oh, that's Fred. He was surrendered when his owners had to move and couldn't take him with them. They weren't very nice about it and didn't tell us anything about the cats. It was kind of a dump and run. He's been here about three weeks and isn't exactly friendly. We're thinking he needs to go into foster care so he can mellow out." She smiled. "Have you looked at those calico sisters over there? They're very affectionate."

Renee dutifully glanced at the pretty calico cats, then returned her attention to Fred. He made no attempt to hide his disdain for her or his circumstances. She didn't need her mother's gift to know he was desperately un-happy, but whether or not that was because he was in a shelter or missed his family or some other reason, she had no idea.

She stayed by Fred's kennel until Brenda returned.

"What did you decide?"

Renee pointed to Fred. "Tell me about him. Another volunteer said he was surrendered because his family had to move."

Brenda looked confused, but nodded. "Fred is about eight years old. He's not really a lap cat. He's not a bad cat, just not very interested in people and he seems upset all the time. I'm not sure he would be a good match for a first-time cat owner. A kitten is going to bond with you more quickly."

Renee looked at Fred. There was something about him. Something she couldn't explain. She pointed to the sign on the wall offering a thirty-day trial on cats over five years old.

"I want to try with him," she said. "I want to see if we can be a family."

"Okay. I'll put him in a room so you two can meet. I wouldn't try to pet him or anything."

Renee and Jasper spent an hour with Fred in the meet and greet room. He stayed in the corner, hissed when either of them approached and refused to play with the feather on a stick toy. When Brenda returned, she smiled at them.

"So, a kitten?"

"I'll take him," Renee said firmly.

"You sure?" Jasper asked, sounding surprised.

"He needs me."

"He needs something, but this is a lot to take on. Don't you want a pet who likes you?"

"He will. Eventually."

Jasper looked doubtful as he said, "It's whatever you want."

It took two volunteers to stuff Fred into a carrier. Renee paid the fees and then shopped at the on-site store where she bought kitty litter, a litter box, food and dishes. She decided toys could wait until Fred was more at home in her apartment.

Jasper helped her carry everything inside.

"Want me to stay for a while?" he asked.

She smiled. "I'm good. Fred and I need to get to know each other. Thank you for coming with me today."

"You're welcome." He kissed her, then glanced at the growling, hissing cat in the carrier. "I guess I don't have to worry about him if he ever meets Koda. He'll send that dog whimpering into the corner."

She grinned and walked him to the door. Once Jasper was gone, she opened the cat carrier. Fred shot out like a bullet, raced twice around her apartment then dove under the bed. She put the litter box in place and added the litter. After setting up a feeding station in a corner of the kitchen, she put out food for him, then prepared her own dinner.

Around ten, she saw movement out of the corner of her eye. Fred had appeared. He investigated the room, careful to keep his distance. She smiled at him and he hissed back.

Right before bed, she checked and saw he'd eaten most of his food and used the litter box. She wished him good-night and got into bed. Sometime after midnight, she woke up to find him sleeping on the far corner of her bed.

"Hey, Fred."

He hissed at her, then deliberately turned his back on her. Slowly, carefully, she reached across the bed and lightly stroked his fur. He growled and promptly jumped off the bed. Renee smiled as she rolled over to her other side. She finally had a pet and while she could guess what was going on with him, she really had no idea what he was thinking. And it was wonderful.

CHAPTER NINETEEN

RENEE DIDN'T EVER want to not like one of her brides, but Asia was really pushing her buttons. The tall, willowy blonde had been difficult from their very first meeting. Not mean so much as demanding in unexpected ways. She would want to start a meeting at 10:22 in the morning and she meant 10:22 a.m. Not 10:15 a.m. or 10:30 a.m. Nope, she would walk in precisely at 10:22 a.m. and things got going.

From Renee's perspective, she overmonitored her fiancé, bossed around her parents and acted like the princess she wasn't. But, Renee reminded herself as she tried to get everyone in place for the rehearsal the Thursday before their wedding, weddings were stressful and maybe Asia was a lovely person in her regular life.

"Jack is late," Asia said, glaring at her parents, the Thursday evening before the Saturday wedding. "I told you he was too irresponsible to put in the wedding, but you said I had to."

"He's your brother, Asia." Her mother's voice was pleading.

"Come on, pumpkin," her father added.

"Don't call me that." She glared at both of them before turning to Andrew, her fiancé. "Do something."

"I'm going to take Buster for a walk."

Buster was the gorgeous golden retriever who would

be acting as best man. The dog belonged to Asia, but Andrew wanted him to participate in the wedding, so the dog wouldn't feel he was replaced. From what Renee had been able to observe, Andrew and Buster were great friends and the new man of the house would be accepted with a wagging tail.

But instead of going with Andrew when called, Buster whined and retreated to a stack of folding chairs and huddled next to them.

"That's the second time he's done that," Andrew said. "Is he feeling all right?"

"How would I know?" Asia snapped.

"He's your dog. Did he eat his breakfast?"

Asia rubbed her temples. "I'm sure he did."

"You can't remember?"

She glared at him. "It was hours ago. Look, you just have to show up and put on a tux. I'm the one handling all the details for our three-hundred-person wedding. It's been a lot, so forgive me if I can't remember how much the dog ate for breakfast."

Her voice rose with each word until she was shouting. Both sets of parents flinched. Out of the corner of her eye, Renee saw Jack, Asia's younger brother, walk into the room, take one look at his sister, then turn on his heel and quickly escape before anyone saw him.

At times like this, Renee really wanted to take the groom aside so he could explain what it was he saw in his bride-to-be. What was she like when they were alone, because out in public, she was a bitch. But she'd never asked the question before and she wasn't going to start now. To almost quote Shakespeare, that way lay madness.

"Why don't we start without Jack?" Renee said,

keeping her voice as soothing as possible. "All he has to do is seat the mothers, then take his place next to Andrew. I'll go over everything with him later."

"No matter how many times you tell him what to do, he'll screw it up," Asia grumbled.

"Asia!"

"You know I'm right, Mom." Asia looked at Renee. "Fine. Let's get going. Come on, Buster. Time to stand with Andrew."

Buster whined, but didn't budge from his place by the chairs.

"He's been upset for a while now," Andrew said.

Asia rolled her eyes. "How would you know? You see him for like five seconds when you come over."

"That's not true. I hang out with him while I'm waiting for you. I take him for walks every night I'm there. When you went away for your bachelorette party, I kept him for three days. I'm the one who took him to the vet for his last checkup."

"Whatever."

Renee realized that both sets of parents had followed Jack's lead and darted out of the room. Great. Twenty minutes into the rehearsal and nearly everyone had disappeared.

"Did you want to take a break?" Renee asked quietly. "I could—"

"Take a break? We just got here. It's a rehearsal. Let's rehearse and be done with it." Asia marched over to her dog. "Dammit, Buster, act right. Go with Andrew."

The dog whimpered, crouching down. Andrew knelt next to him.

"Something's wrong."

"Do you want me to find a local vet?" Renee asked.

She knew of a nice woman with a practice nearby. Renee had taken Fred in to make sure he was all right, but except for the spitting and hissing, he seemed to be in excellent health.

"I don't think he's sick," Andrew said, stroking Buster's head. "But he's sure upset about something."

Renee thought about how they still had the rehearsal to get through, not to mention an entire wedding, and at the rate they were going, nothing was going to happen. She might not be able to fix Asia's attitude but she could help them learn what was wrong with the dog.

"Give me two minutes," she said and hurried out of the room.

"Great," Asia yelled after her. "Now you're leaving, too? What am I paying you for?"

Renee ignored her and quickly texted her mother. Verity replied immediately, saying she would be right over. Renee returned to the main room where Asia stood by herself while Andrew was still huddled by the dog.

"My mom's going to stop by," she began.

"Oh, really? Your mother?" Asia's tone was sarcastic. "Did you forget your lunch or your schoolbooks?"

"Asia, stop it."

Asia turned on him. "This is my *wedding*," she screamed. "No one is taking it seriously."

"Your wedding? Not our wedding?"

"Don't you dare start your damn semantic games with me, Andrew. This is not the time." She spun to face Renee. "What?"

Renee forced herself to relax. She might not be able to change Asia's energy, but she didn't have to feed it.

"My mom is something of an animal expert. I'm hoping she can tell us what's wrong with Buster."

"An expert? Do tell."

Renee smiled. "She has a show on Animal Planet."

"Oh." Asia looked impressed. "Okay, that would be great. Once we get the damn dog fixed, we can move on to where everyone went to."

The last few words were delivered at a shout.

Andrew shifted so he was sitting on the floor. Buster stretched across his lap and closed his eyes.

"We should never have had a dog in the wedding," Asia muttered. "Not that my stupid brother is any better."

Verity walked in. "I came as quickly as I could."

"Thanks, Mom." Renee made introductions, saving the golden retriever for last. "This handsome guy doesn't want to cooperate. I thought maybe you could help us figure out why."

"Of course." Verity started toward Buster. Her warm smile quickly faded as she stumbled to stop. The color drained from her face and she immediately turned and ran from the room.

"This is ridiculous," Asia snapped. "What is wrong with everyone tonight?"

Renee didn't answer. Instead she said, "I'll be right back," and went after her mother.

While she didn't know the details, she could guess the problem. Buster had told Verity something her mother didn't want to hear or share.

She found Verity in the hallway, leaning against the wall. Her mother was still pale and her breathing was shallow.

"I won't," her mother said, closing her eyes. "I won't ruin your life again. I love you and I want you to be happy."

"Mom, what are you talking about?"

"Those people. The wedding. I can't say it. Don't make me say it."

"Since when do you have a choice?"

Renee kept her tone gentle, but her words were true regardless. Eventually Verity would have to blurt out whatever she'd sensed. It was just a matter of time.

"I don't want to hurt you."

Renee hugged her mother. "Mom, you won't. Nothing you're going to say affects me. Even if it does, I love you."

"What's going on?" Andrew asked, hurrying up to them, Buster at his side. Asia trailed behind them.

"This is insane," she said. "You're ruining my wedding."

Renee looked into her mother's eyes. "It's okay," she said. "Just tell us what Buster told you."

Verity looked at the dog. "He's upset. He loves Andrew and knows how hurt he's going to be. He wants to tell him, but he can't, so he's trying to deal with it as best he can." She closed her eyes. "I'm sorry."

"It's okay, Mom."

Verity looked at Asia. "He knows about your affair. I don't know who the man is, but it's not your fiancé. Buster doesn't want to live with you anymore. He wants to live with Andrew."

"What are you doing?" Asia screamed, rushing toward Verity. "You bitch! How could you do this? I'll sue you. I swear to God, I'll destroy you."

Jack stepped into the hallway and grabbed his sister.

"Jesus, sis. An affair? I thought something was up but you told me I wrong. Is there anyone you won't lie to?" He held on to her as she clawed at Verity. "Stop it. Act like a human for a change. It will be good for you."

Andrew seemed more sad than stunned. He sank to the floor and held out his arms to Buster. The dog threw himself into the embrace.

"I guess I suspected," Andrew said, his voice thick with emotion. "I didn't want to believe it." He looked at Renee. "Not her first time. It's kind of her thing. I guess I was the idiot who thought he could change her."

All Renee could think was to ask why on earth he'd proposed if his girlfriend was a chronic cheater, but that wouldn't help anyone. Instead she offered a sympathetic, "I'm sorry," grabbed her mother and headed out of the hallway.

She found both sets of parents huddled in the parking lot. "You need to go inside," she told them. "There's been a development." When they'd disappeared into the building, she looked at her mother.

"Thank you."

Verity's eyes widened. "I ruined everything."

"You're not the bitch who cheated, Mom. You just told the truth."

"You're not upset?"

"No. I like Andrew. Hopefully he'll grow a pair and dump Asia. I figure the odds of there being a wedding on Saturday are slim to none, so I get a day off." She hugged her mom. "I swear, it's totally fine."

"I'm glad. I was afraid you were upset."

"Not even a little. But I do have a favor."

"Anything."

"I need you to come by my apartment. I adopted a cat and there's something going on with him. I'd like you to tell me what."

Her mother looked at her. "You're not cheating on Jasper, are you?"

Renee laughed. "I'm not. I promise."

"All right then. How about after you get this mess cleared up?"

"Perfect."

"OPEN, OPEN, OPEN," Renee chanted the next morning as she waited outside the animal shelter. She was on a mission to heal Fred's kitty heart and she didn't know if she was too late.

A volunteer unlocked the front door and smiled at her. "You're eager. How can we help?"

"I need to adopt a cat."

"Excellent. We have lots of cats."

"No. A specific cat. Her name is Lucille." Renee held in a groan. "Not that you'll know that's her name. She's gray and white and she came in with Fred nearly four weeks ago. She was surrendered by her owner. She was really sick. Skinny and throwing up."

The woman stared at her. "Was she your cat?"

"No." Renee had no idea how to explain what was going on without sounding insane. "Look, my mom has the ability to know what animals are thinking. It sounds crazy, but it's true. She has a show on Animal Planet." Credentials she was tossing around these days. Thank goodness for the network and its shows!

"I adopted Fred earlier this week. He's obviously upset about something, so I asked my mom to talk to him."

"Because she can talk to cats?" the volunteer sounded doubtful.

"Yes. Look, just hear me out. Fred and Lucille were brought in together. They're a bonded pair and he misses her and he's worried about her. She was really sick. I need to know if she's okay and if she's been adopted or not. If she's still here, I'd like to adopt her for Fred."

Another volunteer, an older woman, walked over. "I know who you're talking about. She's a sweet little thing. We're calling her Misty." The woman smiled sadly. "She had a hernia in her diaphragm. It was keeping her from eating. She had surgery and now she's healing nicely. We were going to release her to be adopted in a day or so. Would you like to see her?"

Renee nodded. She was led back into the cat area, then through doors marked Staff and Volunteers Only where there were a dozen or so cats in various stages of recovery. Misty—aka Lucille, or so Renee hoped—was a pretty gray-and-white cat with an inquisitive expression and a soft meow.

"Hey, pretty girl," the volunteer said. "You have a visitor." She pointed to Misty. "Is this her?"

"I don't know. I think so."

Misty rolled onto her back, exposing her shaved belly and a long scar.

"That was a serious surgery," Renee said. "Is she okay?"

"She should be fine. She's eating well and putting on weight. Do you want to take her home and see if she's the cat you're looking for?"

Renee nodded and went to fill out the paperwork. Less than an hour later, she was back at her apartment, the recovering Lucille with her.

"Fred, I've got her. At least I hope I do."

She opened the carrier. Lucille took a tentative step into the living room, offering a soft meow as she walked. Fred raced in from the bedroom. He skittered to a stop and stared at her. Lucille stared back.

At first there was nothing, then they hurried to each other. There was lots of sniffing and then they started to groom each other.

The movements were frantic, but loving. Fred sniffed at Lucille's healing incision, then returned his attention to grooming her face. She tucked her head into his chest. Renee could hear they were both purring.

"So now you have two cats," Jasper said.

"I do. Fred and Lucille. He had a different name before but he told my mom he likes Fred, so we're keeping that."

They were out to dinner, on a Saturday night. Something Renee couldn't remember happening for years. She was never free on Saturday night. There was always a wedding. But perhaps not shockingly, the Halloween wedding had been canceled.

"Is he any more friendly?"

Renee smiled. "He'll never be a lap cat, but he's stopped hissing at me. This morning, he let me pet him without grumbling about it. Lucille is a total lovebug. She slept curled up next to me all night. She's sweet and I adore them both."

"Are you stopping with two cats, or do you want an even dozen?"

She laughed. "I'm happy with my two."

"I heard about the wedding drama. Was the bride really taken away by the police?"

"Who said that? No. There was just a lot of screaming. She threatened to sue us for I'm not sure what. Andrew said he would make sure that didn't happen, but I'm thinking he has a lot less influence with her now. He ended things with her and he kept the dog."

"Do you think they'll get back together?"

"I hope not for his sake, but he already knew what she was like when he proposed, so I don't know."

Jasper frowned. "Why would he do that? Was she really beautiful?"

"She's lovely but she has the personality of a viper. I don't know what he saw in her. At least Buster has a good home now."

"Buster is the dog?"

"Uh-huh." She picked up her drink. "Enough about the wedding or nonwedding disaster. What's going on with you? How's the book?"

"I'm nearly done. I'm working on the ending. It's not going well. I can't figure out what is supposed to happen."

She leaned toward him and lowered her voice. "Isn't your hero supposed to stop the bad guy?"

"Is that it?" He smiled at her. "It's adding the emotional element that's more challenging. I'm still figuring it all out."

"Want me to help you block out the final action scene?"

"Could you?"

"Sure. I'm going to see my mom in the morning, but I could come by after that."

"That works. Thank you."

She smiled in anticipation. She liked helping him with his books. Not that she did any of the actual writing, but blocking out scenes was a lot of fun. Maybe Vidar and Mandy would have sex and Jasper would want to act that out, as well.

She held in a laugh. A girl could only hope!

"I CAN'T BELIEVE it's already time for you to go back to San Diego," Renee said, folding the T-shirts her mother put on her bed.

"I know. The time has gone by so quickly. I'm just glad everything worked out for us."

"Me, too."

Renee thought about how upset she'd been when her mother had first arrived, how she'd been convinced having Verity around would ruin everything, but that wasn't true at all. If anything, having her mother around had been a positive experience. She was closer with her friends, Jasper understood Koda better, Carol knew what was going on with her giraffes and Renee had two cats. It was kind of a miracle.

"I hope you can come to the show's premiere," Verity said. "It won't be for a couple of months. They want to film the first few episodes before rolling out the big reveal." She smiled. "I'm sure they call it something different, but that's what I call it."

"I'd love to be there, Mom." Maybe she could bring Jasper. Oh! She was going to have find a cat sitter for Fred and Lucille. She smiled. Responsibility in her personal life. It felt good.

"The premiere will be in Los Angeles," Verity said. "It's not that far. You could drive out with Ed."

Renee started to ask why she would do that when she realized her mother was avoiding her gaze as she busied herself rolling socks into neat little bundles. Suddenly several pieces of information fit together. How her mother had been so busy in the past few weeks. The late arrivals, the flushed cheeks, the vague answers to "What's new?"

"You're dating Ed?" Renee's voice was a squeak. She cleared her throat. "When did this happen?"

"You were there when we met. At the animal preserve."

"Yes, he gave you a tour but I didn't think…" Renee

shook her head. The meeting wasn't the point. "Is it serious?"

Her mother looked at her. "I think it might be. He's a very nice man."

Renee held up both hands in a gesture of surrender. "Mom, I'm not judging at all. I'm surprised because you've never mentioned a guy in your life. Not since Dad left and that's been decades." She smiled. "I'm happy if you're happy. I don't know him that well, but he's always seemed nice. Carol's my friend and I adore her." She wasn't sure what else to say. Her mother had a boyfriend. While it was good news, it was going to take some getting used to.

"It was unexpected," Verity admitted with a shy smile. "But I couldn't help myself. He's very—"

Renee winced. "No sex talk, Mom. Please."

"But we're both adults."

"Technically, but in my mind, I'm still the kid, so no."

Her mother laughed. "All right. I'll just say things are going very well and we're going to continue to see each other."

"I'm glad. Any other bombshells?"

"I think that's it."

Renee hugged her. "I love you, Mom."

"I love you, too, sweetie. Always."

CHAPTER TWENTY

JASPER REVIEWED HIS PAGES, knowing he was close to figuring out the ending, but still not there yet. If he was just dealing with Vidar and the killer, he would be fine. It was Mandy who was throwing things off. Or rather how Vidar was supposed to deal with Mandy. He just couldn't get the flow of events lining up correctly with dialogue that made sense.

Part of the problem was the book, and part of the problem was him. Or rather his definition of himself, which seemed to be changing by the minute, or at least the day.

He'd been unable to shake Wynn's statement that he wasn't broken anymore, mostly because he didn't know where that left him. Whole sounded nice, but there were expectations. If there wasn't that much wrong with him then why couldn't he fall in love, get married and have a family, just like everyone else? He kept circling back to the question, and he couldn't seem to come up with an answer.

Just as confusing, he didn't know where Renee fit in. He cared about her. He enjoyed being with her. He respected her. He wanted to spend time with her, and not just in bed. So what did that mean? Was it like-plus? The other *L* word? He didn't have a clue and he wasn't sure how he was supposed to figure it out.

He tried to distract himself with a long walk. Koda trotted ahead of him as they made their way through the forest. They were back before eleven and just in time to get a text from Renee saying she was on her way.

"Any suggestions?" he asked Koda.

His dog rolled onto his back for a belly rub.

"I'll take that as a no."

He waited anxiously for Renee to arrive and walked out the front door when she pulled up.

"You'll never guess," she said as she got out of the car. "Seriously, it's not possible. My mother is dating Ed."

It took him a second to remember who Ed was. "Carol's dad?"

"Uh-huh. They're probably sleeping together, which I don't want to talk about, but can you believe it? I don't mind the relationship, but it's weird. My mom never dated when I was growing up. This is new territory. I tried to be all cool and sophisticated, but I think I failed. I want her with someone who makes her happy, but it's so strange to think about. Parents dating. What was God thinking?"

She sighed. "Enough about that." She raised herself on tiptoe. "How are you?"

"Good."

They walked into the house and went through to his office. Koda trailed after them, stopped at his bed and flopped down. Renee pulled the extra office chair close to his desk.

"Tell me where you are in the book."

"The serial killer has Mandy and her daughter, and Vidar is coming to rescue them. There's going to be a fight where Vidar is injured and maybe Mandy, I haven't decided. Vidar gets the killer in the end."

She frowned. "Why do you need help with that?

You do complex fight scenes all the time. You do fight scenes with sticks and all kinds of scary stuff."

She had a point. He liked the fight scenes. He could block them out like a movie, going step-by-step.

"I guess I want them to talk," he admitted. "But I don't know what they're going to say. I don't want Mandy to be completely passive, but it's not like she has any skills."

"Is she tied up?" Renee asked. "Are she and her daughter bait?"

"Maybe. I hadn't thought of that."

"If they were bait, Mandy would be really scared, but also really mad. She doesn't want to be the reason Vidar gets killed, and she doesn't want anything to happen to her daughter. The kid kind of gets in the way of the two of them dealing with each other, though, so maybe the daughter is unconscious. That would scare Mandy even more. And if Vidar's in danger, trying to save them, she's totally on the edge. She cares about him, so she won't want him to take any chances. But he cares about her, too, and her daughter. He can't not save them and he's the kind of guy who will put his life on the line."

"He would do that for anyone."

"I know, but it's different if he's in love with her. It makes the danger personal. He would take chances with her and her daughter that he wouldn't take for anyone else. He's more vulnerable."

Jasper hadn't thought about it that way, but she was right. Vidar was more vulnerable. He might push himself harder or take a different kind of risk.

He could see the scene in his mind. Having Mandy

trapped worked. She would hate it and yet she wouldn't want to die.

"What would they talk about?" he asked, more to himself than Renee. "She would want to warn him."

"I don't think they'd have a regular conversation, if that's what you're asking. I'm about to die, and we need milk?"

Jasper grinned. "I was thinking more about an emotional declaration."

Renee wrinkled her nose. "Don't do that."

"Why not? What if one of them dies? Wouldn't you want to hear you were loved before a serial killer slit your throat?"

"I guess. I'm just not sure how much it's going to matter in those last few choking seconds. Plus, if they don't die, then for the rest of their lives, they're going to remember the first time they said they loved each other. The memory will be tainted."

He wanted to disagree, but he wondered if it was a guy thing versus a girl thing. Would a guy want to say it so it wasn't unsaid and would a woman...

"Would you say it, if you thought you were going to die?" he asked.

"Shout out 'I love you' right before my throat is cut?" She shrugged. "I don't know. It just seems like a tacky way to do it. Why not last night at dinner or two weeks ago when she was folding your socks? If it takes a near death experience for you to get your feelings, then maybe they're not real to begin with. Maybe they're just the adrenaline talking. Love is flashy in the movies and stuff, but in real life, love is steady. It's not the peak moments, it's the everyday grind and how love makes it better. I'm not saying it has to be wine and roses but wouldn't it be better to say it because you wanted the other person to know and not because one of you might die?"

He studied her. "When you fell in love with Turner, how did you know?"

She looked startled, as if she hadn't been expecting the question. "I don't know," she hedged, glancing away. "We were dating and spending time together. He started to matter more and more. I realized over time. It wasn't any one thing—it was a lot of little things. My feelings got bigger until they were love."

He'd never been in love. There'd been the girl he'd left behind when he'd joined the army, but he'd been a kid and she'd been just as young. When things had ended, they'd both quickly moved on. He'd had a lot of short-term relationships in the military but those were never expected to be more than a way to get through the night. After, well, he'd been too shattered to imagine ever being able to function. Love hadn't been an emotion he'd even considered.

And now?

It was a question that had no answer.

"Vidar's scared," he said quietly, turning his attention to his character. "He's been so careful to hold back, to never let anyone in. Mandy got to him in ways he didn't expect and now she's in danger and it's his fault and he's screwed." He stared at Renee. "He doesn't want to tell her he loves her, he wants to apologize. He wants to make it right and the only way to do that is to save her and her daughter, even if he dies in the process. He's always willing to save the victim, but this is different. Saving those two redeems him."

The pieces fell into place and he could see everything that needed to happen. Renee surprised him by smiling, then standing and kissing him on the mouth.

"I'll see you later," she said, already walking to the door.

"Where are you going?"

"You have that look I've come to recognize. You're going to tell me that you need just fifteen minutes to get a few thoughts down and then you'll disappear for three or four hours." She paused in the doorway. "It's okay, Jasper. It's who you are and it's kind of cute."

"Rain check?" he asked, already sliding toward his computer.

"Promise."

He pulled up his word processing program and stared at the screen. After deleting the dialogue he'd written that morning, he started typing.

JASPER FINISHED THE book about ten Sunday night. He spent two days editing it, then sent it off to both his editor and agent. Wednesday morning he woke up, took Koda on a long hike, then returned to his house to begin the ritual of cleaning out his office before he started thinking about his next project, all the while assuming Sara was going to call and tell him what he'd submitted was total crap and that not only wouldn't they publish it, they were canceling the rest of his contract and black-balling him from any future publications. Because an undisciplined imagination was a very bad thing.

He'd just finished breakfast when his phone rang. He stared at the 212 number, wondering if his editor was calling about the book, told himself she couldn't be, and that he would deal regardless, and took the call.

"Hey, Sara."

"Morning, Jasper."

"There's no way you've read the book. You've only had it since last night."

"I started it. I was only going to read the first few pages, and here I am, still at my desk. I had to cancel three meetings to keep reading! I'm eighty pages in and I can already tell it's your best one yet. I love Mandy. She's fantastic. I'll admit it—I wasn't sure you could pull off writing a woman, but you did. She's smart, she's funny, she's caring. I love her daughter. I love how competent she is at her job. The wedding planning behind the scenes is so interesting." She laughed. "So I'm just going to ask. Who is she?"

Relief eased the tightness in his chest. Maybe his career wasn't over.

"Who is who?"

"The woman who inspired Mandy. Come on. I know how you work. Real life influences your stories more than it does for most authors. Mandy is an amazing character and I'm guessing she's based on someone. So who is she?"

Jasper grinned. "Her name is Renee."

"I knew it!"

"She's a wedding planner and the big wedding at the end is based on a wedding here in town. I have the bride and groom's permission to use the details. I'll send you a copy of the releases they signed."

Sara sighed. "No way. The Scottish wedding is real? I want to see that."

"It's this weekend. Want to fly out?"

"I wish I could. So, about Renee. Tell me about her. Was it love at first sight and then you flew off to Rome?"

"What are you talking about?"

"I want the story to be romantic. That would make me happy."

"Okay," he said slowly. "Don't take this wrong, but when it comes to my personal life, your happiness isn't that important to me."

"You're no fun. But you are wildly in love with her, aren't you? You have to be. The way you write about her, what else could it be?"

In love with... In love? He went from relieved to freaked in less than a second and he had no idea what to say. He wasn't in love with anyone. He couldn't be. He was broken and damaged and all things...

"Jasper?"

"What? I'm here."

"Sorry. I crossed a line there. You don't have to tell me about Renee. I just knew one day you'd meet someone and it would be wonderful. I'm glad that's true and I really hope it works out."

"Uh, thanks."

"You're welcome. Okay, I'm going to stop reading because I have meetings I can't cancel. I'll get you notes within a couple of weeks, but I doubt they'll be much. You did great."

"Thanks. Talk to you soon."

He hung up and stared at Koda.

"She liked the book."

He was going to focus on that because thinking about anything else was just too terrifying. In love with Renee? He couldn't be. He wasn't. They weren't. It was just fun and friendship and sex.

Are you in love with my daughter? Verity's words came back to him, making him wonder what was wrong with everyone. Why did it have to be love? Why couldn't it just be what it was and everyone was happy?

Koda stretched out in his bed.

"Nothing to add?" he asked the dog. "No opinion on the matter?"

Koda closed his eyes, which Jasper took as a no.

RENEE WAS DETERMINED that every single detail for Hanna and Graham's Scottish wedding would be perfect. Not only did she really like the couple, she was still dealing with the debacle that had been the Halloween wedding. She needed happy we'll-be-blissful-together-all-our-lives vibes resonating through the entire property.

She and Pallas had already performed their ritual cleansing with the burning of white sage smudge sticks and sprinkling salt on the floors and carpets. A good vacuum later and all the rooms seemed happier. A silly tradition to be sure, but one they followed faithfully whenever a wedding didn't happen. Better to be safe, and all that.

She reviewed her to-do list for the next few days. Friday was the rehearsal and rehearsal dinner. Saturday was the wedding itself and Sunday morning was the goodbye brunch. The Friday and Sunday events were easy. Just setup and takedown, with very little in between. The catering service was in charge of the meals. Silver was sending her smallest trailer to handle the bar service, and there were no special decorations or entertainment.

The wedding on Saturday was a big deal with three hundred guests, so a full house for Weddings Out of the Box. There was a traditional service and a dinner reception following with a live band and dancing until at least eleven. It was going to be a long day.

But a happy one, Renee thought, excited to be a part of the weekend. She and Pallas had divided the duties. Renee would take the rehearsal and the wedding while Pallas would man the Sunday brunch. They'd hired a couple of college kids to work the Saturday night reception, mostly to help out Renee and be another set of hands if needed. Renee wanted everything to be perfect.

She walked through the main building to where the wedding would be. Chairs were already in place, along with the pole where they would string the floral garland at the front by the podium. Outside, the huge white tent was up, and the tables and chairs were in place there, as well. The plates, glasses and flatware had been delivered, along with dozens of flat bowls to be used as the centerpieces. Clematis blossoms would float in the bowls with greenery scattered across the table.

Knowing she'd done all she could for today, she returned to her office and was surprised to find Ed waiting for her. Carol's father was handsome, with dark red hair and an easy smile. Renee hadn't spent a lot of time with him, but what she knew, she liked and he made her mother happy, so that was all that mattered.

"Hi," she said, not sure if she should ask why he was here or—

"I hope it's okay I stopped by." He rubbed his hands against his jeans, looked at her, then away, then back at her. "Do you have a minute?"

"Of course." She motioned to a chair.

He started toward it then shook his head. "I should stand. It's easier."

"Is my mom okay?"

"What? She's fine. Busy getting ready for her show.

It's going to be exciting for her. She'll be successful—I'm sure of it. She's a great woman. A wonderful woman."

He swallowed. "I'm in love with her. I had no idea I could fall in love again. I didn't expect to and I wasn't looking, but suddenly there she was. It was like being struck by lightning. The second I saw her, I knew. It was fate."

Renee hadn't known they'd been going out for more than a few days, so she wasn't prepared to have her friend's father declare his love for Verity. Fortunately, Ed didn't seem to expect an answer.

"I thought I had everything I wanted here, but now that I've met Verity, that's not true anymore. My brother Ted is more than capable of handling things. The recycling center practically runs itself and Carol manages the staff that looks after the animals. There's no reason I couldn't make a change."

Renee had no idea what they were talking about. "You're thinking of moving?"

"What? Yes, to San Diego. I want to marry your mother."

Renee sank down in the visitor's chair. Her mother getting married? "But you've only known each other a few weeks."

Ed nodded. "It's quick, I know, but I've never felt like this before. I'm certain I can make her happy. I want to spend the rest of her life doing that." His expression turned stricken. "It's not about the money. I'll sign a prenup. I just want her."

Renee couldn't gather her thoughts together. She managed to stand and smile at Ed. "I'm not worried that you're after her money or anything like that. It's all happening so quickly. I want her to have everything she wants. What did she say when you proposed?"

"I haven't. I wanted your permission."

"Mine?"

Everything about this moment was surreal. Why would her permission matter? Her mother was a capable woman who knew her own mind and had been making her own decisions for longer than Renee had been alive. Only Renee recognized that Ed wasn't saying Verity couldn't decide—instead he wanted Renee to be a part of things. The gesture was sweet. A little unexpected, but sweet.

"Of course," she said with a smile. "I hope you two will be very happy together."

There was a squeal from the hallway, then Carol raced in and hugged her.

"I was eavesdropping," Carol said happily. "I couldn't help myself. We're going to be sisters. I'm so excited. You can't move away. You have to promise."

Carol's sister, Violet, had moved to England a couple of years back. Carol still complained about it.

"Your mom is so great," Carol continued. "I never thought my dad would find anyone but I knew the first time I saw them together." She clapped her hands. "We're a family."

She kept talking, then Ed hugged them both and it was a happy moment, but all Renee heard was "We're a family."

While she'd always had her mom, there had never been any other relatives. Not since her dad had left. It had just been the two of them. Renee had always wanted a sister, an aunt or uncle, grandparents, and while she wasn't exactly getting anything like that, she was getting family. A place to belong.

Unexpected tears burned in her eyes. "I'm so happy," she whispered.

"Us, too," Ed told her. "I'm driving to San Diego right now. I want to propose right away. You girls take care."

He walked out. Renee stared after him. "You girls." Like they were both his daughters. She loved the sound of that.

"Do you think she'll say yes?" Carol asked, sounding anxious.

Renee thought about how blissful her mother had been and how alone she'd been for so long. Ed was a good guy and from what he'd said, it had pretty much been love at first sight for both of them.

"How could she not?" she asked with a laugh. "Come on. Let's go out and celebrate."

She was going to have a family. Later she would text Jasper and tell him the great news. Maybe he could figure out a way to put it in his next book.

JASPER HADN'T SLEPT in two days. Not because of nightmares or a book idea that wouldn't let go but because he was trying to make sense of his feelings for Renee.

He wanted to say his confusion had started with his editor's questions, but he knew the problem had begun long before that. Maybe when Wynn had pointed out he wasn't broken anymore or even back when he and Renee had first spent the night together. Or maybe the first time she'd understood that he got lost in a book and hadn't been mad about it.

There was something about her. Something that drew him in and made him want to stick around. Something that made him wonder if maybe his life was better with her in it.

God knew he'd screwed up. He still winced when he thought about how he'd horned in on the wedding, going behind her back, and later, how he'd told her to get over her fears of having her mom's gift. He wasn't perfect, but she seemed okay with that. Being with her made him a better man.

Just as important, he liked taking care of her. He liked making her laugh and helping out when he could. He liked being with her and not just for sex. He liked how she'd picked the cat who seemed right, even though Fred hadn't been easy at first. She was so competent at work. She was resourceful and brave and funny. So what was the problem?

He supposed part of the issue could be the fact that he wasn't the man he'd been three years ago. Everything was different now. He'd made a life, he'd found a new career, he'd met a girl. But did he love her?

Jasper wasn't sure what love was—not really. A feeling, yes, but wasn't it more than that? Wasn't it as much about the other person as himself? When he thought about Renee he was happy. When he was with her, he wanted to spend more time with her.

He walked around his office, Koda watching him, as if a little worried.

"I'm okay," he told the dog. At least he would be when he got his act together.

What if she was sick? What if she was dying? Would he want to deal with her then? He'd seen a lot of horrible things on his tours with the army and figured he could handle pretty much anything she had to deal with. He wasn't afraid of fighting with her, he knew she had a good heart. But was that enough?

Did he want to take care of her, no matter what? Did he want to make her happy, even if he had to sacrifice some things? What if she didn't want to live up in the mountains? What if she wanted to live in town?

He thought for a second. He could do the town thing. He would keep the house in the mountains and he might have to come up here to write for a few days at a time, but if living in Happily Inc made her happy, then he wanted to buy her the house of her dreams. He wanted to hold her and be with her and—

He turned to Koda. "I want kids. With Renee. I want kids and car trips and an IRA and a joint checking account and hell, a minivan. I love her. I'm in love with her."

Koda sighed, as if relieved he'd finally figured it out.

"You like her, too, don't you, boy?"

Koda's tail wagged.

"That's what I thought. I think you'd be good with kids. She has cats now, so that will take some getting used to for all of us. I've never had a cat."

Of course he'd never had a dog, either, and that seemed to be going well.

"I love her," he repeated, not sure what to do next. "I guess I should go see her."

They could go out to dinner to celebrate her mom and Ed's engagement and then he could casually mention his feelings. Or maybe that was better done in private. Either way, he should go to town right now and talk to her.

"I won't be late," he told Koda. "I won't stay the night. I'll be home to take care of you."

He quickly fed the dog, made sure the doggie door

was operational, then drove down the mountain road leading to Happily Inc. Along the way he tried to find the right words, but everything he came up with seemed lame, which was not a good sign. He kind of made his living with words—shouldn't he be better at this?

Still not sure what verbal direction made the most sense, he parked by her apartment building, raced across the lawn and took the stairs to her place only to hesitate in front of her door for at least three minutes. Finally he knocked.

She opened the door and smiled when she saw him.

"Jasper! Did I know you were coming by? Come on in. It's a big night here. Fred accidentally sat on my lap for about thirty seconds. Then he came to his senses, hissed at me and ran off. Lucille, on the other hand, sticks close and loves to snuggle."

She looked incredible. She was barefoot and casually dressed in capris and a T-shirt. She'd scrubbed off her makeup. There were freckles on her nose and cheeks. Her mouth beckoned. He wanted her but more than that, he loved her.

Her smile faded. "Are you okay? You have the strangest expression."

"I'm fine."

She didn't look convinced. She pulled him into the living room and sat next to him on the sofa. Once they were angled toward each other, it occurred to him that it would be so easy to slide to one knee and—

He swore under his breath, thinking he was not ready to propose. Besides, he didn't have a ring and he hadn't even told her he loved her. One step at a time, he reminded himself. He didn't want to screw this up.

"Jasper, you're scaring me."

"I don't mean to." He looked at her. "Have you talked to your mom? Is she happy?"

Renee looked slightly surprised by the question but she nodded slowly. "She is. She said they both realize things are moving fast, so they're going to wait several months before setting a date. She sounded so excited and in love. I'm so glad for her."

"Me, too."

He continued to watch her. Renee shifted on her seat. "What is going on?"

He had to do it, he told himself. He would just put it out there and see what happened.

Lucille jumped onto the sofa and curled up next to him. He petted the cat, hoping the action would be soothing.

It wasn't. He sucked in a breath and said, "Renee, I'm in love with you. You are incredible—not just because you're beautiful, although you are, but because of everything else about you. You're smart and caring. You're funny and I want to be with you. I want to make you happy and I hope you want that, too."

Her eyes widened as she stared at him without speaking.

"You make me a better man," he continued, wondering when she was going to say something. "I think we work as a couple and—"

"No!" She sprang to her feet and hurried to the far side of the room. "Why are you doing this? We agreed we wouldn't do this. We talked about it. We have a relationship that we both like but it's not love. We're not supposed to be in love. I don't want you to love me. Love isn't safe. You have to know that."

Tears filled her eyes and her voice softened to a whisper. "Don't, Jasper. Don't make me do this. Don't ask for more than I have. I can't risk it. I just can't."

His happiness evaporated as dread took its place. She wasn't ready. Or she didn't share his feelings. Either was bad.

"What are you afraid of?" he asked, careful to keep his voice neutral. "Your mom isn't an issue. Not with me. I'm not going to break your heart or hurt you."

"Of course you are. That's what people do. They hurt each other. You'll hurt me and then you'll leave. You're going to leave me and it will be over. I'll be shattered and damaged for the rest of my life."

He stood. "I'm not those other guys."

"It doesn't matter." Tears slipped down her cheeks. "You said you wouldn't do this. What we had was great. Don't ask me to change."

"You have to trust me."

"I can't."

"You won't."

She brushed away the tears. "Does it really matter which it is? I can't risk it. I don't have another broken heart in me."

She walked into her bedroom and closed the door behind her. Jasper stood there, alone. *But I love you.* He wanted to shout the words, only he knew they wouldn't matter. Not to her.

Hell of a thing, he thought as he let himself out and walked back to his truck. Hell of thing.

CHAPTER TWENTY-ONE

JASPER SAT IN his truck for several minutes, not sure what to do, think or feel. Renee's response had stunned him. He'd certainly been aware of the possibility that she might not share his feelings, but he'd never thought that she would be that upset and simply walk away from him. Funny how he'd been so worried about healing from his own past, he'd never considered that she might not be over hers.

He wanted to do something, but what? There weren't words to convince her that everything was going to be fine. How could there be? Life was always a crapshoot. If only he didn't already miss her.

His phone buzzed with a text. He grabbed it, hoping it was Renee. But instead the message was from Drew.

San Francisco is kicking the Rams's collective asses my friend. You're going to owe me $20.

At first the message made no sense. It was as if Drew were using a language Jasper didn't speak. Then the meaning sank in. The weekly football pool he was in with his friends. He and Drew always had a side bet on the Thursday night game and tonight it was San Francisco and the Rams.

He scrolled through his contacts, then pushed the call button.

"Twenty big ones," Drew said by way of greeting. "You're going to owe me, my man. Ha!"

"Can I come over?" Jasper asked.

"Sure. I'm home. What's wrong?"

"I'll tell you when I get there."

Jasper made the short drive to his friend's house. Drew had the front door open before Jasper had turned off his truck's engine.

"What's going on?"

Drew sounded concerned. That was nice, Jasper thought. Having someone who would listen, someone who would care. He hadn't had a group of friends in a long time. No matter what happened with Renee, he would get through it. He had his writing and Koda and guys like Drew. If things got really bad, he knew how to ask for help. He was a lucky man. Except for the fact that the woman he loved had kicked him to the curb.

"I told Renee I was in love with her," he said. "It didn't go well."

Drew motioned for him to come inside. "I'm sorry. I thought things were going good with her."

"I did, too. I tell myself it's because she's not ready, but what do I know?"

He followed Drew into the family room of the large house. His friend got him a beer, then joined him on the sofa. The game was on the big TV up on the wall but the sound was muted.

"Start at the beginning," his friend said.

Jasper told him about the one-sided conversation and how Renee had accused him of breaking the rules. He didn't mention the heavy weight of sadness or how all his hope was gone.

"It wasn't supposed to get serious," he said. "She's right about that. I just thought things had changed. I guess they had, but only for me."

He thought about all the times she'd made it clear that she wasn't interested in getting involved. She never talked about getting married or having kids. Maybe she'd been telling the truth all along.

"I should have listened," he said. "I should have paid attention to what she was saying."

"It's not wrong to love her," Drew told him. "It's a gift."

"Renee's not big on gifts."

"Want to stay here tonight? We have a guest room."

"Thanks, but I need to get back to Koda." He'd promised his dog he wouldn't be gone all night. Plus, he knew there was no way he was sleeping. Not with a Renee-sized hole in his heart.

RENEE COULDN'T REMEMBER the last time she'd felt so awful. Maybe after Turner had broken off his engagement to her, but she wasn't sure. Because as much as that had hurt, she'd known the reason had very little to do with her. Yes, her mother's ability was weird, but was it really a reason to dump and run? Or had Turner been looking for an out all along?

She'd never gotten the answer to that question and now, as she huddled on the floor in her bathroom, wondering if she was going to throw up her breakfast the way she'd thrown up her dinner the previous night, she knew that in many ways, this was different. Worse. Because not only was she desperately missing Jasper, she knew she only had herself to blame.

Last night she'd been able to get by on righteous indignation. The man had broken the rules. He taken their perfectly wonderful relationship and twisted it into something she couldn't recognize. He'd been wrong and horrible and how dare he tell her he love her! What was up with that?

But this morning there was too much sadness for her to be mad. She knew she'd done the right thing and now she had to deal with the painful consequences.

She leaned against the side of the bathtub and waited for her stomach to settle. It wasn't as if she could have responded any other way. She'd been burned too many times. Every relationship she'd ever had had failed.

Not with her mom, of course, but that was different. They were family. And her friendships here in Happily Inc were good. She loved working with Pallas and now they were going to be business partners. But her last serious boyfriend had lied about being married and there was Turner and her father had walked out on her and those kids in high school had treated her like a freak so it made sense that she wasn't going to accept that Jasper loved her.

Love was not in the cards for her. She'd made that decision and she wasn't changing her mind now. Her way was safer. Her way made sense. Her way sucked the big one, but life was pain.

She gave herself fifteen more minutes of waiting on her stomach, then got ready for work. No matter how bad she felt, this was the Scottish wedding weekend and she was going to make sure it was magnificent.

She arrived at Weddings Out of the Box in time to

confirm the caterer was doing a great job setting up for the rehearsal dinner. After a quick pass to make sure everything put out the previous day was still in place, she retreated to her office to make her phone calls confirming everything from flowers to the cake delivery.

Normally her final to-do list only took her two or three hours, but today she spent most of the morning working through it. She was slightly less nauseous than she had been, but much more emotionally devastated than she'd thought she would be. She could focus for the moment, then she remembered what had happened with Jasper and she got shaky again. She expected her heart to be battered but what was up with her inability to concentrate?

At noon she made sure the setup for the rehearsal dinner was complete. The caterer had also put out the tables for the reception. They would be decorated in the morning. She'd double-checked on all that she could. The cake would be arriving in the next thirty minutes and would be fully assembled by six that evening when it would be locked in the special cake-only refrigerated space. She was just wondering if she could keep down lunch or if she should simply skip the meal when Silver and Wynn arrived.

"Hi," Renee said, a little surprised to see them. "Everything okay?"

Silver shrugged. "I'm good. How are you doing?"

There was something in her tone. Something… "You know what happened?"

"Jasper stopped by to see Drew and Drew told me when Jasper left. You doing all right?"

"Sure. I mean it's sad and all, but I'm fine." Did that sound as normal as she hoped? Not that she was lying—not really. She was feeling all right, or she would be eventually.

Silver glanced at Wynn. Neither of them looked convinced.

"Did you guys have a fight?" Wynn asked.

"There was no fight. Jasper wanted to take things to the next level and I don't. It's no big deal."

"Are you sure? I thought you were pretty happy together."

"We were. He's great."

More than great. She liked being around him. He could be annoying and bossy and determined to get his way, but when she explained the problem, he really got what he'd done and did better the next time. He admitted his flaws, he'd hung out with her mom, he was a fabulous kisser.

And caring, she thought, remembering how he was so considerate of Koda.

"I miss him, of course," she said, fighting a flood of emotion. "But that will pass." It had to. Time healed and all that. "I know I'm doing the right thing."

Wynn shook her head.

"What?" Renee demanded. "You think I should accept what he said? Just like that? Say sure and go for it? Trust him with who I am? What happens when he dumps me? What happens when there are forty-seven reasons why it won't work? I'm tired of having my heart broken all the time. I won't go through it again. I won't and you can't make me."

"You're scared." Wynn's voice was soft. "I get that. You've had to deal with some stuff in your life and you're scared and it's much easier to pretend you don't want what he's offering because if you do want it then you can be hurt. You can be broken and there are only so many times you can pick up the pieces."

Renee fought against tears. "I know and it hurts." She waited for her friends to hug her.

"Get over yourself," Wynn told her.

"What?"

"You heard me. Get over yourself. Jasper is a great guy and you're going to lose him because you're a coward. Girlfriend, you think you have regrets now? Wait until he's moved on and you wake up and realize you had a chance with him and now it's over. He's done with you and you're alone because you were too afraid to take a chance."

Silver's eyes widened. "Is that what you think about Jasper?"

"Me?" Wynn rolled her eyes. "No and no. Look, he and I had a great time, but it was never going to be anything. I made sure of that with my rules about Hunter. He never loved me enough to fight and I never cared enough to bend. We let each other go without a backward glance. I don't regret Jasper but I do regret keeping myself so closed off all the time. Now it's been so long, I'm not sure I can find my way back."

Her voice softened. "Renee, don't give up on yourself and don't live with regrets. They hurt the most. You're stuck in the past when you have a wonderful man offering you the future. What more do you want?"

"I want to know for sure. I want to believe that it's going to be okay."

"It's not going to be okay if you just sit on your butt, feeling sorry for yourself. Success is about showing up. You're running in the other direction."

"That's easy for you to say. You don't know what I'm dealing with."

Wynn's expression turned sad. "We're all dealing with crap from our past. You think you're the only one? You're not."

"She's right," Silver said softly. "Look at what I went through with Drew. But I toughed it out and now we're married and it's great."

"Which is fine for you, but you can't make me do this," Renee shouted. "I won't let you. You don't understand. You can never understand."

She turned and made her way to her office. As she climbed the stairs, it occurred to her that she was spending a lot of time running from something rather than to something. But being a coward was easy and she wasn't sure at all that she had what it took to be brave.

JASPER HADN'T KNOWN what to do about Hanna and Graham's wedding. Hanna had texted him twice, telling him what time the rehearsal started and inviting him to the Sunday morning brunch. He had already committed to attending the ceremony and reception, but with everything that had happened with Renee, he wasn't sure if he should go to any of it. Late Friday afternoon, he was still undecided, then figured what the hell. He would handle whatever happened. Renee wasn't the type to make a scene—not only wasn't it in her nature, she would never do anything to upset one of her happy couples.

Besides, he had a gift for Hanna and Graham—he was dedicating the book to them for letting him use their wedding as a backdrop for his story.

He unwrapped the pages he'd had mounted on poster board. The first one—the one that mattered most—had two dedications. *To R, with love*, followed by a paragraph thanking Hanna and Graham. The second one only had the thank-you.

He thought about bringing the first one and letting the truth hang out there. Except there would be questions and those questions would detract from the evening. Besides, he didn't want to embarrass Renee or make her feel bad. He only wanted to make her happy, to love her, to know they could be together always.

He grabbed the one with the single paragraph, told Koda he wouldn't be late and walked out to his truck. As he drove down the mountain, he realized he had no idea what was going to happen at the rehearsal and dinner to follow. He missed Renee more today than he had yesterday—which was not comfortable news. At this rate, within a week, being without her would be unbearable. He was already using the breathing techniques he'd learned in his therapy sessions and he was thinking maybe he and Koda should get in the motor home and go somewhere for a couple of months. Being on the road always made him feel better. He could get away from all the Renee-reminders in town and start his next book.

Only he didn't want to go anywhere. Not without her. He had it so bad, he would rather see her and feel the pain of not having her than be away from her. Which left him in an impossible situation.

He arrived at Weddings Out of the Box a few minutes before the rehearsal was due to start. A quick scan of the parking lot told him that Renee's car wasn't there. He knew she and Pallas had divided the duties—with Renee handling the rehearsal and wedding and Pallas stepping in for Sunday's brunch.

They must have switched things up, he thought grimly. Pallas was here tonight, when it was a smaller group. Tomorrow he would be easier to stay away from—and even if he wasn't, Renee would never disappoint Hanna.

Until that very second, he hadn't realized how much he'd been looking forward to seeing her. He loved her. There was no getting around that, he thought as he walked toward the building. He loved her and wanted to spend the rest of his life with her, and she wasn't interested. He couldn't figure out if she simply didn't share his feelings or if she was too scared to take a chance on him, but knew it didn't matter. In the end, they weren't together anymore and he was going to have to figure out how to deal with that and move on.

CHAPTER TWENTY-TWO

RENEE SPENT A LONG, lonely Friday night home by herself. Fred and Lucille were some company but neither was much for conversation and after they got tired of playing with her, they went to sleep, leaving her alone with her thoughts.

Word of what had happened with Jasper had spread and Pallas had insisted on handling the rehearsal dinner so Renee didn't have to worry about running into Jasper at such an intimate setting. Although Renee appreciated the gesture, she couldn't help wondering if being busy would have been easier to deal with. Not that she would have enjoyed having to avoid Jasper at every turn. In fact there was no way she could have avoided him, and yet she really regretted not being at the rehearsal dinner, which meant what? She'd finally slipped into madness?

She spent a restless night and woke up before five on Saturday morning. After taking care of the cats, she left for work and got to Weddings Out of the Box well before seven. She reviewed Pallas's notes on the rehearsal dinner, then walked the venue and made sure everything was as it should be for the Scottish wedding.

The cake was safely assembled and in the refrigerated case. It would be wheeled out midmorning so it had time to come to room temperature. The bottom and top two layers were about three inches each with the middle layer twice as high. Blue, teal and magenta flowers cascaded down one side. Sprigs of heather would decorate the table. It was as beautiful as the pictures and Renee knew that Hanna and Graham would be thrilled.

She went into the groom's room and made sure all the tuxes were hanging in place. Graham's tux had been custom-made for him. The jacket lining had been printed with photographs of the happy couple from the time they met until their engagement photo. It was a wonderful surprise element that would be special to the couple. She remembered how they'd talked about having it done and how Jasper had encouraged them. He'd been right—the lining was perfect.

In the bride's room, Hanna's dress hung on the specially designed rack, leaving plenty of room for the train. Her shoes were there, along with makeup, and everything she would need for her special day.

The flowers arrived at eight. Renee confirmed the order, then helped the florist put the various bouquets in the bride's room and the boutonnieres in the groom's room. Three college-aged guys hung the floral garland in the main room where the ceremony would be, while two more students filled the shallow bowls with the clematis blossoms.

At noon Renee forced herself to eat a protein bar. She wasn't hungry, but knew she would need her energy for later. She drank a couple of glasses of water and told herself that eventually she would stop feeling as if she were slowly bleeding to death. That once she got through the brunch tomorrow, she would retreat to her apartment and spend the next two days seeing what she could do about moving on with her life, but until then, she had to focus on Hanna and Graham.

A little after three, the activity began in earnest. Hanna and her friends arrived. An hour later, Graham and his family showed up, including his twin sister who looked enough like him to almost make things confusing. Hanna's parents arrived separately, each with a spouse. The caterer was in place, getting the food ready, while Silver had two trailers parked by the reception area and was preparing for the post-ceremony deluge.

Renee made a continuous circuit of the event space. She smiled when she saw Hanna in her beautiful elbow-length sleeve, off the shoulder, mermaid style, lace gown. Her hair was up, her makeup perfect and the photographer was already doing her thing. Renee confirmed the quartet were ready to begin as the first guests arrived.

She kept busy enough that she only thought of Jasper every thirty or forty seconds, which was better than it had been that morning. She'd yet to catch sight of him, but she knew he would be around.

At four thirty, guests began to fill the rows of white chairs. At four fifty, the mothers were about to be seated. Hanna's father was waiting for his daughter and a sense of expectation filled the space.

Renee went back to check on Hanna and found all six of her bridesmaids milling in the hallway.

"What's going on?" she asked.

"Hanna asked for a few minutes to herself," one of the bridesmaids said.

Renee went cold. No, no and no. Brides were never to be left alone—too many bad things could happen.

She stared at the bridesmaids. "Do not, under any

circumstances, come into the room. Don't let anyone else in, either. I'll handle this myself."

They all nodded.

She knocked once and pushed the door open before she heard a request for her to enter.

"Hanna, it's me," she called.

Hanna stood by the long vanity, staring at herself in the mirror. Her eyes were wild, her mouth twisted. She spun toward Renee.

"I can't do this. I won't do it. What was I thinking? I can't marry Graham. I need to get out of here. What did I bring? Do I need to pack?" Tears filled her eyes. "Renee, you have to help me."

Renee put down her tablet and poured a glass of water. She handed it to Hanna, then felt her forehead and the side of her face.

"Have you taken anything?" she asked quickly. "Valium, something else to help you relax?"

Hanna stared at her. "Of course not."

Her eyes weren't dilated and there were no other signs of drugs. As far as she knew, no one had brought alcohol into the room.

Renee pulled out a stool and positioned it so Hanna could sit down. "Drink some water," she said, seating herself across from the other woman. "Take deep breaths."

"I don't want to take deep breaths, I want to get out of here."

Renee waited. Hanna glared at her, but she sipped water and drew in a breath.

"Happy?" she asked, her voice both angry and panicked.

"Not yet." Renee kept her posture relaxed, her tone gentle. "Tell me what's going on."

"I can't marry Graham. Isn't that obvious?" The tears returned. "Everything is a disaster. Or it will be. Have you met my family? I don't even know how many of my stepbrothers and sisters are coming. I can barely remember who my parents are married to. I swear, they should wear name tags at all family events."

She clutched her glass in both hands. "That's going to be me," she said helplessly. "I'm going to have to divorce Graham and I don't want to."

"Do you love him?"

"Of course I love him. Now! But what about in two years or five years? What about when things go bad and I end up like my mother?"

She brushed away tears. "He says it will be all right but he can't know. Not really. It's too big a risk."

"Tell me about the first time you met."

"What? Now? No. Besides, I already did."

Renee waited.

Hanna glared at her. "Fine. We were standing in line for a movie. All our friends left so it was just the two of us. We introduced ourselves and started talking."

"Was it cold outside?"

Hanna smiled. "A little, but I didn't care. It could have been a hurricane and I would have stood there. I thought he was so good-looking and when he laughed at something I said, it was the best."

"Butterflies?"

"More than that. I was scared and excited and hopeful and happy. It was wonderful."

"When did you first know you loved him?"

Hanna sipped her water. "I thought it on maybe our

fourth date, but I knew for sure after a month." She laughed. "I wanted to say something, but I knew that sort of thing scared off some guys, so I kept quiet until he said it first."

"Was it magical?"

"More than that. It was everything I'd ever wanted. He was amazing."

"Is he the best man you've ever known?"

The tears returned. "He is. He's kind and strong and he loves me with all his heart. I trust him completely." She stiffened. "What are you doing?"

"Trying to figure out if you're scared and reacting or if you really think you're making a mistake. There's a difference, Hanna. A big one. Weddings are a huge deal and it's not uncommon to have a mini freak-out. I have no problem with that. But if you really think you shouldn't marry Graham, I need to know that, too. Because what you decide right now is going to affect the rest of your life. If you call off the wedding, then realize you do want to marry him, Graham may be okay with that. But no matter what, the memory of what you did will be there, always. You can't take it back."

She leaned toward Hanna. "I will do whatever you want, and I will totally support your decision. I'm not judging. I'm making sure *you* know what you're doing."

Hanna put down the glass and grabbed Renee's hands. "Oh, no. I couldn't just leave him standing there. I couldn't humiliate him like that. You're right—he would always have to live with that. We'd be sitting together having dinner and he would remember. I don't want that. I love him. I don't want to hurt him."

"Do you want to marry him?"

"Of course." She started to laugh. "What have I been doing?"

"Like I said, having a little freak-out. It happens."

"I was so scared. I thought I was making a mistake. But I'm not. He's wonderful and the only bad thing would be not to marry him today."

Hanna stood and flung her arms around Renee. "Thank you for talking me off the ledge."

"You're welcome. Are you sure?"

"Absolutely." Hanna looked at herself in the mirror and shrieked. "My makeup! My dress."

"You're going to be fine."

Renee turned on the steamer, then brought in the bridesmaids. It took only about fifteen minutes to get Hanna bride-ready. Renee got everyone in place and, as the last note of bagpipe music faded, motioned for the quartet to start the processional music.

As the bridal party began the long walk to where Graham was waiting, Renee allowed herself to exhale fully for the first time in nearly three days. She hadn't just been speaking to Hanna back there, she'd been talking to herself. Because she was wrestling with many of the same fears as her bride.

What if it didn't work out? What if they weren't going to make it? What if, what if, what if. Her choices were simple—she could trust herself and Jasper to weather whatever happened and follow her heart, or she could spend the rest of her life being afraid. Because there weren't any guarantees or promises. There was her and the man who had told her he loved her.

She had spent years blaming circumstances or her mother for what had gone wrong—but what if the real culprit was her? What if she was the reason Turner had left? What if it was all on her?

With a little time and self-reflection she might get close to an answer, but so what if she was half to blame or 90 percent? The past was done—what did she want from her future?

Jasper, she thought with a certainty that filled every cell in her body. She wanted Jasper. All of him—the healed and the broken, the laughter and the pain, his past, her past, their future. She wanted him messing up and then growing from the experience. She wanted him busy with his writing, then hanging out with her. She wanted the man who spent time with her mother and came with her to get a cat and who brought her takeout when she was tired and hugged like he would never let go. She wanted to love him with the fearlessness he'd shown her. She wanted to be worthy and happy and giving and strong and she wanted to spend the rest of her life knowing he was exactly where she belonged.

And she couldn't tell him because Hanna and Graham were getting married and she needed to be doing her job.

Somehow she managed to get through the ceremony without bursting out laughing or yelling out his name. She watched as they exchanged rings and shared their first kiss as husband and wife. She got them back into the bride's room so they could have their first toast, just the two of them, then made sure the guests were moving out into the reception area.

When the photographer corralled the families for pictures, Renee ducked away and went searching for Jasper.

She found him in the back of the main building,

standing by the empty white chairs. When he spotted her, she half expected him to walk away, but he stayed where he was, watching her approach.

He looked good, she thought happily. The dark suit, shirt and tie suited him. It was his sexy author look, and it worked for her in a big way.

"I don't have much time," she told him. "I have to get to the reception, but I didn't want to wait any longer to tell you that I'm sorry for what happened before, between us. I'm sorry for how I acted and what I said. I was caught off guard. That's information, not an excuse."

She paused, hoping he would say something, but he looked at her without speaking.

This was her moment to be brave, she reminded herself. She refused to lose out because of fear. Not anymore.

"A lot of things have gone wrong in my life," she continued. "Verity's gift has been a challenge from time to time, and while that's on her, my reaction to those circumstances is on me. I'm pretty sure I learned the wrong lesson. Instead of thinking other people needed to grow enough to accept her, I told myself to be scared. To hide, to not reach out to anyone. I was so afraid of being like her that I stifled any creative thought I had. I wasn't being my best self and when you came along, I didn't realize what an amazing opportunity I had until I messed up everything."

His dark gaze locked on her face, but he still didn't speak. Which made all this really hard, but she wasn't giving up.

Okay, this was it. She was ready to fling herself off the side of the mountain and hope he caught her.

"I love you," she told him. "With all my heart. I love you and I'm so grateful that you were able to see what we could be together. Even if it's too late and you're done with me, I still want you to know how I feel and I hope that you can—"

He pulled her close, breathed her name and kissed her. No, it was more than a kiss—it was a promise. She hung on to him, kissing him back, feeling at home in his embrace, knowing this was all she'd ever wanted.

"I love you, too," he said, pulling back enough to stare into her eyes. "It's not too late. It will never be too late, because I'm not going anywhere. I've just found you, Renee. I'm not letting go ever."

They smiled at each other, then kissed again. After a few seconds, he drew back.

"You have a reception to put on. Go back to work. I'll be waiting when you're done."

She nodded. There was so much to talk about. Them, their future, where they were going to live and how they were going to have to introduce Koda to Fred and Lucille. But that was for later. He was right—she did have a reception to manage and a happy couple to watch over.

She raised herself on tiptoe and kissed him. "I do love you, Jasper Dembenski."

"I love you back, times a thousand. Now go. I'll be right here when you're done."

Three weeks later...

KODA STARED AT JASPER as if asking if this were really necessary. He was in his own home—shouldn't the other creatures be the ones on a leash? At least that was Jasper's interpretation of what Koda was thinking. If he really wanted to know, he was going to have to ask Verity to stop by.

They were in day two of what he liked to think of as the cat invasion. So far Koda had been accepting and the cats weren't overly freaked out.

Fred and Lucille had a small room of their own, so they could have privacy while eating and using the bathroom. The cats weren't allowed in his office, so Koda could have time away from them and relax. Renee was still concerned about the family blending but Jasper knew it was all going to work out.

They'd spent the past few days moving Renee into his house. They'd discussed getting a place in town, but she wanted to see if she could make the mountain retreat work. So far the late fall weather was cooperating, but the real test would be January.

He and Koda headed into the master bedroom where Renee was putting away her clothes. Knowing she'd moved in made him ridiculously happy, although he was trying to act as normal as possible. Thursday would be their first Thanksgiving together as a couple. Ed and Verity were flying in and they would all spend the day with Carol, her husband, Mathias, baby Devon, and Ed's brother Ted. Dinner would be at Carol and Mathias's house, with Koda getting a special invitation to join them.

For once, there were no Thanksgiving weekend weddings, so he and Renee would have several days together. They wanted to trade in her car for something with all-wheel drive, then spend the rest of the time together, just the two of them. Well, the five of them, if he counted the pets.

He had a special dinner planned for the Saturday

after Thanksgiving. Not just the meal and the bottle of champagne he'd put aside, but also the ring he planned to give her when he asked her to marry him.

"You sure I can't help?" he asked.

She smiled at him as she carefully put folded sweaters on a shelf. "With my heart and my life, but not with my clothes."

He grinned. "Just asking."

"I appreciate that, but I'm good." She pointed to the door. "Go write. I know you're dying to get back to your new serial killer." She grinned. "Pun intended."

He crossed to her and kissed her. "I'm setting my timer for two hours. I want to spend the evening with you." And the night and tomorrow and all the tomorrows, but he didn't say that.

"I will start dinner at six and be waiting breathlessly for your return."

He and Koda started for the office. Fred and Lucille raced past, playing some chase game only they understood. He walked through the kitchen, where Renee's purse sat on the counter and her shoes in the middle of the floor. She had a messy streak he wouldn't have guessed.

Everything was different, he thought happily. Everything had changed and very much for the better. He was one lucky guy and later, he was going to be the guy who got the girl. It was his own happy ending—and it was the best one yet.

* * * * *

Celebrate the season with this warmhearted charmer from #1 New York Times bestselling author Susan Mallery

When Princess Bethany's father, the king, sells one of his best stallions, she insists the animal get the royal treatment. Disguised as Beth Smith, a mere stable hand, she takes him to Happily Inc, California, a quaint wedding destination that's especially sparkly over the holidays.

Rich women have no place on Cade Saunders's ranch. He wants a down-to-earth girl-next-door type—like Beth Smith. After a few cocoa-flavored kisses by the Christmas tree, Bethany begins to fall for her irresistibly handsome host. But will Cade still want her when he discovers she's more familiar with a crown than a cowboy hat?

Enjoy *A Very Merry Princess!*

A VERY MERRY PRINCESS

To Hazel, who kept asking for Bethany's story.
At long last!

CHAPTER ONE

DE-PRINCESSING ONE'S life wasn't the easiest thing in the world. There were the obvious items to leave home—tiaras, scepters, ladies-in-waiting. But there were also actual problems. For Bethany Archer, otherwise known as Princess Bethany of El Bahar, the complications included her passport. As in, which one to take on her trip.

She had her American passport by virtue of being born in California and spending the first nine years of her life there. But once she and her mom had moved to El Bahar and her mother married Crown Prince Malik, who two years ago had become the king, Bethany had become an honest-to-goodness princess, with an El Baharian passport. One that under *Occupation* actually said *Princess*.

She looked at the two official booklets on her bed, then groaned and shoved both in her backpack. She would enter and exit the United States with her American passport, but have the El Baharian one with her just in case. Because where she went, complications followed.

If only her mother had fallen in love with an ordinary man. Someone as wonderful and loving as King Malik, but less…royal. Not that Bethany hated living at the famed El Baharian pink palace. Or working in the royal stables, or being with her three younger brothers, or her mother, Queen Liana. As for her adoptive father, the king, Bethany had loved him from their very first meeting when she'd been nine years old. But the monarchy thing really, really sucked.

Bethany's late biological father had raced cars for a living. Looking back, she had no idea how her parents had ever thought they could make their marriage work. After their divorce, Chuck had been far more interested in maintaining his cars than paying child support and he'd forgotten to spend time with his daughter.

In an effort to provide a home and college fund for her daughter, Liana had taken a job as a math teacher at the American School in El Bahar. The well-paying position was to be a temporary thing—just long enough to provide the two of them with a little financial security. But Liana and her daughter had caught the eye of the then–Crown Prince and within a matter of weeks, the couple had been married and Bethany had become a princess.

Bethany added her e-reader to her backpack, along with a few protein bars. The flight from El Bahar to the small airport near Happily Inc, California, would take nearly seventeen hours, including one fuel stop. While meal service would be offered, she couldn't know if she would be able to leave the back of the plane for more than short bathroom breaks. That all depended on Rida and how he handled the journey.

She'd already packed her two duffels. She wasn't going on vacation, or traveling officially, so she wouldn't need much. Jeans, shirts and boots should do it. Her entire skin care regimen consisted of soap, water and sunscreen. Her idea of nonprincess makeup was mascara and lip gloss. The second duffel held her sleeping bag and a pillow.

"Are you ready?"

She turned toward the door and saw her mother walking into her suite. Queen Liana of El Bahar was a beautiful woman in her forties who dressed stylishly and always looked perfectly pulled together. Bethany supposed it helped that famous designers were forever dropping by with new clothes for her mother to try.

Her mother never forgot where she'd come from. One of her favorite charities helped women get an education so they could raise themselves out of poverty and take care of their families. In addition to serving on the board of the charity, the queen purged her wardrobe every year and sold the pieces at a fund-raising auction.

One day, Bethany promised herself. One day she would be as smart and gracious and pulled together as her mother. As of yet, that day had not arrived.

"I see you're packed," Liana said as she hugged her daughter. "I wish you didn't have to go."

"Me, too, but there's no way Rida can go by himself. He'll need me along."

"You'll miss Thanksgiving dinner and I'll miss you."

Bethany tried not to smile. "I'll miss you, too, Mom, but Thanksgiving dinner? Seriously? Do you want me to remind you about last year?"

Her mother's mouth twitched. "I would prefer you didn't. It wasn't my fault."

"Yeah, those wily calendar people tricked you."

El Bahar, known diplomatically as the Switzerland of the Middle East, was a multicultural haven of many faiths. There were always myriad holidays to celebrate and the royal family enjoyed all of them, including Thanksgiving.

After nearly twenty years away from California, and

with no in-palace turkeys and pilgrims to provide a re-
minder, Thanksgiving occasionally took a back seat to
other events. Last year Liana had forgotten completely
until two o'clock on the very day. The staff had been uncomfortable watching the queen run shrieking through
the palace, begging for a turkey with stuffing and gravy,
along with pumpkin pie, all by seven that evening.

The family had agreed to celebrate Thanksgiving on
Friday instead, with Bethany's three younger brothers not
understanding the big deal. Of course they had been born
and raised in El Bahar. Their knowledge of the United
States was limited to a few visits and what their mother
told them. Plus none of them especially enjoyed turkey.

"I have the holiday on my calendar now," Liana said
with a sigh. "I was planning on a big turkey dinner
with lots of leftovers. What will you do? I might have
forgotten last year, but you'll be in the States. It will
be all Thanksgiving, all the time. I don't want you to
be lonely."

"I'll be fine," Bethany promised. "Rida and I will
try to make sense of American football. You know he's
a fan."

"Very funny." Her mother looked around the room
and smiled. "I still like that you're living in this suite."

The huge apartment was the same one Liana and her
daughter had been given when they'd first come to the
palace, all those years ago. The furniture had changed,
but the view of the Arabian Sea was still the same, as
was the decoration on the wall.

The mural of beautiful Arabian horses galloping
across the desert had been the first thing that stirred
Bethany's interest in their new home. Then she'd seen

the Crown Prince's large stable of beautiful horses and she'd been a total goner.

When her mother had married Malik, Liana and Bethany had moved in with him. On her eighteenth birthday, Malik had presented Bethany with this suite to be her own.

"It brings us back full circle," she told her mother, then shook her head. "Mom, I'm going to be fine."

"I know. You're perfectly capable of taking care of yourself."

Bethany knew there was more. With her mother, there was always more. "But?" she prompted.

"I just want you to be happy."

"I *am* happy."

"Fine. Then I'll be more specific. I want you to fall madly in love and I want grandchildren. There, I said it. Now you can hate me forever."

At twenty-six, Bethany kind of wanted the same thing. All right, not grandchildren, but a man who loved her and a couple of babies would be really, really nice.

"Not that I'm trying to pressure you," her mother added primly. "You have to make your own decisions."

Bethany laughed. "Right, Mom. No pressure." As for making her own decisions, to date, she'd done an excellent job of making bad ones. Especially when it came to men.

"I'll always have my career," she said, trying to smile so her mother wouldn't worry.

"Your career won't keep you warm at night."

"It will if I sleep in the stable."

"How you love to torment your beautiful mother," King Malik said as he swept into the room. "I will not complain because you are the daughter of my heart and can do no wrong, but know that she worries about you."

King Malik—relatively new to the title since his own father stepped down a mere five years ago—was tall and handsome, with dark eyes and dark hair. He wore a stylish business suit, with a shirt and tie. He saved his traditional El Baharian garb for his frequent trips into the desert. The country might be incredibly modern and financially successful, but it never forgot its desert roots and neither did the king.

"You are leaving us again," Malik said, kissing Bethany on the cheek. "We will be heartbroken."

"I'm the one whose heart is shattered," she said, only half kidding. "I can't believe you sold Rida. You rarely sell your stallions and technically he's still a colt. He's only four. And to sell him to some guy I've never heard of in California. What's up with that?"

Malik shook his head. "You dare to question the decision of your king? I have failed you as a father."

Bethany groaned. "Dad, this is serious."

Malik's eyes brightened with amusement. "I agree. I am the great and powerful king of all the land, yet you speak to me so impertinently. A punishment must be arranged."

"She's missing Thanksgiving," Liana said with a sigh. "That is punishment enough."

"Ah, so we will be remembering it this year, will we, my sweet?" he asked, taking Liana's hand in his and kissing her knuckles. "I am beyond delighted."

"You two are weird," Bethany said as she picked up her backpack. "I have to go get Rida so we can head to the plane." She looked at her father. "All kidding aside, I'm still not happy you did this, Dad."

"I know, my child. I think Rida will do well in America, but if you are not satisfied with the facilities, then you have my permission to bring him home. I will not question your decision."

"Thank you." She knew she could trust his word. Not once had Malik ever lied to her.

Her father glanced at her mother, then back at her. "As you requested, the stable manager in Happily Inc has been informed that a Beth Smith will be accompanying Rida on his journey and will be staying with him until he is settled."

"I appreciate that."

She knew her parents didn't understand why she sometimes preferred to be a regular person rather than a princess, but they respected her wishes. As her father had never been anything but a Crown Prince and then King, he didn't know any differently, but she did. Despite her occasional appearance in gossip magazines, she was a relative unknown and preferred to keep it that way. Rather than use her before-being-a-princess-real-last-name, she went with an alias to avoid being found on the internet. Plain Beth Smith could move easily through life, unnoticed by all. Princess Bethany of El Bahar took up a lot more room on the stage.

It was like her job at the royal stables. Had she even hinted she was interested, her father would have given her some lofty position, simply because she was his daughter. But Bethany preferred to earn her place, so she was a (somewhat) lowly groom, assigned to a few horses at a time. Rida being one of them.

"You'll be back by Christmas?" her mother asked anxiously. "You have to be."

"Mom, I promise. Rida will need a few weeks to get

settled. I'll know long before Christmas if I can leave him or not. Either way I'll be home."

Her parents hugged her. As they held her close, she felt more like she was six rather than twenty-six, and leaving home for the first time ever. It was always like this, she thought to herself. The palace had become her haven and traveling outside its protective walls meant risking far too much. But Rida needed her and she would be there for him, no matter how much leaving home cost her this time.

BETHANY MIGHT HAVE a few complaints about her princess lifestyle but how she traveled on official business was not one of them. She arrived at the private airport before Rida, then inspected the large stall that had been set up in her father's Boeing 757. A luxurious seating area and private cabins took up the front of the plane, but the rear had been converted to the aviation equivalent of a horse stable.

Thick mats under a generous layer of wood pellets would provide cushioned comfort for the horse. The water trough would sway with any movement, keeping splashing to a minimum. She had a couple of rubber trash cans with lids and the equipment she needed to take care of any bathroom issues.

Although the 757 offered every comfort imaginable, Bethany would stay in the back with her horse. She had a comfortable chair and her e-reader, which were all she needed. Rida had been taken on a couple of short flights to get him used to the experience, but he'd never been in the air as long as he would be today. Her job was to keep him calm and safe. As she'd been a part of his life since the day he was born, just having her around quieted him.

She walked down the long ramp and waited for the entourage that would signal Rida's arrival. She'd already checked that everything necessary for his move to the States was on board. She was bringing her own hay, straw, pellets, blankets. The list went on. His new home would be unfamiliar, but everything that surrounded him would be known. She'd even arranged for fifty gallons of El Baharian water to accompany them so he could get used to the new California water slowly.

She supposed there were those who would say she was being ridiculous—that he was just a horse and would be fine. But he was more than that to her. Not only was it her job to take care of him, she loved him and she would miss him when he was gone.

A truck and horse trailer pulled up to the plane and behind it, a gleaming black Rolls-Royce with royal flags flying. Bethany might adore her equine charge, but she also understood her place in the world order. She walked over to the car and waited while her father stepped out.

"I thought we'd said our goodbyes at the palace," she told him. "Not that I'm not thrilled to see you once again."

King Malik smiled. "I could not bear for the daughter of my heart to leave without us having a few more minutes together."

"And?"

"I'm checking on you. I sense something is wrong. Tell me what it is."

Every now and then her father surprised her by being emotionally perceptive. Not a traditional characteristic in a male ruling monarch. Imperious, yes. Decisive, sure. But aware of the ebb and flow of his daughter's emotions? Why now?

"Dad, I'm totally fine."

"Of course you are. Would you prefer someone else to go with Rida in your place?"

"What? And leave him in the hands of a stranger? I don't think so."

"I doubt any of the groomsmen at the royal stables would be considered strangers," her father said gently. "Is it that you will miss your brothers?"

Of course she would miss her brothers. They were sixteen, fourteen and twelve, and she adored them. Being a big sister was a lot more fun than she would have thought.

"I will miss all my family," she murmured, glancing at the horse trailer. "Dad, we really have to get going."

Her father stayed where he was. "They'll wait."

Right. Because, hey, it was his plane.

"Daughter of my heart, I know there have been difficulties as you have found your way to adulthood," King Malik began. "Unexpected pitfalls."

Bethany stifled a groan. She *so* didn't want to have this conversation. Not now. Not again.

The unexpected pitfalls, as he'd called them, had been a series of hideous events that had left her feeling exposed and incredibly betrayed.

At fourteen, Bethany had been sent to a Swiss boarding school populated by the daughters of presidents, prime ministers and kings. She'd loved her studies and had made plenty of friends. Missing her family had been a drag, but she'd handled it.

At a coed dance with a neighboring school, she'd met a boy. It had been an innocent flirtation, completely age appropriate, and the night had ended with her first kiss. Only a frenemy had found out and had written all about it in an underground school blog. Someone leaked the blog to the European press and the story had grown into a scandal of sex parties and drugs.

Bethany had been humiliated. Her parents had offered her the chance to return to El Bahar and she'd taken it. Private tutors and her love of learning had meant she'd finished high school only two years later. She'd gone to college in Tennessee. Older and wiser, she'd been exceptionally careful about dating.

She'd fallen for a sweet guy—a slightly nerdy engineering major. They'd taken things slow. When they'd finally become lovers, he'd secretly taken pictures and sold them to a tabloid. While there hadn't been actual frontal nudity, there'd been no confusing what—and who—was in the pictures. The headline—I Deflowered a Princess—had added to the clarity of the moment.

Once again a devastated Bethany had retreated to the safety of the palace walls. Her father had threatened to hunt down the young man in question and throw him in the dungeon while deciding which of several horrible ways to punish him.

Her normally even-tempered mother had agreed. When Bethany surfaced from the shame, she'd been more concerned about what *she* was doing wrong.

Other people managed to grow up in the limelight without so much as a misstep. Was it because she was just some kid from Riverside, California? Was there a whole "to the manor born" thing she was missing? Regardless of the reason, she'd accepted that she had to be even more careful. She'd withdrawn from much of what the world considered ordinary life. She could trust her family and the people in the palace and her horses. Everyone else—not so much.

Which was why she would travel as plain Beth Smith and not tell anyone in Happily Inc who she really was. While she helped Rida get settled, she would experience living as a normal, happy young woman before returning to the safety of the palace once again.

Now she looked at her father. "Dad, it's not the pitfalls. It's that you sold Rida. He's wonderful. Fast and smart, with perfect form. He would have been a wonderful addition to our breeding program."

"Yes, he would have been. However, in my stable every horse is perfection. He would have been one of many and I believe he deserves more. He deserves to be special. In America he will have a chance to fulfill his potential—to find out all he is meant to be."

She narrowed her gaze. "We are still talking about the horse, right?"

Her father smiled. "Of course. What else?"

He had a point—it wasn't as if she was staying in Happily Inc. Once Rida was settled, she would be returning home. In time for Christmas, as she'd promised her mother.

She hugged her father. "I'll be okay, Dad."

He held on tight for a second before letting her go. "You know how to get in touch with me if you need anything. If necessary, the El Baharian Air Force is at your disposal."

"I'm going to pretend you never said that."

Her father chuckled, then got back in his car and was whisked away.

With the royal distraction gone, Bethany turned her

attention to the horse trailer. She helped unfasten the latches, then spoke softly to the huge, solid black horse.

"Hey, big guy. How are you feeling? Ready for an adventure? I think we should check out this little town called Happily Inc. It's supposed to be really nice this time of year. What do you say?"

She walked into the trailer and untied Rida, then guided him down the ramp. She gave him a couple of minutes to adjust to being outside, before leading him onto the plane.

He walked confidently at her side and went directly into his stall.

Normally he was left loose, but given that they would be flying, she tied him securely. If she had to enter the stall while they were in flight, she wanted to know where his hooves would reach. Rida had a reputation for being stubborn and difficult—with everyone else. With her, he was docile and sweet. Still, he was a powerful animal who could be unpredictable if frightened or startled.

She stroked his gleaming black coat and received a nuzzle in return. "I still can't believe my father sold you," she murmured into his neck. "I swear, if you don't love this place, you're coming directly home. I promise."

Rida leaned his head against hers, as if telling her he trusted her completely. She lingered for a second before stepping out of the stall. She picked up the phone by the door separating her section of the plane from the main passenger section.

"We're ready," Bethany told the flight attendant who answered. "Whenever the captain is ready to take off."

"Yes, Princess…ah, Ms. Smith," the woman said. "I'll let him know."

"Thank you."

Bethany thought about asking her to remind all the staff that, as of now, she was just plain Beth Smith, an unremarkable groom accompanying an extraordinary horse on his journey. She decided to let it go. The odds of anyone addressing her by name once they reached Happily Inc seemed small. When she got Rida and his things off the plane, the crew would immediately return to El Bahar.

"Please let me know when you'd like meal service and if I can help in any way."

"I appreciate that."

Bethany hung up, then checked on Rida. The horse looked relaxed and sleepy. She settled in her seat and fastened her seat belt before closing her eyes and wishing the stupid trip was behind her. Not that being home was going to be much of a help.

She was twenty-six years old and basically working as a groom in her father's stable. How pathetic was that? With all the opportunities given her, she should be doing something important with her life. Raising money for a cause, going to medical school and curing a disease. Instead she was hiding—afraid to go into the world because someone might pretend to be her friend only to find out something about her that he or she could sell to a tabloid or post on the internet.

She wanted to be useful and figure out what was important to her. She wanted to get on with her life, fall in love and have a family. Disappearing into the palace was getting her nowhere. It was time to grow up and take charge of her own happiness.

She promised herself she would use her time in Happily Inc to come up with a plan. Nothing was off the table—she could go back to college and finish her degree, go to work for a nonprofit, or join an online dating service. At this point the most important thing was to do *something*.

So first a plan, second implementation. She knew her parents loved her. Now she wanted them to be proud of her. And even more important, she wanted to be proud of herself.

CHAPTER TWO

CADE SAUNDERS WAS trying to act cool, but it was nearly impossible. He felt like a kid on Christmas morning. No, that wasn't right. He felt like a kid on five Christmas mornings and six birthdays rolled into one. He couldn't sleep, couldn't eat and he found himself whistling for no apparent reason.

He was an idiot, he thought cheerfully as he stood on the front porch of his house. But that was just fine with him—his good fortune was idiotworthy.

The farm's security system had alerted him to an authorized code being used to open the gate, so it didn't take long for him to see a familiar car pulling up. He waited while his sister got out of the driver's side, then, before he could control himself, he waved happily and jumped to the ground.

His fraternal twin stared at him wide-eyed.

"What is wrong with you?" she demanded. "You look…" She stared at him intently. "I don't know what but you're freaking me out."

"Nothing's wrong." He tried to look totally casual and manly.

Pallas groaned. "It's that horse, isn't it? You're practically giddy with excitement, which would be charming if you were seven, but it's more than a little disconcerting on a guy pushing thirty."

He raced toward her, grabbed her around the waist and spun her in a circle. "I can't help it," he yelled, before putting her down and laughing. "Do you know what this is going to mean? We have a stallion from the El Baharian royal stable, right here in Happily Inc. It's incredible. It's more than incredible—it's a miracle. Do you know how rare it is for the king to sell one of his horses? It almost never happens, and if it does, it's usually a mare. We got a stallion."

His sister shook her head. "You're this excited about horse sex? I'm sorry to have to say this, but you need to get out more."

He swung her around again. She shrieked to be put down, then started laughing with him.

Cade released her. "I've been working on our breeding program, but Rida changes everything. He's going to put us on the map."

"Technically, Happily Inc has been on the map for a while," Pallas said sweetly. "You should Google us. We're right there."

"Ah, sis, it's a great day."

"Then I'm happy for you. And I brought everything you asked for. Although you should have told your fancy housekeeper to take care of the guest room."

"This is important. I need it to be right." He shrugged. "You have great taste, Pallas, and I trust you."

She groaned. "Don't be sincere. It makes it too hard to mock you." She led the way to the back of her car and opened the trunk. "All right. Let's get this stuff inside."

The "stuff" consisted of several boxes, along with shopping bags. The trunk was full, as were the backseat and the front passenger seat. Together they carried it all inside. Pallas sorted through everything, then took charge of telling him what went where.

When Cade had found out King Malik was willing to sell him Rida, he hadn't thought much past getting the stables ready. Three days ago the royal stables master had informed him that Rida would be accompanied by one of the horsemen familiar with the stallion. A not-unexpected occurrence. Cade had known someone would tag along to make sure the horse was comfortable, the surroundings acceptable—that requirement was in his contract with the king. What he hadn't expected was that the horseman being sent would be a woman. Then he'd panicked.

The farmhouse at the ranch was nearly a hundred years old. It had been remodeled a couple of times, but the kitchen hadn't seen much improvement since the 1950s and the bathrooms weren't a whole lot better. He doubted many guys would care, but a woman might be different. Women tended to pay attention to their surroundings and have higher expectations. Not knowing what else to do, he'd called his sister and begged for help, and Pallas had come through.

They carried a couple of boxes and a half dozen shopping bags up to the guest room. His sister stared at the purple-and-green wallpaper, then sighed.

"You weren't kidding when you reminded me how bad it was," she said. "This is some serious ugly."

"They're due later today. There isn't time to take it down." Would the wallpaper upset Rida's handler? Would she want to take the horse home because of it?

"Not to worry. I've got the problem if not solved then at least managed."

She had him strip the queen-size bed and carry all

the old linens downstairs. Together they put on freshly laundered sheets in a pale sage color, topped with a thick cotton blanket. A light beige comforter went over all that.

She pulled out two decorative blankets and had him fold them across the foot of the bed, then added about a hundred pillows. She had him put together a couple of small lamps for the nightstand while she fussed in the bathroom. Thirty minutes later, they were done.

The en suite bath was big, but old-fashioned. The floor was octagon-shaped white tiles, with more tiles going halfway up the wall. A claw-foot tub stood at one end of the bathroom. The cleaning service kept it scrubbed, but it looked like what it was—a tub from another era.

Pallas replaced the old shower curtain with a new one done in sage and beige. A small white shelving unit held stacks of towels in various shades of green. The top shelf had a blow-dryer along with a basket filled with tubes and bottles and creams. She'd tucked a small room heater into the corner—a thoughtful touch someone used to warmer temperatures might appreciate. Happily Inc was in the California desert, but unlike El Bahar, it could get chilly in late November.

They moved downstairs. Pallas had him drape a couple of throws over the sofa, then switched out the place mats on the kitchen table and added a couple of ceramic turkeys to the counter.

When they were done, Cade grabbed her in a hug and kissed the top of her head.

"I owe you," he told her.

"Good. I plan on collecting." She grinned up at him. "Seriously, this was fun. It was a break from wedding planning, and I have to say shopping with other people's money is the best!"

"I couldn't have done this without you. I really appreciate everything."

She shifted so she was standing in front of him. "I've never seen you like this," she admitted. "You're always so laid-back and internally confident. You must really want this horse."

Because that was all Rida was to Pallas, he thought with a smile. A horse. An interchangeable hoofed animal.

"I really do."

"Then I hope this helps."

She tucked her hair behind her ear. As she moved, light caught her new engagement ring sparkling on her finger. Pallas's fiancé was a good guy and Cade was happy to have him in the family. Just as important, he was relieved to know his sister had another person to watch her back and take care of her.

He grabbed her hand and nodded at the ring. "Have we set a date yet?"

"No, and I don't want to think about it right now. I have holiday weddings to plan."

His sister owned a destination wedding business called Weddings Out of the Box. Couples came from all over to have a theme wedding. Everything from princess weddings to pirate weddings to some kind of under-the-sea extravaganza. She worked hard to be successful and he would guess the last thing she wanted to do was plan her own wedding.

"You could elope," he suggested.

"We've talked about it." She sighed. "I just worry everyone will be disappointed."

"We'll get over it," he told her. "Getting married is about you and Nick. Do what feels right."

"Thanks." She looked around the kitchen. "Okay, favorite brother of mine, I'm going to go back to work. Good luck with the girl and the horse."

"I'll let you know how it goes."

He walked her to the front door. As Pallas stepped out onto the porch, she swung back to face him. Her eyes widened.

"You have to invite her to Thanksgiving!"

"No, I don't."

"Yes, you do. It's a huge holiday. She'll be alone."

"She's from El Bahar. They don't celebrate Thanksgiving. Plus, it's a family thing and she'll feel weird with all our family around."

The entire clan got together for Thanksgiving—Grandpa Frank, his *seven* daughters, their spouses and their kids. He and Pallas had over a dozen cousins. It was loud and frantic.

"Plus, there's Mom," he added.

Pallas grimaced.

Their mother, Libby, was a stern woman who believed that all rules were meant to be followed and that the world would be a much better place if everyone simply did as she told them. Cade had always chafed at the restrictions and had learned early to go his own way, while Pallas had spent years trying to please their mother. It had taken her finally breaking free to find peace with their relationship.

"You still have to ask," his sister told him. "She'll probably say no, but an invitation is required."

"I'll think about it."

Which was his way of saying, *No way. Not even for*

money. His goal was to impress Rida's handler, not offend her or terrify her. Besides, he was pretty sure she wouldn't care about an American Thanksgiving dinner.

"Rida will only have been here a few days," he added. "She might not be comfortable leaving him alone for so long."

Pallas's mouth twitched. "Yes, we wouldn't want to upset his delicate horse sensibilities." She hugged him tight, then ran to her car. "Good luck, Cade."

"Thanks. You're the best."

"So I've been told." She was still laughing when she drove away.

Cade retreated to the house. He checked on the guest room again and hoped the mystery woman would find it acceptable, then he went out to the stable. Easier to wait in his office, he told himself. There was always paperwork to be done and if that didn't distract him, he would pace the length of the huge barn until it was time to go to the private airport and pick up the stallion who was going to change everything.

EIGHTEEN HOURS, including a stop for gas, four meals, two movies and half a book later, Bethany felt the plane touch down on the other side of the world. The captain had announced the local time but she wasn't sure if they'd gained a day, lost a day or if it was still Friday. She was exhausted and she was pretty sure Rida felt the same. While the horse had been exceptionally well behaved in his metal stall, he'd also been restless and hadn't slept much.

She waited until the plane taxied to a stop before standing and stretching. The crew would open the huge rear doors and put the ramp in place before Rida was moved. Bethany wanted to make sure the horse had a few minutes to adjust to the brighter light and sniff the fresh air before trying to walk him out. He might be a sweetie—at least to her—but he was still a massive guy who could crush her like a bug if he chose to.

She grabbed sunglasses from her backpack, then headed down the ramp and out into the afternoon. The sky was clear and bright blue. They were in a tiny, private airport. In the distance were mountains. She was pretty sure they were to the east, and to the west, a couple hundred miles away, was the Pacific Ocean.

Everything felt different—from El Bahar and from the eastern part of the country, where she'd briefly gone to college—yet there was familiarity, too. Perhaps because she'd spent the first nine years of her life not that far away in Riverside.

She shook off the memories and glanced around at the small group waiting for her and Rida. There were three good-sized trucks, a regular pickup pulling a horse trailer and a handful of men. One of them walked toward her, grinning as he approached.

He was tall—but at five foot four she found a large percentage of the world was tall to her—with light brown hair and broad shoulders.

"Beth Smith?" He held out his hand. "I'm Cade Saunders."

They shook hands and he removed his sunglasses. His eyes were hazel and he had a scar by his eyebrow. As she stared at him, she felt a weird kind of quiver low in her stomach, followed by a powerful desire to flip her hair—despite her French braid.

No, no, no, she told herself. There would be no hair flipping on this trip. No swooning or thinking Cade was handsome. This was about work and nothing else. The last thing she needed in her life was some semi-charming, cowboy type.

"Nice to meet you," she said, carefully removing her hand from his hold.

Cade glanced anxiously toward the plane. "How's he doing? Did he make the trip okay? How can I help?"

"You can stay out of the way when I bring him out," she told him. "Otherwise, you brought the trucks, so we can get going on offloading Rida's supplies."

"I can't wait to see him." Cade sounded more like a six-year-old than a grown man as he spoke. "I still can't believe the king let me buy him. I'd heard he was for sale and figured it was a long shot, but I had to try, you know. I mean, he's glorious. I watched his video maybe fifty times. The way he moves, the power. I met the king once, in Texas. At a dinner. He was a great guy. Have you met him?"

She stared at Cade. "Once or twice," she murmured. "You're really excited."

"Wouldn't you be? This is a once-in-a-lifetime opportunity. I run a small ranch in Happily Inc, California. Guys like me don't get a chance at a horse like Rida every day."

She did her best not to smile. She liked how happy Cade was and that he understood what had been offered to him. At least Rida would be appreciated, even if knowing that wouldn't make her miss him any less.

"Then let's get you two introduced," she said and started up the ramp.

On the plane, she spoke quietly to the horse. Rida listened, his ears forward, as if he knew he was finally going to get out of his stall. She took a couple of minutes to stroke his head and neck, getting a horse nuzzle in return, then untied him and led him toward the ramp.

Rida walked along easily, inhaling sharply, testing the air. At the top of the ramp, Bethany paused to let his eyes adjust before starting down.

When they reached the tarmac, she walked him in a large circle to get the kinks out. He seemed more interested than apprehensive—as if curious about his surroundings. Cade watched, his expression a combination of awe and gratitude. Finally she led the horse over to his new owner.

"Rida, this is Cade. He's going to take care of you now."

She felt tightness in her chest as she admitted what she didn't want to be true. Of all the horses her father could have sold, why this one? Yes, he'd explained, but she still wasn't convinced that was the reason—not that her father would tell her otherwise.

"Hey, Rida," Cade said quietly, keeping his distance from the horse, letting him get used to his surroundings. "Welcome home."

One of the flight attendants carried Bethany's two duffel bags and backpack down the ramp.

"Did you have any other luggage, Prin…um, Beth?" the woman asked, her gaze darting between Cade and Bethany. "This was all I saw."

"That's all I need," Bethany said, keeping her tone casual. "Rida's the one who has to bring everything with him when he travels."

The attendant smiled before nodding and returning to the plane. The luggage compartments were open, and barrels, boxes and bins moved down the conveyor belt.

The first of the three trucks was filled quickly, then the second took its place.

"You weren't kidding," Cade said, watching the process. "Did you actually bring water?"

"Yes. He's going to have enough of an adjustment with his new surroundings and jet lag. I don't want him getting an upset stomach."

Cade held up both hands in a gesture of surrender. "Just asking. You're the boss. We do filter our water at the ranch, by the way. It's from an underground aquifer and is very pure."

"But still different from what he's used to."

She led Rida into the trailer and secured him. By then, the third truck was nearly full.

"Does someone need to get the crew into town for the night?" Cade asked. "I can arrange for transportation."

"They're taking off right away. We had two crews on the flight, so one is rested and ready to go."

He glanced at the huge 757. "And you were the only passenger? Must be nice to be the king."

She grinned. "So I've heard."

She climbed into the passenger seat of his pickup and fastened her seat belt. Cade started the truck and they drove out of the airport. About ten minutes later, the plane flew overhead as it took off for El Bahar.

Bethany knew that Happily Inc was in the California desert, less than sixty miles from Palm Springs. The town sat in the foothills of the mountains and had a relatively temperate climate. At least Rida wouldn't have to get used to snow and subfreezing temperatures.

"The ranch is only about twenty minutes from the airport," Cade told her, "which is a private one and doesn't get a lot of use. Most people either fly into Palm Springs or drive to Los Angeles to get a flight out."

Unless she was taking Rida home with her, she

would be returning to El Bahar on a commercial flight, she thought. So out of Los Angeles with a change of planes in Amsterdam or Frankfurt.

"Have you been to the States before?" Cade asked, then shook his head. "Sorry. Of course you have. You're American. Where did you grow up?"

"Not far from here, actually," she said. "My mom and I are from Riverside. We moved to El Bahar when I was nine. I came back to Tennessee for a couple of years of college."

"So you're a California girl."

She laughed. "I haven't thought of myself as that in a long time, but I suppose I am."

There were rolling hills on both sides of the two-lane highway, with lots of trees. She saw a flash of movement, stared, blinked, then shook her head.

"What's wrong?" Cade asked.

"Nothing. I would swear I saw... Is it possible there are gazelles?"

She braced herself for laughter and derision. Instead Cade chuckled.

"Look closely and you might see a few zebras and a giraffe. Or maybe three giraffes. I know we're getting some new ones any day now." He grinned. "We have an animal preserve on the edge of town. It's connected to the landfill and recycling center. Weird, I know."

"Unusual," she admitted. "But nice."

After a few more minutes, they turned onto a long, paved driveway. There was a big gate and a keypad. Cade pushed a remote and the gates swung open.

Bethany looked around, anxious to get a first impression of the ranch. She liked the sense of openness. There were huge pastures and lots of trees for shade.

Up ahead was the farmhouse, which looked fine. She was more interested in the stable.

They drove around to the back of the house and she caught sight of a series of outbuildings, including the long, tall barn. The buildings looked well used, but clean and in good condition. She wasn't a huge fan of brand-new when she delivered a horse. It meant a lot of work had been done before her visit and made her wonder what the owners were trying to hide.

Cade pulled in front of the stable's big open double doors and cut the engine. Bethany slid out of the passenger seat, breathing in the familiar scents of horses and outdoors. Without waiting for Cade, she entered the main barn and saw there were stalls on each side. She went left and saw clean stalls, smooth bedding and full water troughs awaiting the horses' return from the pasture.

The stalls had an in-and-out design, allowing each horse to spend the day outdoors if he or she wanted. One of the stalls had the gate latched open. She walked inside and inspected the mats on the concrete floor, the walls, then studied the mechanism on the water trough.

"It tells us exactly how much water flows in during the day," Cade explained, leaning against the entrance to the stall. "That way we can know if someone isn't drinking. There's a switch that allows us to flush the trough once a day so they stay clean."

He nodded at the trough. "They all drain into a cistern we use to water the grass, so we're not wasting water. We also use our own compost for the pastures."

She listened without commenting, then went to the door that led to the outdoor paddock. She checked the locking mechanism, the edges for sharp splinters, before stepping out into the late afternoon sun.

Trees provided shade, but were planted out of reach of curious mouths. There was a light breeze, plenty of space and three exercise paddocks beyond. Cade's ranch wasn't anything like the royal stables back in El Bahar, but that wasn't necessarily a bad thing. So far, she liked what she'd seen. Cade took the time to take care of details. She was more than willing to judge a man by how he treated his horses. Based on that criterion, Cade was one of the good guys. The fact that he was easy on the eye was just a bonus. One that she planned to ignore.

"Okay," she said as she walked back into the barn. "Show me where he's going to be."

She checked on Rida's stall, confirmed the bedding was the kind she'd requested before making sure the central watering pipe was turned off. For the next two days, Rida would only drink El Baharian water before slowly being transitioned to the local supply.

She inspected the outside area for general hazards along with anything Rida might try to eat, then turned to Cade.

"I'm ready to bring him in."

"Great. Let's go get him."

"Aren't you going to tell me I'm being too picky?" A few people had.

"No way. He's the biggest investment I'm ever going to make. Of course I want him taken care of."

Rida backed out of the trailer like a pro. Bethany walked him around for about half an hour before taking him to his stall. He stepped in as if he'd lived there his whole life and immediately went outside.

The sun was low on the horizon. The warm rays

danced on his black coat bringing out the hints of red and gold hidden in the depths. Rida shook his head, then moved next to her and pressed his head to hers. She stroked his neck.

"I'll take your luggage up to the house," Cade told her. "You can check out your room when you're ready."

She looked at him. "I'll be sleeping here for the first couple of nights, just to make sure he's all right."

Cade raised his brows. "You sure?"

"I am. I brought a sleeping bag and a pillow. I'm prepared." She looked around. "I assume there's a bathroom in the barn?"

"Toilets and sinks but no showers."

"I'll shower at the house. Otherwise, I'll be hanging with this guy."

Cade looked from her to the horse and back. "Like I said before, you're in charge." He glanced at his watch. "I'll leave you two to get settled and bring you some dinner in a couple of hours. How does that sound?"

"Perfect."

CHAPTER THREE

CADE HADN'T KNOWN what to expect from Rida's handler. He'd never bought a horse before that he hadn't simply gone and picked up. Beth was competent, professional and obviously knew her way around horses. He would simply have to pretend she wasn't a stunning, curvy, blue-eyed blonde.

Close to six thirty he carried the back patio table and two chairs to the barn, then brought dinner, along with flatware, plates, glasses and napkins. When everything was set up, he walked to the last stall on the right.

Rida and Beth were in the paddock outside Rida's stall. She sat on the fence, the horse standing close to her. There was a young marmalade barn cat perched on a fence post nearby. Beth was speaking to Rida in a low voice, but Cade couldn't make out her words. They were a contrast in sizes, but looked perfectly comfortable together.

He cleared his throat to get their attention. Beth turned and smiled.

"Hi. We were discussing the weather."

Her smile hit him like a kick in the gut. *Not good,* he told himself. *Not good at all.*

"I have dinner ready, if you're hungry."

"I'm starving." She jumped down and petted Rida. "I'll be close by. If you need me, just give a shout."

"Does he answer?" Cade asked, holding the stall door open for her.

"Sometimes."

They walked to the middle of the barn. Beth shook her head. "This is very nice, thank you." She studied the set table, the bowl with salad and the hot chicken and pasta casserole. "Should I be impressed with your cooking skills?"

"Not based on this. I have a housekeeper who comes in two days a week. She cleans, does laundry and leaves things like this in the freezer. A housekeeper comes with the job."

Beth excused herself to wash her hands. Cade poured iced tea for both of them, then waited until she returned to take his seat.

"How long have you worked here?" she asked as she served herself salad.

"I moved back to Happily Inc a few months ago." He took the salad bowl she passed him. "My grandfather owns the ranch. I've been coming here since I was a kid. He taught me to ride and by the time I was six, I knew I wanted to be a cowboy."

She smiled. "It's nice to have direction. You never strayed from your original goal?"

"Nope. I didn't even have a firefighter phase." He thought about his past. "My family has lived in the area for a few generations. Grandpa Frank also owns the biggest bank in town. It's the family business. My mom wanted me to go to work with her, but that was never going to happen. My grandfather had made it clear I wasn't going to get a job on the ranch just because I was his grandson, so when I was eighteen, I left home to learn the trade."

He glanced at her. "You sure you want to hear this?"

"Yes. I love origination stories. Where did you go?"

"Kentucky."

She sighed. "I've been a couple of times with my, ah, some friends. It's beautiful."

"It is and it's horse country. I started out doing the dirty work and learned everything I could. After a few years, I moved to a ranch in Texas."

What he didn't bother sharing was the reason for his move. Not only was it private, it was humiliating. He'd been played by a woman in Kentucky—he'd learned his lesson and had vowed never to repeat it.

"You met the king in Texas, didn't you?" she asked.

"Yes. I was invited to a dinner he attended. I have no idea why I was allowed to tag along, but it was a great experience. We ended up debating horses and when I heard about Rida I took a chance on him remembering me."

She studied him for a second before looking away. "I'm glad it worked out."

"Me, too. Rida's amazing."

"He is. When will you have him checked out by your vet?"

"Tomorrow, then again in a couple of weeks." He picked up his water glass. "How did you come to work in the royal stables of El Bahar?"

Her blue eyes danced with amusement. "It is unexpected, isn't it? My parents divorced when I was little. My dad was into car racing, a lot more than he was into paying his child support, so money was tight for my mom. She was a teacher and found out about a job at the American School in El Bahar. The pay was generous and an apartment was provided, so five years there would have given her enough for a down payment on a house and a good start on a college fund."

She leaned toward him, her thick blond braid falling over her shoulder. "She met someone and fell madly in love. We were living, um, close to the royal stables, so I started taking riding lessons. I never outgrew my love of horses and when I was old enough, I got a job there."

Her smile faded. "I love what I do, but it's hard when I have to give up one of my babies. I was there when Rida was born and I'm going to miss him."

"Trying to make me feel guilty?" he asked.

She laughed. "Maybe a little. Is it working?"

"Sorry, no. He's going to put our little ranch on the map. I have big plans for him. All good, I promise."

Her gaze locked with his. He felt something pass between them, although he couldn't say what it was. The beginning of trust, maybe? Or something more?

Not more, he told himself firmly. He didn't want more. Rida was plenty. Beth's appeal was not part of his plan.

RIDA SETTLED IN much more quickly than Bethany would have expected. He started eating right away and seemed to like spending his day out in the sun. He'd even made friends with the small marmalade barn cat.

"You won't miss me at all," Bethany complained as she trotted him in a circle in the exercise ring. "You'll forget me as soon as I'm gone."

Rida looked at her, his expression both chiding and intelligent, as if pointing out he would miss her, but he knew that he had to be here now.

"You're trying to act like the mature one in the relationship," she complained. "How do you think that makes me feel?"

Rida tossed his head, snorted and continued his morning exercise. Tomorrow she would ride him, but for today this was enough.

Thirty minutes later, she walked him back to the barn for his grooming session. She'd just secured him when she heard a woman calling, "Hello? Is it all right to come into the barn?"

Bethany waited for someone else to answer. When no one did, she said, "It's okay with me, if that's what you're asking."

A pretty brown-haired woman who looked oddly familiar walked over and smiled. "Hi. You must be Beth. It's nice to meet you. I'm Pallas Saunders, Cade's sister."

"Hello."

Pallas eyed Rida warily. "Wow. He's really handsome. And big." She kept her distance. "Doesn't he scare you?"

"No. He's a good guy."

Pallas didn't seem convinced. "If you say so." She looked back at Bethany. "I wanted to meet you and see how you're settling in. You really came all the way from El Bahar to get your horse settled? Is he afraid to fly?"

Bethany laughed. "He did really well." She rubbed Rida's neck. "He's special. Horses of his caliber rarely get sold. My job is to make sure he's going to be comfortable here and well cared for. Once he's acclimated, I'll head home."

"To El Bahar?"

Bethany nodded.

"Wow. I've barely traveled," Pallas admitted. "It sounds so exotic. I've never been a horse person but

Cade has been crazy about them his whole life. We're twins. Fraternal, obviously. Is he making you feel at home? Oh, do you like the room? He asked me to help with a few touches. I hope you're okay with them."

Bethany had no idea what she was talking about. What room— "Oh, the bedroom in the house." She tried to remember what it looked like. "I'm sorry. I've been sleeping in the barn. I've only run inside to use the shower. But I'm sure it's lovely and very comfortable," she added, feeling awkward. One would think being a princess would help her be less of a dweeb socially, but one would be wrong.

Pallas's hazel eyes widened. "You're sleeping in the barn?"

"To keep Rida comfortable. Just the first couple of nights."

"In the barn. On the hay."

Bethany did her best not to laugh. "Technically people put straw in stalls. Hay is what horses eat. Here, Cade uses bedding pellets. It's a wood product that produces less dust and is easier to maintain. But you're probably not concerned about that."

Pallas started laughing and Bethany joined in.

"Now I know where the old saying 'hay is for horses' comes from," Pallas said, shaking her head. "All right, this hasn't gone like I expected. Let's start over. Hi, I'm Pallas, Cade's sister. I know nothing about horses. It's nice to meet you."

Bethany grinned. "Now you know a little something about horses. You should spring it on Cade the next time you see him. He'll be shocked."

"Good idea."

"I have three younger brothers. I get the dynamic

and the importance of always having the upper hand."
That was even more critical in her family what with the
oldest of her younger brothers being the Crown Prince,
a title he loved to flaunt.

"How long have you lived in El Bahar?" Pallas asked.

"We moved there when I was nine, but I was born
in Riverside, so I'm right at home here."

"Good. Want to come to Thanksgiving with Cade
and me?"

The invitation was unexpected. While the holiday
wasn't a big deal in El Bahar and could occasionally
be forgotten, it was still part of her life. Spending it by
herself would be lonely. Rida wasn't much for celebrat-
ing with turkey and dressing.

"Before you answer," Pallas said, "I should warn
you. We have a huge family. My grandfather had seven
daughters and they all come home for the holiday. Cade
and I have over a dozen cousins. There's no telling who
will show up or what will happen. It's loud and crazy
with plenty of drama, but the food's good and you could
sit by me. I'd protect you from the worst of it."

Her words made Bethany miss her own family. "I'd
love to if you're sure it's all right."

Pallas waved her hand. "Trust me, no one'll even
notice and if they do, you'll be a much-needed distraction. Although my second warning is my mother can
be relentless with the questions."

"I'm pretty good with answers." Even if, in this case,
they would have to be lies.

"Then it's settled. Do you have a cell phone here?
Let me give you my number."

Pallas fished her phone out of her handbag. Bethany pulled hers from her jeans pocket. They exchanged numbers.

"Dinner's usually around three, which is a stupid time to eat. I mean seriously, lunch or dinner, pick one. But noooo. It has to be three." She sighed. "I'll let Cade know to give you a ride. He shows up about one, which is really smart. I'll be stuck with kitchen duty starting at eight."

"I'm looking forward to it. Thank you for inviting me."

"It's going to be fun." Pallas laughed. "Or at the very least, you'll have a heck of a story to tell when you get home. See you on Thursday."

"See you then."

Bethany finished grooming Rida, then led him back to his stall. The barn cat was waiting on the pole by the gate. Rida walked over and raised his head. The cat rubbed his face against the horse's nose.

"All right, little guy, you're going to need a name." She smiled. "How about Harry, after England's ginger-haired prince? Like you, he's friendly and very sweet. It will be our little joke."

She petted Harry, who purred loudly.

After making sure Rida was secure in his stall, she went to the house. As she'd told Pallas, she really hadn't paid attention beyond running upstairs to shower. Now she took her time to explore the main level before heading upstairs.

The house was older, but well cared for. Like much of the barn, it had been lived in. She liked the old-fashioned kitchen. The microwave looked incongruous next to the stove from the 1940s or 1950s. The windows were clean, the pantry well-stocked. She went upstairs and paused on the landing. There were two guest rooms at this end of the hall, which meant the master was in the other direction.

For a second she thought about checking out Cade's room, then told herself there was no way she could be that rude and intrusive. Still, she was curious about him. From what she'd discovered in the past couple of days, he was good with horses and ran his ranch efficiently. The animals were healthy and his employees seemed happy. Which made him a really nice guy. And handsome. And funny.

But not for her, she told herself firmly. She was a disaster in the romance department. Even if she wasn't, she was only going to be here for a few weeks, and she was hardly the fling type. Besides, the fact that there wasn't another woman living at the house didn't mean anything. For all she knew, Cade had a girlfriend in town.

The thought was too depressing to consider for long, so she pushed it out of her head and retreated to her room. She paused to notice all the things she hadn't bothered to see until now. The bedding was new and pretty. There were lots of pillows and blankets. A TV sat on the dresser; there was a desk with a card that gave her the house's Wi-Fi password. In the bathroom there was a basket of lotions and hair care items, along with fluffy towels.

When she saw Pallas at Thanksgiving, she would be sure to thank her for all her thoughtful touches. Cade's sister was nice and Bethany wanted to get to know her better. Making friends was on her life's to-do list. She'd become too isolated at the palace. If she wanted to find where she belonged in the world, she needed to get out in it and experience things. Starting with a big American Thanksgiving.

CADE HAD SEEN videos of Rida in action but watching him in person was a whole different experience. The horse was that perfect combination of strength and agility. The same could be said of his rider. Beth and Rida were a well-matched team—anticipating, respecting each other. Seeing them together was a hell of a show.

One of the barn cats leaped up on the railing post and meowed at him. Cade scratched the side of its face. Beth slowed Rida and urged him closer.

"I named that one Harry," she said with a grin. "I hope that's okay."

"Did you make sure he was a boy first?"

"I didn't. It seemed rude. If he turns out to be a she, we'll say it's short for Harriet."

"I like that you're a problem solver," he teased.

She laughed. "Thanks. I try."

She swung her right leg off the saddle and jumped to the ground, then reached for the gate. Cade opened it first and they walked to the barn, Rida trailing behind.

"I met your sister yesterday," Beth told him as they stopped in front of the tack room.

"Pallas couldn't believe the El Baharian royal stables were sending a woman, so she had to come check you out for herself."

"El Bahar is a great advocate of women's rights both at home and abroad," Beth told him. "Girls have been educated alongside boys for over fifty years. University is free to all. While we still value our traditions and culture, women aren't second-class citizens."

Before Cade could react, Beth groaned. "Sorry. That came out way more like a lecture than I'd intended."

"Still, good information," he teased. "I can probably use it on *Jeopardy.*"

"Is that game show still on?"

"It is. Are you a fan?"

"The theme gets in my head for days at a time," she admitted. "Anyway, back to your sister. She seems really nice."

"She is."

Beth hesitated for a second. "She invited me to Thanksgiving dinner. Is that okay?"

"That depends. I have a big, loud family and my mother is weird. If you can handle it, you're more than welcome."

"Will I be in the way?"

"Do you plan to eat over six pounds of turkey, because unless it's that, you'll be fine."

She unfastened Rida's saddle and lifted it off him as if it weighed nothing. "I am unlikely to eat more than five pounds of turkey. I was thinking more about your personal life. Will your girlfriend mind me tagging along?"

He reached for the saddle, but she shook her head. "I'm good. I do this all the time." She carried it into the tack room, leaving him to ponder the girlfriend question.

For a second he allowed himself to pretend she was fishing for information rather than being polite. Then he reminded himself his luck wasn't that good. He'd had his share of women, but very few of them had been as beautiful as the curvy horsewoman walking Rida's saddle blanket into the tack room.

"No girlfriend," he said when she returned. "No wife, either."

"I kind of assumed that last one," she admitted, setting several brushes on the table by the door. "Seeing as I haven't seen one lurking around the house."

"Why would I marry someone who lurks? What are you saying?"

She grinned. "I take that back. You would never marry a lurker."

As they spoke, she patted Rida's front shoulder, then gently nudged him. The huge stallion politely shifted his weight to his other three legs, then raised his front hoof for her to inspect. Beth used a small brush to clean the outside of his hoof, then pulled a hoof pick out of her back pocket.

It was the kind of grunt work they all did every day, but he had to admit on Beth it look sexy as hell. Which made him an idiot. Or possibly something worse.

CHAPTER FOUR

"WHAT ARE YOU going to wear?" Queen Liana asked, her face showing worry on their Skype call.

"Mo-om, seriously? I'm not five. I know how to dress."

"I know you know *how* to dress, Bethany. What I'm asking instead is do you have anything that isn't a T-shirt and jeans? I saw your luggage. I would be thrilled to think you actually packed two duffels worth of clothes, but we both know the second duffel held a sleeping bag and pillow, don't we?"

Bethany suddenly felt like that five-year-old. "How come you know me so well?"

"I love you and you're my favorite daughter."

"I'm your only daughter."

Her mother laughed. "Then you don't have to question my sincerity, do you?"

"I have one nice shirt," Bethany said with a sigh. "And a pair of dark wash jeans. And flats." Not exactly her mother's elegant style but hopefully it was good enough for a family Thanksgiving. "Did you have a nice dinner?" Because while it was still late morning in Happily Inc, it was after ten at night in El Bahar.

"We did. We had a delicious turkey dinner with all the trimmings. Louis outdid himself. I had him freeze leftovers for when you get home, darling."

"Thanks, Mom."

Louis was the family's French chef and a master at both the fancy and the simple. The man made a grilled cheese sandwich that could reduce Bethany to whimpering.

"Enjoy your dinner tonight," her mother said. "I miss you."

"I miss you, too. Give my love to everyone."

"I will."

Bethany hung up, then headed for the shower. She'd already fed and exercised Rida. One of the other stable hands would check on him later that afternoon and Bethany would see him after dinner. With Harry hanging out near his stall all the time, she didn't have to worry about her horse being lonely.

After showering, she blew out her hair, doing her best to use her round brush to add a little curl. It wasn't as if she'd brought her curling iron, so that was all she could do.

She dressed in her good jeans and pulled on her shirt, then reached into her duffel for her flats. There was a plastic folder at the bottom of her duffel. She pulled it out and opened it, then unfastened the heavy cardboard protecting the document underneath.

Handwritten calligraphy covering thick parchment paper detailed Rida's lineage back over five hundred years. Tiny drawings at each corner depicted Arabian horses in four different scenes.

She would give this to Cade before she left. He would receive a bill of sale, along with other documents, but to her, this was the one that mattered most. It didn't just say Rida was his—it explained who Rida was.

Twenty minutes later, Bethany joined Cade in the living room and they went out together to his truck.

Like her, he wore dark jeans, but with a long-sleeved shirt and leather boots. With luck, everyone else would be dressed similarly and she wouldn't have to worry about fitting in.

"Do you know how to drive?" Cade asked as he held open the passenger door. "You're scheduled to be here another three or four weeks. That's a long time to be stuck on the ranch. I can arrange for you to have the use of one of the ranch trucks if you want to head into town or something."

"I'd appreciate that." She settled in the seat. "Thanks. I do know how to drive."

One corner of his mouth turned up. "On our side of the road?"

She laughed. "Yes. We have that in common."

"Good."

He got in and started the engine, then turned to look at her. "So here's the thing. My family is a little bit strange."

"All families are, or so I've been told. Your sister also pointed out there would be a crowd."

"My grandpa Frank is the best. He's funny, active and very unconventional. Libby, my mom, can be a bit more…" He hesitated. "Traditional. She loves working in the family bank and it shows. Seriously, if you were to line up twenty women her age and have to pick out the banker, you'd pick her every time."

"Sounds interesting."

He started down the driveway. "That's one way to put it. You've met my sister, Pallas. Her fiancé, Nick, will be there, too. We have over a dozen cousins. Don't worry about trying to keep them straight. I can't and I've known them forever."

She smiled. Cade was doing his best to make her feel comfortable and welcome. He was a very nice man. The fact that the nice man was packaged in a rather sexy exterior was also appealing. So far she hadn't found a flaw, which was a tiny bit scary. Not that she wouldn't mind meeting someone she could fall for, assuming she could ever trust herself or the guy in question enough for that to happen. She'd been burned more than enough.

Besides, she told herself firmly, it wasn't going to be an issue. She wouldn't be around long enough for anything to happen. Still, a girl could dream...

"You probably know a lot about El Baharian history," Cade said as he drove along the road.

"It was required learning in school. Why? Should I be prepared to dazzle with assorted factoids at dinner?"

"We have a history here, too." He winked at her. "It's pretty interesting."

"Do tell."

"About fifty or sixty years ago, my grandfather realized the town was dying. There was no industry, no tourists, and if the town died, he would lose the family bank. To keep that from happening, he spun a story of how the town was founded. That in the 1800s, during the gold rush, a group of mail-order brides were stranded here when their stagecoach broke down. By the time the parts came from back east, they'd all fallen in love."

"That's lovely."

"It's a crock. Never happened. But the locals liked it enough to change the name of the town and the word spread. Hollywood got all excited and a few stars came here to get married. From that point on, Happily Inc became a destination wedding town."

"Very slick," she murmured. "And innovative. I'm very excited to meet your grandfather."

"You'll like him." He glanced at her again. "And he'll like you. He's single, so be careful."

She laughed. "Is he into younger women?"

"Since my grandmother died, he's pretty much been playing the field."

"Impressive."

They drove through an older neighborhood with large homes on big lots. At the end of the street was the biggest house. There was a long driveway with a dozen or so cars parked on one side. Cade parked at the end and turned to face her.

"You start to freak out, just come find me. I'll change the subject to hoof rot or bloat and that will gross out my mother, who will make a big fuss and forget what she was saying before."

Bethany thought about all the state functions she'd survived. She doubted anyone in Cade's family was even close to as tedious as some of the diplomats she'd been seated next to.

"Thank you for that lovely offer. I think I'll be fine."

"I'm sure you will be. Just know there's an escape hatch."

"Which is an interesting thing to call hoof rot."

He flashed her a smile that made her throat tighten and her knees go weak. Maybe it was the little scar by his eyebrow or the chiseled lines of his jaw. Regardless, Cade was one intriguing man. If only he was into women who had yet to figure out what to do with their lives, oh, and who happened to be princesses.

She got out of the cab and started for the front door.

As they climbed the porch steps, Cade put his hand on the small of her back.

"Just remember, my hoof rot stories are all yours," he said quietly before opening the door.

"And people say chivalry is dead."

He was still chuckling when they walked into the house.

Bethany had a brief impression of a spacious foyer and beautiful curved staircase. She and Cade followed the sound of conversation into a large living room.

At first glance she would have sworn there were at least fifty people sitting, circulating and talking, but then she realized there were maybe twenty or twenty-five. She recognized Pallas sitting on the arm of a club chair, her hand on the shoulder of the man next to her. A woman in her fifties with her brown hair in a tight bun detached herself from the group and approached them.

"You made it," she greeted Cade, smiling, then turned so he could kiss her cheek.

"Hi, Mom. This is Beth Smith. I told you about her. She's an American working in El Bahar. She works in the El Baharian royal stables and came with the stallion I purchased. Beth, my mother, Libby Saunders."

"Mrs. Saunders, it's so nice to meet you. Thank you for your gracious invitation."

Cade's mother looked her over in a second. From the slight twist to her mouth, she was obviously unimpressed. "Libby, please. So, you work in a stable?"

Cade stiffened. "Mom, it's not like that. Beth has a lot of responsibility. Rida's a big deal and Beth's the one who makes the decision whether he stays or not. And it's a royal stable."

Libby's expression didn't change at all. "But you do work in a stable?"

"Yes, ma'am."

Libby linked arms with her son. "We have those cheese puffs you like so much, but don't fill up on them before dinner. Cook outdid herself this year. I'm sure it's because you're home. You know I was talking to one of my sorority sisters the other day. She mentioned her middle daughter is single. I think you'd like Kimberly. She's in her last year of residency. She's a pediatrician."

They moved out of earshot. Bethany stayed where she was, reveling in the sense of being just like everyone else. Cade's mother had totally dismissed her because of her job. It was both sad and wildly funny. No wonder he'd warned her about Libby.

Pallas rushed over to her. "OMG! I'm so sorry. My mom is…" She pressed her lips together. "It's the holidays. I won't say what she is, but I'm thinking it really, really loud."

"Don't worry about it," Bethany told her. "I promise I'm totally fine." Mostly because if Libby knew the truth, she would be beyond mortified. Bethany's own mother would tell her this was the price she paid for deceiving people, but Bethany was okay with that. She would rather be dissed than fawned over any day.

"Come meet Nick, then let's get champagne. Mom went all out with the good stuff. It's because Cade is back. He's so her favorite."

"You sound okay with that."

"I love him, too, so it's hard to be mad. Plus, I'm happy with my life. That makes it easier to deal with her. Nick, this is Beth Smith. I told you about her."

"Hello." Nick was tall, with dark hair and eyes. He

rose and shook her hand. "So you're the little lady with the horse."

"I am."

"How's he settling in?"

"He loves it here. He's made friends with a barn cat and he's eating well."

"Wait until he meets the zebras," Nick said, looking at Pallas.

His fiancée groaned. "Don't remind me." She turned to Beth. "I run a destination wedding business. I do themed weddings and over the summer I had a bride who was all about a black-and-white wedding. She begged me to rent the zebras, so I did. It was a nightmare."

"It wasn't that bad," Nick said calmly.

Pallas's eyes widened. "They escaped. Cade and Carol had to chase them down. They could have been killed."

He pulled her close and kissed her nose. "Always find that rain cloud, don't you?"

Pallas smiled at him. "Is this where I remind you it did, in fact, rain that morning? And the DJ held up the wedding party."

"With a flare gun."

"Still, it was a gun!" Pallas turned back to Bethany. "My weddings are normally much more calm than that, believe me." She pointed to the far side of the room. "Come on. Let's get champagne. I'll introduce you as we go, but don't worry. You won't be expected to remember any names."

Drinks in hand, they circulated through the room as Pallas introduced Beth to her family. Cade joined them a few minutes later.

"Sorry about my mom," he said, moving next to her.

"Don't be. It's fine. I'm not ashamed of what I do and if people have a problem with that, it's not up to me to change them."

Cade studied her for a second, as if thinking about her words, then he held out a plate with several cheese puffs. "These will make you feel better."

"I can't be won over with pastries," she told him, then popped one in her mouth. An unexpected slight tang blended with the smooth cheese and the melting pastry. It was all she could do not to groan or grab the plate.

"I take it back," she admitted. "I can be won over with pastries."

Cade laughed, then looked at his sister. "Thanks, sis. I'll take things from here."

"Introduce her to Drew." Pallas grinned. "Our cousin is very charming. He runs the bank." She lowered her voice. "Which makes our mom crazy but you didn't hear that from me."

"We'll save Drew for later," Cade muttered, leading Bethany away.

For a second she allowed herself to hope it was because he was nervous about her meeting his successful cousin. That he might be worried about her reaction. And while that was probably wishful thinking, it still felt nice to pretend he saw her as more than the person who had accompanied his prize horse to Happily Inc.

IT WAS NEARLY ten o'clock before Bethany and Cade left for the ranch. She'd been seated with the younger cousins at dinner, at what was obviously the kids' end of the table. Cade had started to complain to his mother, but Bethany had intervened, saying she was fine where she was. She'd had a great time talking movies and computer games with the teens and telling them about El Bahar. Years ago she'd learned that stories about her summers with the nomadic tribes often got her out of awkward conversational pauses. When in doubt, mention camping in a desert oasis.

"I'm sorry about my mom," he said for maybe the fourth time.

She put her hand on his arm—to, ah, be nice, she told herself. Not to feel the muscles. "Stop. Seriously, I'm fine. Totally and completely fine. I had a great time. I ate enough for twenty, had champagne and talked kitten heels with three of your cousins. My evening was perfect."

"She's a snob."

"Some people are, but you're not and I'm not, so please let it go. In a few weeks I'm going to be gone. She's your mother and there's no reason to be mad at her. I swear."

"Thank you. Other than that, was it okay?"

She put her hand on her very full stomach. "I'm very happy right now. Full and sleepy. Everyone was nice to me. I love your grandpa Frank. Don't take this wrong, but if he were to ask me out, I'd probably say yes."

Cade chuckled. "I'm not going to pass that piece of information on to him."

"I'm crushed."

He pulled into the long driveway and used the remote to open the gate, then drove past the house and around to the barn.

Before she could ask why he was parking here, he killed the engine and looked at her.

"You're going to check on Rida, aren't you?"

"Of course."

"Now you're closer. I'll leave the back door open for you."

Like she'd thought before—nice. And considerate and really, really good-looking. Those hazel eyes appealed and when he smiled, her whole body tingled.

Without thinking she leaned toward him. Mostly because she could use a few tingles in her life. It had been a long time between tingles, probably because the guys she'd been dating had been uninspiring at best. Oh, but they'd been safe. She'd made the decision to sacrifice love or even attraction for knowing she would never be hurt and at the end of the day, she'd been left with nothing. Her father had scared them all off. Worse, she hadn't actually missed them when they'd been gone.

But Cade was different. She liked a whole lot about him, plus the tingles.

Maybe it was the cheese puffs, or the champagne or the fact that he'd driven her right up to the barn. Whatever the reason, she put her hand on his biceps and raised her chin expectantly. It was only when he hesitated that she had the awful thought that she could have misread the entire situation and he might not be interested in her at all.

Before she could scream and bolt, he slipped his hand into her hair to cup her head and brushed his mouth against hers.

That was it—a brief, almost chaste moment of contact. It should have been nothing, but it was everything. Nerve endings fired, her heart raced and her breath caught.

He did it again and she nearly moaned. On the third

time, she wrapped her arms around his neck and sur-rendered to whatever it was he wanted from her.

He drew her as close as she could get, what with the truck console between them. Hard plastic bit into her ribs, but she didn't care—not when Cade swept his tongue against her bottom lip. She parted for him and he deepened the kiss until she was all fire and need.

A very tiny, sensible part of her brain whispered that she should be careful, but she ignored the soft words. Just once she wanted to be like everyone else. For there not to be consequences. Only the whispering continued and she began to remember that she wasn't like every-one else. While she liked Cade a lot, she didn't know if she could trust him and until she was sure…

She drew back. He did the same. They stared at each other, their breathing loud in the truck cab. Finally she opened her door and stepped out.

"Thank you for everything," she told him. "I'll see you in the morning."

He nodded without speaking. She walked into the stable and went to check on Rida. Partway to his stall, Harry joined her, meowing as if asking about her eve-ning.

"It was good," she told the cat. "I had a nice time."

Harry's expression was quizzical.

She smiled. "All right. Better than nice. Are you happy?"

The cat began to purr.

CADE HAD TO admit so far this was shaping up to be the best November ever. First Rida, and then last night, he'd kissed Beth. He grinned as he checked his email. Sure it was just a kiss, but it had been a *really* good kiss.

He liked her. She could have been upset about his mother's ridiculous behavior, but she'd handled the situation with grace and charm. She was professional with the horses, friendly with the staff and easy to be around.

He hadn't allowed himself to get involved since the debacle with Lynette, the girl in Kentucky. Oh, there had been women, but only casually. He'd vowed to be more careful, to stick with women who were more like himself—hardworking, regular kind of people. He didn't need a show horse—at least not the human kind.

His phone buzzed, letting him know someone was at the gate. He activated the camera and saw a delivery truck.

"Come on in," Cade said as he pushed the button to open the gate, then went out to meet the driver.

There were a handful of deliveries, including a good-sized box for Beth. He signed for them all, then left the rest in the office and went in search of her.

He found her in the stable, cleaning out a stall. Judging by the nearly full wheelbarrow nearby, she'd been at it for a while.

"What are you doing?" he asked without thinking. "You don't work here."

He immediately wanted to call back the words. Not only did the statement sound hostile, this was the first time he'd seen her since last night and their kiss.

She looked good. A little sweaty and dusty but still pretty. Instead of getting upset, she grinned.

"See, questions like that make me wonder if you're really ready to be a horse owner. News flash, horses poop about fifty pounds of manure a day. That's per horse. Of course cows poop about three times that, so we have it easy by comparison. Still, someone has to clean it up. I'm really surprised you didn't know that."

"Sorry. I meant why are you cleaning out stalls?"

"One of your guys had car trouble and with the holiday weekend, I figured you were already shorthanded. I'm just helping."

"You don't have to."

"I don't mind. I'm trying to figure out a few things in my life. Nothing clears the mind like honest, manual labor."

"You got that right. Thank you for helping." He remembered the box he'd brought. "You got a package."

Her mouth straightened and emotions flashed through her blue eyes. "I wasn't expecting anything." She sounded more wary than excited.

He handed over the box. She took it and read the label, then smiled.

"It's from my mom. Liana Smith." Her smile broadened. "Knowing her, it's clothes. She told me to pack more than I did, but would I listen?"

"She sounds like a good mom."

"She is." She set the package outside the stall, then nodded at the rakes and shovels by the door. "You could help."

"I could and I will."

They made quick work of the last two stalls, then put their tools away. Cade took the manure to the composting shed before joining her in the break room. She'd already pulled out a soda for him and put it on the table.

He opened the can. "Thanks, Beth. I mean it. You aren't expected to pitch in."

"No big deal." Her eyes brightened with humor.

"Your barn foreman was very excited that I volunteered."

"If you hadn't stepped in, it would have been up to him."

She picked up her soda. "Don't you dare tell him it's not okay to put me to work."

"I wouldn't think of it."

"I'm not sure if I believe you, but all right." She took a sip. "You run a very efficient barn. I'm impressed."

"Remember that when you fill out my report card."

"I will."

"I'm not used to auditioning," he admitted. "It's not a comfortable position to be in."

"Rida's worth it," she told him.

"I agree. I'm just saying you have all the power."

She flushed, then ducked her head. "I wouldn't say that," she murmured.

Words that were nice to hear. "I liked it, too."

She raised her chin and stared at him. "I wasn't... If you're..."

He waited until she was done sputtering. "So you liked the kissing?"

More color stained her cheeks. "We are not having this conversation."

"All evidence to the contrary. Come on, Beth. It's an easy question."

She scrunched up her face, then relaxed. "Fine. Yes, I liked it."

"Good. Me, too. But just to be clear, I have no expectations. A few wishes and dreams, but no expectations. You strike me as the kind of woman who takes things slow. I respect that."

She cleared her throat. "Good. I mean, thank you. I do. It's just, you know, better that way."

She was so confident and in charge when she was with Rida, and she'd handled his family like a professional diplomat. It was nice to see her squirming a little now.

He heard the sound of crickets. Beth pulled her cell phone out of her pocket. "That's weird. Who would be texting me? It's night in El Bahar." She glanced at the screen, then beamed at him.

"It's your sister. She's inviting me to lunch with her and her friends next week."

"Sounds like you want to go."

"I do. Pallas is great and I'd love to meet her friends." She quickly typed her response, then smiled at him. "You think she'll serve those cheese puffs?"

He laughed. "You should ask her to."

CHAPTER FIVE

BETHANY HADN'T KNOWN what to expect when she first heard her father was selling Rida to some guy in America. She'd been devastated at the idea of losing her horse, but more than that, confused by the choice of buyers. Now that she'd met Cade, she was more comfortable with her father's decision. Yes, she would miss Rida, but he would be happy in his new home. Cade ran his ranch the way she would—with a lot of attention to detail. He was careful and smart and a pretty great kisser.

She smiled as she drove into town in her borrowed truck. The day was sunny, the temperature warm, the scenery pleasant, and everywhere she looked she saw signs of the upcoming holidays.

At a large intersection by the river, there was a huge faux chimney sitting on the sidewalk, the bottom half of Santa spilling out of the top as if the man was stuck. As she waited at the light, she saw his mechanized boots waving oh so slowly. On the opposite corner was an equally impressive menorah. The shops all had wreaths on their doors and twinkle lights in the windows. Thanksgiving was over, and the rest of the holiday season had begun in earnest. Maybe she should take an afternoon off and do some shopping for her family. It would be fun to have gifts under the tree from Happily Inc.

But before all that, she was off to have lunch with Pallas and her friends. A "girls' lunch" was a rarity for her and one she was looking forward to.

She followed the directions Cade had given her and found herself in front of an interesting building. From one side it looked like a castle and from the other, it seemed to be a villa. The Christmas decorations reflected the architecture—traditional on the castle side and more airy and whimsical on the villa side. The structure itself was large, with a high roofline and a cute balcony. She pulled into the huge parking lot just as a red truck drove up next to hers.

There were two women inside—one a platinum blonde, the other a brunette. They both waved at her.

"You must be Beth," the blonde said as she climbed out of her truck. She was tall, slender and gorgeous—all of which was slightly intimidating to Bethany. "I'm Silver and this is Natalie."

The other woman was shorter, with brown eyes to match her hair. She wore red glasses and had an easy air about her. "Hi, Beth. Pallas told us you were joining us. You're really from El Bahar?"

"I am, although I was born in California."

They collected big tote bags from the truck, then all three of them walked toward the building together.

"Do you know anything about us?" Natalie asked. "Pallas didn't say."

"Not really. She just invited me to lunch. She's been very sweet to me since I arrived."

"That's our Pallas," Natalie said as she held open the front door. "Okay, so I'll make this super easy. This is Pallas's place. Weddings Out of the Box. Theme weddings of all kinds. Silver here owns a business called

AlcoHaul. It's a cool trailer-slash-bar that she hires out for events and various venues."

"I'm a party on the move," Silver said with a laugh.

"Carol and Wynn are coming. Carol works at the local animal preserve. We're in the process of getting more giraffes, which is very cool. Millie was by herself for too long. A girl needs her peeps, right?" She flashed a grin. "Wynn owns a graphics and printing company. And then there's me." Natalie sighed dramatically. "I'm an office manager at a gallery by day and a struggling artist by night."

"Don't let her fool you," Silver said as they walked down a wide hallway. "She's incredibly gifted. One day she's going to be famous and leave all this behind."

"I won't be leaving anything," Natalie corrected, "but I'm happy to deal with the famous part. As long as the fame comes with nice-sized checks. This girl has rent to pay."

They passed through an open doorway that led to a grassy courtyard. Pallas was there, setting up a table and chairs in the shade. She looked up and hurried over to them.

"You made it," she said excitedly as she gave Bethany a hug. "I'm so glad. I see you've already met Natalie and Silver."

"I explained our very complex relationships," Natalie said with a laugh.

"You did well," Bethany said. "This is a lovely setup."

"Thanks. It's fun rotating locations for our lunches. If it had been Carol's turn, we would have been picnicking on the Happily Inc savanna out at the animal preserve," Pallas said. "It's beautiful, but can take a bit of getting used to."

"I like having semiwild animals stroll by," Natalie said.

"They're great until one of them poops." Silver wrinkled her nose. "If you're downwind, it's not pretty."

Bethany grinned. "I'm around horses all day. I'm not easily offended by that sort of thing."

Carol and Wynn arrived and more introductions were made. Bethany saw that everyone brought something to the lunch while Pallas provided a chicken and pasta main course.

Once they were all seated, dishes were passed around.

"So," Natalie said, leaning toward Bethany. "Tell us what it's like in El Bahar. Where do you live? Do you really work in the royal stables? What's that like? Have you ever seen the king in person? Oooh, what about the princes? Are they cute like William and Harry?"

"That's a lot of questions," Bethany said, wondering how many she could answer without actually lying. She liked these women and didn't want to deceive them.

"You don't have to answer any of them," Carol told her. "We're all just so curious about you. You're so exotic, while our lives are ordinary."

Silver rolled her eyes. "Don't listen to her. She's madly in love and that's never ordinary. Oh, and that one, too." She pointed at Pallas.

Pallas waved her left hand, showing off her engagement ring.

Bethany wondered if her envy showed. Finding the right guy and falling in love was what most women wanted at some point in their lives, including her. Being who she was added a whole layer of complications she had yet to navigate successfully.

Natalie turned to Bethany. "So… El Bahar. Tell us."

"It's very beautiful, right on the Arabian Sea. The people are warm and friendly and the country is progressive." She added salad to her plate. "I do work in the royal stables and I have a nice apartment nearby."

Which wasn't technically a lie. The palace was close to the stables.

"My mom and I moved there when I was nine. She was hired to be a math teacher at the American School. She met a man and fell in love, so we stayed."

"What about the princes?" Wynn asked. "I'm not sure I'm up for a real relationship but a fling with a prince sounds nice."

Bethany shook her head. "I'm sorry to have to say that the king's oldest son is only a teenager and the king's brothers are married."

"Foiled again," Wynn said. "Please tell me someone brought dessert."

Everyone laughed.

Conversation moved on to more neutral topics. Pallas talked about an upcoming wedding and how she and Nick were heading to Italy in a couple of months. Carol mentioned her sister, Violet, who had just moved to England with her fiancé. Natalie's car was hanging on by a thread and she was hoping it held out until she could afford a new-to-her replacement.

Bethany listened more than she talked. She liked the easy friendship between the women and the way they included her. Sure, it was only one lunch but she had a feeling she was going to miss a lot more than just Rida when she returned to El Bahar.

CADE SAT ON the fence watching Beth canter Rida around the ring. His attention was neatly torn in two. The male part of him appreciated how she moved with the horse and how good she looked doing it. That side of his brain was remembering their kiss and wanting more.

The rest of him coveted her relationship with the stallion. He wanted that easy communication and trust. He'd always had an affinity for horses—why would it be different with Rida?

She eased him into a walk, then directed him to the fence.

"I know what you're thinking," she said as she brought the horse to a stop. "I guess it's going to have to happen eventually."

Cade's gut tightened. "What are we talking about?" he asked, keeping his voice light. He doubted his luck was good enough for her to be thinking sex.

"You want to ride him. I can tell." Her expression was doubtful. "We've had trouble with him before, just so you know. But he's your horse and I guess this is as good a time as any."

So not sex, he thought as he jumped to the ground and approached the horse. But a close second.

He stroked Rida's neck, then shoulder. Beth slid to the ground and moved to Rida's head.

"I need you to be a good boy," she murmured. "Cade's your new owner. You're going to have to get along with him eventually."

Cade adjusted the stirrups to the right length, put his left foot in one and swung onto the saddle. He found his seat immediately and kept a light but firm hold on the reins.

Even standing still, Rida was powerful. He could feel the controlled energy, the potential. Running flat out with him would be—

One second he was comfortably seated, the next he was flying through the air. The ground rushed up to meet him and he landed flat on his back with a thud. Rida casually trotted to the far side of the ring while Beth hurried to Cade's side.

"Don't move," she said as she dropped to her knees. Concern darkened her blue eyes. "You've had the wind knocked out of you. It's going to seem like you can't breathe, but you're fine. Just take it slow. Let your body relax for a second, then inhale. Shallow at first but deeper with each breath."

While the words were designed to be comforting, this was not his first rodeo. He waited until he'd caught his breath to say, "I've been thrown a time or two."

He shifted on the ground to make sure all the moving parts were still working, then sat up and looked at the horse.

"I didn't see that coming."

She sighed. "I had a feeling."

"You didn't want to warn me?"

"I told you we'd had trouble with him before. What do you think that meant? That he'd been pouty?"

Cade felt himself start to smile. "You have some attitude on you."

"Well, yeah. I'm not the one who was just thrown by a horse. How are you feeling?"

"Nothing's broken and you only have one head, so I'd say I'm fine."

She scrambled to her feet and held out her hand, as if to help him to his feet. Seriously? Of course it was an excuse to touch her, even for a second, so he took it and stood.

She released him, but stayed close. "Still okay?"

"Never better." He glanced at Rida. "Although he and I are going to be having a conversation, man-to-man."

"Good luck with that."

She whistled. Rida's ears perked up, then he turned and walked directly toward her.

"Show-off," Cade grumbled.

"I know. I can't help it." She reached for the reins. "He's really sorry."

"No, he's not. Does he let anyone ride him but you?"

"My father's been on him and he wasn't thrown."

"Good. I just need to know I stand a chance."

Rida would have to get used to multiple riders. It might take a while, but Cade knew the horse could be trained. He was intelligent and had a good temperament, and both would work in Cade's favor.

He returned his attention to Beth. "You know what you're doing. Let me know if you're ever looking for work."

Her eyebrows rose as a dozen different expressions chased across her face. "You're offering me a job?"

"Would you take it if I did?"

"I would be tempted, but it's…complicated."

What did that mean? Her family in El Bahar, or was there a man waiting for her? He considered the latter, then decided that Beth wasn't the type to kiss him while involved with someone.

"How about dinner?" he asked impulsively. "Tonight."

She smiled. "That I can say yes to."

BETHANY WOULD MAKE a point to thank her mother when next they spoke. The box of clothing she'd sent contained a couple of dresses from Bethany's wardrobe, including a pretty pale pink sleeveless A-line dress that had always been one of her favorites.

Her mother had sent along high-heeled sandals, a curling iron and plenty of makeup and hair products, all taken from Bethany's bathroom. She was too grateful to be exasperated. Plus it was her own fault—she was the one who hadn't moved out of the palace.

Not that she wanted to. She liked living close to her family. She spent a couple of afternoons a week with her brothers and had dinner with her parents just as often. She had independence and yet was still with her family. It was great—only every now and then she wanted something more. Something of her own.

She was nearly twenty-seven. Shouldn't she have a life plan in place, or at least some goals? Her family situation was, as she hinted to Cade, a complication, but she was starting to think the bigger problem was that she was using it as an excuse. And if so, shame on her.

She checked her appearance in the mirror. Her hair had curled nicely and she liked how the dress fit. She slipped on her sandals and picked up her small clutch, then went downstairs to meet Cade.

He was standing in the living room, looking out the window. He'd put on khakis and a light green, long-sleeved shirt. When he turned and looked at her, she felt her heart give a little flutter. The flutter increased as his eyes widened.

"You look great," he told her. "No one would ever guess you can carry a hundred-pound sack of grain with the best of them."

She laughed. "I'm more comfortable with forty-pound sacks, but I can lift a hundred-pound one in a pinch."

They walked outside to the truck. Cade looked concerned when he spotted her shoes, but before he could say anything, she stepped expertly on the running board and eased into the passenger seat.

"I'm a girl," she told him primly. "We're all multi-talented."

"I see that and I won't question you again."

Cade drove them to a steak house in town. He put his hand on the small of her back as they walked inside. His mother might not approve of Bethany but she'd raised her children well. Cade had excellent manners.

"Why are you smiling?" he asked as they were shown to a table by the window.

She waited until they were seated to say, "I was just thinking your mother raised you right. You take charge, but in a polite way, yet you must have a wild streak. You told me you left home when you were eighteen."

"I have my moments," he said. "It was an easy decision when I didn't have any responsibilities. It would be more difficult now." He hesitated, then added, "I'm buying into the ranch. Every year I earn ten percent ownership. I want to expand the breeding program, which is why Rida's so important to me. I've been talking with my old boss in Texas and we're going to work together. Right now I have to run a lot of the big decisions past my grandfather, but once I'm the majority owner, it will be on me."

She saw the passion in his eyes, along with determination and confidence. "You can't wait," she said.

He raised a shoulder. "I like working with Grandpa Frank, but yeah, I'm ready to be in charge. You've been around horses enough to know that you have to take the long view of things. It can take years to know if a gamble is going to pay off. I've learned to be patient.

I've got a lot of years ahead of me and I'm going to make it all happen."

"I don't doubt you for a second. You never would have been happy in the family bank."

"It took a while for my mom to figure that out, but she's finally stopped asking me to reconsider my career choices."

"What about your dad? You never mention him."

Cade's expression tightened. "He died when Pallas and I were kids. He's the one who first brought me to the ranch. We were close." He hesitated. "When I was little, I idolized him. As I got older, I began to wonder if he'd married my mom to get an in with my grandfather and the bank." He shrugged again. "I can't know for sure without talking to my mom and that's not a conversation I want to have with her."

An unexpected confession, she thought. "I'm sorry you have to deal with that. Is it why you're so conscientious? Just in case?"

"Probably. I want to make the right decisions and not screw up. But every now and then it all comes tumbling down."

"Tell me about it. I had a horrible experience with a guy in college. I was devastated and went back to El Bahar." She grimaced. "That's when I started working in the royal stables. While I love what I do, I can't see myself staying there for the next twenty years. Yet I have no idea what else I want to do."

"No room for advancement with the king?" he asked, his voice teasing.

"Not really." She supposed she could use some of her trust to simply buy a horse ranch of her own, only somehow that seemed like cheating. She didn't want to step into a position of ownership, she wanted to earn it. Or at least feel she was a part of it.

Their server stopped by the table and told them about the specials. They each ordered a glass of wine.

Conversation flowed easily. Before she knew it, they were done with their meal. She'd had a great time and didn't want the evening to end. There was something about Cade, something that made her wish their circumstances were different. That she could…

What? Date him? Why couldn't she? It had been forever since she'd been this attracted to a guy. From everything she'd witnessed so far, Cade was totally honorable. Why not explore the possibilities?

Bethany told herself if she wanted something, she had to be brave enough to go after it, so she took a deep breath and asked, "So why isn't there a Mrs. Cade Saunders?"

Cade studied her for a second, before smiling. "That's direct."

"I'm curious, so I asked."

"It's a long story."

"We could order coffee."

"Okay." He reached for his water glass, then drew back. "I always had girlfriends in high school," he began. "When I moved to Kentucky, I started dating the daughter of the owner of the ranch where I worked. Lynette was different from anyone I'd ever known. More sophisticated, I guess. She had a cute accent and knew exactly what she wanted from me."

Bethany wondered if she'd made a mistake, asking for details about his past.

"The chemistry was instant," he continued, "and we both fell hard. Or so I thought. She worried about what her parents would say, so we kept our relationship secret. I missed her when she traveled with her friends or her family, but then she'd be back and it was as if she'd never been away."

Bethany drew in a breath. She already knew the story wasn't going to end well.

"We'd been together nearly two years when Lynette came back from one of her trips with a fiancé."

"Oh no."

He grimaced. "I was surprised, too. And pissed. The guy was a jerk, but rich. When I confronted her, she told me that I was fun to play with, but that we were never going to get serious and I was only good for sex. She needed to marry someone from her social circle. Or as she put it, I was a workhorse and she was a Thoroughbred."

"I'm sorry," she said, wishing she'd kept her mouth shut.

"It got worse. I was mad—she got scared I was going to say something to someone, and she told her mother I'd attacked her. Her family had a lot of influence in town, so I was arrested and charged. Two days later, her father returned from a business trip. Turns out he knew all about our relationship and confronted his daughter."

Bethany couldn't believe it. Who would do a thing like that? If she'd ever tried to pull anything like that, Malik would have killed her. Okay, not killed, but she would have been in big trouble.

"The charges were dropped," Cade said. "I was released, and then fired."

"How could he do that?"

"How could he keep me around? He helped me get a great job in Texas and told me to stick to my own kind. I didn't like the message, but I knew he was right. I packed up and left without looking back." He offered her a humorless smile. "The kicker? Lynette got in touch with me about four months later and wanted to know if we could get together. I told her no. I'd learned my lesson. Next time I'll fall for a good-hearted, honest woman who knows exactly who she is and exactly who I am."

Bethany did her best to keep breathing. Her chest was tight but for once not because of her attraction to Cade. Instead she was fighting a sickening realization and doing her best not to bolt from her chair and keep running until she found her way home.

Then the sensation faded and all she could think was that life was incredibly unfair. If Cade didn't want any more Lynettes in his life, he sure wouldn't want anything to do with her. A princess from El Bahar was going to be way worse than some heartless, rich man's daughter.

Worse, she'd lied about who she was and if he found out… Well, she didn't know what, but it would be really, really bad.

"Beth? Are you okay?"

She swallowed and looked at him. "I'm sorry. My stomach just turned on me. Must be the combination of the rich food and hearing about your horrible ex-girlfriend. I'd say you're lucky to be rid of her, but you already know that."

His expression turned to concern. "You look pale." He waved over the server and asked for the check. "Give me a second and we'll head back to the ranch."

"I'd appreciate that." She tried to smile. "I'm sorry for messing up the evening."

"You didn't. It's fine. I had a good time."

"Me, too." Right up until the end when she'd discovered that hoping for anything like a relationship with Cade was never going to be possible.

CHAPTER SIX

BETHANY SPENT THE night tossing and turning only to end up where she'd started—knowing that she was totally to blame for her current situation. While it would be nice to say it was someone else's fault, it wasn't. She could have sent someone else to get Rida settled—the royal stables was filled with excellent, caring workers who would have gladly accompanied Rida, but she'd insisted only she could do the job. Given how easily he'd settled into his new home, she knew now she'd been ridiculous.

Maybe it was more than the horse, she realized sometime before dawn. Maybe she enjoyed the drama of her situation a little too much. Maybe she'd been putting off having to make some hard decisions about what she wanted to do with her life. Regardless of which or all of the reasons, she was now stuck in a difficult situation and she had no idea how to fix things.

Telling Cade the truth made the most sense. It was the mature thing to do. The right thing to do. Only she didn't want to. For one thing, she knew everything would change. While she was pretty sure he liked Beth Smith, he would have nothing but disdain for Princess Bethany. He would see her as Lynette-like, judge her and dismiss her, which would be devastating, because the even-bigger problem, at least to her, was she had feelings for Cade.

He was so funny and charming and capable. She liked how he respected her job and made her laugh and was easy to be around. She liked how his kisses made her feel. She liked pretty much everything about him. Which meant lying to him had been beyond dumb.

She got out of bed and went to the window. As she saw it, she could go one of two ways. Come clean or not. If she told him the truth, she would lose everything they had. If she continued to lie, she betrayed him and everything they had. It wasn't much of a choice.

By the time she'd showered and dressed, she'd decided to come clean. She would accept whatever consequences there were with her head held high.

That decided, she went downstairs. Cade was already in the kitchen starting the coffee. He looked up as she came in and smiled.

She told herself it wasn't even a special smile, but wow, there was something about the way he looked at her. With affection and kindness, with concern.

"How are you feeling?" he asked. "Did you sleep?"

"I'm better, thanks. I'm sorry about last night."

"Don't worry about it. I'm just glad you're okay."

She opened her mouth, then closed it. She couldn't do it. She couldn't have him think less of her—it would hurt too much. Which made her a coward, but she could live with that easier than seeing disdain in Cade's eyes. However, she also couldn't allow things to move forward between them. It would be wrong. She would keep things as they were, which was the very least he deserved.

"Thanks." She nodded at the pot. "Coffee. My favorite."

He chuckled and poured her a mug. "Mine, too."

By ELEVEN, Bethany had convinced herself everything was going to be all right. She took care of Rida, then retreated to the small office where she dealt with her email, including a note from her youngest brother complaining that he wasn't too young to learn to drive and asking her to talk to their father. She wrote back pointing out he was only eleven and while being a prince did come with privileges, it didn't mean their parents were idiots. No on the driving.

She was still laughing quietly when the door opened and John, the stable foreman, pushed into the office.

"He's gone! Rida's gone. I just went by his stall and it's empty. I know you weren't going to exercise him until this afternoon, so unless you gave someone else permission to take him out, he's gone."

Beth went cold. No one had talked to her about taking Rida. Had one of the guys in the stable tried to ride him? That wouldn't go well—Rida was very particular about who he accepted on his back.

She hurried out of the office. Cade came running around the corner and stopped when he saw her.

"I heard," he told her. "You didn't let anyone take him, did you?"

"N-no."

Fear blended with worry that something had happened to Rida. Had he escaped or had someone taken him? He was a valuable horse and could easily be ransomed for seven figures. There was no way Cade had that kind of money, which meant she would be calling her father.

"Should we phone the police?" she asked. "Or wait for them to contact us?"

"You think he was stolen?" Cade shook his head.

"I have security cameras all over this place. No one came in the gate and there's no other way for a horse trailer to get on the property without being seen. I'm sure he got out."

"But how? I latched the door. I always latch the door."

"You need to breathe. We're going to find him."

Having Rida escape was marginally better than having him kidnapped, but no less panic inducing. What if he got lost? What if he got hit by a car?

"I can't—"

Before she could finish her sentence, Cade put his hands on her shoulders. "Look at me. We're going to find him. I will not stop looking until we do. I give you my word."

She was still terrified, but some of her tension eased. Cade wouldn't lie to her. He would make sure Rida was found.

She nodded and he led her outside. Several of the stable workers gathered around. Cade gave them instructions and they began to fan out. He grabbed Rida's bridle, then led Bethany to his truck.

"If I had to guess," he said as he started the engine, "I would say he's going to head downhill. That will take him directly onto the animal preserve. Let me call Carol and have her meet us at their main offices. We'll take off from there."

Bethany nodded because she couldn't speak. She was too scared. Part of her hated to commit to heading one way or another, but a decision had to be made.

Fifteen minutes later, Cade pulled into the animal sanctuary parking lot. Carol and a tall, older man stood by a pair of golf carts. As soon as Bethany stepped out of the truck, Carol waved her over.

"My dad will take Cade. You come with me." She offered a reassuring smile. "Don't worry. If he's on our property, we'll find him."

Bethany hoped that was true, but she had no way of guessing which way Rida had gone and she doubted anyone else would, either.

"We're going to search in a grid," Carol said as the electric golf cart moved forward silently. "My dad and I studied a map of the acreage and we think the most likely area to find Rida is in the northeast quadrant."

"Are there any dangerous animals there?" Bethany asked anxiously. "I know you have giraffes, but what else is there around here?"

"Gazelles, zebras and a water buffalo. No one will bother him."

Which was only a partial relief. There were a thousand other things that could go wrong. He could be heading in another direction and they would miss him completely. He could step into a gopher hole and break a leg. He could head up into the mountains and eventually starve or freeze to death.

She'd never considered herself overly dramatic, but having Rida gone was fueling the darkest side of her imagination.

Carol drove along a dirt path. "We'll check in with the zebras first. They're fairly skittish, so we'll know right away if Rida's with them. I can't see them accepting any intruder, even a horse. The gazelles are more easygoing. Bronwen, especially."

"You name your animals?" Bethany asked, more to distract herself than because she cared.

"I do. They're not pets, but we still have a bond."

They slowed at the top of a rise. Bethany could see

several zebras grazing in the distance. Had she not been so worried, she would have appreciated the incongruity of the animals living in the middle of the California desert. As it was, she only scanned for Rida, then shook her head.

"He's not here."

"No problem. We'll keep looking."

Bethany nodded. "Thank you for your help. I'm sure you had a different day planned."

"I'm happy to help. I know he means a lot to you."

They drove for five or six minutes, then passed through a grove of thick trees into an open grassy area. She saw four gazelles and right in the middle of the field, a tall, black horse nibbling on grass.

Relief rushed through her, leaving her slightly light-headed. She smiled at Carol. "I'm so giving him a talking-to when I get him back home."

"I'll radio my dad and Cade. You go get your boy."

"Thank you."

Bethany got out of the golf cart and walked toward her horse. She was careful to move at a normal pace and keep her body language comfortable. She didn't want Rida to sense any tension or get spooked.

He raised his head and watched her approach. After a couple of seconds, he started toward her, his head and tail high as if he was pleased with himself.

"Annoying twit horse," she murmured in a soft voice. "You scared me to death."

He stopped in front of her. She wrapped her arms around his neck and he lowered his head as if hugging her back.

"How did you get out? Did I forget to lock the gate or do you have mad skills?"

Rida snorted in response.

A few minutes later, Carol's father and Cade drove up. Cade walked over with the bridle. Bethany slipped it on.

"Can you give me a hand up?" she asked, standing on the horse's left side.

"You're going to ride him bareback with just a bridle?"

"It'll be faster than bringing a trailer out here. Plus the trailer would startle the other animals. I've done it before. He'll be fine."

"If you're sure."

Cade linked his fingers together, forming a step. Bethany put her left foot on his hands, counted to three, then pushed off the ground with her right foot. She swung onto Rida's back and settled into place.

"Do you know where you're going?" Cade asked.

She waved her phone. "I have the ranch's address on my GPS. I'll use the app to guide me."

"If you're sure."

"We'll be fine."

Carol joined them. "There's a gate at the north end of the property." She handed over a key. "This is for the lock. Just bring it back when you can."

"Thank you for everything."

"That's what friends are for," she said easily.

BETHANY GOT RIDA back to the ranch and into his stall. John discovered that two of the screws had come loose in the latching system, allowing Rida to jiggle the door open. The problem explained and solved meant she could relax. She groomed Rida, then left him in his stall with Harry sunning himself nearby. She retreated to the small office and sent thank-you flowers to Carol before making a sizable donation to the animal preserve. Then she went in search of Cade.

She found him with John. They were checking all the stalls for loose screws.

"How's our guy?" he asked as Bethany approached.

"He's fine. I'm still feeling a little shaky. Thank you so much for your help and for staying calm. I was totally freaked."

"You were on edge, but it's not surprising. We were lucky to have found him so quickly. John and I are going to go over all security procedures to make sure nothing like this ever happens again."

She nodded, confident he would take care of things. Between not sleeping and the stress of the morning, she was ready for a quiet afternoon and an early night.

"Pallas texted me," Cade said. "She's invited us over for dinner tomorrow, if you're interested. I thought maybe you could help me pick out a Christmas tree before we meet them." He flashed that sexy smile of his. "I'd like a woman's opinion so I get the right one."

Hope, need and just plain liking smacked her upside the head. She'd promised not to get involved with him, to take a step back and retreat to the safety of the friendship zone. Only she really, really wanted to go to dinner with him and his sister and her fiancé and she wanted to pick out a Christmas tree even more.

Was it wrong to want to create a few memories before she headed home? Was she totally horrible for not simply blurting out the truth and letting the chips fall and all that?

"Beth, it wasn't supposed to be a difficult question."

"Technically it was two questions," she said lightly. "Cade, I really want to go with you."

"But?"

"But I'm leaving and…" *And I'm scared to tell you the truth because then you won't like me anymore and I really need you to keep liking me.*

"I have a feeling you're not worrying about my delicate sensibilities," he teased, then his humor faded. "I get it. You're going home and I'm staying here. As it's only a couple of weeks, a case could be made to go for it. On the other hand, it's easy for a situation to get out of control, and then someone gets hurt."

Or that, she thought, preferring his line of reasoning to her own.

He touched the side of her face. "I'm willing to risk it if you are. And if you're not, come to dinner with me as my friend simply because we enjoy each other's company."

"You are very good company," she admitted.

"And a great kisser."

"There is that."

"So yes to dinner?"

"Yes to dinner and the tree," she said, promising herself that whatever happened she would have no regrets.

HAPPILY INC'S CHRISTMAS tree lot was amazing. Not only did it smell like heaven, but there was a snow machine in one corner, producing a pretty impressive dusting of snow. If Bethany ignored the warm temperature, she could pretend she was in a forest, maybe in Germany or Colorado. She wanted to run from end to end, inhaling as deeply as she could, and maybe make an angel in the snow. Everything was magical and transported her back to her childhood when she and her mother had waited until the trees were marked down to buy one.

"You okay?" Cade asked, sounding worried.

"I'm giddy." She spun in a circle, listening to the Christmas carols. "I love this. I'd forgotten what it was like to pick out a tree. My mom and I did it every year, of course, but when we moved to El Bahar, everything changed."

"Don't they celebrate Christmas?"

"A lot of people do." She touched the branches on the nearest tree and felt the firm needles. The snow was cold and damp. "But at the palace, trees are delivered and decorated professionally. It's not like I got to do anything."

Cade stared at her. "Did you just say 'at the palace'?"

Crap! Double crap! She closed her eyes, then opened them. "I have a small apartment on the palace grounds. It's near the stables."

"They'd probably frown on you dragging in a tree of your own," he said easily.

"They would." Talk about a close call! She reminded herself to be more careful. "What about that one?"

Cade shook his head. "Too small. We've got that spot at the house where we're open a good two stories. Let's get the biggest tree we can."

"Men are obsessed with size," she murmured.

He laughed. "With good reason."

They wandered around the tree lot, picking then discarding options. Eventually Cade admitted that the tallest trees had the fewest branches and they settled on one that was just over ten feet.

"Do you have decorations?" she asked.

"I have a couple of boxes of them. My mom gave me all the ones I made when I was a kid." He grinned. "She said it was so I could start my own traditions, but

I'm pretty sure it was more about them not fitting in with her classy decor."

"What other family traditions do you have?"

"We pick a name out of a hat and that's the only family member we buy a gift for. It has to be less than twenty bucks and if it's funny, that helps."

"Your grandfather's idea?" she asked.

"Yeah. I like it. We take the rest of the money we would have spent on gifts and donate it to the charity of our choice."

He paid for the tree, then helped the guy carry it to his truck. Once it was secure in the bed, he turned to Bethany.

"What's your story? To quote you, why isn't there a Mr. Beth Smith?"

"Oh, that." The truth, she told herself. She would stick to the truth. "I have trouble picking the right guy."

"What kind of trouble?"

It was just after six and already dark. Christmas carols played from tinny speakers. The temperature was in the fifties, the night clear with the first of the evening stars making their appearance. Not exactly the time and place for her great confession, but she wanted to be as honest as she could, within reason.

"I had a serious boyfriend in college. I thought I was in love with him and I'd sort of been saving myself for the *in love* thing, so he was my first, well, everything."

Cade's gaze was steady. "How did he let you down?"

"What makes you think he did?"

"If he didn't, you'd still be with him. There's no way he was stupid enough to let you go."

She wasn't sure how Cade meant what he said, but she chose to read it as the sweetest thing a man had ever said to her. Somewhere deep in her chest, her heart crossed the line from maybe to yes.

"The first night we made love, he took pictures of me and put them up on the internet." She shook her head. "You couldn't really see anything but it was clear I was naked."

Cade's body tensed. "Tell me who he is and I'll go beat the crap out of him."

"Thanks, but my father already flew into a rage."

She hadn't wanted the king to find out, but there was no way to keep the information from him—or anyone. Her parents had flown out the same day and she'd gone home with them. She still didn't know what her father had said to the guy, but Bethany had never heard from him again. Still, the pictures lived on as all things internet related did.

"Since then I've chosen relatively quiet, meek men who would never dream of doing anything like that."

"I don't see you as liking the meek type."

"I don't, which is a problem. They can't stand up to me and they certainly can't deal with my father so it all becomes a disaster fairly quickly. I know I'm afraid," she added quickly, before she could stop herself, "of trusting again."

"Makes sense."

"Maybe, but it makes me feel like a coward. I'm genuinely lost when it comes to my future. Return to college? Start a business? Move somewhere? I like my work, but I should be doing more with my life. I hate to give up horses, though. I've thought of breeding and working on bloodlines. I don't know."

His hazel eyes were unreadable. "Have you come to any decisions?"

"Not really."

She thought longingly of Cade's ranch. She would live there with him, if he asked her to. If he wanted her in his life. Because she could do good there—working with the horses she loved while improving the bloodlines.

The image of their future was so clear she was surprised he couldn't see it, too. Only it was all in her head. Cade didn't even know who she was.

"Okay, this is not Christmas talk," she said with a laugh. "Let's go to your sister's now. On the way we'll sing 'Jingle Bells' and get back in the mood."

For a second Cade didn't move. Then he reached for her hand, drew her close and kissed her lightly on the mouth.

"Do you know the words to 'Jingle Bells'?"

"I know the first verse."

"Then that's what we'll sing."

CHAPTER SEVEN

SEVERAL HOURS LATER, Cade drove them back to the ranch. Dinner with Pallas and Nick had gone well. Cade enjoyed his sister and her fiancé and liked how Beth fit in with them so easily. She and Pallas had brainstormed ideas for an upcoming wedding while he and Nick had talked sports.

He and his sister had always been close. He'd missed her while he'd lived out of state. Coming home to the ranch had been its own reward, but being near Pallas again was a nice bonus. Nick was a good guy and he appreciated knowing Pallas was with someone who loved and respected her.

Beth leaned back in her seat with her eyes closed. As he glanced at her, she smiled.

"What?" he asked.

"Just enjoying the moment. I had a good day. Shopping for the tree was fun, dinner was great, the company was even better. Plus there was that second glass of wine." She opened her eyes and looked at him. "I appreciate you driving."

"Happy to stick to one beer."

"When do you want to decorate the tree?"

"How's tomorrow night? We'll leave it out in the garage until then. I'll get out the lights and ornaments and we can have at it."

"It's a date."

He liked the sound of that, along with having her close by. She was easy to be with, good with his horses. An unexpected find, and he was going to miss her when she returned to El Bahar.

Thoughts formed in the back of his mind. No, not thoughts, questions. Would she be willing to stay? She hadn't jumped at his hint of a job offer—and hiring someone he wanted to date seemed too weird anyway—but there had to be something to keep her here. She wasn't sure about what to do with her life—couldn't she be thinking about that here as easily as back in El Bahar? And most important of all, was it too soon to be having that conversation?

He pulled into the driveway and hit the remote for the gate. When they reached the house, he drove around to the garage. Beth got out of the truck and began unfastening the ropes holding the tree in place. Once the tree was untied, they carried it inside. It was only when they were halfway to the garage that Cade realized she was carrying the heavy end.

Beth, being Beth, hadn't said a word about it. She was certainly strong enough—you couldn't work around horses the way she did without developing muscle, but still. His mother would slap him upside the head if she knew.

Once they had the tree in the garage, she held it steady while he cut a couple of inches off the trunk, then put it in the tree stand before going into the house.

At the bottom of the stairs, they looked at each other. She smiled.

"I had a really nice time today. Thank you."

"You're welcome. I did, too."

There was a lot more he wanted to say—like how much he was going to miss her and how he wanted to talk to her about maybe staying. Only the words suddenly didn't seem all that important, not when he could lean over and kiss her.

Her mouth was soft and yielding. When he drew her close, she sank into him and kissed him back. They stood there at the base of the stairs, holding on to each other, tongues tangling in the soft light of the living room lamp.

After a few minutes, need threatened to overwhelm common sense and he drew back.

"You should go up to bed," he said, his voice husky. "I'm going to take care of some paperwork in my office."

Because if he went upstairs with her, he knew exactly what was going to happen.

She stared at him, her blue eyes dark with passion. He read the indecision on her face and knew the right thing to say and do.

"Go to bed."

She raised herself on tiptoe and pressed a chaste kiss to his mouth, then hurried up the stairs.

He watched her go before retreating to the relative safety of his office. Once he was behind his desk, he leaned back in his chair and tried to figure out what to do next.

Beth was an unexpected complication. Ever since the disaster that was Lynette, he'd avoided entanglements and had kept his relationships short and uncomplicated. Since returning to Happily Inc, he hadn't dated anyone.

In his head he knew that one day he was going to have to get over what had happened if he wanted to settle down and have a wife and family. In his heart, he'd been unwilling to take a chance. Until Beth...

"YOU LOOK BEAUTIFUL, MOM," Bethany said as she smiled at her computer.

"I look old and tired," Queen Liana said. "I usually

enjoy a state dinner, but one of my tablemates was especially tedious tonight. International monetary policy has its place, but after two hours, one should learn to speak about something else."

"I'm sure you tried," Bethany told her mother.

"At least six times. He was not getting the hint." Her mother pulled off her tiara and began to unfasten her earrings. "How are you doing, darling? Is everything all right?"

"Rida threw Cade again."

"That horse. You spoiled him and now everyone has to pay the price."

"I know. I should have been more firm with him, but he never threw me."

"Yes, and he's also not your horse, is he?"

"Ouch."

Her mother looked contrite. "I'm sorry. That came out more harshly than I'd intended. I'm going to blame the monetary discussion. By the way, I spoke with your aunt Dora yesterday. The University of El Bahar is starting an International Women's Studies program in the fall that goes through to the doctorate level." Her mother paused expectantly.

"That is very like Aunt Dora. Tell her congratulations."

"I did already, but that's not the point."

Bethany pretended surprise. "It's not?"

Liana sighed. "You do love being difficult."

"I do. Very much. It's fun."

"You could come home and go back to college right here in El Bahar," her mother said pointedly. "Wouldn't that be nice?"

"Yes, living with my parents and waiting for my father to arrange a marriage. It would be beyond great. How many camels do you think I'm worth?"

Her mother studied her. "Bethany, you know we worry about you. You're obviously not happy with what you're doing and we want to help."

"I know, Mom. And while college is something I'm thinking about, I'm still not sure."

She hated to give up her work with her horses. But working at the royal stables wasn't a long-term solution. Buying her own place was an option, but where? If she stayed in El Bahar, she would always be the king's daughter. If she moved to the States, she wouldn't know anyone. Maybe she should be more independent, but the thought of dropping herself into unknown territory was more than a little scary. As for Happily Inc, well, she was more than a little interested in any opportunities here, but what could they be? It wasn't as if she could go to Cade and say "Hey, have you thought about taking on a partner? I happen to have a royal trust fund. Yay me."

"What, darling?" her mother asked. "You're upset about something."

"I wish I hadn't lied to Cade about who I am." She held up her hand. "I know, I know. It's on me. I'm the one who wanted to travel under an assumed name."

"You like him."

Not a question, but she answered anyway. "I do. He's sweet and funny and he doesn't get mad when Rida throws him."

"So tell him the truth."

"It's not that simple."

"Your grasp of English is excellent. I'm sure you can find the words." Her mother's smile faded. "Bethany, he's going to find out eventually. Better to hear it from you."

"How is he going to find out? I head home in a few

days and he'll never see me again." A reality that made her feel sick to her stomach. "It's okay," she added quickly. "I'll be fine. I miss you and Dad and the boys."

"We all miss you, as well. Hurry home."

"I will. Bye, Mom."

They hung up. Bethany turned off her computer, then walked to the window. The truth was getting to be a heavier burden every day. She would decorate the tree with Cade tonight and tell him in the morning, no matter what. She had to. She really cared about him and until she came clean, she couldn't begin to express her feelings. He would probably hate her, but that was her own fault. Every decision had consequences.

IT TOOK NEARLY an hour to untangle the lights. Bethany kept laughing at Cade's frustration.

"Why didn't you coil them up last year?" she asked, doing her best not to grin.

"I wasn't here last year," he grumbled. "This isn't my fault. The tree should come prelit."

"You'll have to take that up with God. To be honest, a prelit real tree would freak out most people."

"I'd like it."

"Well, then. It must be done."

They managed to string the lights. Cade opened boxes of ornaments. Some were old and delicate, wrapped in yellowing tissue paper. Others were from when he'd been a kid. One was a tiny handprint and there were several made of Popsicle sticks, and one kind of strange creature made from pipe cleaners.

"I think that's supposed to be a reindeer," he said, sounding doubtful.

"It kind of looks like a lizard, and it's green. Why would a reindeer be green?"

"I can't believe you're being critical of my work."

"I know. I'm a horrible person."

He opened another box filled with shiny ornaments from a discount store. "Are you mocking my creative ability? It's already a sore subject. Nick is a famous artist. I'm doing the best I can, but sure, crush my childhood dreams."

She laughed. "Poor broken bunny."

"That's me."

"Shall I kiss it and make it better?"

She'd meant the comment to be teasing, but the second she spoke, the air became charged. Cade's gaze sharpened and everything inside of her went still.

Wanting flared to life. Wanting and need and a thousand other emotions that made her realize that sometime, when she hadn't been paying attention, she'd fallen for this man.

He reached for her and in that split second before his hand touched her body, she knew she had to make a choice: a single night or the truth. Because she couldn't have both. And even knowing it was the wrong decision and one she might regret forever, she took a step toward him and raised her face for his kiss.

BETHANY HAD ONLY been with two men in her life. Cade made three. But to compare making love with him to what had gone on before was to compare a great ocean to a glass of water.

He touched her gently, almost reverently, but with confidence that had her surrendering to him. He explored every inch of her, finding the places that made her gasp and moan, then taught her the same about himself. By the time dawn broke over the horizon, she was satiated, weak and unable to hide from the fact that she'd fallen totally in love with him.

She got up to check on Rida, then returned to his bed. They slept nearly until noon before waking up to make love again. Finally they made it to the kitchen for something to eat.

He'd pulled on jeans and a T-shirt, while she wore one of his long-sleeved shirts over panties. They kissed and touched as much as they cooked, which meant the eggs were well-done and the pancakes had burnt edges, but that didn't seem to matter to either of them.

They sat across from each other at the small table. Cade smiled at her.

"You okay?" he asked.

Because he wanted to be sure. Because no matter what, he would take care of the people in his life. For a second, she let herself pretend it was all going to be okay, that she would tell him who she was and he would forgive her. Only it wasn't going to be like that.

"I am," she told him. "Last night was…amazing."

"Yeah?" His grin turned smug. "For me, too."

"I'm glad." She drew in a breath for courage. "You've been an unexpected part of my trip here." She plucked at the collar of his shirt. "I don't usually do this sort of thing."

"Dress like a man?" he asked, his voice teasing.

She wanted to smile back and laugh with him. She wanted to know it was going to be all right, but it wasn't. She'd put off telling the truth long enough.

"Cade, I've really enjoyed my time with you. More than I should have, I think. I like you a lot." Which was the coward's way of avoiding saying she loved him, but one confession at a time seemed the most reasonable path.

He leaned toward her and took her hand in his. "I feel the same way, Beth. I like to tease, but the truth is you've made a big impact on me. I know it's happened fast and we have to get to know each other better, but I'm hoping we can figure out a way to make that happen."

"First I have to tell you something."

He stiffened slightly and drew back. "What?"

"It's not bad." Or maybe it would be to him. "I mean, I'm not married or dying or anything else. I'm exactly who I said, with one small difference."

His phone beeped. They both glanced at the screen and saw the gate notification.

"I'm not expecting anyone," he said, pushing the button to activate the speaker at the gate.

"Can I help you?"

"Cade? It is I, King Malik. Good morning. Or should I say good afternoon? I was in the neighborhood and thought I would stop by to check on how things are going with you and Rida."

Bethany fought against sudden nausea. She couldn't breathe, which was fine because if she passed out she wouldn't have to face what was about to happen.

Cade stared at the phone in obvious surprise. "Um, okay. Let me buzz you in." He pushed a button on his phone, then glanced at her. "Did you know about this?"

"No. I talked to my mother last night and she didn't say a word." Her mother had been dressed for a state dinner. How on earth could her father have attended that, then flown all the way here? He must have gotten on a plane the second she and her mom had hung up. But why? What had she said to make this happen?

She tried telling herself that she was imagining the connection, but couldn't make herself believe it. She knew her father too well. The timing was more than suspect. He had a reason for showing up today and now she would have to deal with a lot more consequences than she'd anticipated.

"Why would your mother know if King Malik was coming here or not?" Cade asked.

Bethany glanced down at what she was wearing—or not wearing. She thought about bolting for her room, only there wasn't time. Even as she considered her options, she heard a car pulling up in front of the house.

"You'd better go let him in," she said quietly, willing Cade to…to… What? Believe in her? Trust her? She'd had her chance. She'd had chances every second of every day since she'd arrived. Whatever happened now was her fault and no one else's.

Cade gave her a confused look as he got up. She started to follow, then stopped halfway as Cade opened the door.

King Malik wore a dark suit with a white shirt and red tie. He looked powerful and successful, very much the man in charge. Cade shook hands with him and said something she couldn't hear before they both turned to her.

Her father looked her up and down, then raised his eyebrows but didn't say anything.

In her gut she sensed he might play along if she introduced herself as Beth Smith and pretended they barely knew each other. She had a feeling she might be able to stretch out the lie a little longer—only she was done playing that particular game.

She crossed to her father and raised herself on tip-toe to kiss his cheek.

"Hi, Dad. This is unexpected."

"Bethany." Malik glanced between the two of them. "It seems I came at a bad time. Would you like a moment to go get changed?"

"Yes."

She drew in a breath, grabbed on to what little courage she had left, then faced Cade.

Anger darkened his hazel eyes. Anger and something else. Something cold and unforgiving and very much like a sense of betrayal.

"I'm sorry you had to find out like this," she began. "I'm not Beth Smith. I'm Bethany Archer, otherwise known as Princess Bethany of El Bahar. King Malik is my adoptive father."

Cade opened his mouth but before he could respond, Malik moved to stand between them.

"Think carefully, young man, about what you're going to say. Whatever you and Bethany have going on, she is still my daughter and I protect what is mine."

Bethany winced. Of all the things her father could have said, that was absolutely the worst. It would remind Cade of everything Lynette did and make him hate Bethany even more. But it was too late now. Still, she had to try.

"Cade, could I speak to you for a moment?"

He looked at her as if he'd never seen her before, then slowly shook his head. Without saying a word, he turned and walked out of the house.

CHAPTER EIGHT

CADE WASN'T SURE how he got through his unexpected
meeting with King Malik. He knew they discussed Rida
and how well he was adjusting, along with the training
program Cade and Bethany had developed for the horse.
But for the most part, he was simply going through the
motions.

He couldn't believe it—he'd been played again. And
by Beth. No, he told himself. Not Beth. Princess Bethany of El Bahar.

She'd known. That was the real killer in all this. He'd
told her about his past and she'd sat there, blinking at
him, when all the while she'd known. Damn her. He
wasn't sure if he was more hurt or angry. He'd trusted
her, believed in her. He'd thought they had something
together. He'd thought about asking her to stay. He'd
been worse than a fool—he'd actually believed in her.
At least Lynette hadn't lied about who she was.

"I'm very pleased," King Malik said as they walked
out of the stables. "Rida has settled in nicely. Selling
him to you was a wise decision. I hope we can continue
to do business together."

"Thank you, Your Highness."

The polite response when the real one was "Are you
kidding? It will be years before I can afford another
horse like him."

He thought about Bethany, then tried *not* to think about Bethany. He wanted to say something to her father, but what? There were no questions he could ask, nothing to be said. Not when—

He swore silently. King Malik wasn't here because of a horse—he wanted to check on his daughter. Only he wouldn't say that. Cade would be a moron to think otherwise.

"You came a long way to check on a horse," he finally said, wondering if the older man would take the bait.

"I was in the neighborhood."

"Happily Inc isn't close to El Bahar."

"Distance is a matter of perspective, as is much of life. Rida has left our stable to become part of yours, yet he will live on in both. At first, he would have been uncomfortable here, but now this is his home. So it is with life."

"You're not making any sense."

King Malik surprised him by smiling. "I'm the king. I don't have to."

"I guess no one's going to argue with that."

King Malik surprised him again by putting his hand on Cade's shoulder. "You have done well and I am pleased."

Words that shouldn't have mattered, yet somehow eased a tiny fraction of the gaping hole inside his heart.

"Thank you."

With that, Malik walked back to his car, nodded at his driver and got in. Seconds later, they were gone.

Cade stared after them wondering what on earth had just happened. Malik had flown halfway around the world for a ten-minute visit? He hadn't even spoken to Bethany—there hadn't been time.

He started toward the house, only to realize that if she hadn't left with her father, she was still here. He stopped outside the back door, not wanting to go inside, yet wanting to see her. Only he couldn't want that because the Bethany he'd known, the Bethany he'd started to care about, wasn't real.

He'd understood Lynette was vain and selfish, but he'd told himself her love for him would overcome all that. He'd ignored the problems in their relationship, her willingness to sleep with him without ever talking about the future. He'd assumed she would grow up a little and see they belonged together, and he'd been wrong.

In hindsight, he'd been lucky to escape as easily as he had. If she hadn't dumped him, he might have been tempted to hang around and try to change her mind. What a disaster if he had.

But with Bethany, everything was different. He *knew* her. Knew she was a hard worker, knew she was kind and funny and determined. She was fearless, affectionate and it had all been a lie.

Maybe not all of it, but enough. He had no idea which parts of her were real and which were just a game—the princess playing at being like everyone else.

He walked into the house and found her waiting in the kitchen. She'd dressed in jeans and a T-shirt—her usual work uniform. He took in the thick braid, the big blue eyes and felt a stabbing sensation in his gut. He wanted to tell himself he'd gotten off easy a second time, that his luck was holding, but he knew better. Forgetting Lynette had taken a couple of weeks and then he'd been over her. With Bethany it would take longer. Possibly several lifetimes.

She stood with the kitchen counter between them.

She placed her hands on the worn tiles—hands that were almost as strong and scarred as his own.

"I'm sorry," she began. "I want to be clear that I'm not going to say I didn't mean to lie to you. Of course I did. I came here as Beth Smith. I didn't want you to know who I was. I didn't want anyone to know."

"Everyone has fun in her own way."

She flinched. The movement was small, but he caught it. Caught the intake of breath, as if he'd hurt her. He tried to find pleasure in that, and couldn't. Instead he wanted to go to her, pull her close and tell her he was sorry. That they would figure it out. Only he knew that forgiving her would begin a spiral from which he would never escape. Better to let her talk, then send her packing.

"It wasn't for fun," she told him. "From my perspective, it was for survival." She hesitated. "At the risk of playing the 'poor little princess' card, it's not easy being in my position. I'm an American at heart, living in El Bahar as the daughter of the king. I straddle both worlds and I don't do it well. I love my family but I want more from life than an arranged marriage and having babies. The problem is there are limitations to what I can do as Princess Bethany."

Her expression turned pleading. "Imagine how things would have been different if I'd come here as her. You wouldn't have talked to me or let me stay at the house. You would have treated me differently."

He wanted to say that wasn't true, but it was. He wouldn't have teased Princess Bethany or taken her to dinner with his family. He wouldn't have kissed her or...

"You lied," he said, more to distract himself than accuse her.

"I did." She continued to hold his gaze. "I'm sorry about that. I was wrong, but I'm not sure I could have made another decision." She drew in a breath. "I *like* being plain Beth Smith. I like being the same as everyone else. I like being accepted for me and not having to worry that people are pretending to like me because I'm a member of the royal family. I'm not famous enough to be recognized in my regular life. Not outside of El Bahar and I want to keep it that way."

She glanced down, then back at him. "Do you remember when I told you about the guy in college who took pictures of me?"

He nodded.

"He didn't just post them on the internet. He sold them to a tabloid. It was a big juicy headline." She made air quotes. "'I Deflowered a Princess.'"

Rage exploded. Cade took a step forward, then realized he had no one to attack and no reason to defend.

"I was so humiliated. My parents never said anything, but I knew they were disappointed. It was horrible. I left college. Maybe I should have stayed, but the press was everywhere. I felt so naked every second of every day. I just wanted to hide. That's when I started working in my dad's stables. There nobody cared. When I delivered my first horse to a new buyer, I went as Beth Smith and it was great. I wasn't recognized. I was just that girl with the horse. It never mattered before. Not until I came here."

He wanted to believe her. That was what got him. He wanted to say it was fine, that he would forgive her and they would go on as before. Only he knew that was a joke. Just like them.

"I get it," he told her. "You wanted to escape the whole royal thing and you did. Good for you."

Her expression turned wary. "What aren't you saying?"

"That it doesn't matter. You had your reason, Princess Bethany, but at the end of the day, you lied about everything and we have nothing. We never did."

BETHANY SUPPOSED THAT on her list of sins, taking one of the ranch trucks without asking was the least of it. She would have told Cade she wanted to borrow it, but since he'd walked out of the kitchen two hours before, she hadn't seen him.

She was already packed and had a car coming to pick her up and take her LAX. From there she would fly home. But until the car arrived, she had unfinished business.

She drove through Happily Inc, doing her best to memorize all the cute businesses, decorated for the holidays. It was a great little town with lots of character and warm people. She thought maybe she could have been happy here.

She parked outside of Weddings Out of the Box. She'd already texted Pallas to ask if she could stop by. She didn't want to leave until she'd spoken with her friend. Although to be honest, she wasn't sure if she and Pallas would still be friends after Bethany told her the truth.

Pallas greeted her on the stairs and brought her up to what looked like a small break room. "What brings you to town?"

"I wanted to talk to you."

Pallas grinned. "I should probably be subtle, but I think I can guess the topic. I saw the way you and my brother were looking at each other at dinner the other night. There were some serious sparks." She paused, then laughed. "Okay, I want to know everything right up until the kissing starts. Not that I'm not going to be a good friend, but Cade is my brother and there are some things a sister simply doesn't want to know."

Pallas poured them each a cup of coffee, then opened a small box of Oreos. They settled at a round table.

"So?" Pallas beamed at her. "You're crazy about him, aren't you?"

Bethany was shocked to feel her eyes fill with tears. Pallas was at her side in a second.

"What?" her friend demanded. "Did Cade do something stupid? I hate it when men are stupid. What happened?"

Bethany sniffed. "It's not him, it's me. I lied to him." She looked at her friend. "I'm sorry. I lied to you, too."

"Oh, please. About what?"

"About who I am."

Pallas returned to her seat and grabbed a cookie. "What does that even mean? You're an alien? You have antenna and a tail?"

"I'm a princess."

Pallas froze, the Oreo partway to her mouth. She stared at Bethany, then put down the cookie. "A what?"

"Princess. My father is the king of El Bahar. My mom met him when I was nine and we moved there so she could teach at the American School. They got married and when my biological father died, Malik adopted me. I'm really Princess Bethany of El Bahar."

"Wow. That's so cool." Pallas picked up the cookie again. "No offense, but you don't act like a princess at all. You're so like a normal person."

"Thanks." Bethany felt some of her tension ease. "I'm sorry I lied to you and everyone. There are a lot of reasons."

Pallas waved her hand. "You don't have to explain it to me. Of course you wouldn't want everyone to know. That must be a drag. As Beth Smith you got to be yourself. No one fawned, you didn't have to guess if we liked you, you could burp in public."

Despite everything, Bethany laughed. "Exactly." Her humor faded. "Your brother doesn't see it that way. He feels betrayed."

Pallas rolled her eyes. "Then he needs to get over it. I mean, come on. It makes perfect sense."

Not to Cade, Bethany thought. He would only see that she lied about who she was. He would feel that she tricked him, mostly likely for sport. He would judge her by Lynette.

"Thank you for understanding," Bethany said. "I wanted you to know the truth. I hope we can stay in touch."

"That sounds like you're leaving."

"I am."

"What? Why? I thought you were happy here."

"I don't belong." Bethany shook her head. "Sorry. I need to be honest. I love it here, but Cade doesn't want me and at the risk of sounding too much like a pathetic coed, without him, there's no point in staying."

Pallas narrowed her gaze. "Okay, I'll accept all the rest of it, but not that. You are both too involved for you to just walk away. Have you told him how you feel?"

Bethany didn't bother wondering how Pallas had guessed. When it came to love, everyone was smarter than her.

"He won't care."

"You don't know that. Bethany, I'm serious. You have to tell him. If you don't, you're going to regret it for the rest of your life. Cade's one of the good guys. He's worth fighting for."

On the drive back to the ranch, Bethany couldn't stop thinking about what her friend had said. That Cade was worth fighting for. She turned the idea over and over in her head, wondering if she'd ever had to fight for anything before.

So much had been handed to her. So much simply given by virtue of who her mother had married. When there had been trouble at her boarding school, she'd run home. The same in college. Had she ever once stood her ground?

She found Cade at his office in the stable. He didn't look happy to see her, but she didn't care. What she had to say couldn't wait for him to be in a better mood.

She carefully closed the door behind her, then sat at his desk across from him.

"I'm sorry," she began. "I think you can understand why I did what I did, but you can't get past it. It brings up too much hurt from your past. I agree that there were so many times when I could have told you who I was and a bunch of times I should have told you the truth. I was wrong. I guess I've always let circumstances dictate who I was and what was going to happen. I never made any of the hard decisions myself. I've drifted, which is ridiculous. Poor little rich girl with too many options. I want to be different. I want to change."

She took a breath. She was going to have to lay it all on the line and hope that Cade would give her a second chance.

"I know you're hurt and angry. At the end of the day, whatever my reason, I lied. I take responsibility for that and I ask for your forgiveness. I hope you'll consider giving me a second chance because what we have together is good and special, and as far as I'm concerned, it doesn't happen all that often."

Now came the hard part, she told herself.

"I've fallen in love with you," she told him. "With you and this town and I hope you're feeling, if not the same, then maybe you can see yourself..."

Her voice trailed off. Instead of softening, Cade's expression hardened. His eyes became icy and his mouth formed a straight line.

"Don't," he told her. "It's not going to work, Bethany. You should have stopped with the apology. That I might have believed. But this crap—it's not gonna happen."

"It's not crap," she whispered, feeling heat on her cheeks. "It's not. I love you. Why would I lie about my feelings? How does telling you the truth make this crap?"

"It just is. Sell it somewhere else. I'm not buying it for a second."

And that was it, she thought numbly. The end of what could have been. Being brave was highly overrated.

"Okay." She brushed the tears from her cheeks. "I guess this is goodbye."

"I guess it is."

There was so much else she wanted to say but what was the point? She walked out of his office and went to the stable to see Rida one last time before going to the airport. Once she was home, she would figure out what to do next. And how to stop being in love with Cade.

CHAPTER NINE

RIDA CANTERED DOWN the trail but Cade could tell his heart wasn't in it. Bethany had been gone for nearly a week and Rida continued to miss her. The stallion had allowed Cade to ride him for the past three days without putting up any kind of a fight. Cade suspected that was more about being lonely than because of Cade's training skills.

Together they turned back to the barn. Rida knew the way and kept to the main path. When they reached the stable, he looked around, as if searching for someone. Then his head lowered slightly and he walked to the paddock.

Cade walked him to cool him off, then groomed him and checked for injuries before turning him out into the pasture. He would put him in his stall after he'd had a chance to relax in the sun.

Harry jumped up on the railing and walked over to get his head rub, then meowed for Rida. The horse trotted over and stood close so the cat could rub against his face. Rida looked at Cade, as if asking him to fix the problem.

"I can't, big guy," he told the horse. "I'm sorry."

Rida didn't look convinced.

Cade thought about pointing out he was suffering, too. That he missed everything about Bethany, but there was no point. Not only wouldn't the horse understand, if he could appreciate the sentiment, he would most likely tell Cade to take care of business. It wasn't as if Rida could text or call.

Cade knew he couldn't, either. He had all the reasons and he was determined. In time, he would forget her. Only that hadn't happened yet.

Cade headed for his office, then stopped when he recognized his sister's car by the back of the house. He saw her sitting on the porch and went to join her.

"Hey," she called as he approached. "How's it going?"

He'd texted her after Bethany had left to let her know her friend was gone. Pallas's response had been to say that she was around if he wanted to talk. Apparently she'd gotten tired of waiting for him.

"I'm good. How are you?"

She studied him for a second. "You're going to be a jerk about her, aren't you?"

"I see you're getting right to the point."

She waved a folder. "You're my brother and I love you, so yes, I'm going to try to convince you not to be an idiot."

"You have no idea what happened between me and her."

"I know she's in love with you and I'm pretty sure you feel the same way about her."

No, he told himself. He didn't love her. He refused. She'd lied and nothing else mattered.

Pallas waved the folder at him again. "I thought you might retreat into strong-silent mode. It was always your way of dealing with stuff. When Mom got on your nerves, you went to the ranch. Before that, you'd hide out somewhere in the backyard. You don't believe in confrontations. You walk away. Well, walking away this time is a big mistake, Cade, because if you take too long to figure out what she means to you, you could lose her forever."

She opened the folder. "The internet is an amazing place. Nothing ever dies, it just gets harder to find." She picked up a piece of paper. "When Bethany was fourteen, a friend wrote a blog about how Bethany had a crush on a guy at a neighboring boarding school. The supposed friend gets into details about how Bethany wanted him to kiss her at the school dance and he didn't. The friend posted the story online and it went viral. Remember your first crush? Wouldn't having the whole world know be special?"

Cade knew what Pallas was trying to do and he told himself he was immune. He just hoped he wasn't lying.

She took out a second piece of paper. "This one is from a few years earlier. Some reporter got one of Bethany's tutors to talk about her study habits, how she did on tests, what she liked to eat. Apparently our girl had trouble learning French. The tutor mocked her accent. This was published in a magazine. She was twelve."

His stomach knotted and his hands curled into fists. He consciously relaxed. Not his problem, he told himself.

"Did she tell you about the college boyfriend?" Pallas asked. "The one who put naked pictures of her online and wrote about deflowering a princess?"

"She mentioned that," he admitted, still feeling sick for her.

"Yeah, want to see the pictures? Because they're right there for the whole world to look at. Forever." Pallas glared at him. "No matter what she does or where she goes, those naked pictures live on. They're great. She looks fabulous and technically her boobs and crotch don't show, but wow, Cade. What would that be like? Want to see?"

He turned away. "No. I don't."

"You're in the minority. Want to know how many times the pictures have been downloaded? Want to think about all the jackasses in the world staring at her naked eighteen-year-old self? And that happened because she was stupid enough to trust a guy who said he loved her. But hey, why should that matter? She lied to you about who she is. Let's hate her forever."

With that Pallas rose. She slapped the folder against his chest, then kept on walking. He stayed where he was until she'd driven away, then he sank down on the porch steps and dropped the folder to the ground.

He didn't want to feel sorry for Bethany. He didn't want to understand what had happened to her. He wanted to wallow in his pain and blame her for everything. Then he wanted to forget he'd ever met her. Only... Only... That wasn't going to happen. Not any of it. He couldn't forget her, wouldn't forgive her. Sure, she'd had some bad things happen, but so what? She should get over it. She shouldn't have lied to him about—

He picked up the folder, then dropped it again. One of the pictures slipped out, showing part of a bare leg and hip. He closed his eyes as rage and revulsion swept through him. Who would do that? Who would betray someone he was supposed to care about for a check and five minutes of notoriety?

He grabbed the picture and studied it. Bethany looked so damned young and defenseless. She was asleep, half under the sheet. He wondered if the boyfriend had arranged her that way. The pose suggested more than it showed, but it was still a violation. She would still see it every time she closed her eyes.

She should get over it. Had he really thought that? Was she supposed to get over something like this while he was allowed to whine about what had happened with Lynette? Yes, he'd learned a hard lesson, but so what? It had worked out in the end. He'd gotten a great job in Texas that he'd liked a whole lot better. He'd learned more, had a chance to have dinner with then Crown Prince Malik, which had led to him being able to buy Rida for basically pennies on the dollar. Yeah, that was a drag. At least no one had tried to destroy his life by exposing his most intimate acts on the internet.

She'd been what, eighteen? And a virgin until that night? Cade wanted to call King Malik and ask what he'd done, just to make sure it was enough. Because if the jerk who'd done that was still breathing and walking, it wasn't.

Cade carefully put the picture into the folder, then stood and walked into the house. He'd been a fool. No, he'd been worse than a fool. He'd been cruel and insensitive and Bethany deserved a whole lot better than him.

Still, she'd said she loved him. If that was true, if he was so lucky that she'd offered her heart, then what was he still doing in California? It wasn't every day a man met a woman like her. Given that he'd fallen completely and totally in love with her, being without her was wrong on every level.

There was only one thing for him to do—get his ass to El Bahar and grovel like the worm he was. Beg her to forgive him and ask for another chance. This time he wouldn't blow it. This time he would do everything in his power to convince her that he was going to spend the rest of his life proving how much he loved her. He was going to take care of her and protect her and be impressed by her and hope it was enough. Because at the end of the day, he would be offering all that he had.

CADE HAD NEVER been to El Bahar before and didn't know what to expect. The airport was large and modern. He went through customs easily, and then got a cab. It was only when the driver asked him where he wanted to go that he realized he still hadn't come up with a plan.

He'd gotten the first flight he could out of LAX. That meant changing planes first in New York and then in Frankfurt. Including layovers, he'd already traveled more than twenty-six hours and he still didn't know how he was supposed to get in touch with Bethany.

She'd disconnected the phone she'd used in Happily Inc. If she'd given Pallas her real number, his sister hadn't bothered sharing the information with him, so he was on his own.

"Take me to the royal palace, please."

The driver nodded and pulled away from the curb.

They quickly merged onto a multilane highway. Traffic flowed briskly in both directions. The exits were clearly marked, the road signs were in English. To the southwest was the Arabian Sea and up ahead were the modern high-rises of the downtown area.

They drove past what he would guess was a large financial district, judging by the names of banks on several of the tall buildings, followed by more office buildings. When they exited the highway, there was a large park on one side and a shopping center on the other.

They passed several residential neighborhoods, more

parks, schools, a sprawling university, then entered what seemed to be an older part of the city. Streets became more narrow, buildings closer together. The traffic was denser here.

Thirty minutes later, the cab drove down a long tree-lined street. At the far end was the fabled pink palace of El Bahar. Cade stared at the turrets and domes, the walls, the gardens and the tourists' buses.

The cab pulled over and the driver pointed to the amount due. Cade groaned.

"I didn't have time to exchange my money," he said, pulling out his wallet. "Are US dollars all right?"

The driver smiled. "Of course. Very welcome here." He pushed a button on his meter and the amount was converted to US currency. Cade paid him, grabbed his duffel and got out.

The sun was high in the sky, the temperature warm. He could see the blue water to his left and the palace in front of him. Tourists swarmed, taking pictures. Guides held colored signs aloft in an attempt to keep their groups together.

How was he supposed to find Bethany is all this? He knew she lived in the palace, but it wasn't as if they were going to simply let him in. Should he have gone to the stables instead? Called Pallas to beg for Bethany's number? Not knowing what else to do, he walked up to the information booth and spoke to the woman inside.

"May I help you?" she asked.

"Yes. I'm Cade Saunders, from the United States." He pulled a business card out of his wallet. "I was hoping to see the king."

He waited for hysterical laughter, or the guards to pull out their guns and force him back into a cab. Instead the young woman looked at the card, then him, before asking, "May I see your passport?"

"Sure." Cade handed that to her, as well.

"One moment," she told him, and picked up the phone.

"BUT IT'S INTERNATIONAL WOMEN'S STUDIES," her mother said for maybe the sixth time. "Wouldn't that be interesting?"

"Mom, if you're that intrigued, *you* go get your degree." Bethany smiled to soften the words. "I love you, but you're making me insane. I'm fine. You don't need to hover."

Only part of a lie, Bethany thought. She wasn't fine, but she really didn't need the hovering, either. Eventually she would be fine. Or at least all right, which was close. Right now the wounds were too fresh. She'd only been home a few days and she ached for Cade with every breath. But in time, she would heal—of that she was sure.

Her parents had welcomed her with open arms, as had her brothers. She'd given herself twenty-four hours to sulk like a five-year-old, then she'd told herself it was time to grow up and take responsibility.

Feeling more than a little ridiculous, she'd spent a morning taking an online aptitude test that also measured what she liked and disliked. The test had confirmed what she already knew—women's studies were not for her. She liked being outdoors; she loved horses, whether it was caring for them, training them, showing them or breeding them.

"But Texas?" her mother asked, her voice rising only a little. "It's so far. They have lovely horses in England. England is so much closer."

Bethany had already resigned from her job at the royal stables and looked for a college offering a degree in ranch management. While there were several, the one at Texas A&M gave her more options. Once she had her degree, then she would figure out what to do with it. Maybe buy a ranch or get involved with horse rescue. In the meantime she would get a job at a ranch. She had experience and good recommendations.

"I know England is closer," Bethany said lightly. "But it's not for me."

"I'll miss you so much." Her mother hugged her. "But I understand why you have to go." Liana hesitated. "Have you heard from Cade?"

Bethany shook her head. "No, and I don't expect to. It's over. He's not going to forgive me for what I did."

"Then he's not worth it, darling, and I suspect you know that."

Sensible words, Bethany told herself. And while her head knew her mother was right, her heart was not so willing to let go of the man who held it captive.

CADE WAS OKAY with the guy in the suit who led him through the palace—it was the uniformed and armed guard who stayed close that made him nervous.

He'd waited nearly twenty minutes before the guy in the suit had reappeared. He escorted Cade through carved double doors that had to be nearly twenty feet high, then through a foyer the size of a basketball court. Cade had to show his passport at two different checkpoints before leaving what were obviously the public parts of the palace and entering the working section of the compound.

Ancient blended perfectly with modern. The floors

were stone, several of the doorways arched. There were mosaics and murals, tapestries and carvings along with offices and computers and people talking on cell phones. The business of running a country was still a business and a large staff was required.

They passed what he would guess was a large lunchroom. A small raised platform held a Christmas tree, a large menorah and a red-and-white-striped mailbox with a sign saying *Direct mailings to the North Pole.* Cade felt the beginning of cultural dizziness and realized he actually knew very little about the country or its people.

Too late now, he thought as he was led into a very large, very impressive waiting area. Two men sat behind massive desks. They were both wearing headsets and speaking. One of them finished his call, then looked at Cade.

"Mr. Saunders, His Royal Highness, the King of El Bahar, will see you now."

Cade swore under his breath. He really hadn't thought this through. Once he'd figured out how incredibly stupid he'd been to let Bethany go, all he could think about was getting to her to tell her he'd been wrong. He hadn't considered the fact that he was going to have to face an actual king.

Yes, he'd met King Malik before, but at a casual dinner or at the ranch. Not like this.

One of the carved double doors opened and yet another suited minion appeared to escort Cade inside. The guard who had been with him since he entered the palace took Cade's bag from him, then Cade was in what he guessed was Malik's working office and alone with the king.

The monarch sat at his aircraft-carrier-sized desk. He wore a shirt and tie with his suit jacket hanging behind him. Windows looked out onto impressive gardens with the Arabian Sea in the distance.

Cade approached the desk. Malik looked up from the papers he'd been reading and raised his eyebrows.

"Cade, you are most unexpected."

The tone wasn't exactly warm and welcoming. Cade wondered how much Bethany had told her parents.

"I'm here to see Bethany," he began.

Malik shook his head. "That is not going to happen. You have broken my daughter's heart. Consider yourself lucky that I don't in turn break parts of you."

"I never meant to hurt her. I was wrong…what I said to her. I… There are things from my past and they got in the way."

"How fortunate that you had this revelation after sending her away."

Sarcasm was a lot more intimidating when the speaker was a king, Cade thought. He was also aware of not being invited to take a seat.

"I can't help the timing. The things from my past are information, not an excuse. I need to see Bethany."

Malik's dark gaze remained icy. "So you said and yet your request is of no interest to me. You may go."

Now Cade was the one to shake his head. "No, I won't. You have to hear me out."

"Surprisingly, I do not have to do anything." Malik smiled tightly. "It is one of the advantages of being the king. Did you know we still have working dungeons in the palace? They are below ground and most unpleasant."

Cade ignored the threat. "I'm in love with your

daughter and while you won't care about that, you may want to know she's in love with me."

"She'll get over it. She's always been a very smart young woman. In a few weeks, you'll be nothing to her."

Cade had to take the chance—there was no other way to get through to Malik. "We both know that's not true. Bethany doesn't give her heart easily. I don't, either. I want to see her, Your Highness, and I'm not leaving until I do."

"To quote you, we both know that's not true. You will leave when I decide we are done."

Cade swore silently. This wasn't going well and he didn't know how to get through to the angry, protective father in front of him. The man who—

Cade felt himself relax. Of course. Malik might be the king but he was also a dad. What he cared about more than anything was his precious baby girl.

"I love her," Cade said simply. "I was a fool to let her go. Worse, I hurt her and there is no way to take that back. I made a mistake—one I've learned from. Your Highness, Bethany is amazing. She's kind and funny and hardworking. I love everything about her."

He moved closer to the desk. "I'll admit the princess thing threw me. It's not what I was expecting and something I'll have to get used to, but it's part of who she is. I love her. I know I have to apologize to her and work to earn her trust, but once that happens, I want to marry her."

Malik rose, his brows drawing together. "She is Princess Bethany of El Bahar," he roared. "The daughter of my heart. How dare you presume to come here and tell me you want to marry her? What makes you think you can begin to provide for her?"

Cade stayed right where he was. "You would have had me vetted before you let me buy Rida, so that's not what this is about. I get she's your daughter, but do you have any idea who she is inside? Bethany doesn't care about the palace or the trappings of royal life. If she did, she wouldn't have been working in your stable. She wants to be normal. I can give her that, and while you may not think it's enough, she does. For you, I can promise I will take my last breath protecting and loving her. Every second of every day for the rest of my life, she will be my world. It's all I have and it's hers."

Malik continued to glare. "You offer your word. What if I want your head instead?"

"You don't scare me."

"Don't I?" He grinned. "Then perhaps I should try harder."

CHAPTER TEN

BETHANY STOPPED BY the Giving Tree set up by the entrance to the palace offices. Buying dolls and trucks for kids she would never meet wasn't making her feel much better, but at least it was something. For those moments when she went to the bazaar, she could almost forget how much she missed Cade. Almost.

She wound her way through the offices and ended up in front of her father's door. She had been summoned. No doubt he was going to give her his "time to get over the man" speech. He'd delivered it after the debacle with her college boyfriend. To be honest, it had worked. If only it would do the same now.

Her father's secretary told her to go in. Bethany opened the door and stepped into her father's office, only to realize he wasn't alone. Then her heart stopped as she recognized the man sitting across from him.

"Cade," she breathed. "What are you doing here?"

Cade looked from her to her father and back, then crossed to her and took her hands in his.

"Bethany, you're here. I can't believe it. I came all this way only to realize I had no idea how to get in touch with you."

Because she'd disconnected the phone she'd used in Happily Inc, she thought, still dazed by seeing him. "I have a phone with local service for when I'm home. I just went back to that. Pallas has the number." Which was all totally inane. What she should really be asking was *why are you here?*

Hope stirred, pushing away doubt. Both made it hard to breathe.

"I've missed you," he told her, staring into her eyes. "From the second you left, I knew I'd made a mistake, but it took me a couple of days to figure out why. I knew you were wonderful, but I didn't know I'd fallen in love with you."

Tension eased as hope grew stronger and brighter.

"I love you," he repeated. "I was wrong about what I said and how I acted. I apologize and I hope that, in time, you can forgive me. Not right away—I don't deserve that. But eventually."

He drew her close and smiled at her. "You *should* have protected yourself the way you did. It made sense. My past is my problem, not yours. You're nothing like Lynette. What can I do to earn a second chance?"

She started laughing, then crying before finding herself being held tight by the man she loved. Her fears and pain healed as if they had never existed.

Her father walked over and patted her shoulder. "I'll leave you two alone to finish this. He seems like a good man, Bethany. He stood up to me when many would not have been so strong. When I met him, I thought he might be worthy of you."

When the door closed, Cade drew back enough to stare into her eyes. "I'm sorry."

"It's okay. I know why you did what you did."

"That doesn't make it right. I hurt you. Please forgive me."

"Of course. I love you, Cade. That hasn't changed."

He kissed her. She wrapped her arms around him and hung on as if she would never let go, which she hoped was the point. Then he stunned her by pulling back and dropping to one knee.

"I love you, Princess Bethany of El Bahar. I'm not the least bit worthy, but I love you and I'm asking you to marry me."

Her eyes filled with tears as she nodded and pulled him to his feet.

"Yes," she whispered as she pressed her mouth to his. "Yes, of course I'll marry you."

THE FEW DAYS leading up to Christmas passed in a blur. Cade called his mother to explain he would be staying in El Bahar through the holidays and that he was engaged. Libby Saunders had trouble grasping the fact that "the girl who worked in the stable" was really a princess. Bethany found her phone call with her future mother-in-law much warmer than her Thanksgiving conversation had been.

Pallas had shrieked into the phone when they'd called her and made them promise not to elope. Their wedding was her only chance to see a real live princess wedding and she didn't want to miss it.

In deference to tradition, Cade accepted the large diamond engagement ring Queen Liana offered him. It had belonged to Malik's beloved grandmother Fatima and he wanted his daughter to wear it.

Bethany winced when she saw the six carat stone. "There's no way I can wear this while I'm mucking out stables," she said. "But it's important to my folks. You sure you don't mind?"

Cade kissed her. "I figured you'd use it for official

occasions. I'm going to buy you a ring as soon as we get home. And plan better next time."

She laughed. "There shouldn't be another time when you need to pack an engagement ring."

"Excellent point."

They were in her suite, sitting on the balcony. The family's Christmas dinner was in an hour. They'd already exchanged presents that morning. Bethany was thrilled that her younger brothers seemed to adore Cade. Given the fact that he was having to deal with a couple of thousand years of tradition, he was doing great.

Cade took her hand in his and smiled at her. "So here's the thing. About your ranch management degree," he began.

"I've already found an online program that will be perfect for me. It's not as if I need a lot more hands-on training with horses."

"I'm glad. I'd go with you to Texas so you could go to school there, but I really appreciate you being willing to get your degree from Happily Inc."

They'd talked about that, about working together on the ranch. She thought about the paperwork her father had given her that afternoon and wondered if this was the time to share it with Cade. Before she could, he spoke.

"You know I'm buying into the ranch," he began. "When we get married, I'm going to add you to my share, so we'll eventually own it together. We've talked about our plans and I want to get going on growing the operation."

She pulled the envelope out of her back pocket. "Yes, well, there's a small twist to your plan. Your grandfather doesn't own the ranch anymore."

Cade stared at her. "What are you talking about?"

"My father bought the ranch from Grandpa Frank and deeded it to you. I think it's my dowry."

Cade took the paper he offered, then shook his head. "Tell him I won't accept unless he deeds it to both of us. We'll be equal partners in everything." He kissed her. "I love you, Princess Bethany."

She laughed. "I love you, soon-to-be Prince Cade."

"What are you talking about?"

"Yeah, I should have mentioned that, too. My dad wants you to be a prince." She held up a hand. "There aren't any duties or anything. It's kind of honorary, although you might end up owning an island. He wasn't clear."

Cade started to laugh and she joined in. He pulled her close and she let herself get lost in the joy of being loved by him. Yes, there would be details. Where to hold the wedding, how long to wait to start a family, and how to convince her father to give them her favorite mare as a wedding gift, but those tiny problems would be solved in time. For now, there was only this amazing man and the incredible future they would have together.

"I'm so lucky to have you in my life," he told her softly.

"Thanks. I feel exactly the same way."

He rose and pulled her to her feet. "Let's go celebrate our El Baharian Christmas. Later, I'm going to sneak into your room."

She laughed. "I'll be counting the hours." And the days and years to follow. Bethany knew she'd been blessed more than most and she would be grateful for the rest of her life.

* * * * *

HQN™

Don't miss out on these great books by #1 *New York Times* bestselling author Susan Mallery!

One of today's most beloved authors, Susan Mallery mixes her signature cocktail of love, laughter and family drama in this must-read novel of the year. For anyone who has survived the wedding of a sister, mother, friend or daughter, don't miss

Daughters of the Bride

Available now!

Susan Mallery delivers a captivating novel about the problem with secrets, the power of love and the unbreakable bond between sisters.

Secrets of the Tulip Sisters

Available now!

Susan Mallery masterfully explores the definition of a modern family—blended by surprise, not by choice—and how those complicated relationships can add unexpected richness to life.

When We Found Home

Available now!

Did you know that Harlequin My Rewards members earn
FREE books and more?
Join
www.HarlequinMyRewards.com
today to start earning your FREE books!

Connect with us on Harlequin.com for info on our new releases, access to exclusive offers, free online reads and much more!
Other ways to keep in touch:
Harlequin.com/Newsletters
Facebook.com/HarlequinBooks
Twitter.com/HQNBooks
HarlequinBlog.com

PHSM0819

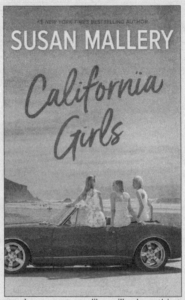

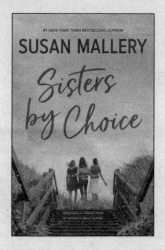

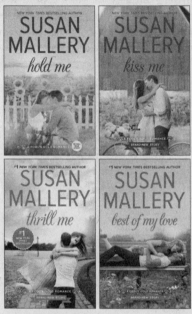